The Grass Is Singing
This Was the Old Chief's Country (*stories*)
The Habit of Loving (*stories*)
In Pursuit of the English
Going Home
Fourteen Poems
The Golden Notebook
A Man and Two Women (*stories*)
African Stories
Particularly Cats
Briefing for a Descent into Hell
The Temptation of Jack Orkney and Other Stories
The Summer Before the Dark
A Small Personal Voice
Memoirs of a Survivor
Stories

CHILDREN OF VIOLENCE

Martha Quest
A Proper Marriage
A Ripple from the Storm
Landlocked
The Four-Gated City

CANOPUS IN ARGOS: ARCHIVES

Re: Colonised Planet 5, Shikasta

THE MARRIAGES BETWEEN ZONES THREE, FOUR, AND FIVE

DORIS LESSING

CANOPUS IN ARGOS: ARCHIVES

THE MARRIAGES BETWEEN ZONES THREE, FOUR, AND FIVE

(As Narrated
by the Chroniclers
of Zone Three)

ALFRED A. KNOPF   NEW YORK   1980

This *is* a BORZOI BOOK

Published *by* ALFRED A. KNOPF, INC.

Copyright © 1980 *by* Doris Lessing

All rights reserved under International and Pan-American Copyright
Conventions.

Published in the United States by Alfred A. Knopf, Inc., New York.

Distributed by Random House, Inc., New York.

Library of Congress Cataloging in Publication Data

Lessing, Doris May [date]

The marriages between zones three, four, and five

(as narrated by the chroniclers of zone three).

(Canopus in argos: archives)

I. Title.

PZ3.L56684MAP 1980 [PR6023.E833] 823.'9'14

ISBN 0-394-50914-5 79-16515

Manufactured in the United States of America

First Edition

This is the second in the series of novels
with the overall title of CANOPUS IN ARGOS: ARCHIVES.
The first was *Re: Colonised Planet 5, Shikasta.*
The third will be *The Sirian Experiments.*

THE MARRIAGES BETWEEN ZONES THREE, FOUR, AND FIVE

Rumours are the begetters of gossip. Even more are they the begetters of song. We, the Chroniclers and song-makers of our Zone, aver that before the partners in this exemplary marriage were awake to what the new directives meant for both of them, the songs were with us, and were being amplified and developed from one end of Zone Three to the other. And of course this was so in Zone Four.

> Great to Small
> High to Low
> Four into Three
> Cannot go.

This was a children's counting game. I was watching them at it from my windows the day after I heard the news. And one of them rushed up to me in the street with a "riddle" he had heard from his parents: If you mate a swan and a gander, who will ride?

What was being said and sung in the camps and barracks of Zone Four we do not choose to record. It is not that we are mealy-mouthed. Rather that every chronicle has its appropriate tone.

I am saying that each despised the other? No, we are not permitted actively to criticise the dispensations of the Providers, but let us say that we in Zone Three did not forget—as the doggerel chanted during those days insisted:

> Three comes before Four.
> Our ways are peace and plenty.
> Their ways—war!

It was days before anything happened.

While this famous marriage was being celebrated in the imaginations of both realms, the two most concerned remained where they were. They did not know what was wanted of them.

No one had expected the marriage. It had not reached even popular speculation. Zones Three and Four were doing very well, with Al·Ith for us, Ben Ata for them. Or so we thought.

Quite apart from the marriage, there were plenty of secondary questions. What could it mean that our Al·Ith was ordered to travel to the territory of Ben Ata, so that the wedding could be accomplished on his land? This was one of the things we asked ourselves.

What, in this context, was a wedding?

What, even, a marriage?

When Al·Ith first heard of the Order, she believed it to be a joke. She and her sister laughed. All of Zone Three heard how they laughed. Then arrived a message that could only be regarded as a rebuke, and people came together in conferences and councils all over the Zone. They sent for us—the Chroniclers and the poets and the song-makers and the Memories. For weeks nothing was talked of but weddings and marriages, and every old tale and ballad that could be dug up was examined for information.

Messengers were even sent to Zone Five, where we believed weddings of a primitive kind did take place. But there was war all along their frontiers with Zone Four and it was not possible to get in.

We wondered, if this marriage was intended to follow ancient patterns, whether Zones Three and Four should join in a festival? But the Zones could not mingle, were inimical by nature. We were not even sure where the frontier was. Our side was not guarded. The inhabitants of Zone Three, straying near the frontier, or approaching it from curiosity as children or young people sometimes did, found themselves afflicted with repugnance, or at the least by an antipathy to foreign airs and atmospheres that showed itself in a cold lethargy, like boredom. It cannot be said that Zone Four had for us the secret attractions and fascinations of the forbidden: the most accurate thing I can say is that we forgot about it.

Ought there perhaps to be two festivals, simultaneously, and each would celebrate that our two lands, so different, could nevertheless mirror something, at least in this way? But what would be the point of that? After all, festivals and celebrations were not exactly pleasures we had to do without.

Should there then be small wedding parties among us, to mark the occasion?

New clothes? Decorations in our public places? Gifts and presents? All these were sanctioned by the old songs and stories.

More time passed. We knew that Al·Ith was low in spirits, and was keeping to her quarters. She had never done this before, had always been available and open to us. The women everywhere were out of temper and despondent.

The children began to suffer.

Then came the first visible and evident manifestation of the new time. Ben Ata sent a message that his men would come to escort her to him. This curtness was exactly what we expected from his Zone. A realm at war did not need the courtesies. Here was proof of the rightness of our reluctance to be brought low by Zone Four.

Al·Ith was resentful, rebellious. She would not go, she announced.

Again there was an Order, and it said, simply, that she must go.

Al·Ith put on her dark blue mourning clothes, since this was the only expression of her inner feelings she felt she still had the latitude to use. She gave out no instructions for a Grief, but that was what was being felt by us all.

Felt confusingly and—we suspected—wrongly. Emotions of this kind are not valued by us. Have not been for so long we have no records of anything different. As individuals we do not expect—it is not expected of us—to weep, wail, suffer. What can happen to any one of us that does not happen at some time to everyone? Sorrow at bereavement, at personal loss, has become formalised, ritualised, in public occasions seen by us all as channels and vehicles for our little personal feelings. It is not that we don't feel!—but that feelings are meant always to be directed outwards and used to strengthen a general conception of ourselves and our realm. But with this new dispensation of Al·Ith the opposite seemed to be happening.

Never had our Zone known so many tears, accusations, irrational ill-feelings.

Al·Ith had all her children brought to her and when they wept she did not check them.

She insisted that this much must be allowed her without it being considered active rebellion.

There were those—many of us—who were perturbed; many who began to be critical of her.

We could not remember anything like this; and soon we were talking of how long it had been since there had been any kind of Order from the Providers. Of how previous changes of the Need— always referred to by us simply, and without further definition, in this one word—had been received by us. Of why, now, there should be such a reversal. We asked ourselves if we had grown into the habit of seeing ourselves falsely. But how could it be wrong to approve our own harmonies, the wealths and pleasantness of our land? We believed our Zone to be the equal at least of any other for prosperity and absence of discord. Had it then been a fault to be proud of it?

And we saw how long it had been since we had thought at all of what lay beyond our borders. That Zone Three was only one of the realms administered generally from Above, we knew. We did think, when we thought on these lines at all, of ourselves in interaction with these other realms, but it was in an abstract way. We had perhaps grown insular? Self-sufficing?

Al·Ith sat in her rooms and waited.

And then they appeared, a troop of twenty horsemen, in light armour. They carried shields that protected them against our higher finer air which would otherwise have made them ill, and these they had to have. But why head protection, and the famous reflecting singlets of Zone Four that could repel any weapon? Those of us who were near the route chosen by our unwelcome guests stood sullen and critical. We were determined not to give any indications of pleasure. Nor did the horsemen greet us. In silence the troops made their way to the palace, and came to a standstill outside Al·Ith's windows. They had with them a saddled and bridled horse without a rider. Al·Ith saw them from her windows. There was a long wait. Then she emerged on the long flight of white steps, a sombre figure in her dark robes. She stood silent, observing the soldiers whose appearance in this manner, in her country, could only have the effect of a capture. She allowed plenty of time for them to observe her, her beauty, her strength, the self-sufficiency of her bearing. She then descended the steps slowly, and alone. She went straight to the horse that had been brought for her, looked into his eyes, and put her hand on his cheek. This horse was Yori, who became celebrated from this moment. He was a black horse, and a fine one, but perhaps no more remarkable than the others the soldiers were riding. Having greeted him, she lifted off the heavy saddle. She stood with this in her arms, looking into the faces of the men one after another until at last a soldier saw what it was she wanted. She threw the saddle to him, and his horse shifted its legs to adjust the weight as he caught it. He gave a comical little grimace, glancing at his fellows, while she stood, arms folded, watching them. It was the grimace one offers to a clever child trying something beyond its powers, yet succeeding. This was of course not lost on Al·Ith, and she now showed they had missed her real point, by the slow deliberation with which she removed the bridle and tossed that, too, to a soldier.

Then she shook back her head, so that the black hair that was bound lightly around it cascaded down her back. Our women wear their hair in many ways, but if it is up, in braids or in another fashion, and a woman shakes her hair loose, in a particular manner, then this means grief. But the soldiers had not understood, and were admiring her foolishly; perhaps the gesture had been meant for the onlookers who were by now crowding the little square. Al·Ith's lips were curling in contempt of the soldiers, and with impatience. I must record here that this kind of arrogance—yes, I have to call it that— was not something we expected from her. When we talked over the incident, it was agreed that Al·Ith's bitterness over the marriage was perhaps doing her harm.

Standing with loosened hair and burning eyes, she slowly wound a fine black veil around her head and shoulders. Mourning—again. Through the transparent black glowed her eyes. A soldier was fumbling to get down off his horse to lift her on to hers, but she had leapt up before he could reach the ground. She then wheeled and galloped off through the gardens in an easterly direction, towards the borders with Zone Four. The soldiers followed. To those of us watching, it looked as if they were in pursuit.

Outside our city she pulled in her horse and walked it. They followed. The people along the roads greeted her, and stared at the soldiers, and it did not look like a pursuit now, because the soldiers were embarrassed and smiling foolishly, and she was the Al·Ith they had always known.

There is a descent off the high plateau of our central land through passes and gorges, and it was not possible to ride fast, apart from the fact that Al·Ith stopped whenever someone wanted to talk to her. For when she observed this was so, she always pulled up her horse and waited for them to approach her.

Now the grimaces among the soldiers were of a different kind, and they were grumbling, for they had expected to be across their own frontier by nightfall. At last, as another group of her people waved and called to her, and she heard the voices of the soldiers rising behind her, she turned her horse and rode back to them, stopping a few paces before the front line of horsemen, so that they had to rein in quickly.

"What is your trouble?" she enquired. "Would it not be better if you told me openly, instead of complaining to each other like small children?"

They did not like this, and a small storm of anger rose, which their commander quelled.

"We have our orders," he said.

"While I am in our country," said she, "I will behave according to custom."

She saw they did not understand, and she had to explain. "I am in the position I hold because of the will of the people. It is not for me to ride past arrogantly, if they indicate they want to say something."

Again they looked at each other. The commander's face showed open impatience.

"You cannot expect me to overturn our customs for yours in this way," she said.

"We have emergency rations for one light meal," he said.

She gave a little incredulous shake of her head, as if she could not believe what she was hearing.

She had not meant it as contempt, but this was what transmitted itself to them. The commander of the horsemen reddened, and blurted out: "Any one of us is capable of fasting on a campaign for days at a time if necessary."

"I hadn't asked as much," she said gravely, and this time, what they heard was humour. They gratefully laughed, and she was able to give a brief smile, then sighed, and said, "I know that you are not here by your own will, but because of the Providers."

But this, inexplicably to her, they felt as insult and challenge, and their horses shifted and sidled as the emotions of their riders came into them.

She gave a little shrug, and turned and went to the group of young men who stood waiting for her at the road's edge. Below them now lay a wide plain, behind them were the mountains. The plains still lay yellowed by the evening sun, and the high peaks of the mountains sun-glittered, but where they were it was cold and in dusk. The young men crowded around her horse as they talked, showing no fear or awe, and the watching horsemen's faces showed a crude disbelief. When a youth put up his hand to pat the horse's cheek briefly, the men let out, all together, a long breath of condemnation. But they were in doubt, and in conflict. It was not possible for them to despise this great kingdom or the rulers of it: they knew better. Yet what they saw at every moment contradicted their own ideas of what was right.

She held up her hand in farewell to the young men, and the men behind her put their horses forward at this signal which had not been to them. She rode on, before them, until they were all on the level of the plain, and then turned again.

"I suggest that you make a camp here, with the mountains at your back."

"In the first place," said the commander, very curt—because he had been annoyed his soldiers had instinctively answered her gesture by starting again, instead of waiting for him—"in the first place, I had not thought of stopping at all till we reached the frontier. And in the second . . ." But his anger silenced him.

"I am only making the suggestion," she said. "It will take nine or ten hours to reach the frontier."

"At this pace it will."

"At any pace. Most nights a strong wind blows over the plain from the east."

"Madam! What do you take these men for? What do you take us for?"

"I see that you are soldiers," said she. "But I was thinking of the beasts. They are tired."

"They will do as they are ordered. As we do."

Our Chroniclers and artists have made a great thing of this exchange between Al·Ith and the soldiers. Some of the tales begin at this point. She is erect before them, on her horse, who hangs his head, because of the long difficult ride. She is soothing it with her white hand, which glitters with jewels . . . but Al·Ith was known for her simple dress, her absence of jewels and splendour! They show her long black hair streaming, the veil streaming with it and held on her forehead with a brilliant clasp. They show the angry commander, his face distorted, and the jeering soldiers. The bitter wind is indicated by flying tinted clouds, and the grasses of the plain lie almost flat under it.

All kinds of little animals have crept into this picture. Birds hover around her head. A small deer, a great favourite with our children, has stepped on to the dust of the road, and is holding up its nose to the drooping nose of Al·Ith's horse, to comfort it, or to give it messages from other animals. Often these pictures are titled "Al·Ith's Animals." Some tales tell how the soldiers try to catch the birds and the deer, and are rebuked by Al·Ith.

I take the liberty of doubting whether the actual occasion impressed itself so dramatically on the soldiers, or even on Al·Ith. The soldiers wanted to ride on, and get away from this land they did not understand, and which continually discomfited them. The commander did not want to be put into the position of taking her advice, but nor did he want to ride for hours into a cold wind.

Which in fact was already making itself felt.

Al·Ith was more herself now than she had been for many weeks. She was seeing that while she mourned in her rooms, there had been other things she should have done! Duties had been neglected. She remembered that messages had come in to her from all over the country, which she had been too absorbed in her fierce thoughts to respond to.

She was seeing in herself disobedience, and the results of it. This made her, now, more gentle with this troop of barbarians, and its small-boy commander.

"You did not tell me your name," she asked.

He hesitated. Then: "It is Jarnti."

"You command the king's horses?"

"I am commander of all his forces. Under the king."

"My apologies." She sighed, and they all heard it. They thought it weakness. Throughout these experiences with her, they could not help feeling in themselves the triumph that barbarian natures show when faced with weakness; and the need to cringe and crowd together when facing strength.

"I want to leave you for some hours," she said.

At this they all, on a single impulse, and without any indication from their leader, crowded around her. She was inside a ring of captors.

"I cannot allow it," said Jarnti.

"What were your orders from the king?" she enquired. She was quiet and patient but they heard subservience.

And a great roar of laughter went up from them all. Long tension exploded in them. They laughed and shouted, and the crags behind them echoed. Birds that had already settled themselves for the night wheeled up into the skies. From the long grasses by the road, animals that had been lying hidden broke away noisily.

What Ben Ata had finally shouted at his commander of all the forces, was: "Go and get that —— —— —— and bring her here. I'm for it if I don't —— ——" For while Al·Ith had been weeping and rebellious in her quarters, he had been raging and cursing up and down the camps of his armies. There was not a soldier who had not heard what his king thought of this enforced marriage, while the camps commiserated with him, drinking, laughing, making up ribald toasts which were repeated from one end of Zone Four to the other.

This scene is another favourite of our storytellers and artists. Al·Ith, on her tired horse, is ringed by the brutal laughing men. The cold wind of the plains is pressing her robe close around her. The commander is leaning over her, his face all animal. She is in danger.

And it is true that she was. Perhaps for the only time.

Now night had fallen. Only in the skies behind them was there any light. The sunset sent up flares high towards the crown of the heavens, and made the snow peaks shine. In front of them lay the now black plain, and scattered over it at vast distances were the lights of villages and settlements. On the plateau behind them that they had travelled over, our villages and towns were crowded: it was a populous and busy land. But now they seemed to stand on the verge of nothingness, the dark. The soldiers' own country was low and mostly flat, and their towns were never built on hills and ridges. They did not like heights. More: as we shall see, they had been taught to fear them. They had been longing for the moment when they could get off that appalling plateau lifted so high among its towering peaks. They had descended from it and, associating flat lands with habitation, saw only emptiness. Their laughter had panic in it. Terror. It seemed they could not stop themselves laughing. And among them was the small silent figure of Al·Ith, who sat quietly while they rolled about in their saddles, making sounds, as she thought, like frightened animals.

Their laughing had to stop at some point. And when it did nothing had changed. She was still there. They had not impressed her with their noise. The illimitable blackness lay ahead.

"What was Ben Ata's order?" she asked again.

An explosion of sniggers, but the commander directed a glance of reproof towards the offenders, although he had been laughing as hard as any of them.

"His orders?" she insisted.

A silence.

"That you should bring me to him, that was it, I think."

A silence.

"You will bring me to him no later than tomorrow."

She remained where she was. The wind was now howling across the plains so that the horses could hardly keep their footing.

The commander gave a brief order which sounded shamefaced. The posse broke up, riding about on the edge of the plain, to find a camping place. She and the commander sat on their tired horses, watching. But normally he would have been with his men who, used to orders and direction, were at a loss. At length he called out that such a place would do, and they all leapt off their horses.

The beasts, used to the low relaxed air of Zone Four, were exhausted from the high altitudes of this place, and were trembling as they stood.

"There is water around that spur," said Al·Ith. He did not argue, but shouted to the soldiers to lead the horses around the spur to drink. He got off his horse, and so did she. A soldier came to lead both animals with the others to the water. A fire was blazing in a glade between deep rocks. Saddles lay about on the grass at intervals: they would be the men's pillows.

Jarnti was still beside Al·Ith. He did not know what to do with her.

The men were already pulling out their rations from their packs, and eating. The sour powdery smell of dried meat. The reek of spirits.

Jarnti said, with a resentful laugh, "Madam, our soldiers seem very interesting to you! Are they so different from your own?"

"We have no soldiers," she said.

This scene, too, is much celebrated among us. The soldiers, illuminated by a blazing fire, are seated on their saddles among the grasses, eating their dried meat and drinking from their flasks. Others are leading back the horses, who have drunk at a stream out of sight behind rocks. Al·Ith stands by Jarnti at the entrance to this little natural fortress. They are watching the horses being closed into a corral that is formed by high rocks. They are hungry, and there is no food for them that night. Al·Ith is gazing at them with pity. Jarnti, towering over the small indomitable figure of our queen, is swaggering and full of bravado.

"No soldiers?" said Jarnti, disbelieving. Though of course there had always been rumours to this effect.

"We have no enemies," she remarked. And then added, smiling straight at him, "Have you?"

This dumbfounded him.

He could not believe the thoughts her question aroused.

While she was still smiling at him, a soldier came out from the entrance of the little camp and stood at ease close to them.

"What is he standing there for?"

"Have you never heard of a sentry?" he enquired, full of sarcasm.

"Yes. But no one is going to attack you."

"We always post sentries," he said.

She shrugged.

Some soldiers were already asleep. The horses drooped and rested behind their rocky barriers.

"Jarnti, I am going to leave you for some hours," she said.

"I cannot allow you."

"If you forbid me, you would be going beyond your orders."

He was silent.

Here again, a favourite scene. The fire roaring up, showing the sleeping soldiers, the poor horses, and Jarnti, tugging at his beard with both hands in frustrated amazement at Al·Ith, who is smiling at him.

"Besides," he added, "you have not eaten."

She enquired good-humouredly: "Do your orders include your forcing me to eat?"

And now he said, confronting her, all trouble and dogged insistence, because of the way he was being turned inside out and upside down by her, and by the situation, "Yes, the way I see it, by implication my orders say I should make you eat. And perhaps even sleep, if it comes to that."

"Look, Jarnti," said she, and went to a low bush that grew not ten paces away. She took some of its fruit. They were lumpy fruits sheathed in papery leaves. She pulled off the leaves. In each were four segments of a white substance. She ate several. The tightness of her mouth showed she was not enjoying them.

"Don't eat them unless you want to stay awake," she said, but of course he could not resist. He blundered off to the bush, and gathered some for himself, and his mouth twisted up as he tasted the tart crumbly stuff.

"Jarnti," she said, "you cannot leave this camp, since you are the commander. Am I correct?"

"Correct," he said, in a clumsy familiarity, which was the only way he knew how to match her friendliness.

"Well, I am going to walk some miles from here. Since in any case you intend to keep that poor man awake all night for nothing, I suggest you send him with me to make sure I will come back again."

Jarnti was already feeling the effects of the fruit. He was alert and knew he could not fall off to sleep now.

"I will leave him on guard and come with you myself," he said.

And went to give orders accordingly.

While he did this, Al·Ith walked past the sleeping soldiers to the horses, and gave each one of them, from her palm, a few of the acrid fruits from the bush. Before she had left their little prison they were lifting their heads and their eyes had brightened.

She and Jarnti set off across the blackness of the plain towards the first of the glittering lights.

This scene is always depicted thus: there is a star-crowded sky, a slice of bright moon, and the soldier striding forward made visible and prominent because his chest armour and headpiece and his shield are shining. Beside him Al·Ith is visible only as a dark shadow, but her eyes gleam softly out from her veil.

It could not have been anything like this. The wind was straight in their faces, strong and cold. She wrapped her head completely in her veil, and he had his cloak tight about him and over the lower part of his face; and the shield was held to protect them both from the wind.

He had chosen to accompany this queen on no pleasant excursion, and he must have regretted it.

It took three hours to reach the settlement. It was of tents and huts: the herdsmen's headquarters. They walked through many hundreds of beasts who lifted their heads as they went past, but did not come nearer or move away. The wind was quite enough for them to withstand, and left them no energy for anything else. But as the two came to within calling distance of the first tents, where there was shelter from low scrubby trees, some beasts came nosing towards Al·Ith in the dark, and she spoke to them and held out her hands for them to smell, in greeting.

There were men and women sitting around a small fire outside a tent.

They had lifted their heads, too, sensing the approach of strangers, and Al·Ith called out to them, "It is Al·Ith," and they called back to her to approach.

All this was astonishing to Jarnti, who went with Al·Ith into the firelight, but several paces behind.

At the sight of him, the faces of the fire-watchers showed wonderment.

"This is Jarnti, from Zone Four," said Al·Ith, as if what she was saying was an ordinary thing. "He has come to take me to their king."

Now there was not a soul in our land who did not know how she felt about this marriage, and there were many curious glances into her face and eyes. But she was showing them that this was not her concern now. She stood waiting while rugs were brought from a tent, and when they were spread, she sat down on one and indicated to Jarnti that he should do the same. She told them that Jarnti had not eaten, and he was brought bread and porridge. She indicated that she did not want food. But she accepted a cup of wine, and Jarnti drank off jugs of the stuff. It was mild in taste, but potent. He was showing signs of discomfort if not of illness: the altitude of our plateau had affected him, he had taken too many of the stimulant berries, and he had not eaten. He was cut through and through by the winds that swept over their heads where they all leaned low over their little fire.

This scene, too, is one much depicted.

It always shows Al·Ith, alert and smiling, surrounded by the men and women of the settlement, with her cup of wine in her hand, and beside her Jarnti, drowsy and drugged. Above them the wind has scoured the sky clean and glittering. The little trees are leaning almost to the ground. The herds surround the fireside scene, looking in and wondering, waiting for a glance from their queen.

She said at once: "As I rode out from the capital today, and down through the passes, I was stopped by many of you. What is this that they are saying about the animals?"

The spokesman was an old man.

"What have they told you, Al·Ith?"

"That there is something wrong."

"Al·Ith, we have ourselves sent in messengers to the capital, with information."

Al·Ith was silent, and then said, "I 'm very much to blame. Messages came, and I was too much preoccupied with my own trouble to attend."

Jarnti was sitting with a bent head, half asleep, but at this his head jerked up, and he let out a gruff triumphant laugh, and muttered, "Punish her, beat her, you hear? She admits it!" before his head dropped again. His mouth hung open, and the cup was loose in his hand. One of the girls took it from him gently. He snatched at it, thrust forward his bottom lip and lifted his chin belligerently at her, saw she was pretty, and a female—and would have put his arms around her, but she swiftly moved back as he submerged again in drunkenness.

Al·Ith's eyes were full of tears. The women first, then the men, seeing this oaf and his ways, saw too what was in store for her—and they were about to raise their voices in lament, keening, but she lifted her hand and stopped them.

"There is no help for it," she said, in a low voice, her lips trembling. "We have our orders. And it is clear down in Zone Four they don't like it any more than we do."

They looked enquiringly at her and she nodded. "Yes. Ben Ata is very angry. So I understood today from something that was said."

"Ben Ata . . . Ben Ata . . ." muttered the soldier, his head rolling.

"He will have the clothes off you before you can get at him with your magic berries and your tricks."

At this, one of the men rose to his feet and would have dragged Jarnti off, with two hands under his armpits, but Al·Ith raised her hand to stop him.

"I am more concerned with the animals," she said. "What was in the messages you sent me?"

"Nothing definite, Al·Ith. It is only that our animals are disturbed in their minds. They are sorrowful."

"This is true everywhere on the plains?"

"It is true everywhere in our Zone, or so we hear. Were you not told of it up on the plateau?"

"I have already said that I am much to blame. I was not attending to my duties."

A silence. The wind was shrieking over them, but not as loud.

Jarnti was slumped, his cup leaning in his hand, blinking at the fire. Really he was listening, since the berries have the effect of preserving attention even while the muscles are slack and disobedient. This conversation was to be retold everywhere through the camps of Zone Four, and not inaccurately, though to them the emphasis must be that the queen of all the land was sitting "like a serf" by the fire. And, of course, that "up there" they spoke of animals as if they were people.

Al·Ith said to the old man, "You have asked the animals?"

"I have been among the herds since it was noticed. Day after day I have been with them. Not one says anything different. They do not know why, but they are sad enough to die. They have lost the zest for living, Al·Ith."

"They are conceiving? Giving birth?"

"They are still giving birth. But you are right to ask if they are conceiving . . ."

At this Jarnti let out a muttering, "They tell their queen she is right! They dare! Drag them off! Beat them. . . ."

They ignored him. With compassion now. He was sitting loose and rolling there, his face aflame, and they saw him as worse than their beasts. More than one of the women was weeping, silently, at the fate of their sister, as they watched him.

"We believe they are not conceiving."

A silence. The wind was not shrieking now. It was a low wail. The animals that were making a circle all around lifted their muzzles to sniff the air: soon the wind would be gone, and their nightly ordeal over.

"And you, the people?"

They all nodded, slowly. "We believe that we are the same."

"You mean, that you begin to feel in yourselves what the animals feel?"

"Yes, Al·Ith."

And now they sat quiet for a long time. They looked into each other's faces, questioning, confirming, allowing their eyes to meet, and to part, letting what each felt pass from one to another, until they all were feeling and understanding as one.

While this went on, the soldier was motionless. Later, in the camps, he was to say that "up there" they had vicious drugs and used them unscrupulously.

The wind had dropped. It was silent. In a swept sky the stars glittered cold. But wisps of cloud were forming in the east, over the borders with Zone Four.

One of the girls spoke up at last. "Al·Ith, some of us have been wondering if this new Order from the Providers has something to do with this sadness of ours."

Al·Ith nodded.

"None of us remember anything like it," said the old man.

Al·Ith said, "The Memories speak of such a time. But it was so long ago the historians knew nothing about it."

"And what happened?" asked Jarnti, suddenly finding his tongue.

"We were invaded," said Al·Ith. "By Zone Four. Is there nothing in your history? Your tales?"

At this Jarnti wagged his pointed beard at them, grinning— triumphant.

"Is there nothing you can tell us?" asked Al·Ith.

He smirked at the women, one after another, and then his head fell forward.

"Al·Ith," said a girl who had been sitting, letting her tears run, "Al·Ith, what are you going to do with such men?"

"Perhaps Ben Ata won't be so bad," said another.

"This man is the commander of all the armies," said Al·Ith, and could not prevent herself shuddering.

"*This* man? *This?*"

Their horror and shock made itself felt in Jarnti, and he would have punished them if he could. He did manage to raise his head and glare, but he was shaking and weak.

"He is going to have to get back to the camp at the foothills," said Al·Ith.

Two of the young men glanced at each other, and then rose. They grasped Jarnti under the armpits, hauled him to his feet, and began walking him up and down. He staggered and protested, but complied, in the end, for his brain, clear all this time, told him it was necessary.

This scene is known as "Jarnti's Walk," and gives much opportunity for humour to our artists and tellers.

"I don't see that there is anything we can do?" asked Al·Ith of the others. "If this is an old disease, nothing is known of it in our medicine. If it is a new disease, our doctors will shortly come to terms with it. But if it is a malady of the heart, then the Providers will know what to do."

A silence.

"Have already known what to do," she said, smiling, though not pleasantly. "Please tell everyone on the plain that I came here tonight and we talked, and what we thought together."

We will, they said. Then they all rose to their feet, and went with her through the herds. A young girl called three horses, who came and stood willingly, waiting, while the young man put Jarnti on one, and Al·Ith mounted another, and the girl herself got on a third. The animals crowded around Al·Ith on her horse, and called to her as the three rode past.

Out on the plain, headed back towards the camp, the grasses were now standing up grey in a dim light, and the eastern sky was aflame.

Jarnti had come awake, and was sitting straight and soldierly on his horse.

"Madam," he asked, "how do you people talk to your animals?"

"Do you not talk to yours?"

"No."

"You stay with them. You watch them. You put your hands on

them and feel how they feel. You look into their eyes. You listen to the tones of their cries and their calling to each other. You make sure that when they begin to understand that you understand them, you do not miss the first tones of what they say to you. For if you do not hear, then they will not trouble to try again. Soon you will feel what they are feeling, and you will know what they are thinking, even if they do not tell you themselves."

Jarnti said nothing for a while. They had now left the herds behind.

"Of course we watch them and take notice of how they look, if they are ill or something like that."

"There are none among you who know how to feel with your animals?"

"Some of us are good with animals, yes."

Al·Ith did not seem inclined to say any more.

"Perhaps we are too impatient," said Jarnti.

Neither Al·Ith nor the girl said anything to this. They trotted on towards the foothills. Now the great peaks of the high lands were pink and shining from the wild morning sky.

"Madam," he said, blustering, because he did not know how to be on an equality with her, or with anyone, "when you are with us, can you teach some of the soldiers who are in charge of the horses this way of yours?"

She was silent. Then: "Do you know that I am never called anything but Al·Ith? Do you understand that I have never been called Madam, or anything like it before?"

Now he was silent.

"Well, will you?" he asked gruffly.

"I will if I can," she said at last.

He was struggling with himself to express gratitude, pleasure. Nothing came out.

They were more than halfway between the herds and the camp.

Jarnti put his heels into his horse suddenly, and it neighed and bucked. Then it stood still.

The two women stopped too.

"Did you want to go on ahead?" asked the girl.

He was sullen.

"He won't carry you now," she said, and slid off her horse. Jarnti got down from his. "Now get on mine." He did so. She soothed the bewildered horse he had kicked, and mounted it.

"*Think* that you want to go on in front of us," said the girl.

He had an ashamed, embarrassed look. He went red.

"I'm afraid you will have to put up with us," said Al·Ith at last.

When they were in sight of the camp, she jumped down from her horse. It at once turned and began cantering back towards the herds. Jarnti got off his. And this one too cantered back. He was standing looking in admiration at the lovely girl on her horse, who was turning around to go.

"If you ever come to Zone Four," he shouted at her, "let me know."

She gave a long look of commiseration at Al·Ith, and remarked, "Luckily for me I am not a queen." And she sped off across the plain with the two other horses neighing and tossing up their heels on either side of her.

Al·Ith and Jarnti walked towards the camp with the sunrise at their backs.

Long before they reached the camp, the smell of burning meat was strong on the air.

Al·Ith did not say anything, but her face spoke.

"Do you not kill animals?" he asked, unwillingly but forced to by his curiosity.

"Only if it is essential. There are plenty of other foods."

"Like those horrible berries of yours," he said, trying to be good-humoured.

In the camp they had killed a deer. Jarnti did not eat any of it.

As soon as the meal was over, the horses were saddled, all but Al·Ith's. She stood watching the beasts adjust their mouths and their teeth uncomfortably as the bit went in.

She vaulted onto her horse, and whispered to it. Jarnti watched her, uneasy.

"What did you say to it?" he asked.

"That I am his friend."

And again she led the way forward, into the east, back across the plain.

They rode to one side of the herds they had been with in the night, but far enough off to see them as a darkness on the plain.

Jarnti was riding just behind Al·Ith.

Now he was remembering the conversation around the fire last night, the tone of it, the ease of it. He yearned for it—or something in it, for he had never known that quality of easy intimacy. Except, he was saying to himself, with a girl, sometimes, after a good screw.

He said, almost wistfully, to Al·Ith, "Can you feel that the animals out there are sad?" For she was looking continually towards them, and her face was concerned.

"Can't you?" she asked.

He saw she was weeping, steadily, as she rode.

He was furious. He was irritated. He felt altogether excluded from something he had a right to.

Behind them clattered the company of soldiers.

A long way in front was the frontier. Suddenly she leaned down to whisper to the horse and it sped forward. Jarnti and the company broke into speed after her. They were shouting at her. She did not have the shield that would protect her from the—to her—deadly atmosphere of Zone Four. She rode like the wild winds that scoured the plains every night until early dawn, and her long hair swept out behind her, and tears ran steadily down her face.

It was not for miles that Jarnti came up with her—one of the soldiers had thrown the shield to him, and he had caught it, and was now riding almost neck and neck with her.

"Al·Ith," he was shouting, "you must have this." And held up the shield. It was a long time before she heard him. At last she turned her face towards him, not halting her mad pace in the slightest, and he wilted at the sight of her blanched, agonised face. He held up the shield. She raised her hand to catch it. He hesitated, because it was not a light thing. He remembered how she had thrown the heavy saddle the day before, and he heaved the shield towards her. She caught it with one hand and did not abate her pace at all. They were approaching the frontier. They watched her to see how she would be affected by the sudden change in the density of the air, for they had all been ill to some extent, the day before. She went through the invisible barrier without faltering, though she was pale, and did not seem well. Inside the frontier line were the observation towers, rising up at half-mile distances from each other, bristling with soldiers and armaments. She did not stop. Jarnti and the others fled after her, shouting to the soldiers in the towers not to shoot. She went between the towers without looking at them.

Again they were on the edge of a descent through hills and rocks above a wide plain. When she reached the edge of this escarpment she at last stopped.

They all came to a standstill behind her. She was looking down into a land crowded with forts and encampments.

She jumped down from her horse. Soldiers were running to them from the forts, holding the bridles of fresh horses. The jaded horses of the company were being herded off to recover. But Al·Ith's did not want to leave her. He shivered and whinnied and wheeled all about Al·Ith, and when the soldiers came to catch him, would not go.

"Would you like him as a present, Al·Ith?" asked Jarnti, and she was pleased and smiled a little, which was all she could manage.

Again she removed the saddle from this fresh horse, and the bridle, and tossed them to the amazed soldiers. And she rode forward and down into Zone Four, with Yori trotting beside her and continually putting up his nose to nuzzle her as they went.

And so Al·Ith made the passage into the Zone we had all heard so much of, speculated about, and had never been in.

Not even with the shield could she feel anything like herself. The air was flat, dispiriting. The landscape seemed to confine and oppress. Everywhere you look, in our own realm, a wild vigour is expressed in the contours of uplands, mountains, a variegated ruggedness. The central plateau where so many of our towns are situated is by no means regular, but is ringed by mountains and broken by ravines and deep river channels. With us the eye is enticed into continual movement, and then is drawn back always to the great snowy peaks that are shaped by the winds and the colours of our skies. And the air tingles in the blood, cold and sharp. But here she looked down into a uniform dull flat, cut by canals and tamed streams that were marked by lines of straight pollarded trees, and dotted regularly by the ordered camps of the military way of life. Towns and villages did not seem any larger than these camps. The sky was a greyish blue and there was a dull shine from the lines of water. A wide low hill near the centre of the scene where there seemed to be something like a park or gardens was all the consolation she could find.

Meanwhile, they were still descending the escarpment.

A turn in the road showed an enormous circular building of grey stone, squatting heavily between canals. It seemed recent, for rocks and earth near it were raw, broken. Her dismay that this might be where she was bound for brought her horse to a faltering stop. The company halted behind her, and she looked back to see a furtive triumph on every face. Jarnti was suppressing a smile as a leader does when he wishes to indicate he would like to join with his juniors in a show of emotion. Then as they remained there, with no sound but the horses shifting their hooves for relief, on the stony road, she saw that she had been mistaken: what she feared was not matched by the particular variety of triumph these captors of hers were showing.

"When may we expect to reach the king?" she asked, and Jarnti at once interpreted this as a reminder from her of higher authority. He rebuked his company with a strong look and adjusted his own face to obedience.

All this she watched, understood—and it came to her what a barbarous land this was.

They had imagined she had been intimidated by the sight of the rumoured "round fortress of the deadly rays" as one of our songs described it.

She told herself, not for the first time, or the tenth, that she was not likely to adjust herself quickly to these people with their slavish minds, and to make a test of them, moved her horse on and towards the road that led to the building. At once Jarnti was beside her, and his hand was reaching out for her horse's head. She stopped. "I would like to see into one of the famed round fortresses of your Zone," she said.

"Oh, no, no, you must not, it is forbidden," said he, still full of importance.

"But why? Your weapons are not directed against us, surely?"

"It is dangerous . . ." but at this moment, around the side of the building came some children running, and in scattering for some game, two of them darted into an open doorway.

"So I see," she said, and rode on, without looking again at Jarnti or at the soldiers.

When nearly at the level of the plain, there were grazing cattle near the road, and a half-grown boy attending them.

Jarnti shouted at the boy to come forward, and the boy was already running towards them, before Jarnti said, "You could teach him your ways with the animals," and as the boy arrived at the roadside, pale and startled, Jarnti was shouting, "Down on your face! Can't you see who this is we are taking to the king?"

The lad was face down, full length on the grass, and this was no more than a half-minute since he had first been hailed.

Jarnti was giving her half-pleading, half-commanding looks, and his horse was dancing under him, because of his master's eagerness to learn her lore.

"Well," she said, "I don't think we are likely to learn or teach anything in this way."

But he had seen himself that he had mishandled the occasion and because of it was red and angry. He shouted, "The lady here would like to know if your beasts are well."

No reply, then a whimper which sounded like, "Very well, yes, well, sir."

Al·Ith slid down from her horse, walked over to the boy, and said, "Stand up." She made her voice a command, since commands were what he understood. He slowly shivered his way to his feet, and stood, almost collapsing, before her. She waited until she knew he had seen, from his furtive glances, that she was not so frightening, and said, "I am from Zone Three. Our animals have not been well. Can you say if you have noticed anything unusual with yours?"

His hands were clenched at his chest, and he was breathing as if he had run several miles. Finally he brought out: "Yes, yes, that is, I think so."

From behind them Jarnti's voice, jocular and loud: "Are they having sorrowful thoughts?" And the entire company sniggered.

She saw there was nothing that could be done, and said to the boy, "Don't be frightened. Go back to your beasts." She waited until he sped off, and she returned to her horse. Again, Jarnti knew he had behaved clumsily, and yet it had been necessary to him, for the sight of her, small, unarmed, standing rather below them near the defenceless and frightened boy, had roused in him a need to show strength, dominance.

She swung herself onto her horse and at once rode on, not looking at them. She felt very low, our poor Al·Ith. This was the worst time of all. Everything in her was hurt by the way the poor boy had been treated: yet these were the ways of this land, and she could not believe then, in that bad hour, that there could be any way of communicating with these louts. And of course she was thinking of what she was going to find when she was led to Ben Ata.

They rode on, through the middle of the day, across the plain, with the ditches and the lines of dull bunchy trees accompanying them all the way. She went first. Yori, the riderless horse, was just behind, with Jarnti, and behind them the company. They were all silent. She had not said anything about the incident of the boy, but they were thinking now that she would be soon with the king, and were not expecting she would give a good report of them. So they were sullen, sulky. There were few people on the roadside, or in the flat boats of the canals, but those who saw the little company go past reported that there was not a smile to be seen: this wedding party was fit for a funeral. And the riderless horse caused rumours to spread that Al·Ith had fallen and was dead, for the slight figure on the leading horse that they did see, had nothing about her to command their attention. She seemed to them a serving woman, or an attendant, in her plain dark blue, with her head in its black veils.

There was a ballad about how the horse of the dead Al·Ith had gone with the troop of soldiers to the king to tell him that there could be no marriage. The horse stood on the threshold of the wedding chamber and neighed three times, Ben Ata, Ben Ata, Ben Ata—and when he came out, said to him:

> Cold and dark your wedding bed,
> O King, your willing bride is dead.
> The realm she rules is cold and dark.

And this was popular, and sung when everyone knew that Al·Ith was not dead, and that the marriage was a fact. That it was not the smoothest of marriages was of course known from the beginning. How? But how do these things get themselves known? The song was always being added to. Here is a verse that came from the married quarters of the army camps:

The Marriages Between Zones Three, Four, and Five

> *Brave King, your realm is strong and fine.*
> *Where beasts may mate, then women pine.*
> *I will be your slave, brave King.*

Not anywhere with us, or at any time, have such verses as these
been possible, though there were plenty of compassionate and tender
ballads made up about Al·Ith. There are some who say that where
there is rulership, there has to be criticism of this ribald kind, because no matter the level of the ruler, it is in the nature of the ruled
to crave identification of the lowest sort. We say this is not so, and
Zone Three proves it. To recognise and celebrate the ordinary, the
day-to-day levels of an authority, is not to denigrate it.

Such Zone Four ballads, travelling upwards to us, found themselves transformed as they crossed the frontier. For one thing, there
was no need of the inversions, the ambiguities, that are always bred
by fear of an arbitrary authority.

We may almost say that a certain type of ballad is impossible with
us: the kind that has as its ground or base lamentation, the celebra-
tion of loss.

In their Zone the riderless horse gave birth to songs of death and
sorrow; in ours to songs about loving friendship.

The road, which cut straight across the plain, and was intersected
at about the middle by one running equally straight, began to lift a
little to reach the small hill that Al·Ith had seen with relief from the
top of the escarpment. The canals were left behind, with their weight
of dead water. There were a few ordinary trees, which had not been
hacked into lumps and wands. At the top of the hill were gardens,
and here the water had been forced into movement, for they rode
now beside channels where it ran swiftly, fell from several levels to
others, and broke into fountains. The air was lively and cool, and
when she saw ahead of her a light pavilion, with coloured springing
pillars and arches, she was encouraged. But there was no one to be
seen. She was contrasting this empty garden and the apparently deserted pavilion with the friendly amplitude of her own courts, when
Jarnti called an order, and the whole company came to a stop. The
soldiers jumped off their horses, and surrounded Al·Ith, who, when
she got down from her horse, found herself being marched forward in

their midst, like a captive of war—and she saw that this was not the first time they had done this, from the ease of their arrangements.

But as they had enclosed her, Jarnti in front, she put out her hand to hold the horse she had been given, Yori, by the neck.

And this was how she arrived at the steps of the pavilion, when Ben Ata came out to stand in the doorway, arms folded, legs apart, bearded soldier, dressed in no way different from Jarnti or the others. He was large, blond, muscular from continual campaigning, and burned a ruddy brown on the face and arms. His eyes were grey. He was not looking at Al·Ith but at the horse, for his first thought too was that his bride had been killed.

Al·Ith went quickly through the soldiers, suspecting that there were precedents here she might not want followed, and arrived in front of him, still holding the horse.

And now he looked at her, startled and frowning.

"I am Al·Ith," said she, "and this horse has been kindly given to me by Jarnti. Please, will you give orders for him to be well treated?"

He found himself speechless. He nodded. Jarnti then grasped the horse's neck and attempted to lead him away. But he reared and tried to free himself. Before he would allow himself to be taken away, Al·Ith had to comfort him and promise she would visit him very soon. "Today, I swear it." And, turning to Jarnti, "So you must not take him too far away. And please see he is well fed and looked after."

Jarnti was sheepish, the soldiers grinning, only just hiding it, because Ben Ata's face gave them no guidance. Normally, on such occasions, the girl would have been bundled across a threshold, or pushed forward roughly, according to the convention, but now no one knew how to behave.

Al·Ith said, "Ben Ata, I take it you have some sort of place I can retire to for a time? I have been riding all day."

Ben Ata was recovering. His face was hard, and even bitter. He had not known what to expect, and was prepared to be flexible, but he was repelled by this woman in her sombre clothes. She had not taken off her veil, and he could not see much of her except that she had dark hair. He preferred fair women.

He shrugged, gave a look at Jarnti, and disappeared into the room behind him. It was Jarnti then who led her into another room, which was part of a set of rooms, and saw that she had what she needed. She refused food and drink, and announced that she would be ready to join the king in a few minutes.

And she did join him, emerging unceremoniously from the retiring rooms just as she had arrived, in her dark dress. But she had removed the veil, and her hair was braided and hanging down her back.

Ben Ata was lounging on a low divan or settee, in a large light airy room that had nothing very much in it. She saw that this was a bridal room, and planned for the occasion. Her bridegroom, however, sprawling on one edge of the divan, his chin on his hand, his elbow on his knee, did not move as she came in. And there was nowhere else to sit, so she sat down on the edge of the divan, at a distance from him, resting her weight on her hand in the position of one who has alighted somewhere for just a moment and has every intention of leaving again. She looked at him, without smiling. He looked at her, very far from smiling.

"Well, how do you like this place?" he asked, roughly. It was clear he had no idea of what to say or do.

"It has been built specially then?"

"Yes. Orders. Built to specification. Exactly. It was finished only this morning."

"It is certainly very elegant and pleasant," she said. "Quite different from anything else I've seen on my way here."

"Certainly not my style," he said. "But if it is yours, then that's the main thing."

This had a sort of sulky gallantry, but he was restless, and sighing continually, and it was evident all he wanted to do was to make his escape.

"I suppose the intention was that it should be suited to us both?" she remarked.

"I don't care," said he violently and roughly, his inner emotions breaking out of him. "And obviously you don't either."

"We're going to have to make the best of it," she said, intending consolation, but it was wild and bitter.

They looked at each other with a frank exchange of complicity: two prisoners who had nothing in common but their incarceration.

This first, and frail, moment of tolerance did not last.

He had flung himself back on this marriage couch of theirs, arms behind his head, his sandalled feet dusty on the covers, which were of fine wool, dyed in soft colours, and embroidered. Nowhere could he have seemed more out of place. She was able to construct his usual surroundings by how he slouched there, gazing at the ceiling as if she did not exist.

She examined the place. This was a very large room, opening out on two sides into gardens through a series of rounded arches. The other two sides had unobtrusive doors leading—on one—to the rooms for her use where she had already been, and on the other, presumably, to his. The ceiling was rounded and high, fluted at the edges. The whole room was painted a softly shining ivory, but there were patterns of gold, soft red, and blue, and beside each archway embroidered curtains were caught back with jewelled clasps. The fountains could be heard, and the running of the waters. This was not far from the gaiety and freshness of the public buildings of Andaroun, our capital, though her own quarters were plainer than these.

The great room was not all one empty sweep of space. A column sprung up from its centre, and curved out, and divided into several, all fluted and defined in the same gold, sky blue, and red. The floors were of sweetly smelling wood. Apart from the great low couch, there was a small table near one of the arches, with two graceful chairs on either side of it.

A horse whinnied. A moment later, Yori appeared outside one of the arches, and would have come in if she had not run across and stopped him. It was easy to guess what had happened. He had been confined somewhere, and had jumped free, and the soldiers set to guard him did not dare to follow into these private gardens with the pavilion all the country had been talking of for weeks. She put her hands up to his cheeks, pulled down his head, whispered into first one ear, and then the other, and the horse swung around and went out of sight, back to its guard.

When she turned, Ben Ata was standing just behind her, glaring.

"I can see that it is true, what we have heard here. You are all witches in your country."

"It is a witchcraft easy to learn," she said, but as he continued to glare, her humour went, and now she crossed swiftly to the bed and,

throwing down one of the big cushions, sat on it cross-legged. She
had not thought that now he must do the same, or remain above her
on the bed, but he was uncertain, seemed to feel challenged by her,
and in his turn pulled a cushion off the bed, pushed it against a wall,
and sat.

They sat opposite each other, on their two cushions.

She was at home, since this was how she usually seated herself, but
he was uncomfortable, and seemed afraid to make any movement, in
case the cushion slid about the polished floor.

"Do you always wear clothes like that?"

"I put this on especially for you," she countered, and he reddened
again: since her arrival she had seen more angry, embarrassed men
than ever in her life, and she was on the point of wondering if they
had some disorder of the blood or the skin.

"If I had known you were going to arrive like this I would have
ordered dresses for you. How was I to know you'd turn up like a servant?"

"Ben Ata, I never wear elaborate clothes."

He was eyeing the plain looseness of her robe with annoyance and
exasperation.

"I thought you were supposed to be the queen."

"You cannot be distinguished from one of your own soldiers."

Suddenly he bared his teeth in a grin, and muttered something that
she understood meant: "Take the thing off, and I'll show you."

She knew he was angry, but not how much. On their campaigns,
when the army reached new territory, into his tent would be thrust
some girl, or she was thrown down at his feet. She would nearly
always be crying. Or she might be hissing and spitting. She might bite
and scratch as he entered her. She could weep throughout and not
cease weeping. A few gritted their teeth, and their loathing of him
did not abate. He was not a man who enjoyed inflicting suffering, so
these he would order to be returned to their homes. But those who
wept or who struggled in a way he recognized he did enjoy, and
would tame them, slowly. These were the conventions. These he
obeyed. He had penetrated, and often impregnated, women all over
his realm. But he had not married, he did not plan to marry, for the
present arrangement did not come within his notions of marriage,
about which he had the sentimental and high-flown ideas of a man

ignorant of women. This woman with whom he was to be afflicted almost indefinitely, at least at intervals, was something outside his experience.

Everything about her disturbed him. She was not unbeautiful, with her dark eyes, dark hair, and the rest of the usual appurtenances, but there was nothing in her that set out to challenge him physically, and so he was cold.

"How long am I supposed to stay with you?" she enquired next, in exactly the cut-and-dried way he now—dismally—expected of her.

"They said, a few days."

There was a long silence. The great pleasant room was full of water sounds, and watery reflections from the pools and fountains.

"How do you do it in your country?" he enquired, knowing this was clumsy but not able to think of anything else.

"Do *what*?"

"Well, we hear you have a lot of children, for a start."

"I have five of my own. But I am the mother of many. More than fifty."

She could see that everything she said put greater distance between them.

"It is our custom, if a child is left an orphan, that I should become its mother."

"Adopt it."

"It is not one of our words. I become its mother."

"I suppose you feel about them exactly as you do about your own," he said, and this was a mimicry. But of something she had not said.

"No, I did not say that. Besides, fifty children are rather more than one can keep very close to."

"Then how are they your children?"

"They all have the same rights. And I spend the same time with each of them, as I am able."

"It's not my idea of a mother for *my* children."

"Is that what is expected of us, you think?"

This infuriated him! He had not *thought* very much at all about this appalling, affronting imposition, he had been too emotional. But at the least he had supposed that there would be children "to cement the alliance"—or something of that sort.

"Well, what else? What did you have in mind? Amorous dalliance once every few weeks? You!" And he snorted out his disgust with her.

She was trying not to look at him too closely. She had seen that a close steady look—which was her way—discomfited him. And besides, he appealed to her less than she did to him. She found this great soldier gross, with his heavy overheated flesh, his hot, resentful eyes, his rough sun-bleached hair which reminded her of the fleeces of a much prized breed of sheep that flourished on a certain mountain.

"There's more to mating than children," she observed.

And the commonsensicalness of this caused him to groan out loud and strike his fists hard on the floor beside him.

"Well, if so, one wouldn't think you knew much about *that*."

"Indeed," she retorted. "But in fact it is one of the skills of our Zone."

"Oh, no," he said. "Oh, no, no, no, no." And he sprang up and went striding about the room, beating the delicate walls with his fists.

She, still cross-legged on her cushion, watched him, interested, as she would have done some strange new species.

He stopped. He seemed to make an effort. Then he turned, teeth gritted, strode across to her, picked her up, and threw her on the couch. He put his hand across her mouth in the approved way, twitched up her dress, fingered himself to see if he was up to it, thrust himself into her, and accomplished his task in half a dozen swift movements.

He then straightened himself, for he had not removed his feet from the floor during this process and, already embarrassed, showed his feeling that all was not right by a gesture of concern most unusual in him: he twitched her dress down again and removed his hand from her mouth quite gently.

She was lying there looking up at him quite blank. Amazed. She was not weeping. Nor scratching. Nor calling him names. Nor showing the cold relentless repulsion that he dreaded to see in his women. Nothing. It occurred to him that she was *interested* in a totally unsuspected phenomenon.

"Oh, you," he groaned out, between his teeth, "how did I get saddled with you."

At which she suddenly let out a snort of something that was unmistakably amusement. She sat up. She swung her legs down over the couch, then she all at once burst into swift tears that shook her shoulders quite soundlessly, and then, just as suddenly, she stopped crying, and crept to her cushion, where she sat with her back to the wall, staring at him.

He noted that she was afraid of him, but not in any way that could appeal to him.

"Well," he said, "that's that." He gave her uneasy sideways glances, as if waiting for a comment.

"Is that really what you do?" she enquired. "Or is it because you don't like me?"

At this he gave her a look which was all appeal, and he sat on the bottom of the bed, and pounded it hard, with his fists.

She saw, at last, that he was a boy, he was not much more than a small boy. She saw him as one of her own half-grown sons, and for the first time, her heart softened.

Looking at him with the tears still full in her great eyes, she said, "You know, I think there might be something you could learn from us."

He gave a sort of shake of his great shaggy head, as if too much was reaching his ears all at once. But he remained leaning forward, not looking at her, but listening.

"For one thing, have you never heard that one may choose the times to conceive children?"

He winced. But only because again she talked of children. He pounded the bed with one fist, and stopped.

"You did not know that the nature of a child may be made by its conception?"

He shook his head and hung it. He sighed.

"If I am pregnant now, as I could be, then this child will have nothing to thank us for."

He suddenly flung himself down on the bed, prone, and lay there, arms outstretched.

Again, a long silence. The smell of their coupling was a small rank reminder of lust, and he looked up at her. She sat leaning against the wall, very pale, tired, and there was a bruise by her mouth, where his thumb had pressed.

He let out a groan. "It seems there is something I can learn from you," he said, and it was not in a child's voice.

She nodded. Looking at each other, they saw only that they were unhappy, and did not know what to expect from the other.

She it was who got up, sat by him on the couch, and laid her small hands on both sides of his great neck as he still lay prone, chin on his fist.

He turned over. It was an effort for him to face her.

He took her hands, and lay there on his back, she sitting quietly close to him. She tried to smile, but her lips trembled, and tears rolled down her face. He gave an exclamation, and pulled her down beside him. He was astounded that his own eyes had tears in them.

He tried to comfort this strange woman. He felt her small hands on his shoulders, in a pressure of consolation and pity.

Thus they fell asleep together, worn out by it all.

This was the first lovemaking of these two, the event which was fusing the imaginations of two realms.

He woke, and was at once alert. His senses were anxiously at work, mapping the space that surrounded him where it should not, coming to terms with sounds that suggested whispering, danger. His tent flap had been left open . . . but the opening was higher than it should be: his tent had been torn away by a wind, or an attack? Water . . . water flowing, and rising: the canals were overflowing, would he find himself standing in water? Ready to accept the cold wet clasp of a calamitous flood around his ankles, he swung his feet over on to a dry floor, and had taken several strides forward, calling out in the hoarse shocked voice of nightmare for his orderly, when he saw that he had mistaken the high curve of the central pillar where it met the ceiling for the tent opening. At once he remembered everything. He turned around in the dark, believing that the woman Al·Ith could be mocking him. But it was too dark even to see the couch. What he wanted then was simply to stride out of that place and not come back. With the understanding it was the fountains tinkling he had been taking for floods and inundations, the panic thought overcame him that he was not himself. He was undermined, unmanned, and made a coward. Bitterness shook him; his mouth was dry with it. Quite simply he was appalled—by the situation, by himself, by *her*. Yet, if he knew nothing else, he knew obedience. An order had brought him here to this effeminate pavilion, and duty must take him back to that couch. Convinced that *she* was lying awake and somehow watching him, he nevertheless took cautious steps in the dark until his shins encountered the softness of the couch. He slid himself to a half-sitting position, and began feeling the couch for her limbs—for her. Then he was groping all over the surface for her and finding nothing. She had escaped! Relief! That could only be her fault, and not his! He did not have to do anything! But then, these thoughts were chased away by indignation, and by chase lust. If she had escaped she must be caught. The confusions and indecisions of the last minutes came together in a surge of energy. He actually began a lively whistling— then thought she might be somewhere in the room, perhaps behind the pillar, watching him. And laughing. He swung around and strode to the pillar and felt all about with his hands. Nothing. Again he was about to raise his voice to call his orderly, and remembered that there were to be no servants here, no regular attendants. He did not mind about that: this king was happiest on campaign, a soldier among soldiers, and not marked out from them except that it was his task to make decisions. What he did mind was having to be alone with *her* without attendants. Shut up with a woman. This woman. Who as a witch might certainly be somewhere in the room, seeing where he could not. Anger fed his decisiveness. He pulled his army cloak about him and strode to the door opening on to the fountains.

Awaking in the dark, he had not known the time. In the camps a sentry was ordered to halt outside his tent and to announce—not call out, but state—each half-hour. If he was awake, he needed to know where he was in the countries of the night. Which he did not enjoy: distrusted, in fact. He liked to put his head down soon after the evening meal and to sleep until first light, and to know nothing in between—but if awake for some reason, then he would wait for the low reassuring voice of the sentry.

Now he stood square in the archway, with the dark room behind him, looking out past the arches of the porticoes, and he knew at once that it was about an hour before dawn, although the sky had no moon or stars in it and low clouds hurried past. An irregular streak showed the long rectangle that was the pool where seven jets of water played. Irritation was remembered—almost claimed him again. The dimensions of this pavilion, its adjacent rooms, the approaches, the galleries surrounding it, the gardens, the many pools and fountains, the walks, and the steps and the levels—every one exactly specified, prescribed, measured, and all in the damnedest of measurements—everything in halves and quarters and bits and pieces, irregularities and unexpectedness. The architects, none of whom of course had built anything but army forts and towers and barracks for years, had been expected to mutiny. At any rate, this particular very long and narrow pool, or ditch, as he had muttered when he had seen the plans, had had seven jets prescribed for it. Not ten, or five, or twenty, but seven. And the long oval pool beyond it had three, of different sizes from each other . . . a clump of nine spice trees stood to one side of the pools, and under them he saw something shadowy and disturbing. But it was too big to be a woman. He heard movements, though. Just as he realised it was a horse—that damned horse! —his eyes had come to life enough to see that she was sitting quietly at the end of the long pool, between it and the oval pool, on a raised stone dais, or terrace, which was a circle that had a radius of exactly seven and a half feet. The masons building it had joked it would make a good bed. Oh, the jokes, the jokes, he had been sick of them, was sick to death of them, of the whole thing . . . he could not make out if she had seen him. But it occurred to him that if he had seen her, she could be expected to have seen him.

However, there was nothing ridiculous about his stance there, legs apart, arms folded, everything soldierly and correct.

It occurred to him that he was still alert and poised because his expectations of a chase, a pursuit, were not quieted in him: if there she sat, then he would not have to chase after her, poor draggled fugitive, across the marshes and puddles, with half the army after her, and he heading them all . . . so he let himself relax.

He was *not* going to make the first move, or greet her. He did not want to greet her. He did not feel friendly in the slightest. He did not remember the moment of tenderness they had shared, and his present self could only have repudiated it . . . he had been standing there for some time. Minutes. She had made no move. He could see her face glimmering whitely there. That dreary dark dress of hers was of course absorbed by the night. He believed she might be sitting there hating him. He could smell now the damp breeze that always stirred just before dawn. He loved to be awakened by that little wind, which crept so softly over the earth, setting the bushes astir, bringing the smell of grass and water. When sleeping out on marches he always woke to it, contrasting it pleasantly with the rainy winds that drove across this flat land of his sometimes for weeks at a time . . . he had, without knowing he was going to, taken a few steps out and along the edge of the pool. He had not taken his sandals off at all, and now he was unable to walk quietly and surprise her. But still she said nothing. He had come up to her, past the seven silly jets of water, and up to the edge of the little terrace, before she turned her head, and remarked, "It is pleasant sitting here, Ben Ata."

"You didn't sleep well, I see!"

"I never sleep more than two hours, or three."

This annoyed him: of course she would be at home in the night—what else!

As there was nothing else to do, he sat down on the dais, but on the edge of it, away from her.

Now he could see that there were two horses under the spice trees, hers—the black one—and another, white: the black one he could see only because it stood very close to the other, making a black horse-shaped shadow against the white.

"I see that in your country you have horses the way we have dogs!"

"No, Ben Ata." He could hear from her voice—he could hardly see her face—that she was conciliatory, or even afraid? His blood did leap a little at the thought she was afraid, but lay subdued again. He heard himself sigh. A dismal weight seemed to press him down. All his elation had gone. He was sensing with the whole of him, his memories and his hopes too, how alien was this woman: how the strangeness of her did weigh him down, how she oppressed him. He was feverishly casting about in his memories for girls like this one, that he could match with her, to make some sort of guide for himself, for he really did intend to try and understand her. But there was nothing there remotely like her. Like his mother? Certainly not! She had been foolish—he supposed. But then he had not seen her, really, since he was seven and had been sent to the soldiers to train. His sisters? He had not seen them either since then, except for brief glimpses on trips home; and they had married far away on the outer reaches of the Zone. The wives of his officers? The point was, he could not remember being discommoded by a woman, and above all it was what this one did. She never reacted as his expectations dictated. He was as jumpy and edgy as a badly handled horse . . . horses again. He did not really like horses. Not that he remembered wondering before if he liked them or not, they were there.

"Ben Ata, when I got up out of bed and came out here, I saw my horse standing here by the fountain. I thought he had not been properly looked after but it was not that. He was not hungry or thirsty . . ."

He, and she, both heard the breath let slowly out of his lungs, not so much in exasperation as in sheer wonder at it all, a sort of stunned imposed patience.

". . . but he was disturbed in his mind and he had jumped out of the enclosure and come to try and find me. That is why I woke, I expect. But while I have been trying to find out exactly what's wrong, it isn't easy. I told him to go and fetch one of his friends from the enclosure . . ."

He had let out his breath again: it was a cautious sigh.

"I am surprised," said he, in a soft, tentative voice, as if trying out this new key in sarcasm, "that you didn't go down to the stables and fetch the horse yourself."

"But, Ben Ata, you know that I cannot leave this place. Not without my shield. I am confined to the pavilions and the gardens. Otherwise the air of your Zone would make me very ill."

"All right, all right, I had forgotten. No, I hadn't . . . but . . . oh, for goodness' sake, do . . ."

Oaths and expletives of all kinds were dying on his tongue, and he heard what he had said as if some foreigner had spoken.

"He went off. It took some time, but he has brought this white horse with him. Do you know this horse?"

"No."

"They came up the hill just before you came to stand in the door there. Now look, Ben Ata."

He could in fact see now that the two beasts stood quietly side by side, their heads hanging. They were the picture of despondency.

"I shall go to them." And she was off down through the fountains on bare feet. He could see her easily now against the eastern sky. A vast greyness covered the land. Shreds of cloud sped past low overhead. He followed her, not at all willingly, and the two beasts, seeing her there, came together up from the trees and stood before her, their heads drooping. He watched her caress her black horse, and the white one; bend to speak to the white horse and the black one. He saw how she laid her hands on their damp slow flesh, and put her arms around their necks as she stood between them. Then she came away, and clapped her hands, once, and they turned and cantered off down the hill, both rising at the same moment in a great jump that took them over the stone walls of their corral.

She turned to face him. He could now see her clearly. Her small face was very pale, and worried. Her hair was loose and damp down her shoulders, with a fine mist on it. By her mouth was the bruise. As he saw it the wildest need seized him to crush her to him—but not in lust or in love, far from it. A wave of brutality almost conquered him. But he felt her small hand in his, and he was utterly stupefied by it. Perhaps as a small child another had put a confiding friendly hand in his, and not since.

He could not believe it! While he had been holding in impulses of pure disliking hostility, she put her hand in his, as if it was a natural thing to do. His own hand remained stiff and rejecting.

She then hastened her pace and went on in front of him, past flowers, past the many jetting fountains, till she reached the raised round place where she sat, tucking her bare feet in under her skirt.

His thoughts were all a riot of amazed expostulation. This great queen, this conquest—for he could not help feeling her being here as one—was more poor and plain than the girls who herded the deer.

She looked straight up at him, insistent, troubled. "Ben Ata, there is something very wrong."

Again the heavy sigh from him. "If you say so."

"Yes. Yes, there is. Tell me, your herds, your animals, have there been reports of illness?"

He now looked straight at her, serious, in thought. "Yes, there were reports. Wait though—no one seemed to know what was wrong."

"And the birth rate among them?"

"It's down. Yes, it is." Even as he confirmed her, he could not resist the jeer: "And what did the two nags have to tell you?"

"They don't know what is wrong. But they are low in spirits, all of them. They have lost the will to mate . . ." As the obligatory jest became imminent, she pressed on, dismissing it—and *him*, he felt, in wild rebellion at her—with, "No, do listen, Ben Ata. It is all the animals. All. And the birds. And as we know, that means the plant kingdom, too, or if not now, soon . . ."

"Do we know?"

"Yes, of course."

Despite the feeble attempt at a jeer, in fact his eyes most seriously engaged hers, in responsible enquiry. He believed her. He was alerted, and ready to do what he could. This seriousness brought him down beside her, closer than before, but not as if he felt any likelihood of comfort or reassurance from her touch.

"Are as many children being born?"

"No, there are not. There has been a long steady decrease."

"Yes, and with us, too."

"Outlying parts of our Zone are lying derelict."

"Yes, and with us, too."

They were silent a long while. Through the drenched air of the eastern sky, light struggled from the rising sun. The clouds were a pale wet gold, and a yellowish haze lay everywhere. The spice trees were spangled with rainbows, and shafts of opaline light pierced the banks of fog rising from the marshes. The fountains splashed on water, and their noise seemed subdued by the general damp.

"I suppose it is quite pretty," she said in the smallest of dismayed voices, and suddenly he let out a bellow of a laugh, but it was not unfriendly, far from it. "Oh, come now, it isn't as bad as that," he said. "You'll see, when the sun is up, and things have dried off. We have some very pleasant days down here, you know."

"I hope so! Feel my dress, Ben Ata!"

But this invitation put them back again. It was certainly not coquetry, and to be invited to feel her dress for any other reason affronted him. He took a fold of the dark blue stuff between thumb and finger, and pronounced it damp.

"Ben Ata, we have gone wrong somewhere. Both our Zones. Badly. What are we going to do?"

His hand dropped away. He frowned. "Why don't they tell us what is wrong, quite simply, and be done with it. And then we could put it right." He observed her very small wry smile. "Well, and what is wrong with that?"

"I think we are supposed to think it out for ourselves."

"But why! What for! What is the sense of it! It wastes time."

"That's not how things work—I think that must be it," she almost whispered.

"How do you know?" But as he asked, he observed himself that his question was already answered. "How long is it since you had an Order?"

"So long that no one can remember. But there are old stories. And songs," she said.

"Well, I certainly can't remember anything. When I became king nothing of the sort was told me. When the Order arrived I remembered that they have to be obeyed. That I did know. But that was all."

"In my lifetime there has been nothing. Nor in my mother's."

"And hers?"

"Not for generations of the Mothers."

"Ah," he said, brisk and noncommittal.

"You know, I think that things are very serious. Very bad. Dangerous. They must be!"

"You think they are?"

"Well, for us to be together like this. Ordered to be. Don't you see?"

Now he was silent again. He was frowning. He sighed, without knowing he did, and it was from the effort of unaccustomed thought —he was not used to speculation on these lines. As for her, she watched him: this Ben Ata, the man who sat quiet, thinking, trying to puzzle out the meaning of their dilemma—this man she felt she could like. Respect. Again her hand went out and into his, in an impulse of friendliness, and his great hand closed over hers like a bird trap. It opened at once and she saw him look down at their two hands in incredulity. Then he gave her the most helpless, unhappy glance.

Now she sighed, briskly withdrew her hand, and stood up.

She turned her back on the yellow and gold skies of the east, and stared up past him into the sky. She was looking up at the peaks and heights of her own realm. "Ohhhh," she sighed out, "look . . . I had no idea . . . I did not have any idea. . . ."

The mountains of Zone Three climbed more than a third of the way to the zenith. She stood with her head bent back, gazing up at the towering lit heights there. The rising sun was making them blaze and glitter, and the sharp points of the uttermost peaks seemed to be heaped with clouds that shone pink and red and gold—but they were not clouds, these were the piled snows of a thousand years. And low down against this mass lay the dark edge, rock-fringed, fort-fringed, which was the edge of the escarpment she had ridden down only the day before. The vast plain that lay between the escarpment and the foothills of the plateau, which was itself the low base for the in-numerable mountain masses of our land—this was not visible at all. One would not know it was there. The inhabitants of this low watery Zone could never imagine, gazing up at that scene of a hundred mountain ranges, the infinite variations of a landscape and country that were not to be seen by them at all. Al·Ith was standing there, her hands cradling her bent back head, gazing up, up, and she was smiling with delight and longing, and weeping with happiness as she gazed.

Ben Ata gazed at her. He was uncomfortable.

"Don't do that," he said gruffly.

Reluctantly, she returned her gaze downward, and saw him dis-approving. "But why not?"

"It is not right."

"What isn't?"

"We do not encourage it."

"What?"

"Cloud gathering, we call it."

"You mean, people don't look up at all that . . . that *glory*?"

"It is weakening."

"But I don't believe it, Ben Ata!"

"It is so. Those are the laws."

"If I had to live down here I don't think I would be able to take my eyes away. Look, look . . ." and she flung her arms wide and exulted at the vast panoramas of light, of colour, that filled all the western skies. "Clouds!" she sang out. "Those are not clouds, that's our country, it is what we are."

"We have times for looking up there. Definite times. Festivals. Once every ten years. Otherwise people caught spending too much time looking up there are punished."

"And how do you punish them?"

"We put heavy weights on their heads so that they cannot look up."

"Ben Ata, that is wicked."

"I did not make the law. It has always been our law."

"Always, always, always . . . how do you know?"

"I do not think that any one of us has ever questioned it. You are the first."

She sank down beside him. Close. Again there was the small shrinking from her that he could not control. This exultation of hers, this rapture, was abhorrent to him. He could hardly bear to see her enhanced smiling face. Though on the other hand he did feel the beginnings of relief that she was not always so pale and serious. Her face, now illumined by the rosy light from those far peaks, was as pretty a pink as any girl's he could remember, and her heavy hair, still pearled from the mists, was in wisps around her face.

But: "You must not stare like that. It is against our laws. While you are here, you must obey our laws."

"Yes, that is proper," she whispered, and turned her eyes away.

"When you are in your own country, you can of course do as you like." He sounded to her like her brother, who had been steward of her household for many years before he had asked to be transferred to the post of Keeper of the Memories.

"But in our country that is what we *are*, Ben Ata."

Suddenly, and like light striking into her brain, she was dazzled. "Ben Ata, I've just had a . . ." but it had gone. She put her hands over her face and rocked back and forth, trying to remember what had just fled past her.

"Are you ill?"

"No, I am not. But I *almost* understood something."

"Well, let me know when you have."

At this the soldier got to his feet, and—just for a moment—took a glance at the glories of the mountainous paradise in the skies. Muttering to himself, "Quite right, of course people shouldn't waste their time on *that*—" he resolutely turned his head and marched off towards the pavilions. Al·Ith came behind, slowly, along the narrow pool, passing the jets, one, two, three—she, too, took one last look at her own country, and as resolutely averted her eyes, and looked instead at how the seven jets blurred the gleaming surface of the pool which was trying to reflect the heavy grey skies.

Inside the pavilion, everything awaited them. The large, silent, airy, white-gleaming room, with its delicate embroideries, and its bright paint patterns. The deep couch, hardly rumpled from their encounter. Through the arches at the other side could be seen nothing but grey. It was raining, and the gardened hillside that sloped to the camps was blotted out.

Ben Ata stood in the middle of the room by the pillar, looking at her, in the most comically disconcerted way in the world. And she stood similarly looking at him.

They felt for each other at that moment friendship. Comradeship. If they were nothing else, these two, they were representatives and embodiments of their respective countries. Concern for their realms was what they were. This concern, in him, took the shape of obedience. Duty. In her these tight compulsions were lightened to responsiveness to events, situations, but they were of the same kind, nevertheless. Their people were what *they* were, their thoughts were. Their lives could be nothing else, or less . . . yet now both were aware, and deeply, so that they were shocked and stirred to their depths, that all this concern and this duty of theirs had not prevented them from going very wrong. . . . They were looking at each other, not shrinking from each other's gaze at all, but both trying to enter in behind the sober, thoughtfulness of his grey eyes, the soft gleam of her black eyes, so that they could reach something deeper, and other.

"What are we going to do, Ben Ata?" she whispered.

This time it was he who extended his hand, just a little, and she went to him, and took it in both of hers. "We have to think," she said. "We must try and find out . . ."

Now he put his great arms lightly about her, almost as if afraid the size and weight of him might crush her, and as if he were attempting, or trying out, entirely new and not altogether welcome sensations and, avoiding the bruise beside her mouth, he gazed into that face of hers which seemed to him as if it were made of a substance or a light that he could never hope to, or even want to, encompass. He kissed her, as clumsily as a boy. He felt that her mouth was coming alive and responding in ways that could still only alarm him. Quick light kisses, the subtle tastes and touches of a smiling and easy companionship, the teasing and the response on response on response—all this was too much of an imposition, and after a few moments, he again carried her to the couch. He did not miss that, as he held her still so that he could enter her, she shrank from him and tightened as if everything in her and of her repudiated him. He felt this and contrasted it with the beginnings of the sensuous exchange which he had cut short. Her ways seemed too difficult for him, or at least unfamiliar, or out of his reach just then. And his were striking him as crude . . . he could only complete the entry and the possession by taking a furtive glance at the bruise he had inflicted, and this itself now shamed him so that as he spurted he groaned and then lay still. He was filled, amazingly, with grief.

She was quite still, and a look at her face showed her eyes open and desolate.

"All right," he said. "I know you think I am a boor."

"You have very bad habits in your country," she remarked at last, and it was cold. Though he believed there was at least the possibility of a revival of her friendliness.

He jumped up, pulling the cloak all around him, and covering her legs with the blue dress.

"You know what I'm going to do," he positively hissed at her, "I'm going to order you up some dresses from the town."

At this she began to laugh. Weakly, her head turned to one side, and her hand at her mouth, but she laughed. He smiled, in relief, though he knew this laugh of hers might just as well be weeping.

"It's time we both ate, anyway," he said. And he sounded even more like her brother the steward, so that now she laughed harder, and then turned over, put her head under her arms and called out to him, "Get out of here, get out, and leave me alone."

He went, marching briskly, into the rooms set aside for him, on the right of this central pavilion.

There he bathed, and changed his garments. He put on a tunic used for ceremonies and special occasions, because there was nothing else in his cupboards that seemed suitable for this tryst, or wedding breakfast.

Then he went back into the central room. She was in her rooms. He sat at the little table in the window against the arches where grey rain was sweeping in front of a pouring wind, and almost at once put his chin in his hand and fell to thinking of their dilemmas as rulers. There she found him later, so deep in thought he did not hear her.

She had found in her cupboards a light white linen wrapper that had been left there by one of the maids who had swept and tidied the pavilion. She had left her dark blue garment behind and had come in to him dressed in what he recognized as a maid's overall—so he saw when at last he did realize she was there.

He said nothing, however. He thought that the fresh white became her. He thought that she was quite pretty, he could suppose, if only she was able to make her face more ready to meet his needs. But she was serious again, and this matched his real mood.

Between their two chairs was a small square table, inlaid with coloured woods and carved. This, too, had been exactly specified by the Order.

Now he said, "What do you want to eat?"

As she seemed about to answer, he clapped his hands, and there appeared before her fruit, bread, a hot aromatic drink.

"Very frugal," said he, and clapped his hands again. Before him appeared cold meats and the hard biscuit they used on their campaigns.

"Very frugal," said she.

"You aren't impressed at my little trick?" he enquired, brisk and as it were brotherly-sarcastic.

"Very, but I suppose it is part of the furnishings of the Order."

"Yes, it is. Do you have anything like it?"

"Never."

"Well, we just think of it and it arrives." And she could see from the boyish pleasure he was showing that he was about to cause something else to materialise.

"No, don't," she said. "We mustn't abuse it."

"You are right. *Naturally*." And he began eating, in efficient and large mouthfuls.

This meal of theirs was prolonged deliberately by them. Both liked each other best when in their roles of sovereign responsibility— thoughtful, serious. He told himself that he longed for her to behave like the girls he was used to, but the truth was, he was already used to her, and had begun to rely on her. As for her, her natural antipathy to his physical type and kind could only be set aside when she was able to watch him thinking, and trying to approach her to share what she knew faced them both.

They talked more than they ate, and sat watching the interminable rain sweeping past the arches and enclosing them in steady hush.

Towards midafternoon it stopped and, with bare feet, they walked around and between and among the faithful fountains, still plashing into the pools that had overflowed everywhere, so that they walked through inches of warm water. Ben Ata was kicking and dragging his feet through the shallows like a child. He had the look of someone let off a long leash: it was a foolish look, and Al·Ith was repelled by it. This was a man who did not know how to play without self-consciousness. He felt guilty, he had even the air of someone who needed punishment. Soon she suggested they should go indoors and then he put on stiffness and a correct manner like a child rebuked too harshly. She took a quick glance at the peaks of her own country, already slightly tinted by the sun going down behind them in a crystalline blue, and saw him tighten his lips and shake his head. With him there was no midway—licence or prohibition, one or the other! But inside they were able to regain a balance, and to talk again.

They had reached no conclusions about what was wrong in their two realms, or where they had taken false decisions—for it was clear to them both that this must be the case. But it seemed to them that they were all the time on the edge of some understanding that nevertheless continually eluded them.

The evening shadows enclosed the pavilions, and lights sprang up in the fluted edges of the ceilings. The two were walking about their —prison. For both knew that this was how the other felt. But they were not able to put themselves enough into each other's place so as to understand why. Ben Ata, with every particle of himself, felt a need to throw off these surroundings, and to push away her whose very presence seemed to set up an irritable resistance in him as she moved to and fro, passing him, so that as she came near all the flesh on that side was protesting and shrinking. He had not experienced anything like this in his life. But then he had never spent such a long time alone with any women, let alone one who talked to him, and behaved "like a man," as he kept telling himself. These waves of emotion were so strong that as they lessened, he felt astonished at himself, and wondered if he were not ill. Thoughts of her possible accomplishments in the dark arts returned. As for her, she was sorrowful, grief-struck, she wanted to weep. These emotions were foreign to her. She could not remember ever feeling a low, luxurious need to weep, to succumb, to put her head on a shoulder—not anyone's, let alone Ben Ata's. And yet she caught herself wishing more than once that he would carry her to that couch again, not to "make love"—certainly not, for he was a barbarian—but to enclose her in his arms. This need could only amaze and disquiet her. She believed herself afflicted by the airs of this Zone, so enervating and dismal. Despite her shield, despite the special dimensions of this place, she must have become perverted in some way. With all her being she longed to be free and back in her own realm where an easy friendly lightheartedness was what everyone expected to feel, and where tears were a sign of physical illness.

Their pacings back and forth and up and down became such a frenzy that both even laughed, and tried to joke about it—but suddenly he let out a muffled shout, which she recognised easily as the sign of an organism reaching breaking point, and he said, "I must go and see about something . . ." with which he disappeared into the dark down the hill.

She knew he had gone to the encampments—they were his home.

As for her, his going left her breathing more easily. But as she still paced to and fro, the words came into mind as clearly as if they had been spoken into her inner ear: "It is time for you to go home now, Al·Ith. You will have to come back later, but now go home."

She could not doubt that this was the Order. Her spirits rose in a swoop. Not even stopping to put on her dark dress, but staying as she was in her white maid's wrapper, she ran out in the other direction from that taken by her husband, Ben Ata, and standing among the fountains called to her horse. Which she did by thinking him to her. Soon she heard him cantering up the hill, and then picking his way through the flowers and the pools. She was on his back and off down the hill and on the road westwards before Ben Ata could have reached his soldiers.

She was not afraid of being stopped. It was dark. She had only to follow a straight road that ran without branching or even curving, straight on, and on, with the straight line of trees on one side looking like bunches of leafy twigs in the dark, and the canal lying on the other. Very few people went out at night here. In fact Ben Ata was quite shocked that in her realm the night was valued for visiting, feasts, and all kinds of enjoyments. He allowed that with them the air might be less dangerous, which he assured her it was down here. Al·Ith did not find it more than unpleasantly heavy and damp, and long before dawn the road rose steadily before her, to where the escarpment's sharp lift began. It was necessary for her not to be stopped by the soldiers and on this side of the frontier. She ripped the sleeves out of her wrapper, tore each in half, and bound these around the hooves of her faithful horse. Then she rode on, making no sound.

She did not see the flocks and herds as she passed them, but she heard them, and thought of the poor subdued boy she had seen face down before her. She did not see the great pile of the "dangerous" place, and told herself that on her next visit, which alas was inescapable, she must ask Ben Ata about it. She saw no one on the road. She heard soldiers singing and carousing not far from the frontier, but went past them without hindrance.

As the dawn lightened the sky far behind her, and she was lifting her eyes to wonder and marvel at the snow lands of her mountains, she heard a horse racing behind her, and thought it must be Ben Ata. She pulled in her horse and waited patiently for him to come up. It was Jarnti. He was without his armour, but had his shield, and was covered by the regulation cape.

"Where are you going, madam?"

"Home. As I have been ordered."

"Ben Ata does not know it. He is in the mess tent with the officers."

"I am sure he is," she said, but he did not respond to her humour. He was not looking at her, but rather to one side. He had the furtive shamefaced look she remembered as being peculiarly his. But he seemed to be straining to move his eyes further to one side . . . then with the same difficult movement, he was turning his head to the other side. And then he seemed to be attempting to lift his head, and failing.

She suddenly felt on the verge of an understanding.

"Jarnti, do you ever look at the mountains?"

"No," he said, making his black horse wheel about, in protest.

"Why not?"

"We are forbidden."

"It seems there is a great deal you are forbidden. Look now, look, how beautiful it is."

Again his horse wheeled and swerved all about the road, and she could see that he was trying to force his eyes up. But while they kept flickering to one side and then another, he did not raise his head. *Could* not.

"Did you cloud gather when you were a child?"

"Yes."

"And you were punished with the heavy helmet. For how long?"

"For a very long time," he blurted, with sudden reminiscent anger. And the obedience took over again.

"Do a lot of children disobey, and watch the mountains?"

"Yes, a great many. And sometimes young people."

"And they all wear the punishment helmet and thereafter are obedient?"

"That is so."

"How did you know I had gone?"

"This horse was left alone, and he jumped over the wall and was cantering after you. I knew you had gone, and so I got on him."

"Well, I shall now ride on, Jarnti, and I daresay I shall see you again. But tell Ben Ata that if it is he who gets the Order that we must meet again, and here in your Zone, then he doesn't have to send a company of soldiers."

"We do what we think is correct."

"How many soldiers did the Order specify were necessary to fetch me? None, I think."

"It is not safe for you to ride alone."

"I have ridden safely to this point, and once over the border and into my country I can assure you I have no need to fear."

"That I know," he said softly, and in admiration and with a longing in his voice that told her that he would dream of his visit to her Zone for all his life. Even though he might not know why he did.

Al·Ith examined this man while he kept his eyes averted.

He was built like Ben Ata, strong, brown-skinned, though his hair was black and so were his eyes. But she knew him, intimately, because of Ben Ata. He would be the same with his woman or women —blustering, and a boor. Yet for one moment, astounding her by its strength, she wished she were inside those arms like pillars, "safe," "sheltered." She called, "Goodbye, Jarnti, and tell Ben Ata I will see him when I have to." The grimace on Jarnti's face was quite enough reward for her brief flare of spite, and she at once felt remorse. "Tell him . . . tell him . . ." but she could not think of anything softening and sweet. "Say I left because I was told to go," she brought out at last and sped up the road between the cliffs of the escarpment. Turning her head, she saw him trying to lift his on its stiff neck to gaze up into the forbidden mountains. But he could not: he forced it up a little way, and then his face fell forward again.

She rode over the frontier with her shield held before her, and then when she was in the fresh high singing airs of her own country, she threw down the shield, flung herself off the horse, and danced around him, shieldless, laughing so that she could not stop. And on the peaks that stretched halfway up the sky now, the sunrise was scarlet and purple.

She wanted more than anything to be on the plateau, close under the mountains, but first she wished to make sure of certain facts. So when she had sung and danced herself back to her usual frame of mind, she got back on the horse, and turned off the road that ran to the plateau so that she would make a circle around it from right to left, through the outlying regions of the Zone. These were mostly pastoral, and farming, and she always enjoyed travelling there . . . but it was some time since she had made such a tour . . . how long? Prickling at the back of her mind was the knowledge that it had been a very long time. What had happened? How was it she had got slack like this? For she had. *Irresponsible*. There was no worse word. She was being stung, whipped along by it. Normally, after such a delight of dancing and retrieval of her self to the point where every atom sang and rejoiced, she would have expected to ride, or walk, or run through the long scented grasses of the steppe with nothing at her heels but the pleasures of the day, sunlight, crisp aromatic winds, the lights changing, always changing, on the peaks . . . but no, it was not so. She had been very wrong. Why? She even jumped down off her horse and stood with her arms around his neck and her face pressed into the slippery heat there, as if the horse's strength could feed understanding into her. She had been particularly busy? No, she could not believe so. Life had been as it always was, delightful, with the children, her friends, her lovers, the amiable pace of this realm setting the rhythms of the body and the mind into good humour, kindliness . . . thinking of the smiling, contented faces of her life, she rebelled that there might be something wrong—how *could* there be!

A man's voice said, "Are you in need of help?" She turned and saw he was an agriculturalist from one of the communal farms. Young, healthy, with that particular glistening warmth to him that was the mark of well-being and good humour, and which was so singularly lacking in Ben Ata's realm.

"No, I am well," she said. But he was examining her in doubt. She remembered she still wore the brief white wrapper, now sleeveless and ragged, and that the horse's hooves were bound in cloth. She pulled the rags off his hooves, and as she did so, he asked, "Ah, I see who you are. And how is marriage in Zone Four?" This was the sort of friendly enquiry that she would normally have expected, but she gave him a quick suspicious glance, which she was categorising as "a Zone Four look." But no, of course he meant nothing "impertinent" —a Zone Four word! Oh, she had been very much changed by her day and a half in that low place.

"You are right, I am Al·Ith. And I had forgotten I was wearing this thing. Tell me, would one of the women of your household lend me a dress of some kind?"

"Of course. I'll go now."

And he ran off to where she could see a group of farmsteads surrounded by flocks and herds.

Meanwhile, she found a small tree, set the horse free to graze, and sat down.

When he came running back, with a garment in his hand, he saw her there, and the horse cropping, but close enough that he could lift his nose often to nuzzle and caress her.

"What is your horse's name, Al•Ith?"

"I haven't thought of a name good enough for him."

"Ah, then, he is a special friend!"

"Yes, he chose me as a friend almost from the first moment."

"Yori," he said. "Your companion, your friend."

"Yes, that is very good!" And she stroked the horse's nose and whispered his name, Yori, into his ears.

"And I, too," said the man. "Of course I have always known you, but when I saw you, I felt at once that you were of me. My name is Yori, too." And he sat down on the grass opposite to her, and rested his arms on his knees, and leaned forward smiling.

And now Al•Ith was altogether thrown into doubt. She smiled, and nodded, but kept silent. If things had been normal, these words were of the sort she would have responded to at once. This man was her kind, and her flesh and his flesh communicated easily, and had from first glance. Sitting there with him among the warm drily scented grasses, the shade from the little tree sifting gently over them, it would have been the easiest thing to put out her hand, to his, and start a delicious hour or two of play. But voices seemed to ring through her, saying No. No! Why? Was she then already pregnant? Oh, she hoped not, for it was not in such a way that she had chosen children in the past. And if she were pregnant, then it was in the order of things and, indeed, required, and prescribed, to allow herself to be bathed and sustained by this man's particular and individual being, so that the child would be fed by his essences and so that it would hear his words and be nourished. When she had been pregnant—and after what care, and thought, and long careful choices—in the past, she had, as soon as she had been sure, chosen as beneficial influences for her child, several men who, knowing why they were chosen, and for what purpose, co-operated with her in this act of blessing and gracing the foetus. These men had a special place in her heart and in the annals of her Zone. They were Fathers of the children just as much as the Gene-Fathers were. Every child in the Zone had such exactly chosen Mind-Fathers, who were as responsible for it as were the Gene-Fathers. These men formed a group who, with the Gene-Mother, and the women who cared for the child, considered themselves joint-parents, forever available to her, or him, any time they were needed, collectively and individually. If she were indeed pregnant, then she could not begin too soon to choose her child's good influences.

"Yori . . ." and the horse pricked up his ears and moved forward, so that the two people both smiled and touched him gently to soothe him, "do you think I am pregnant?"

"I don't know."

"Would you know, in the normal run of things?"

"Yes, I have always done until now."

"Are you many times a father?"

"Twice a Gene-Father—and I expect to be one again in five years' time when my turn comes around. And seven times a Mind-Father."

"Have you always known?"

"Yes, from the first."

They looked at each other reflectively, in the way that would have led to play, but there was a barrier between them.

"If I were myself, it is you I would choose above any man, and I would choose you, too, for a Gene-Father, if a Gene-Child were required of me, but . . ."

Shadows came racing across the great steppe, the grasses rippled and hummed, the tree above them rustled, Yori the horse lifted his head and whinnied as if letting out into the air thoughts too painful to keep in, and she sat there with tears running down her face.

"Al·Ith! You are weeping," he said, in a low, appalled voice.

"I know! I have done nothing else these last days. Why? I don't understand myself! I understand nothing!" And she put her face in her hands and wept, while Yori the man caressed her hands, and Yori the horse snuffled at her arm.

Waves of understanding passed between her and the man through their hands, their severed flesh mourned because their two bodies knew they should be together, and she said, "That is a terrible place down there. Have I been poisoned by it?"

"Why is it? What is its nature?"

"How should I know?" She sounded peevish, and this shocked her. She sprang up. "I am irritable! I am angry! I feel the need to fling myself into strong arms, and weep—yours . . . oh, don't be shocked, don't be afraid. I shall of course not do any such thing. I have become suspicious of words and looks—now you tell me what the nature of Zone Four is!"

"Sit down, Al·Ith." This command, which was as she heard it, brought her to sit down: and she sat thinking that he had not meant an order, a command, but it was the sort of suggestion a friend made, yet she had *heard* an order.

"It is a place of compulsion," she said. "There are pressures we do not have here, and know nothing about. They can respond only if ordered, compelled."

"*Ordered?*"

"No, not *the* Order, not *Order*. But *do* this. *Do* that. They have no inner listening to the Law."

"Have they always been like that?" he asked, with a sudden illumination which she felt at once, so that she sat up and leaned forward, searching his face.

"Yes," she said. "That may be it. I think you are right."

"Al·Ith, things are very bad with us here."

"Yes, I know it. I know it *now*. I should have known it before. If I had not been remiss."

"Yes, we are saying now that you must have been remiss. Only now. For it is only now that these different events have come together to make the understanding."

"Why was it no one came to tell me . . ." and she remembered that they had, and she had not been listening. "Oh, it is right that I am being punished . . ." she cried out, and the amazingness of the words caused her to say in a low bitter voice, "Did you hear that? That's what I mean."

"I heard."

Again, they were quiet, sitting close, enclosed in harmonies.

"Perhaps if we came together you might be cured?" he suggested.

She said, "As you said that my first thought was suspicion—no, wait, listen. 'He is saying that for self-interest.' No, you must *not* be shocked at me. I am trying to explain . . . that is how it is with them down there and I am infected by it. . . . I believe that perhaps, if we joined, completely, I might be cured, improved at least. But there is some other obligation on me, an imposition I have to obey. . . . I feel it would not be honourable."

"Honourable?" And his smile was quizzical.

"Yes. Honourable."

"You do not belong to Ben Ata and his kingdom."

"Who knows!" And she got to her feet again. The thin white wrapper left her almost naked. She might as well have been. He wore the comfortable loose clothes of his calling, loose trousers, and singlet. They stood close together, hands joined. The black horse Yori stretched out his nose to them from a few paces away. This is a very favourite scene among Chroniclers and artists of our realm. It is called "The Parting." Or, for the subtler minds, "Al·Ith's Descent Into the Dark."

"I would ask you to travel with me," she said. "But I am not going to. I do not know myself. I do not trust myself. I must go alone. Meanwhile, tell me quickly how things are with you in this part of the steppe."

Holding her hands, he talked for a while about the sadness of the animals, the poor crops, the falling-off of the weather, the lessening in conception among animals and people.

"Thank you. And now I shall put on this dress. Tell me to whom I shall return it."

"It is my sister's. She sends it with her friendship."

"I shall send one to her in gratitude when I get back to my home."

He saluted her with a smile, and a gentle kiss on her cheek, and went off. She took off the white wrapper, standing naked, for comfort, among the sunny plants, and then put on the sister's robe, which was a dark red, shaped as she liked best, close-fitting in the bodice and sleeves, loose in the skirt.

She got back on Yori and rode on towards the northern parts of her kingdom.

Everywhere she stopped her horse, and went to homestead or farm or herdsmen's shelter, to talk and make enquiries, she heard the same news. Either things were worsening fast everywhere, or they were worse here, in the north, where already the chills of an early autumn thickened the air.

She spent only the time she needed to everywhere. She was welcomed with a kindness that had not lessened, though there was not one woman or man or even child who did not speak in the understanding that she had been at fault, and that this new marriage, or mingling, with Zone Four, was to do with this fault or falling-off.

And as she rode through the wilder country of the northern regions, hilly, many-watered, often precipitous, she remembered—only remembered—the easy, slow-pacing times of the past, for now Ben Ata, Ben Ata, Ben Ata rang in her blood, she could not forget him, and yet every reminder of him was painful and brought a bitter load with it: she knew, she knew better every day and every hour, that she was on the verge of a descent into possibilities of herself she had not believed open to her. And there was nothing she could do to avert it.

Leaving the north, she swung around, with the central massif always at her left, and entered the west. Here it was late summer again, and the sun warm and still. She rode among scenes of plenty and fullness, yet the information was the same, and woman, man, and child greeted her: Al·Ith, Al·Ith, what is wrong? Where have we gone wrong, where have you gone wrong?

The weight of discomfort on her was guilt. Although she did not know it, for she had not known of the possibility of such a state. Recognising, among the many calamitous and heavy emotions that moved in her, taking so many different shades and weights and colours, this one that returned, and returned, seeming at last to become the ground or inner substance of all the others, she learned its taste and texture. Guilt, she named it. *I, Al·Ith, am at fault.* Yet whenever this thought came, she started to back away from it in dislike and mistrust. How could *she*, Al·Ith, be at fault, how could *she*, only she, be in the wrong . . . she might be in bondage to Zone Four, but she had not lost the knowledge, which was the base of all knowledges, that everything was entwined and mixed and mingled, all was one, that there was no such thing as an individual in the wrong, nor could there be. If there was a wrong, then this must be the property of everyone, and everybody in every one of the Zones—and doubtless beyond them, too. This thought struck Al·Ith sharply, like a reminder. She had not thought, not for very long, about what went on beyond the Zones . . . for that matter, she thought very little now about Zones One and Two—and Two lay just there, to the northwest, beyond a horizon that seemed to fold and unfold in blue or purple. . . . She had not looked there for . . . for . . . she could not remember. She was on a slight eminence, in the centre of the western regions. She got off the noble Yori, and with her arm flung across his neck for comfort, allowed herself to gaze northwest, into Zone Two. What lay there? She had no idea! She had not thought! She had not wondered! Or had she, a long time ago? She could not remember ever standing as she did now, gazing there, wondering, allowing her eyes to be drawn into those long, blue, deceiving distances . . . her eyes seemed to be drawn and follow, and become dissolved in blue, blue, blue . . . a mingling, changing, rippling blue. . . . Al·Ith came to herself after a lapse into the deepest regions of herself, with a knowledge born that she knew would hatch out. Not yet, but soon. . . . "It's there," she was whispering to herself. "There . . . if I could only grasp it. . . ." She got back on her horse and rode on always in her wide curve, bending to the left hand, and passed out of the western regions into the south. Her favourite, always her favourite, yes, she had made excuses to come here more often than the other regions . . . she had been here quite recently, with all her children, and her court and, it seemed, half the population of the plateau. And what a time they had had—festivities, singing—it seemed looking back that they had sung and danced and feasted for all the summer months. And never standing for long pauses in her busy life to rest her eyes in the blue reaches of the Zone which was as much higher than Zone Three as this one was to Zone Four. . . . This idea shook her, shook her as strongly as a conception did—*should*, if it were a properly designed and orchestrated conception—here was some very strong and urgent need, that she should be attending to, reaching out towards. . . .

And yet as she rode among the farms and ranches of the south, greeted by everyone with such kindness and recognition for the good times they had all enjoyed, it was there again, and more than ever— "You are at fault, Al·Ith, at fault. . . ."

And she rode on, saying to herself, I am not, I am not, how can I be, if I am queen here, it is because you have chosen me, and you have chosen me because I am you, and you recognise it—I am the best part of you, my people, and I call you *mine*, as you call me *ours*, our Al·Ith, and therefore I cannot be at fault any more than you can—the fault is somewhere else, somewhere deeper, somewhere *higher*? And she kept riding up on to hills covered with the rich vineyards of the south so that she could stand and gaze towards the northwest, into the azure ranges of that other land—or she did until she rounded the central massif and could no longer gaze there, nor could she expect to until she climbed up into the plateau where she intended to ride fast straight across it, only briefly stopping in the capital to greet her children and us all, so as to stand on the very edge there, overlooking the west and the northwest to gaze into the blue hazes, until what she had to remember—and she knew that this was it—came into her mind.

All through the southern Zones she rode up and down and back and forth. Several times she encountered the men who, if things were right, she would have approached to irradiate her with their various and many qualities for the sake of the child which she might have conceived—but had she? And here again was a source of utter self-reproach and self-lack—for it was now nearly a month since she had been with Ben Ata, and she had no idea if she was pregnant or not. For of course one knew it, understood such a fact, through the responses and heightened intuitions of one's entire being, not because of any purely physical thing. Guilty, oh, guilty . . . yet she was *not*, such a thought was in itself a reason for guilt—it was so foolish and self-fixated and self-bounded. And so rode Al·Ith, all seethe and conflict. Her mind was calm, clear, and in balance, while below rioted and writhed and moaned and gibbered emotions she judged as ludicrous.

And as for the rest of her, the higher regions in which she normally dwelt, and on which she relied—those distances in her which she knew to be her own real being—well, they seemed far enough these days. She was a fallen creature, poor Al·Ith, and she knew it.

Meanwhile, Ben Ata, Ben Ata rang in her blood and in the pounding of her horse's hooves.

When she again reached the road that ran from the borders of Zone Four straight across the plain to the central plateau and its mountains, she turned her horse to her left hand, so as to ride on and up home. But the unmistakable voice spoke suddenly and clearly into her mind: "Turn round and go back to Ben Ata . . ." and, as she hesitated, "Go now, Al·Ith."

And she turned her horse and went east. On emerging from Zone Four, in her dance of relief and triumph, she had flung down her shield and been pleased to forget it. She could not ride into Zone Four now without protection. Not knowing what to do, she did nothing: *they* would know of her predicament and provide.

As she rode she turned around continually to look back at the vast mass of the core of her land with its brilliances, its lights, its shadows . . . and now there was a thought that had not been there before . . . she was thinking at the same time of the blue distances beyond. So that this beautiful realm of hers was held in her mind extended, or lengthened: it had been finite, bounded, known utterly and in every detail, self-enclosed . . . but now it lapped and rippled out and upwards beyond there into hinterlands that were like unknown possibilities in her own mind.

As often as she turned to gaze back, she resolutely made herself look forward and confront what waited for her. Behind, all heights, distances, perspectives: before, Zone Four.

And Ben Ata. She found the thought in her mind that this great lump of a man so newly introduced in her life must balance in some way those far blue heights of Zone Two—but she did not smile. She did not seem now a creature who could laugh. What she did observe in herself, though, was a most unfamiliar impulse towards silliness. Never before in her whole life had she met any being, woman, man, or child, without an opening of her self to them, for the flow of intimacy to start at once—and now arts and tricks she had known nothing of were working in her without her volition, or so she believed. She would meet Ben Ata so, and so, and so—and she was imagining little glances, smiles, evasions, offers of herself. And she was revolted.

At the frontier she saw, as she had expected, a figure on a horse, and it was not Ben Ata, nor was it Jarnti. On a fine chestnut mare was a strong dark-haired powerful woman, with her hair done up in braids like a coronet round her head. Her eyes were straight and honest. But they were wary, and her whole being expressed a need for acceptance that was being kept well in check. Before her, on the heavy saddle that was Zone Four's indispensable horse furniture, was set two glittering metal oblongs: she had brought a shield for Al·Ith.

"I am Dabeeb, Jarnti's wife," she said. "Ben Ata sent me."

The two women sat on their horses facing each other, in open and friendly examination.

Dabeeb saw a beautiful slender woman, her hair flowing down her back, with eyes so warm and kind she could have wept.

Al·Ith saw this handsome female who in her own Zone would have been put, at first sight, in positions of the most responsible and taxing kind—and yet here she had on her every mark of the slave.

Her eyes never left Al·Ith's face, for she was watching for signs of rebuke, or dismissal. Even punishment . . . yet she was, as it were, tripping over herself in eagerness and liking.

"Are you wondering why I am here, my lady?"

"No . . . oh, please don't! My name is Al·Ith . . ." and this reminder of the ways of this Zone made her whole self sink and shrink.

"It is hard for us," remarked Dabeeb. But she spoke in a small stubborn self-respecting way that made Al·Ith take note of it.

"I have not heard the name Dabeeb before."

"It means something that has been made soft by beating."

Al·Ith laughed.

"Yes, that is it."

"And who chose that name for you?"

"It was my mother."

"Ah—I understand."

"Yes, she liked her little joke, my mother did."

"You miss her!" exclaimed Al·Ith, seeing the tears in Dabeeb's eyes.

"Yes. I do. She understood things the way they are, that's what she was like."

"And she made you very strong—the one-who-has-been-made-soft by beating."

"Yes. As she was. Always give way and never give in. That's what she said."

"How is it you are here alone? Isn't it unusual for a woman to travel alone?"

"It is impossible," said Dabeeb. "It never happens. But I think Ben Ata wanted to please you . . . and there is something else. Jarnti had already got ready to come and fetch you . . ."

"That was kind of him."

A shrewd flash of a smile. "Ben Ata was jealous—" with the swiftest of glances to see how this was being taken. And she sat, head slightly lowered, biting her lip.

"Jealous?" said Al·Ith. She did not know the word, but then remembered she had read it in old chronicles. Trying to work out what it could mean in this context, she saw that Dabeeb had gone red, and was looking insulted: Dabeeb believed that Al·Ith meant Jarnti was not on her level.

"I don't think I have ever been jealous. We do not expect to feel that emotion."

"Then you are very different from us, my lady."

The two women rode together down the pass. They were assessing each other with every sense, visible and invisible, they had.

What Dabeeb felt made her exclaim, after a short distance, "Oh, I wish I were like you, if only I could be like you! You are free! Will you let me come with you when you go home again?"

"If it is permitted." And they both sighed, feeling the weight of the Order.

And Al·Ith was thinking that this woman had in her a core of strength, something obdurate, enduring: sufferings and pains that she, Al·Ith, had never imagined, had made her thus. And so she was curious, and eager to learn more. But she did not know how to ask questions, or what to ask.

"If you, a woman, can ride to meet me, and with Ben Ata's permission, does that mean that women now will be more at liberty?"

"Ben Ata permitted it. My husband did not." And she gave a short shrewd laugh that Al·Ith already knew was characteristic.

"So what will he do about it?"

"Well. I am sure he will find a way to make himself *felt*." And she waited for Al·Ith to join her in a certain kind of laugh.

"I don't think I know what you mean." But as she saw the humorous patience on Dabeeb's face, she understood.

"Have you ever thought of rebelling?"

Dabeeb lowered her voice and said, "But it is the Order . . . is it not?"

"I don't know."

"You don't?"

"I find there is a great deal I don't know that I thought I did. For instance, can you tell when a woman is pregnant?"

"Yes, of course, can't you?"

"Always until now. But not now. Not here."

Dabeeb instantly understood this, for she nodded, and said, "I see. Well, you are not pregnant, I can assure you."

"Well, that is something."

"You plan not to get pregnant?" And again her voice was lowered and she gave furtive glances all about her, though they were now at the foot of the escarpment and on the point of starting their ride across the watery fields and there was not a soul in sight.

"I think we use the word *plan* differently."

"Will you teach me?" came the whisper just audible over the horses' thud-thudding on the dirt road.

"I'll teach you what I can. What is permitted."

"Ah, yes . . . I know." And the sigh she let out then held in it everything Al·Ith needed to know about women in this Zone.

Resignation. Acceptance. *Humour.* And always a pull and a tug from within these armours of watchfulness, patience, humour, of a terrible need.

Al·Ith pulled up Yori. Dabeeb did the same. Al·Ith put out her hand. After a struggle with her cautions and resistances, Dabeeb did the same. Al·Ith whispered across the space between them: "I will tell you everything I can. Help you as I can. I'll be your friend. As far as I can. I promise you." For she had seen that words were necessary. This kind of speech. She had never used them in her own land, had never imagined the need to use them. But now she saw tears fill the handsome black eyes of Dabeeb, and trickle down her ruddy cheeks. The words had been right, and necessary.

"Thank you, Al·Ith," she whispered, her voice broken.

When they reached the place in the road where they could easily see the pavilions on the eminence, Al·Ith said, "I would like you to lend me one of your dresses. Ben Ata thinks I am unsuitably dressed."

Dabeeb looked longingly at the dark red, embroidered dress of Al·Ith and said, "That is more beautiful than anything I have ever seen with us. But they would never understand that in a thousand years!" She spoke with the affectionate indulgence Al·Ith could not imagine offering to anyone other than a small child. And there was, as well, a dreadful contempt in it.

"You are elegant, Al·Ith, I wish I could know how to be as elegant . . ."

And she looked in dismissal at her own dress, which was a patterned material, pretty enough, but without the rightness and flair that stamped the garments of Zone Three.

"You needn't worry about what you are to wear. Everyone is talking about the clothes Ben Ata has ordered up for you from the town. There are cupboards full of them . . . though I don't know what you will make of them, I am sure."

She rode with Al·Ith up the rise of the hill, to where the gardens and fountains began, then leaned forward and suddenly and emotionally embraced Al·Ith. "I will be thinking of you, my lady. We all will, all the women, we are with you, and don't forget it!" And she rode off down the hill, and her tears scattered back on the wind like rain.

Al·Ith rode gently across the end of the gardens, dismounted, told Yori to find his way to the corrals, and walked back through the gardens, looking at the pavilion and waiting for the moment Ben Ata would show himself. She noted in herself the most remarkable constellation of unfamiliar emotions, which, regarded as a whole, amounted to a sort of antagonism that was quite unfamiliar. There was a sort of mocking, amused, intention there: "I'm going to show you!" and, "You think you are going to get the better of me!"

It went not with dislike of Ben Ata, but a quite pleasant challenge and combativeness.

She even looked forward to seeing him, so that this new exchange could begin. There were no tears on this horizon, certainly not!

She was full of confidence, and calm, all her powers reined in and held.

There was also in her an inner core of unassailability which she recognised because she had been sensing and assessing just this quality in Dabeeb, all across the plain.

It was in this state of mind that she waited for the encounter with Ben Ata.

Who was lounging against the central pillar, arms folded, in a pose that mirrored her own mood. He smiled, hard and mocking.

"Did you like your escort?" he enquired, reminding her he was supposed to be jealous.

"Very much. Not as much of course as I would have enjoyed the handsome Jarnti!"

With which he came forward fast, eyes momentarily aglitter, and she saw that he could easily have struck her. But instead he smiled in a way which told her she would pay for it later, and held out his two hands. She took them and swung on them lightly, from side to side, smiling and mocking.

"That is a pretty dress," said he, for he had determined to be complimentary about it.

"You like red then?"

"I think I like you," said he, in spite of himself grabbing at her—for he did not, he liked her even less than before, for while his senses in fact were informing him that this girl in a red, provokingly fitted dress could easily be to his taste, he had in fact forgotten the independence of her, which informed every smile, look, gesture.

She evaded him and slid away into the room, with a mocking backward look over her shoulder which quite astounded her—she did not know she had it in her! And he, to tease, did not follow, but stood his ground, a pillar of a man, in his short green belted tunic, and bare head, arms folded. She, then, smiling "enigmatically"—though feeling this smile on her lips she was amazed at it—put two hands around the slender central pillar and swung there lightly, in a way that was bound to set him all aflame. And it did, but he was not going to budge.

He stood grinning, while she swung and smiled . . .

When Al·Ith had left him that evening all those weeks ago, he had returned, reluctant, at midnight, having refreshed himself among his soldiers, and found her gone. Furious, he understood there must have been a summons she had obeyed, and then he felt in all of himself a lack and a need and a disability that he in no way knew how to diagnose or to feed. It was not Al·Ith he was missing, he was sure of that.

He was nothing if not a painstaking man.

He had understood that in certain practices he was quite lacking in understanding and indeed in any sort of knowledge.

He despised men who went into the stews of the town, as self-indulgent. But that is where he went now. Having made methodical enquiries of Jarnti and others of his officers, he went to a certain establishment, and demanded an interview with its madam. She understood exactly what he wanted and had done so from the moment the rumours entered her house that he was about to visit them. But she sat smiling through his rather clumsy, but determined explanations.

She sent him into a room that was already furnished with a girl who had been given all kinds of detailed instructions. For the capacities and lacks of Ben Ata had of course been discussed up and down the land from woman to woman. After all, so many campaigns, so many army exercises, so many sacks and rapes and loots had given plenty of opportunity for ravished or disappointed girls to spread their news.

Ben Ata found himself bedded with an expert young woman, who had quite surprised him. It could not be said that he found such prolonged dedication to pleasure entirely to his tastes, for he persisted in regarding all this as hardly the occupation for a real man.

But the fact was that Ben Ata had been pleasured, the only word for it, during the month that Al·Ith had been riding around her realm making investigations. He had been taught, as in a school, a large variety of lessons, to do with the anatomy, the capacities, the potentialities of the body, male and female. He was not a particularly apt pupil. But on the other hand he was certainly not a sluggard, for once he had decided on a certain course of duty, nothing much was likely to deflect him.

This courtesan, for she was no common whore, having been chosen among very many by the most expert madam of the whorehouse, and even brought here from another town because of her reputation, had taught him everything she could.

What Elys had achieved in a month of pretty hard work was to adjust Ben Ata's mind to the notion that pleasure could be multifunctional. This was at least a basis.

He had believed that he now knew everything there was to know.

But the moment Al·Ith had sauntered so charmingly and mockingly into the pavilion, he had remembered something entirely blotted from his mind during that enervating month. The light, glancing, inflaming kisses that he had not known how to answer, had gone from his mind. The invitation, the answer and question, the mutual response and counter-response—none of this had been within the provision of the courtesan Elys, since she had never in her life enjoyed an equal relation with anyone, man or woman.

As Al·Ith swung there, lightly, and delightfully, on her pillar, smiling, and waiting, he understood that he was now to start again. There was no help for it. He could not refuse, for his month as apprentice, and a willing one, had already said yes to what was to come.

As he challenged and antagonised, an equal—at the same time his look at Al·Ith told her all this. And so she left her pillar, and came to him, and began to teach him how to be equal and ready in love.

It was quite shocking for him, because it laid him open to pleasures he had certainly not imagined with Elys. There was no possible comparison between the heavy sensualities of that, and the changes and answerings of these rhythms. He was laid open not only to physical responses he had not imagined, but worse, to emotions he had no desire at all to feel. He was engulfed in tenderness, in passion, in the wildest intensities that he did not know whether to call pain or delight . . . and this on and on, while she, completely at ease, at home in her country, took him further and further every moment, a determined, but disquieted companion.

He could not of course sustain it for long. Equality is not learned in a lesson, or even two. He was heavy and slow in response by nature: he could never be anything else. Impossible to him would always be the quicksilver pleasures. But even as far as he could stand it, he had been introduced to his potentialities beyond anything he had believed possible. And when they desisted, and he was half relieved and half sorry that the intensities were over, she did not allow him to sink back again away from the plane of sensitivity they had both achieved. They made love all that night, and all the following day, and they did not stop at all for food, though they did ask for a little wine, and when they had been entirely and thoroughly wedded, so that they could no longer tell through touch where one began and the other ended, and had to look, with their eyes, to find out, they fell into a deep sleep, where they lay becalmed for another twenty-four hours. And when they woke, at the same moment, at the beginning of a nightfall, they heard a drum beat, beat, from the end of the garden, and this rhythm they knew at once was signalling to the whole land, and beyond it to her land, that the marriage was properly accomplished. And the drum was to beat, from that time on, from when they met, until they parted, so that everyone could know they were together, and share in the marriage, in thought, and in sympathetic support—and, of course, in emulation.

They lay in each other's arms as if in the shallows of a sea they had drowned in. But now began the slow and tactful withdrawals of the flesh, thigh from thigh, knee from knee . . . it was partly dark and while each felt their commonplace selves to be at odds with the marvels of the days and nights just ended, luckily any dissonances could not be seen. For already they were quick to disbelieve what they had accomplished. He, with an apologetic and almost tender movement, pulled his warm forearm from under her neck, sat up, then stood up, stretching. Relief was in every stretch of those sturdy muscles, and she smiled in the dark. As for her, she was becoming herself again the same way. But it was clear he felt it was ungallant to leave her at once, for he pulled around himself his soldier's cloak and sat at the foot of the couch.

"If we tidied up a little bit," said he, "we could meet for supper."

"What a very good idea!" And her voice came from the door to her apartments, for she had crept there without his seeing her. And she had gone.

Nothing had changed in the weeks since she was here, except that the length of a wall was exposed to show row after row of dresses, robes, furs, cloaks. She had never seen anything like it, and muttering that this was clearly some kind of storehouse for a whole houseload of whores—for the word had already been learned from him—she pulled out one after the other. The materials were fine enough, and she examined silks, satins, woollens, with a professional eye for their quality—certainly this country knew how to manufacture these goods. But she could only marvel at the awfulness of their making-up. She could not find one that wasn't exaggerated in some way or another, that didn't emphasise buttocks or breasts, or expose them, or confine them uncomfortably, or if not, the material or the colour was wrong for the conception. There was nowhere here the instinctive feel for the rightness of a match of style and cloth, and no subtleties. But, thinking that instant seduction was hardly so soon to be the order of the day, she found a commonsensical green dressing robe that amazed her for its infallible wrongness in everything, but was better than most. She bathed, arranged her hair something as she had seen Dabeeb do hers—womanly was probably the word for it— and put on the green robe. Then she returned to the centre room, where Ben Ata was moodily awaiting her at the small table by the window. Seeing her attire he brightened, then was disappointed.

"Is that one of ours?" he enquired doubtfully, and she replied, "Indeed it is, great king," and they exchanged the comradely, knowledgeable smiles of the thoroughly mated. For looking at each other now, returned to their absolute separateness, their otherness, these two denizens of their different realms could not believe what they had won together during their hours of submersion in each other. She was to him, again, a foreign woman, everything about her alien, though dear now in a way that estranged him more than bound him, for he feared, most deeply, where she might lead him. And she, looking at this great ox of a soldier, with his hair plastered to his head after the bath, thought that she was much to be congratulated in leading him as far as she had.

They mentally summoned hefty meals, which came, and they ate hungrily, for some time.

Meanwhile, the drum from the gardens beat, beat, beat.

No sooner had they ended their meal, than they sprang up and went out and wandered everywhere over the garden, from one end to the other. They could see no drummer and no drums. But the sound was there—somewhere—here?—no, there—they were always on the point of coming on the source of it, but always failed.

Realising that they were not ever going to learn where this sound came from, they returned to the pavilion. Not hand in hand. Not even very close. Each felt sealed, whole, self-locked, absolutely impenetrable by the other, that foreigner.

"However," said she, as if in continuation of a conversation, "I am certainly pregnant."

"You are? Are you sure? Splendid!" Feeling that an embrace of some kind was due, he made as if to approach her, but as she clearly felt no such impulse he thankfully forgot about it.

"Of course I am sure."

"Why? How?"

"As the women of your country, but certainly not as we know." And with this she laughed. She laughed, while he maintained polite looks and waited for her to finish.

"Well, good, I am delighted."

"Well, so am I, since it is probably what is required of us."

"Are you sure?"

"No, of course not. I am not sure of anything."

"What are we supposed to do next?"

"How should I know? But perhaps they will tell me to go home?"

At the look of instant relief on his face, she rolled with laughter, pointing at him, and he, realising what she had seen, and that she was willingly confessing to the same, laughed with her. This feast of laughter having ended, they were forced to acknowledge that it was still far from midnight, and that if left to their own devices they would certainly separate.

"Chess?" he suggested.

"Why not."

He beat her, then she beat him. They were both very good and in fact master and mistress of the game respectively, in both their two realms. This meant the games took a long time and it was dawn when they were finished.

Both wondered (and hoping the other did not guess) if more lovemaking was yet appropriate, but decided against it.

Walking again in the mists and splashings of the gardens, with the drum everywhere, in their blood, and in their minds, she called his attention to the files of soldiers down below, deploying among the wet hazes of the meadows. She watched his face, respecting what she saw on it: it was a complete knowledge of what he saw, and she knew he was marshalling praise and criticism and orders, for the perfection of that work of his, the army.

"And who," she asked, in a way that would make him know she was in earnest, "are your enemies?"

He tensed, and she understood he had been thinking hard on this question ever since she had first asked it of Jarnti, who had transmitted her words jeering, but inwardly disturbed, to his king.

"If we have no enemies, then why do we have armies?" he asked her, not at all in jest, but in respect for her questioning of him.

"Who do you fight?"

He was tense and silent. She knew he was remembering the pillage and the rapine of innumerable campaigns, and thinking if these had in fact been for some ghost of a mistaken idea then. . . .

"We are not your enemies—it is not even possible for one of us to cross the border without bad effects—yet you have forts all along our frontier from one end to the other, just as close as you can get to it without the soldiers being made ill by its proximity."

He gave an odd little shrugging movement of his shoulders.

"How long is it since anyone fired so much as a single warning shot there?"

He laughed, shortly, in acknowledgment. "So long that we can't remember. Mind you, we do sometimes arrest someone as a spy . . . but then let him go again."

She laughed. "Then why?"

"We have large, and efficient armies."

Down among the golden fogs that were rising straight up into the air and dissipating at about their eye level, the glittering brightly coloured soldiers wheeled and marched, and the sharp barking sounds of the orders seemed to fade at about the same level, as if the sounds and the mists were one.

"And Zone Five? You have forts there? A frontier?"

"And skirmishes and even battles."

This startled her: she had forgotten there was a war there.

"Surely," she said, "but surely . . ."

"Yes, I know." Awkward, embarrassed, apologetic, as if he were at fault before her and not before Them—the Providers and the Orderers—he was stammering. "I have been wondering since you brought the matter up. It is true . . . of course we are not supposed to fight . . ."

"Real battles?"

"Yes. Well . . . nothing very serious . . ."

"Wounded? Casualties?"

"Wounded and dead."

Her breath was a long, dismayed, and even frightened sigh. He turned on her the bleakest of faces. "Yes, I know. But I swear it—it grew up like that. I never thought . . . none of us did . . . it was not until you . . ." And he crashed his great fist down on a low parapet that bordered a pool.

"Who starts it? The fighting? Is it possible for people from this Zone to cross into that one—and back—without damage, or danger?"

"At one time I know that it was as impossible to cross from one Zone to another, as it is now for us to move back and forth between your Zone and ours, without shields. But something seems to have changed. I'm not saying that it is easy. There isn't large-scale movement across the frontier. Nor does it happen often. But the fighting takes place along the borders, sometimes on this side, and sometimes on that—never far inside their Zone."

"You've been there?"

"Yes. More than once."

"What is it like, Zone Five?"

He shuddered, and rubbed his hands up and down his forearms, to warm them. He was quite pale with dislike of Zone Five.

"It is as bad as that," she said, not without irony, for she knew that he was feeling for that place what she and all of us in Zone Three felt for this one. He caught the irony, acknowledged it, nodded, and put his arm around her, in affection. "Yes, it is as bad as that."

And, drawing her close, he put his face down into the coils of her hair and she heard him muttering, "But what are we to do, Al·Ith? What? Bad enough that I have only just begun to think of it."

"As I have of the deficiencies in our Zone. Do you know, Ben Ata, I have not had time to tell you, but I have ridden all around the outer regions of our Zone since I saw you last . . ."

"Alone?" said he, incredulous and sharp, despite himself, and was not able to laugh when she said, indulgent, "Of course alone, since I wanted to . . . but that isn't the point, Ben Ata. When I was on a certain high point of country, below the central massif, but where I could look straight out northwest, I could see . . . but the point is, that none of us have done that for so long I don't think anyone could say when we last did. You need punishment helmets to prevent your people looking *there*—" and she pulled him around so that his dazzled eyes rose to the great heights of Zone Three, now all the colours of a fire opal. "Your people won't look up there, no, keep your eyes on it, Ben Ata, but our people *never* look beyond our borders, and this is without any punishments or forbiddings. It never occurs to us. We are too prosperous, too happy, everything is so comfortable and pleasant with us, Ben Ata . . . I don't know what to say or to think . . ." and she was astounded, utterly appalled, to find that again tears ran down her cheeks, while he bent over her, forgetting the beguiling colors of the great peaks, making small concerned noises at these so foreign tears. And he even brushed a tear from her lid with one large forefinger and looked at it, as if this tear could not be like any other he had seen.

In song, in picture, and in story, this scene is known as "Al·Ith's Tear." It is popularly believed to have to do with the tender emotions of this pair when she told him she was pregnant, but the truth of the matter is as I tell it here.

There lay Al·Ith, rocked on the man's strong breast, all cradled and comforted, sobbing away, just as she had wanted to do on so many occasions recently. That she didn't believe in the efficacy of it, did not prevent her enjoying it, while it lasted.

As for him, he was both delighted that this dreadfully self-sufficient girl could have a good cry, just like any other, and at the same time he didn't believe in it either. It simply wasn't like her, and he was relieved when she stood up, sniffed, wiped the wet off her cheeks with two small hands, and again stood upright by him at the parapet.

"And what is Zone Two like?" he enquired.

"You know more about our Zone than I can tell you about *there*. All I can say is that you stand and gaze and look, and never have enough of it. It is as if you looked at blue mists—or waters or—but it is blue, blue, you've never seen such a blue . . ."

"Well, I don't see the point in *that*," said he shortly, "it doesn't get anything done."

Which was so exactly what she expected of him that she went into a fit of laughter, in which he joined: and this led back to the couch. This exchange was by no means on the level of the last days, but was more of a confirmation that the thing was still possible—for their differences were so great that they were both always being overtaken by feelings of astonishment that they could be there together at all. And so they were to feel until the very end.

They were now at midday again: a steamy day, and she shocked him by jumping nude into one of the fountains. He had not seen fountains as containing any such possibility and he joined her, but not with abandon. He complained that the goldfish were tickling him, that they themselves were disturbing the fish, and that in any case, "if anyone were to see them . . ."

But who could?

"There's that drummer," he complained. "There must be someone there, it stands to reason," for the drum went on, on, on, no matter what they did or said.

"What we have to do," she said, when they were dressed and again seated on either side of their little table, "is this. You know that there was a time when it was not possible for Zone Four and Zone Five to mingle. Now you do—and even fight. So what has happened? We must find out. And having done that, we must find out what your armies were for, originally. Why do you have armies? All the wealth of your land drains into the armies. No wonder you are so poor."

"We are poor? What do you mean!"

"Ben Ata, you are poor! You don't know it, but you are pathetic! The poorest of our herdsmen lives better than you do, the king. As for the clothes in those cupboards! Oh, I'm not saying that they aren't solid and well-sewn—or not adequate. For their purpose. But if those are the clothes thought fit for a queen, according to your ideas—for with you of course a queen would have to wear one richness of garment and the wife of a soldier another—"

"But of course. There have to be ranks."

"Of course—according to you. But I tell you it is not necessary. Why do you have to have ranks, and a hierarchy? It is because you are so poor. Why do you have to wear that great brooch holding your cloak that says you are Ben Ata? With us, everyone knows I am Al·Ith. And they would if I wore sacking. Don't you see? You are poor, poor people, Ben Ata. Everything I see as I ride here—oh, I'm not talking of this pavilion here, which has been created for just this time and this place and will probably vanish when we part—"

"Are we going to part again?"

"But of course! What do you imagine? That we are together for ever, Ben Ata? We are here for a purpose—to heal our two countries and to discover where it is we have gone wrong, and what it is that we should be doing, really doing . . ."

She was leaning forward, her eyes all persuasion and passion.

He was leaning back, watching her satirically. He was offended. He had never, not ever, imagined his country could be described as poor and strike foreigners as backward and lacking. He did not mind that this woman found him—as she clearly did—rough and unsubtle. He was a soldier! Soldiers were—soldiers. But he had believed his realm a model of what it should be. He was cold against her. Cold and furious. He was looking at her shining eyes and illumined face, from a distance—one of total repudiation.

He suddenly got up, and strode furiously around the chamber.

"You think luxury is what matters, you said so yourself. Comfort. Ease. All that—you said it, you said it . . ."

"Yes, I did." And of course he pounced on it, an admission being weakness, and he was standing rocking with derisive laughter and pointing.

"You are like a half-grown boy, Ben Ata," said she, and got to her feet. "If we are rich and have everything it is bad only insofar as it has made us forget our proper purposes. But if you are poor and barbaric, it is because all your wealth goes into war—a needless, stupid, senseless war . . ." She stood there, confronting him.

His loathing for her culminated in lifting his hand to hit her. The great fist that looked the size of her small head was poised to crash down—she stood her ground and looked at him.

"Ben Ata, I am very much less strong than you, and you can do what you like in the way of violence. I can't stop you. And nor, in this awful country of yours, can I use any of the real strengths to stop you . . ."

He of course now had to carry her to the bed and to treat her as he had treated the most weakly girls of his looting nights.

She did not resist for she could not, but turned her head away and closed her eyes and was quite absent from him, as if she were dead.

He was raping a dead woman, or so he felt it. And he was loathing himself. And her—for forcing him into this act. And then he remembered that she was pregnant and that he might be damaging the foetus. All this prevented him from doing it twice, which he would otherwise have done. He rolled off her and, shaking with his dislike of her, he said, "And that's that. That's that."

In the silence, both heard that the drum was silent.

She painfully pulled herself up, went into her rooms, and came out almost at once in her own dark red dress. She did not look at him.

"You can't go unless they tell you," he said, stupid and threatening.

"The drum has stopped, can't you hear?" she said in a voice that was drained of any life.

She went out and stood calling for her horse. At once he could hear the beast coming, clip-clop among the fountains.

"Then don't come back," he said, broken. He could not believe what had happened. He could not make the early part of their being together match what he had just done.

It seemed to him that he had been standing on the verge of some landscape that he had never even imagined and that it had vanished.

"You can go back to your damned whores," she said, swinging herself up onto Yori. And added, almost at once, hearing these words that certainly were not hers but were Zone Four words, "Oh, I must get out of this dreadful place," cutting him absolutely to the heart because of the sincerity of them.

She cantered away. He ran down to get his horse, and rode like fury after her, not catching her up till she was a good way along the west road. The two horses, white and black, fled along side by side, and it being early evening, and still daylight, there were people on the roads and on the boats in the canals. They saw the queen of Zone Three riding "like a she-demon" out of their country, with their king in pursuit, "as pale as death, the poor man."

That was only on the first part of the road, for she had forgotten to take the shield, and near the frontier she leaned forward, senseless, clinging to Yori's mane, knowing what was happening and that if she did not hold fast she would be killed as she fainted. Yori, feeling her slacken there on his back, slowed, and walked carefully on, while Ben Ata, seeing his wife lolling senseless, picked her up off Yori's back, and carried her. The people on the second part of the road told how the queen was ill, because of her grief at leaving the Zone, and the king cradled her "like a baby" and was weeping as they rode.

Yori came along behind the king. At the frontier, he set her on the ground, just on the other side—but not too far, for he could no more travel unguarded in her realm than she could in his, and as soon as she showed signs of coming to herself, stood back, with just one hand on her shoulder to steady her. What she found, when she opened her eyes, was a wild dark night, and the sharp wind that always swept up from the east into her country already strong enough to push her along. She saw Ben Ata, white and grim, and believed him angry, not seeing his concern for her.

Her horse was beside her, she climbed onto it and fled into the dark, she and Yori both vanishing like straw in a storm. And Ben Ata rode back to his camps wondering when she would be ordered to come again.

She had not gone far along the road when she understood, by thinking hard, and with sympathy, what had happened. Now she felt sorrow because she knew that Ben Ata did, and she wished she could reassure him by even a word that she knew he had carried her to her frontier and put her across it and that he could no more believe now he had crushed her down and punished her than she could like in herself the hard accusations and criticisms of his country.

How could she! She, Al·Ith, who was not capable of a cruel or even careless word to anyone at all in her own realm, yet, with this man who was neither more nor less culpable than she, who was—for no fault of his own—king of that sad and sodden and poverty-struck land, she had let venom rule her tongue.

He back with his army, she riding to her capital, thought of each other, and with compassion.

When she reached the top of the pass that led from the plain to the plateau, she reined in Yori, and looked up at the heaped mountains all around. Her life had been lived among these mountains; and watching how they changed and deployed inside their moulding atmospheres had been her recreation and her mind's nourishment. Now, as she gently turned her horse about and about she saw them as she always had—but saw them, too, as she had from far down in the lowlands, looking up with Ben Ata. She knew that at this moment, now, he would be gazing at those peaks, forbidden or not: he would not be able to help himself. And seeing him stand there, momentarily lost to himself among the tents and picket lines of the camps, his officers, first glancing at each other, with raised eyebrows, would one after another themselves look upwards—and then, following them, the soldiers. Al·Ith was wondering about the women, whom she suspected of being custodians of all kinds of private beliefs. Probably they, or many of them, had never ceased, when no one could see them, to watch the skies westwards, where the mountain snows lay so high in the heavens it was hard to tell them from clouds.

Now she remembered a song—yes, hearing it as she lay in Ben Ata's arms, not taking it in then, but retaining enough to hear it again now. The song had been part of the mounting delights of their two astonished bodies:

> *How shall we reach where the light is,*
> *Come where delight is?*
>
> *High on the peaks light changes,*
> *Hope ranges.*
>
> *Clouds?—no,*
> *Snow . . .*
>
> *Rain here,*
> *Snow there:*
>
> *Freeze-fire white,*
> *Flake light.*
>
> *How may we go there*
> *Climb in the air there*
>
> *Up, up, up from this flat land,*
> *Into the high land*
>
> *That is our way*
> *That is our way . . .*

A woman's high sweet voice had rung through their lovemaking, and these words would now always be melded with their memories of each other.

And yet she knew that the words actually heard by any *casual* person listening, soldier or uninitiated soldier's wife, would not have

been these—the initiated women would hear them, and she with Ben
Ata had heard them—but had he? Well, she would ask when they
met next!

She rode forward again and now all along the roads groups of
people called out to her, welcoming her back. And she stopped to
talk, to listen to their messages, and to tell them, too, that she was
pregnant by Ben Ata. The news flew across the plateau as they called
to each other, and when she rode into the streets of our capital, the
crowds were lining the way and singing and calling out a welcome to
the new child, and by the time she had reached her home, she was
back in the high easy friendliness which is the common mood of
Zone Three.

On the wide steps were waiting her sister Murti· and all the children who called her Mother. She was enclosed by them in love and
welcome, and was with them all for a day and night, to hear their
tales of what had happened while she was gone. Meanwhile, the bells
were ringing out from our information tower, so that no one in all of
our Zone could fail to know that she was home and safe and that
there would be a new child.

Then, retiring with her sister, leaving the children to their Mind-
Fathers and their lessons and games, she went right to the very top of
the palace, where the roofs stretched everywhere, level on level, and
where it was possible to climb up even farther to a spire higher than
any other in the capital. Right at the top of this tower she stood with
Murti· and she said to Murti·, who was wondering at this exertion
to visit a place she could not remember ever having tried to reach
before, "Look, look there . . ." and she pointed northwest between a
deep gap in the mountains there. The blue of Zone Two gleamed like
sapphires. Murti· could see nothing at first but a gap in the mountains with a haze in it.

Al·Ith gazed, letting her eyes fill with the blue, and thought fondly
of how Ben Ata had said it was a waste of time, so that she was
smiling, and Murti·, glancing at her, knew that she was thinking of
her husband, for that smile could mean nothing else. She laughed,
and was about to turn to her sister and tease her, begging for facts
and bits of news of this famous Ben Ata, the great soldier, but Al·Ith
said, "No, no, just stand and look. . . ." For all of her life, she,
Al·Ith, had had the possibility of climbing up to this high place and

finding Zone Two with her eyes. No one had said she should not! But no one had ever mentioned Zone Two! And yet—yes, as a child she had come here. Now she remembered. She had been a very young girl, before menarche. She had been impelled to climb up and up, first to the immensities of the roofs spreading all over the tops of the many paláces so that she could, if she had wanted to, have jumped from one to another, and around and about for weeks of days. But instead she saw the tall spire, and the little door at its foot and she had crept up and up. And up. And at last had reached the end of the interminably swirling stairs and stood breathless and giddy on the little platform they stood on now, enclosed by the lights of the evening sky. Birds sped past, and called to them. High over the mountains the eagles swung and swerved. She had clung here and looked up and out and it had been as if her whole self had filled with a need to leave here and let herself be absorbed by that endless blue—the blue, the blue, the blue! And it was hours before she had crept down again, her head filled with blue air, and—then, what? She could not remember! She had told someone and been warned? She had not told, but had simply forgotten?

Did it matter? The fact was, all her life the possibility had been here for no more effort than the climb up flights of difficult stairs. And yet it had been as if her own mind had closed itself off to what it could do. Should do. Wanted to do. . . .

Her sister was clinging to the rail with both hands, her fine clear profile lifted, her eyes shining. She seemed to shine everywhere; the strong evening light polished her soft gold hair, and the embroideries on her yellow dress glowed. She had seen!

When she turned to Al·Ith all she said was, "Why did we forget it?"

And Al·Ith had no reply.

Next, Al·Ith ordered the bells to peal out an invitation for all the regions to send in messengers, and as quickly as was comfortably possible. Then she took supper with her sister, who wanted to know about this new husband, and while normally she would have told Murti· everything, without any feeling of disloyalty, or betrayal, she found her tongue weighted. Why? Only partly because news about Zone Four must be so foreign to Murti· that it would be necessary to say everything again and again from a dozen different angles before she could begin to understand it, but also because she could feel Ben Ata thinking of her. She did not like this connection with him. She could not remember ever before, with any man, whether for parenthood or for play, feeling this yearning, heavy, disquiet. She judged it unhealthy—a projection of that Zone where all the emotions were so heavy and so strong. But this is what she *did* feel, and it was no use behaving as if she did not. Murti· felt the resistance in her, did not blame her, but was excluded, and she went away early to her rooms where her own children awaited her.

Surely a relation with one person that narrowed others must be wrong? How could it not be wrong?

But Al·Ith knew the real questions that faced her now were more urgent than these disquiets about that husband of hers, to whom she would certainly be ordered to return in due time—and she could not say whether she abhorred the thought or longed for him.

And she put herself to sleep so as to be fresh for the day ahead, which she hoped would bring her the insights she so badly needed.

The main Council Chamber of our Zone is not very large, for there is no necessity for it to contain more than twenty or thirty of us at a time, since this number adequately represents us: of course the representatives are different, according to their function. It is a square room, its ceiling not very high, situated where windows show sky, clouds, mountains, on three sides.

The floor has on it very large flat cushions, where we sit according to no order except of preference, and Al·Ith may sit anywhere: there is no need for her to be elevated or on a prominence with such a small number of people.

On this day she was in the Chamber before anyone else, and moved from window to window, looking down at our streets, and up at the mountains, and then for a long time at a certain spot towards the northwest. I was there that day, and found her when I entered —the second to arrive. I was struck at once by her restlessness, her anxiety. This was not the contained woman I had known since she was a baby: I am one of Al·Ith's Mind-Fathers.

I stood by her at the window, and she gave me the wildest saddest look, and then sank her head on my shoulder, snuggling like a small

child. But as a small girl she had been too independent and striving
for such an action and I was disturbed more than I can say.

She soon pulled herself away. "Lusik, I don't know myself."

"Yes, I can see that."

Down below in the main square was a commotion, and we both
leaned forward to watch, thankful to be taken out of our anxieties.

Delegates were arriving from all our regions, on horses and don-
keys, and there were children on goats. These animals were being
taken into the care of some young people whose task this was, and
led under trees that shaded the square's southern side. I had come in
by camel, since I live in the extreme south of our lovely southern
region. This beast, who did not often have the chance to make the
acquaintance of animals other than her own kind, since camels
thrive so well with us they are our main transport, was standing nose
to nose with a fine black mare from the eastern herds.

It was such a pleasant and familiar scene that we were both
cheered, but she said, "All the same, we are in bad trouble and I
don't know at all what it is."

The room filled with our people, men, women, and two small girls
who had already shown a proclivity for the arts of management and
were being given opportunities to learn them.

There were twenty-five of us that day. Al·Ith sat down at once,
under the west window, spread her yellow skirts around her, for she
knew we liked to see her beautiful and well presented, and began.

"We all know the situation. I take full responsibility." She waited,
then, and looked around at us. Everyone had nodded, not in animos-
ity, but saluting a fact. She smiled, slightly, and it was a bleak little
smile.

"What we have to know is this. In the last thirty-nine days, has
there been any change in our situation?"

She paused again, looked carefully from face to face, and making
sure to smile at the two little girls, who of course smiled back in
adoration and total submission to their desire to be like her, and
better.

"In every region it has been the same. Animals have ailed, and
lost their fertility. And we, too, have not been as we were. This I
know. This we all know. And I might have known it before I did had
I taken as much notice as I should of your reports."

We all nodded again: it was the truth.

"It is clear that everyone believes that my marriage with Ben Ata is in someway connected with this decline. We do not know why or how, but we may expect to see an improvement among us. As has already been announced to everyone, I am pregnant. This presumably is part of the prescription for our recovery."

After every statement she paused and looked around, for signs of disagreement, or that anyone wanted to add to what she had said.

"Well then, it is thirty-nine days since I was taken to Ben Ata." The *was taken* came out of her with a bitter emphasis, and she at once regretted it, offering us a quick apologetic smile. By now there was no one present who had not seen her inner distress. There was an atmosphere in the Council room I had not experienced before. More than anything could have done, Al·Ith's state told us how things were in our realm.

She waited quietly. "There has been no change at all in that time? No? Now, I have been pregnant for five days. Has there been any change in that time?"

At this one of the little girls said, "My sheep had twins yesterday."

We laughed, and the proceedings halted while Al·Ith explained to her the gestation time for sheep.

Meanwhile, we were wondering if there had in fact been any change in the last five days? Discussion began. Al·Ith was listening carefully. And then she jumped up and went fast from one window to another, returning to the west window where she leaned, gazing out and up. This was not what any one of us had observed in her before. After a time I, as the only one of her parents present, went to the window and looked where she did. I could see only the massed piles of the western ranges.

She was reminded by my being there of her duty, and sat down again.

The little girl who had spoken about her sheep was humming.

It was one of our children's games.

> *Find the way*
> *And find the way*
> *And follow on and through.*

Through the pass
There we must pass
And gather in the blue . . .

Al·Ith was leaning forward, listening. There was not one of us who had not heard it a thousand times. The children made patterns of stones and hopped through them in certain definite rhythms which kept varying according to the rules of the rhyme.

We believed Al·Ith was as usual paying especial attention to children and waited.

But she was still leaning there, intent on the little girl, who was quite oblivious of Al·Ith, but sat swaying a little, humming, and even softly clapping her hands. She was a child typical of the eastern regions: a sandy little thing, with bright blue eyes and pale hair. These scraggy chickens tended to grow up into the wildest beauties, oddly enough, and the men, too, were handsome. When we had our festivals, hearts tended to beat faster when the companies from the east came riding in, smiling charmers all of them, conscious of their power over us, ready with their songs of a much harder fiercer past . . .

"What is your name?" asked Al·Ith.

"Greena."

"Well, my little green one, come here."

The child skipped forward and sat at Al·Ith's knee. She took her hand.

"What is the rest of that song?"

"What song, Al·Ith?"

"You were singing. What comes after 'And gather in the blue'?"

The child tried to think. She glanced around at her sister for help.

By now we all understood that something important was happening.

As for me, I had been present at certain heightened moments in that room, but nothing like this. The air was snapping with excitement, and Al·Ith's lassitude had gone. She was as she normally was: alert, lively, all attention.

"Is there any more of that song?" Again the child looked for help at her sister, another little wisp of a girl, but she shook her head. Then, she scrambled to her feet. "Yes, yes, there is . . . I think . . ." and sank back to the floor.

"Listen," said Al·Ith, "what I want you to do is this. Go down to the square there—where the animals are. Forget about us up here for a time. Play that game. Just play it as if you were at home with your herds and your families. And try to remember what comes after 'And gather in the blue.'"

The two little girls sprang up, and ran together out of the Council Chamber, hand in hand. We were smiling and we all knew it was because every one of us was seeing them as they would be in such a short time.

"What is all this about, Al·Ith?" asked a young man from the north. He was in fact her son by adoption, and had grown up near her. He even looked like her, as adopted children so often did.

"I'm on the verge of it," she said, looking fast and close into all our faces. "Can't you feel it? There's something! What!" And in her urgency she was up again and pacing all around the room, this time standing at the windows without seeing out. "What is it?" We said nothing, but waited. We all know that when one of us is on the edge of an understanding that we help by thinking with her, him, and waiting. "I just don't know, don't know . . ." and then she whirled round to the west window and leaned over. As many of us who could, crowded there and looked down. The two children had laid out their pattern of pebbles and were skipping and singing.

We could not hear the words.

Feeling our eyes on them they stopped, and looked up. We drew back out of sight.

"We must wait," said Al·Ith.

We sat down. Of course we hoped to know more about her visits to the other Zone, but did not want to say anything that would bring the shadow down over her again.

She knew what we were thinking, and with a sigh, met us.

"It is very hard to describe it," she said courageously, and we saw the animation had left her. "It is easy to describe it outwardly. Everything in it is for war. Fighting. It is a poor place. We have nothing in our realm to compare with it. As for the spirit of the people . . ." She was faltering, with pauses between words. Again we recognised that she was in the grip of something. "War. Fighting. Men . . . every man in the whole realm is in the army. . . ." She tailed off, silent. She had virtually stopped breathing. "Every man in uniform . . ." She stopped again, and her eyes lost all their lustre while she went deep inside herself. As for us we sat absolutely still.

"An economy entirely geared to war . . . but there is not much war . . . hardly any fighting . . . yet every man a soldier from birth till death . . ."

Again the tight silence, and she sitting there, straight and tense, eyes blank. She was rocking back and forth, on her cushion.

"A country for war . . . but no war . . . they are bound by a hard, strict Law . . . their Law is hard indeed . . . war. Men . . . all men for fighting . . . but no war, no wars to fight . . . what is it, what does it mean . . ."

The tension in her was frightening to see. An elderly woman who had been watching her keenly now went forward, sat by her, and began to soothe her, stroking her arms and shoulders. "That's enough, Al·Ith. *Enough.* Do you hear me?" Al·Ith shuddered and came to herself.

"What is it?" she said to us, in a whisper.

The woman who held her said, "It will come to you. Quieten yourself."

Al·Ith smiled and nodded at the woman, who went back to her place and said, "The best thing we can do is to keep the thought whole in our minds and let it grow." Al·Ith nodded again.

That was the end of the hard part of the Council. Murti· brought in a tray of jugs with fruit juices, and went out to bring in some light food. She then joined us, sitting by her sister.

And then the little girls came in. They seemed disappointed.

They stood before Al·Ith and Murti· and Greena said, "We played it. Over and over. We could not remember. But there are words that come after. We have remembered that."

Al·Ith nodded. "Never mind."

"Shall we play the game when we get home again and see if we remember then?"

"Please do . . . and I have had an idea . . ." All of us were alert, thinking she had achieved the understanding that had eluded her, but she smiled and said, "No. I am afraid not. But I have had a good idea. We shall have a festival. Soon. And it will be for songs, and stories—no, not the way we always have them. This one will be for songs and stories we have forgotten. Or half forgotten. All the regions will send in their storytellers and singers, and their Memories . . ." Here she smiled at me, to soften it, and said, "Lusik, it seems to me that you have all been remiss. How is it that children can play games and *know* that verses have been forgotten?"

I accepted it. Of course it was true.

Shortly after, we all went home.

Now I take up the tale again, not from firsthand, as is my remembrance of the events of the Council Chamber, but pieced together the best way I can, as Chronicler.

The sisters went up to Al·Ith's apartments, where Al·Ith said she was tired: this pregnancy was already proving more taxing than her others. She had set in train the events that were necessary, and now she wanted to retire for a few days and rest.

Murti· was concerned for her.

The two beautiful women sat hand in hand in the window that overlooked the western mountains. Al·Ith said she wanted to go up to the spire again, but Murti· asked her not to go. Al·Ith submitted. Usually, at such moments of relaxation the women would have petted each other, done each other's hair, tried on each other's dresses, planned new ones, discussed what innovations and developments they had noticed in the clothes of the girls and women who had been present that day, in case any might be useful to clothing generally. These were true sisters, with the same Mother, the same Gene-Father, and even sharing the same Mind-Fathers. There had never been secrets between them. Now Al·Ith said, "You are right to feel hurt. I can't help it." Murti· kissed her and went away.

Al·Ith had not been home a full day when she knew she had to return to Ben Ata. The words came into her mind: The drum is beating. She even heard the drum, faint, but there. She put her hand to cup her lower belly, thinking she heard that small heart but it was the drum.

She went through her cupboards, this time trying to find clothes that would soothe and please Ben Ata. She put together some of these and ran down to the first floor where she would leave a message for Murti·.

There were five persons coming up the great stairs, to see her: a girl just out of childhood, her Gene-Father, and three of her Mind-Fathers. Al·Ith was her mother.

There was a problem to do with this girl, but it is not of concern here. This event is being related because just at the time when Al·Ith was in mind already on her way to Ben Ata, with all the disturbance and adjustment this meant, she had to go aside to a quiet room, with a man with whom she had had, and for years, a close friendship, the child's real father, and three men who had been as close, but whom she had not seen for some time, as it happened, because they had been in distant parts of the country.

The room was off the main Council room, and had the usual cushions and low tables. Al·Ith embraced the girl, and held her close, and then kept her beside her when they sat down. But almost at once she felt her own churning emotions communicate themselves to the girl, and this she could not allow: she quickly got up and sat apart from her, and the girl felt she was being disliked, and sat with an unhappy face turned away from her mother. This disturbed Al·Ith even more.

These six persons, woman, four men, and the girl, had often been together thus. And Al·Ith had very often been with the men, all together or singly. These men were among the closest people to her, not even excepting her sister. It was not possible for her now to shut them out, even for her own protection. She was quite open to them, just as she was at the same time open to the demands of Ben Ata, which were claiming her fiercely. She was trembling.

The men all embraced her, and sat close. They congratulated her on the new pregnancy. All the time she was looking, and feeling, worse.

"You are ill," said the girl's real father, Kunzor, and Al·Ith said she was, she could not help it, she was sorry. And she fainted clean away.

They called Murti·, who explained that Al·Ith's state of mind was beyond anything they were likely to understand. Murti· undertook to stand in for Al·Ith on this occasion and set herself to be kind to the poor girl, who was astounding them all by wringing her hands and saying that "it was her fault" her mother was ill. This struck them as a sort of lunacy: they had never heard anything like it.

When Al·Ith came to herself, she was attended only by Kunzor, who was trying to understand her. He had known her in many complex ways, but this was entirely beyond him. Al·Ith weeping and distraught was something he had never imagined possible.

She said she had to get on her horse and go, and he took her down the steps to the square, called for Yori, and saw her ride off.

It did not help that it was early night when she reached the plain, and had to ride in the face of the cold wind from the east all the way to the frontier.

She hoped that it would be Ben Ata at the frontier to meet her, and it was. He sat cold and silent, in his black army cloak, waiting, gazing up the road, pale, intent, fixed.

At the first sight of him, her spirits sank. What had happened within her was that riding across the plain in the bitter wind, comforted only by the warmth of her horse, she had been thinking of the long friendship she had known with Kunzor, and the men whom she had been close to—she was already wondering about these words that people used. She had, in the past, not used words, not even in her mind. She had *felt* her closeness to them, as part of the fabric of her life. Meeting one of them again, by plan or by chance, they would at once move together as they had always, according to the intuitions of the moment. She had not said they were this and that, beyond *friends*. Now, she wondered, were they husbands? Certainly not if Ben Ata was one! But, during that cold ride, she had been thinking of Ben Ata, whom she was so soon to be with, as a *friend*— with all the simplicity of good sense and responsibility that word meant to her.

Seeing him there, the bonds in her flesh and being with the men who sustained her in Zone Three snapped and left her vulnerable.

Ben Ata waited till she had crossed into his Zone, and handed her a shield—he was right in thinking that she was likely again to have forgotten hers. Then he put out his hand to grasp her bridle—but she did not have one—and put his horse forward so that he was side by side with her, she facing into Zone Four, he into Zone Three. His eyes searched her face as if for a hidden crime.

"What is the matter?" she asked, irritated.

"The matter is that I've understood something."

"And what is that?" She rode forward, sighing, meaning him to hear it, and he came after her, and rode so close her foot had to be curled in on poor Yori's side to avoid being crushed.

"You don't love me," he announced.

Al·Ith did not respond at all.

The words had simply gone past her. She had seen that Ben Ata was in a fine old state about something, and that there was no point at all in expecting any comfort or sustaining from him. She was engaged in strengthening her inner self.

He rode close, casting dramatic looks into her face, and trying to lean forward so that he could see into her eyes.

It was early morning. They were riding down the escarpment, looking into fields where as usual mists were rising, admittedly very pretty in the weak sunlight.

"You do not love me. Not really," he was shouting.

This time Al·Ith heard the word love. She was making a note that the two Zones used it differently.

What had happened to Ben Ata was this.

When she had left him on the frontier, he had been shaken by emotions he had not known existed. If Elys had indicated to him that in the physical realm there were facts that perhaps he might have missed, he now saw that there was a world of emotions that had been kept from him until now. He visited the madam of the whorehouse with this problem who, after a brisk diagnostic exchange, said that it wasn't Elys he needed—she in fact had gone back to her own town, much congratulated and very pleased with herself—but a serious affair.

He had of course been aware that affairs were what some people had, but not, surely, soldiers!

Seeing Dabeeb brushing down her husband's uniform, where it hung on a line behind the married officers' quarters, he speculated on her possibilities. At once appropriate emotions invaded him in swarms, quite amazing him, for he could not imagine where he had got them from.

Dabeeb was disconcerted, of course, and enjoined caution, common sense, and then secrecy. It goes without saying that she was frightened of her husband. Affairs she had had, but not for the purpose of stimulating Jarnti. She was even more afraid of Ben Ata. She had no intention of yielding him her person, but kept him off with a variety of kisses and touches of the hand, all nicely adjusted to holding the situation while she could think what best to do.

Jarnti found his king in a compromising situation with his wife.

Violent scenes. Jealousy. Reproaches. The men fought, decided that the friendship of men outweighed the love of women, clasped hands, drank together for the whole of a night, fell together into a canal at dawn . . . all according to the book.

Ben Ata was now violently in love with Al·Ith.

Riding together through the golden mists, he ground his teeth and yearned towards her, while she murmured, "Is there a dictionary in the pavilion?"

"What?"

"It is the word love. We use it differently."

"Cold. Cold and heartless."

"Cold, I certainly am. I am frozen through."

Compunction touched him but was inappropriate to the moment.

"Very well then, *how* do you use the word love?"

"I don't think we do. What it means is being with someone. Taking the responsibility for everything that happens between you. Between the two people in question and of course all the other people involved or who might be involved."

It occurred to him that during these tumultuous six days he had forgotten what Al·Ith was like.

His elation drained away. He rode apart from her, and with a good distance between them the two horses cantered together up the hill to the gardened pavilions where the drum had been beating since the evening before.

As they let the horses go to find their own way to attendants, they were in a welter of wet, and ran through it to the pavilion, where she fled shaking water everywhere to her rooms. The cupboards were empty again of the dresses from the town, and she dried herself and looked through those she had brought for one that would be right for this dejected mood she found in herself. The bright gold of yesterday was like a bird's plumage in a wrong season. A brown was too lowering, but she raised that note a little with a tawny-orange, which seemed something she could aspire to, if things went well. Having put her hair up into Zone Four's matronly braids, she took herself to the central room as Ben Ata came in from the other side. There was not a suggestion of armour about him. His under-tunic looked as if it had been put on with a view as to how it would look to her, and his hair had been brushed close to his handsome head. All this, together with his needy and hostile looks, made her sink down as far away from him as she could get, which was at the table. He, having had no other idea in his head for the last twenty-four hours at least, strode over, and was about to haul her to the couch when it occurred to him that this was exactly what had set off all the turmoil of the last few days which, matched against the appraising reality of Al·Ith, seemed now, to put it mildly, inappropriate.

Swearing vigorously, he sat down opposite her, looking as ever on his side of the little table as if an incautious movement might collapse not only it, but the whole pavilion. He leaned back, sighed, and seemed to return partly to himself.

They were both considering, with fortitude, the uncertain term that they faced during which they would have to sustain their incompatibility.

"I would like to know," said he, "all about your arrangements for this sort of thing—in your country."

Now Al·Ith had already given thought to this problem. She could not imagine that he would accept the proprieties of Zone Three, not in any terms. She tackled the immediate point of his disquiet with: "There is absolutely no doubt at all—there can be no doubt—that this child is yours."

"I said nothing about that," he protested, while his pleased face showed she had been right.

He waited.

Having discovered she needed food, she had thought her requirements, and what had arrived before her was a delicacy of her country made of honey and nuts. She began to crumble bits off it. Without ceremony, he put his finger out, scooped up a fragment, tasted it, rolled up his eyes, and was resigned.

"It is very good for pregnant women," she said.

"I hope that you are taking proper care of yourself! After all, this child will be the ruler of Zone Four."

This thought, too, had not been overlooked by her. She contented herself with: "If the Providers so decide."

His checked gesture of rebellion told her what his thoughts were—what his actions might be.

"I take it," said he, positively radiant with sarcasm, "that I am only one of your lovers."

At this she leaned back, held up her two hands, and began counting on her fingers, with a look of pretty self-satisfaction, hesitating on the third finger with a little *moue*, returning to the second, going back to the third with a nod, then on to the fourth, the fifth—changing hands, with deliberation, six, seven, eight—allowing her counting forefinger to dwell lovingly with a reminiscent smile on the ninth; heard his indrawn and outraged breath, wondered if she dared to count back again, eleven, twelve, thirteen, and did so, rather perfunctorily, fourteen, fifteen, and ended on nineteen with a competent little nod, like a steward who hasn't forgotten anything.

She looked at him, inviting him to laugh—at her, himself, but he was quite yellow with disastrous thoughts.

"You know," she began, but he finished for her, savagely, " 'Things are not the same with you as they are with us!' I give thanks for it. Decadent, spoiled, immoral . . ."

"It is true I can't imagine you making much of our ways."

"Very well, how many lovers have you had?"

She winced at the word and he noted it. Not without interest, a dispassionate interest. This encouraged her to try and explain, openly—though she had previously decided against any such attempt —with a real intention to persuade him out of his barbarity of perception.

"First of all, that word means nothing to me. It would mean nothing at all, to any woman in our Zone. Even the worst of us, and of course we have our failures as you do . . ." She noted him noting that word as being different in emphasis from any Zone Four might use. "Even the worst of us would be incapable of using a word that described a man as some kind of a toy."

This earned a glance of appreciation. Finding she liked him enough, she continued, and explained the sexual arrangements of Zone Three to him. As she went on, his pose, his fists, tightened until she was almost brought to a stop; then he became absorbed, and listened carefully, missing—she could see—nothing.

There were moments when she was afraid that all his self-pride was going to mount to his head and explode in fresh violence against her, but he contained it. By the time she had finished, aggression had left him, and there remained only the philosopher.

She thought herself some wine, and at a gesture from him, some for him as well, but stronger. He took the glass from her, with a nod of thanks.

"It's no good pretending that I can go along with any of that," he pronounced at last.

"It seems to me," said she humorously, "that you are going to have to." But, as a threat of trouble reappeared, she told him that since their first association, claims (she was not going to say "higher" ones) had made their appearance, and it looked as if absolute fidelity to Zone Four was going to be the order of her day. "It seems," said she, "that there is some sort of prohibition laid down in my flesh— laid down somewhere—and that it is not merely the touch of another man I cannot allow, but the touch of anybody." He was smiling, and she said, "And that is not good, oh great king, it is not. I regard it as pernicious, and unfriendly, but we are both stuck with ways not our own and we have got to get on with it."

On the tip of his tongue hovered words such as "then you must love me after all," but this calmly explanatory mode seemed to forbid it. Melancholy settled on him. It had enclosed her. The reason was, simply, that whenever a natural spring of vitality flourished in either of them, it was instantly suppressed by the natural disposition of the other.

Melancholy took them to the couch in fellow-feeling, made them love each other with many whispers of condolence for their unfortunate linking, caused sympathy to flow from one to the other, made their sexual play—if that could possibly be the word for such sorrowful exchanges—so unlike their previous encounters that neither could recognise the other in them, and culminated in groans and cries from both of them that were nothing less than expostulations at the mismanagement of absolutely everything.

But Al·Ith had noted in herself, and with dismay, the sharp—as if with an ambiguous wound—pleasures she felt in being ground and pounded into these ecstasies of submission to fate. She had not known anything like it before, and could not believe that she could ever want them again.

Meanwhile, it rained. They lay in each other's arms listening to squelches and wallows of rain, and both marvelled at the infinite possibilities of variation there were that neither had expected of themselves.

Still under heavy rain they rose and bathed, and dressed, and returned themselves—she this time using the bright orange dress in a quite desperate attempt to bring some sunlight into this marriage of theirs—to the central room.

They were as close and connubial as any Order could have wished.

But there was also the edge of asperity in both voices that goes so ineluctably with this marriage mood.

She wished to get at the truth of this martial Zone of his.

Do you mean to say—her questions began, while he sat with his chin in his hand, elbow on the table, with the air of one admitting to everything because he was forced to, but nevertheless preserving inner independence.

"Do you mean to say that those singlets of yours you make such a great thing about are all a fake? They don't do anything at all? They can't repel weapons?"

"They are very good at keeping off the rain."

"Do you actually mean to say that these hideous grey round buildings you've got all over Zone Four don't make death rays? That's a fake, too?"

"Everyone believes we've got them. It comes to the same thing."

"Ben Ata, sometimes I can't believe my ears!"

"Why are you in such a fuss about it? For one thing, building one of those death ray fortresses is a major undertaking. We have so little stone. It has to be carted right across Zone Four, sometimes. I don't know how often I've had the army pestering for a campaign, and I've got them building a couple of death ray fortresses instead. They were the best idea I've ever had!"

"Do you mean to say it was your idea?"

"Well . . . I heard about something of the sort."

"Who from? When?"

"A man came through here once, and he mentioned them. All sorts of ideas like that."

"What man? From Zone Five?"

"Zone Five! They didn't so much as know about spears till they saw ours. Even so they like catapults best. No. A man came through. That was in my father's time. I was a boy. I listened. He said he had come from—where was it? Not Zone Five. Was it Zone Six perhaps?"

"I know a little about Zone Six. It can't have been from there."

"A long way, I am sure of that. He talked of a place where they had weapons we hadn't even imagined. They can use the air itself to make weapons of."

"But if they can use air to make weapons, they can use it to make things that are useful?"

"He said nothing about that. It is a place somewhere. A planet. It is an evil race. They kill and torture each other all the time, for the sake of it . . . no, Al·Ith, I'm not taking that look from you! We are *not* like that in Zone Four—not anywhere near it. But I thought it all over, and that is when we spread the rumours about our invulnerable vests and our deadly rays."

"They don't seem to impress Zone Five much."

"Anyway, that isn't the point. I've told you it keeps a lot of men busy."

"Well," she summed up, "this is how it seems to me. Nine-tenths of your country's wealth goes into the preparations for war. Apart from the actual growers of food, and the merchants for food and household goods, everyone is in the employ of the army, in some capacity. Yet you have not in living memory had a war. When you do have a war, I have only to make a list of the supposed reasons for it, and you admit to their inadequacy. Even these wars were in previous generations. Your skirmishes on the borders of Zone Five are because if you have two fighting forces in close connection both will, by their nature, attack, and will similarly accuse the other. The standard of living of your people is very low—" here he groaned, admitting it—"but, Ben Ata, all this goes on under the Law. Under the Providers. All for each and each for all. So what has gone wrong?" She noted that in this somewhat hectoring analysis, she felt not an inkling of the rush of nearness to understanding she had felt yesterday. You put one person with another person, call it love, she was thinking, and then make do with the lowest common denominator.

He yawned.

"It's much too early to go to bed, you know," she said. "It can't be even late afternoon yet—if we were able to see where the day had reached in this downpour." For it was still pelting down.

"Very well, Al·Ith, I want you to picture your affairs to me, just as you have ours to me."

She was hesitating because it occurred to her to wonder why she had not actually made such an analysis—for while such a way of thinking did not conduce to intimations of a higher kind, they were certainly useful for clearing the mind.

"Now come on, Al·Ith, you are ready enough to criticise me."

"Yes, I was just . . . very well. The economy of our country does not rely on any single commodity. We produce many varieties of grains, vegetables, and fruits. . . ."

"But so do we," he said.

"Not to anything like the same extent."

"Go on."

"We have many different kinds of animals, and use their milk and meat and their hides and their wool . . ." And, as he was going to interrupt her again, said, "It is a question of degree, Ben Ata. A half of our population produces these things. A quarter are artisans, using gold, silver, iron, copper, brass, and many precious stones. A quarter are merchants, suppliers, traders, and tellers of stories, keepers of Memory, makers of pictures and statues, and travelling singers. None of our wealth goes into war. There are no weapons in our country. You will not find anything beyond a knife or an axe for household use or the use of a herdsman, in any home in our country."

"And what if you are attacked by a wild animal? If an eagle takes a lamb?"

"The animals are our friends," she said, and saw the incredulity on his face. Also, he found her account lacking in any drama.

"And where has all this got you? Except where we are, in trouble . . . or so you say we are—"

"Is your birth rate falling or is it not?"

"It is. All right, things are unhealthy. I admit it. And now Al·Ith, in this paradise of yours, I want to know what are the men doing?"

"They are not making war!"

"What do they do with themselves all day?"

"Exactly what every one of us does—whatever it is their work is."

"It seems to me that with women ruling there is nothing a man can do but—"

"Make love, you were going to say."

"Something of the sort."

"And bake, and farm, and herd, grow, and trade and mine and smelt and make artefacts and everything there is to do with the different ways of feeding children, mentally and emotionally, and the keeping of archives and maintaining Memory and making songs and tales and . . . Ben Ata, you look as if I had insulted you."

"All that is women's work."

"How is it possible that *They* expect us to understand each other? If you were set down in the middle of our land you would not understand anything that was going on. Do you know that as soon as I cross into your land I cease to be my real self? Everything I say comes out distorted and different. Or if I manage to *be* as I *am*, then it is so hard, that in itself makes everything different. Sometimes I sit here, with you, and I think of how I am, at home, with Kunzor, say, and I can't—"

"Kunzor being your husband?"

She was silent, helpless at the utter impossibility of saying anything that could keep in it the substance of truth.

"Well then, out with it? He is, isn't he? Oh, you can't fool me."

"But didn't I tell you myself that Kunzor is the name of one of the men I am *with*?"

But he kept on his face the look of a man who has with penetration discerned the truth. His stance, arms folded, knees set apart, feet planted, announced that he was not in the least undermined or intimidated.

Yet she could see that he was in fact really trying to understand: she would be wrong to allow herself to be held off from him by his automatic defensiveness. Something she could respect, and from the most real part of her, was at work in him.

Again, automatically, he jeered: "And this Kunzor of yours, of course he is a finer fellow than me in every way possible. . . ."

She did not respond to this, but said, "If we were not meant to understand each other, what are we doing here at all?"

From within deep thought, thought that was being protected, in fact, by his derisiveness, the stances of what he had always considered "strength," he said, or breathed out, slowly, "But what is it . . . I must understand . . . *what*? We have to understand . . . what . . ." He lapsed into silence, eyes fixed on a cup on the table. And she realised, with what delight and relief, that he was in fact operating from within that part of him which meant that he was open and ready for understandings to come into him—as she had been, in the Council Chamber. She sat absolutely still, subduing her breathing, and not allowing her eyes to rest too long on his face for fear of disturbing him.

His own breathing was slower, slower, he was stilled, his eyes fixed on the cup had no sight in them—he was deep within himself. "*What* . . ." he breathed. "There is something . . . we have to . . . *they* want us to . . . here we are soldiers . . . soldiers with no war . . . you are . . . you are . . . what are you? What are we . . . *what are we for* . . . that's it, that's it . . ."

Like someone in sleep, he brought out these words, slow, toneless, each one only a summary, a brief note or abstract, as it were of long processes of inner thought.

The slow rain soaked down, they were inside a bright shell drowned in water, they were inside a hush of wet sound. Neither moved. He breathed now hardly at all. She waited. A long time later he came to himself, saw her there, seemed surprised, glanced around at the cool spaces of this meeting place of theirs, remembered everything, and at once restored face, eyes, and body to alert disbelief.

He did not know what had just happened. Yet she could see on his face a maturity that spoke for the deep processes that had been accomplished in him.

She did not now feel helpless in the face of a diminishing of herself she could not control or direct: she was sustained and comforted, knowing that despite everything, they were in fact achieving what they should . . . and, speaking from the highest of intentions, from out of *her* best understanding of what was needed, she now destroyed this precious mood of mutual benefitting.

What she said was this: "Ben Ata, I wonder if it would be possible for me to see Dabeeb—you know, Jarnti's wife."

He stiffened and stared. This was so violent a reaction that all she could do was to acknowledge that she was back on that level where she could not expect to understand him.

"You see, we—I mean, in our Zone—we are going to have a festival of songs and tales . . ."

His face was working with suspicion. His eyes were red, and glared.

"What is the matter?"

"Oh, you are a witch all right. Don't pretend you are anything else."

"But, Ben Ata, it seems to me that we may find out what we want to know—or at any rate get some inkling, by listening to old songs. Stories. Not the ones that everyone sings all the time. Ones that have . . . fallen out of . . . use . . . and—" But he had got up violently, and was leaning over her, gripping her shoulders, his face six inches from hers.

"So you want to interview Dabeeb!"

"Any of the women. But I've met Dabeeb."

"I can tell you this, I'm not going to share one of those orgies of yours, everyone having each other."

"Ben Ata, I don't know what has happened, but you are off again on some wrong track . . ."

"So I am! What happens when a group of you and your Fathers get together? I can imagine!"

"You are imagining something you've experienced yourself, Ben Ata, something like what happens when your soldiers invade some wretched village and . . ." but she saw there was no point in going on. She shrugged. Stung by her contempt, for it was that, he straightened himself, and strode to the arched door which led out to the hill at the foot of which lay the army camp. He shouted into the rain, again, again, again . . . an answering shout, the sounds of feet running through water, then Ben Ata shouting, "Tell Dabeeb to come here. At once."

And he turned there, arms folded, leaning his weight back on the archway, smiling triumphantly at her.

"Well, I want to speak to Dabeeb, and I am glad she is coming. But I've got no idea why you are behaving like this."

"Perhaps you fancy having Dabeeb yourself? Who knows what you and your filthy lot get up to."

"*Having. Having.* What is this word of yours, having. How can one *have* another person. No wonder you can't—" but she had been going to say, "No wonder you can't make love when you think in terms of having—" but of course had to check it.

"You had better get the shield to protect her, or something like that," she said. "She won't be able to stand up to the air in here."

"Thank you so much. It had occurred to me, you know. How do you suppose all these arrangements were made here?"

And he indicated the devices for the protection of the people who had worked, or who still worked in here from time to time—in this case, large clasps or brooches, which were for fastening at throat level.

Soon the sound of squelching feet, and Dabeeb appeared, wrapped in a vast dark cloak, one of her husband's old army cloaks. She stood in the entrance, *not* looking at Ben Ata, but very closely, and shrewdly at Al·Ith, who smiled at her. She accepted from Ben Ata the brooch—which was of a yellow dull substance, very heavy—and pinned this at the opening of her dress at the throat, and stepped lightly in, dropping the wet cloak outside the arch on the floor of the portico.

She still did not look at Ben Ata, but was waiting for Al·Ith. Who had suddenly understood what was the probable cause for all the drama. Dabeeb had not looked at Ben Ata. In this awful place, with the antagonisms inseparable from being *with*—from sex, as they put it—this probably meant they had *had* each other. She had *had* him, or he had *had* her—however these barbarians saw it—but she was not disposed at this particular time even to wonder.

Seeing Dabeeb, the neat, handsome, capable matron, with her air of shrewd humour, standing there waiting for direction, Al·Ith decided to make as much as she could of the situation.

"Please sit down, Dabeeb," she said, nodding at the chair Ben Ata had left empty. And now Dabeeb did glance at Ben Ata. The real danger of this situation—as she had momentarily seen it—had not been enough to allow her to raise her eyes to him, but now that she needed an order, a direction, she did look towards her lord.

But he had left it all to Al·Ith, and stood like a sentinel, watching the scene.

Dabeeb sat.

"In our country we are going to have a great festival of songs and of stories. We have them often, but this one will be different."

Already Dabeeb was alert and on guard: the eyes of the two women had engaged, and Dabeeb's were warning. Al·Ith very slightly nodded, saying, "I understand, don't be afraid." Ben Ata did not catch this minutest of nods, but he had seen that he had been mistaken. The sight of these two women, sitting opposite each other, both ready to catch from each other the best they could, did not fail to soothe him, and at the same time to disturb him. Their instant understanding made him feel left out, shut out.

He exaggerated his sarcastic look and soldierly straightness.

"We want to try and find out if there are songs which perhaps we have forgotten or half forgotten that can tell us things."

"I see, my lady."

Again the two pairs of eyes searched each other.

"But there is no need to be afraid . . ." here Al·Ith paused a moment, and then continued, "if you don't remember any. That is why I asked Ben Ata if you would come up to talk to me. You really mustn't worry . . ." here Al·Ith paused again, and waited until Dabeeb had, in her turn, given the very slightest of nods, "about it. It is just an impulse I had. A whim!" And she put on the look of one who was subject to whims and to having them indulged—a bit fatuous, self-congratulatory.

"I see, my lady."

"I wish you would call me by my name."

"It is hard to remember." This was in an apologetic voice, almost a plea.

"We have all kinds of songs, but for instance only the other day listening to some children some of us realised that parts of songs might have been forgotten, or changed—or something like that. And perhaps it is like that with you."

"Perhaps it is."

"There is a song I believe I heard the other day when I was here. The beat is like this—" And Al·Ith rested the heel of her hand on the table's edge and tapped with her fingers: — ·· — ·· — ·

Dabeeb had caught it and nodded.

"Perhaps it is a woman's song?"

"All manner of people sing it, my lady."

"Perhaps it has a tune that different words are set to, at different times," said Al·Ith casually.

"I think that sometimes is so, with us," said Dabeeb.

Meanwhile, Ben Ata was as awake as he had never been in his life.

He knew quite well that this encounter between the two women was accommodating levels of understanding he did not, at the moment, in the least grasp. But he had every intention of doing so. But strongest in him, raging among thoughts and intuitions of a quite different character, was suspicion. And he was as forlorn and excluded as a small child that has had a door shut in his face.

"Is it something to do with light?" suggested Al·Ith.

"Light? Oh, I don't think so. I haven't heard that one."

But her eyes had said yes, and begged and pleaded for Al·Ith not to betray them. Al·Ith was seeing that her idea about the women was not only correct—but had been far from adequate. She saw that here was something like an underground movement.

"Shall I sing one of the versions for you? It is very popular."

"I wish you would."

"It is a very old song, my lady." And Dabeeb cleared her throat, and stood up behind the chair, holding on to it with one hand. She had a clear strong voice, and evidently used it often.

> "Look at me, soldier! He's looking!
>   It's at me he is looking!
>
>   Soon I shall smile, not quite at him,
>   That'll catch him!"

And now both women heard Ben Ata's breathing, thick, angry.

Neither looked at him: they knew they would see a man in frenzies of jealousy. Everything was now perfectly clear to Al·Ith. She marvelled at her own clumsiness; and also at the aptness of events,

which always pleased her, so inevitably and satisfyingly proceeding
from one thing to another, turning facets of truth, the possibilities of
development, to the light one after another.

She knew that Ben Ata had wanted to *have* this woman, and that
she had not wanted to be *had*. She knew that Ben Ata's mind was
inflamed with jealousies and suspicions. There was nothing for it but
to go along with whatever was happening and—and wait and see.

Dabeeb was singing:

> *"Eyes shine—*
> *His, mine . . .*
>
> *I know how to please him,*
> *Simple and tease him.*
>
> *I'll make him hunger,*
> *And languish and anger,*
>
> *And give me his pay,*
> *A corporal's pay."*

Her strong voice left a strong silence, supported by the hushing
rain.

"We sing that at the women's festivals—you know, when women
are together."

Seeing that Al·Ith was smiling and pleased, she said, obviously
daring and delighted with herself—and even looking at Ben Ata and
allowing herself a half-humorous shudder at the black rage on his
face—"There is another version, but of course it isn't fit for your
ears, my lady."

"Oh, don't worry," said Ben Ata. "Don't run away with that idea.
If you knew what they get up to in that Zone of theirs . . ."

Dabeeb had winked at Al·Ith, then blushed at her audacity, and
had begun the song.

> *"Come husband! Smooth out my—cushion . . ."*

"You are not to sing that," said Ben Ata. He was now sustained by
a calm, moral loftiness.

"Perhaps the lady Al·Ith would like to know the worst of us as
well as the best, my lord," said Dabeeb, in a cosy comfortable voice,

motherlike. As Ben Ata did not persist, but merely strode about, snorting, she began again:

"Come husband, smooth out my—cushion.
Quick, get a push-on . . ."

Dabeeb interrupted herself, and drummed rapidly on the table's edge.

"I'm hungry as—winter.
No sin to . . ."

She drummed again:

"Warm me up
Fill my cup . . ."

She drummed.

"Now—go.
Quick. Slow."

She drummed. She winked at Al·Ith again and, animated with the song, winked at Ben Ata, too, who could not suppress a brief appreciative smile.

"Hard as a board this
Good old bed is . . ."

She drummed.

"One two three four
One two three four . . ."

She drummed, smiling, alive with challenge and invitation.

"That's how we do it.
That's how we do it.

That is our way.
That is our way."

A long sustained drumming, while all her white teeth showed.
"A fine idea you'll have of us, my lady."
Ben Ata was standing with arms folded, feet planted, smiling. As

a result of this song, the current was running strong between him and Dabeeb, whose looks at him were confident, inviting.

Al·Ith watched with interest. Rather as she would have done the mating approaches of a couple of horses.

"There's a song we have . . ." she began casually, and Dabeeb allowed the tension between her and Ben Ata to slacken, and she became attentive to Al·Ith.

Who was thinking that this lie she was telling would not have been possible in Zone Three at all. Occasions for lies did not arise.

Now she was saying: "There's a song we have . . ." when they did not, nor anything like it.

"How shall we reach where the light is,
   Come where delight is . . ."

"Oh, no," Dabeeb broke in, "we have nothing like that. We don't go in for that kind of thing." She was obviously afraid.

"You don't think it might be a good idea if you had a song festival here?" said Al·Ith.

"Oh, a very good idea. A very good idea indeed," said Dabeeb enthusiastically. And her eyes pleaded with Al·Ith.

"Perhaps we'll talk about it, Ben Ata," said Al·Ith, and at once went on, speaking to him: "Dabeeb was kind enough to agree to give me one of her dresses. I'd like to give her one of mine."

"But she has had dozens of dresses. She had all those that weren't good enough for you. What did you do with them, Dabeeb? Flog them?"

"I sold some of them, my lord. They didn't all fit me." And to Al·Ith, "I'd be so grateful. If we could—I mean, I could, have one of your dresses . . ."

"Then come with me," said Al·Ith, on her way to her rooms.

"My lady, if I could have the one you have on now? I've never seen anything like it . . ."

The two women went into Al·Ith's rooms and Ben Ata bounded across and leaned to listen. He could hear the two women, talking about clothes, weaving, sewing. Al·Ith was taking off her dress and Dabeeb was exclaiming over it.

"Oh, this is too fine for me, oh, it is so beautiful, oh, oh, what a beautiful . . ."

"When you make dresses for ordinary wear, do you always make copies for special occasions?"

A brief pause.

"Nearly always, Al·Ith."

"It must be nice wearing a plain dress and thinking of the one that you'll wear on a special occasion."

"Yes, it is. But, of course, we don't have all that many special occasions. We are poor people here."

Oh, we are, are we? Ben Ata was thinking. And he returned rapidly to sit down at the table, where Dabeeb had been. He was tapping out rhythms on the table. He had not been fooled. He did not know what was going on, though he knew something was. He would get it all out of Dabeeb. If he had not got it out of Al·Ith by then.

The two women returned to find him sitting and smiling, the picture of good nature.

He was stung into admiration by both of them. Dabeeb's swarthy and energetic beauty was well accommodated by the tawny silky dress Al·Ith had just taken off. Al·Ith had on her bright yellow dress that seemed to take in all the light there was in the great softly lit room—and to give it out again. Her loose black hair shone, her eyes shone, she was full of mischief and gaiety. Ben Ata was thinking, frankly, to himself, of the pleasures there would be in having them both at once—a possibility that had not entered his head until recent instructions with Elys. He remembered Al·Ith's scorn of the word *have*. He sat head slightly lowered, looking up from under his brows at the two—and his mind was full of a painful struggle suddenly, as if it were trying to enlarge beyond its boundaries. He was having a flash of understanding—into the way Al·Ith scorned him for using the language he did. But it did not last. A gloomy suspicion came back, while he watched Al·Ith go with Dabeeb to the arch, and Dabeeb wrap herself tightly in the old dark cloak, and then with a smile at him and something intimate and quick with Al·Ith, run off to be enclosed in the pelting grey of the rain.

Al·Ith watched her go, and smiled. And turned to him, and smiled. In her sunny yellow, she was lovelier than he believed—at that moment—he deserved. He could see that she was a quick, volatile, flamelike thing, and understood how he subdued and dimmed her. But jealousy was undoing him.

She was inviting him. Everything about her, as she stood smiling, enticed him. He got up clumsily and heavily and rushed at her. She evaded him, not out of coquetry, but from real dismay. "No, no, Ben Ata, don't spoil it. . . ." And she was trying to meet him lightly, and gaily, as they had not long ago, during hours which now to Ben Ata seemed so far above anything he had thought and been since that he would not believe in them, any more than he was able easily to lift his gaze to the vast mountainous region that filled all the western skies. He grabbed her, and she withheld him. "Wait, wait, Ben Ata. Don't you want to be as we were then?" Oh, yes, he did, he did very much, desperately, he was all inflamed with wanting just that and nothing else—but he could not help it, or himself, or her—he had to be, just then, all grab and grind, and he extinguished all the possibilities of sweetness and the playfulness, and the slow mounting of the exchanges. He had her. And then, all the light gone out of her, she had him. It was not a new experience for him, since Elys, but all the time he was remembering that other time and he made this one obstinate and heavy because, simply, that other time had gone and was not here. This time Al·Ith did not weep, or allow herself to be pulverised into submission. She gave as good as she got, words which she chose, carefully, out of many, and handed to him, with a smiling air of indifference, scorn even.

They ended some hours of this kind of obdurate interchange unfriendly to each other, and inwardly depressed.

When they rose to bathe and dress and arrange themselves, the lovely airy room seemed denuded of its sparkle, and the drum had stopped beating.

This time, all was efficient and considered. She wrapped herself in a cloak, she remembered her shield, and stepped out into the gardens from the opposite door Dabeeb had run down into the rain from. There the fountains played coldly under a cold low blue sky.

Ben Ata came after her, similarly cloaked and ready. She called, and the two horses, black and white, came cantering up, and they leapt onto their backs and rode off, soberly, down towards the road west. They used the time of the journey to discuss what was seen along the road—the crops, the canals, the fields.

Nothing more sensible and connubial could be imagined. But Al·Ith was so far inwardly from Ben Ata that he could get from her not one little moment of real recognition. It was clear to him that she did not want anything from him—only to be rid of him. He knew perfectly well he was to blame.

At the frontier, they reined in their two horses, and Al·Ith was about to shoot forward into the sunny immensities of that plain below the mountains when he called to her hoarsely, "Al·Ith, wait."

She turned and gave him the coolest of mocking smiles.

"I suppose now you are going to Kunzor," he shouted, enraged.

"And others," she called back, and rode off.

He muttered to himself that he would order Dabeeb back, but in fact, knew he would not. He was thinking. He had realised that while jealousy and resentment and suspicion worked in him, poisoning everything, there were other things he could be understanding. And he was determined that he would.

The people on the roads who saw him returning to the camps, remarked to each other that the king seemed subdued. That foreign one was not cheering him up, not much, that was for certain, whatever else she might be doing!

Exactly as had happened before, both Al·Ith and Ben Ata, separated from each other, one riding on into Zone Three, one riding back into Zone Four, felt that the burden of their emotions for one another was not lightened, as they had wanted, but was heavier. Together, they provoked each other into unwanted feelings, apart, thoughts of the other tormented and stung. Ben Ata felt that he was carrying around with him a curse, or a demon, who prevented him from being with Al·Ith in a way that would lead to an incredible happiness. Al·Ith felt a most painful bond with her husband—a word she was examining, turning over and over, as if it were a new ring of a complicated design or a new metal made in the workshops of the northern regions where the mines were. Ben Ata was a weight in her side, no, in her belly, where the new child was, but that was still no more than a speck or a dab of new flesh, so it could not be that which made her so heavy. Riding forward, she was in mind with Ben Ata, whose face was set towards the low, damp fields. . . . She could have asked him this, found out that . . . if she had done this instead of that . . . for, away from him, she could not truly believe that her behaviour had been as she remembered it was. When she had come back into the tall light central room she was vibrant and strong because of the exchange with Dabeeb, which had made her alive and confident, so that she had felt far from the gloomy moods of Ben Ata. Her yellow dress had fitted her like happiness. And yet nothing had come of it but the punishments Ben Ata called love.

And now, as she rode through the plain with the grasses shimmering on both sides of her, and the sky a soft blue over her, she felt as if this land of hers was foreign to her, or she foreign to it. This was so unexpected that she got off her horse and stood by his head, her cheek against his, murmuring, Yori, Yori, what are we to do? But it seemed as if even this dear friend her kind horse was impatient with her.

She walked forward along the soft dust of the road, Yori following behind. This was her home, she was this land, she was its heart and soul—and yet she felt like a ghost in it, without substance.

When she came to the road that crossed this one, running north and south, she turned northwards, still walking, and slowly walking, like one who does not want to reach a destination. She walked all day, her horse following her, and sometimes touching her cheek with his nose, as if questioning her. But she did not want to get on his back. She was feeling something like: if I walk, one foot after another, on this soil of mine, then perhaps I can *will* that it take me back, accept me into itself. . . .

Towards evening she saw a man on horseback coming to her and soon saw it was Kunzor. He jumped down, took her hands, and looked into her face.

The two horses stood nose to nose, telling each other their news.

"I felt you were in trouble, Al·Ith."

"Yes, I am, but I don't know what it is."

They moved off the road, and after searching, found a small stream, with some low bushes marking its passage, and they sat there, hand in hand.

Al·Ith was trying with all of herself to reach out to Kunzor, to feel what he was, how he was . . . she observed herself doing this, with some dismay. For this was not how she usually had to be. Encountering anyone, but particularly those she was most close to, what she or he was, their real selves, impressed themselves on her—sharp, clear, and unmistakably, uniquely, him, her. . . . She had always taken it for granted—the moment of recognition. Kunzor's own self, his individual and unique self, had a flavour that she could never have confused with anyone else's. It was a strong, quick, dry, male force. Tangy and energetic, like the winds coming down off the snows at a certain season, just before fresh snowfalls were expected.

But she had not had to think about it before, to make efforts, to reach out—and to fail. Unable to make a match with him inwardly, she examined him, carefully, as if this outward appraising could be a substitute.

Kunzor was, of all the men she was *with*, the nearest to her. In appearance, too. His body build was the same, light and slender, his way of moving lithe and quick, and his eyes, like hers, were dark, deep, reflective. Together they had always known what each other thought. Their feelings passed always through their linked hands like shared blood. They might spend days, or weeks, and hardly need to talk. Now even the sound of the running water seemed a barrier to their being together, and when she began to weep, he simply nodded.

"You are different," he said. "You do not hear what I am. And all I can hear of you is that you are troubled and heavy."

"The worst is that I don't want to go on up into my own home, my own realm. It's as if it were *not* mine. Do I seem a stranger to you, Kunzor?"

"Yes. It is as if you, Al·Ith, the shell of you, had taken in a new substance. And yet I can talk to you, and you can understand."

"There are moments when I don't. Your voice seems to come and go, sometimes I know it all through me, just as I feel your thoughts in me when I am myself. But then I look at you and you are outside myself and not in."

He said in a low difficult voice, "But you are now host to a child from *there*."

"Yes. When it is delivered, then I shall be delivered, too? Do you think that?"

"You cannot host a soul from a land as far from us as that place is, and not lose yourself to it, Al·Ith."

"What am I to do?"

"Al·Ith, you know there is nothing you can do."

Soon the sky lost its light, and became a soft grape colour, and the winds from the east began rustling the grasses. The two horses stepped down carefully till they were close to the stream and sheltered from it. And the girl and the man sat close, holding hands, deep in trouble, sustaining each other.

When this scene is portrayed, the two are always shown sitting apart from each other, not touching: Al·Ith with her head bowed, in sorrow, and Kunzor watching her in brotherly concern. And I think that this is the truth of how it was. For if she felt remote from him, this man who had been ever since she could remember part of her, for they had known each other as children, he was thinking that until she came out from under the dark shadow of Zone Four—for that is how he was experiencing being near her—he would not be able to do more than go through the motions of being close. Yet he held her hand through that long night, and tried to reassure her when she wept.

When the sky lightened again, and the searing winds dropped suddenly, she rose, brushing off the grass seeds and dust the wind had left on her sunny yellow dress, which contrasted so much with her wan face, and thanked him for riding out to meet her.

But she had to go on up into the plateau whether she liked it or not.

They parted, she riding back towards the road that would take her west. Her horse was happy to go, and trotted along, alert and full of energy, but she knew the pressure of her knees on him was telling him of her mood, and she tried, so as not to dim his pleasure, to be as willing as he.

As they climbed up the long pass on to the plateau, she was thinking that when they reached there her land would take her into itself again. And then, when it didn't happen, that it would when she passed some people who would know her and greet her—but she saw a group of young men on the roadside, walking to a town on a hill, and she slowed so that they could see her and call to her, as always happened, but it seemed that they did not notice her at all. They were coming towards her, and she waited, but they looked everywhere else, and did not stop their talking and laughing. She called out to them: "Greetings! Is everything going well with you?" And they did call back: "Greetings, thank you, and we trust with you . . ." and she realised she was not recognised as Al·Ith. Never had this happened before, and in the deeps of the thought that now took her, she was not conscious of how she and Yori crossed the distance to

Andaroun. She was vaguely aware that they were passing people who did not recognise her, and that the horse was slowing, and becoming depressed, because of her. And she entered our capital as slowly as if she were expecting to be ill-treated there, or even punished. And still she felt as if she were not part of her beloved realm, she felt like a stone on the top of her horse, like a sack of ill-fated heaviness, with nothing to give out in response to the friendly charm of our streets and avenues and gardens. Her land did not know her. She had become filled with a substance foreign to it—even hostile, but how, she did not know! And when she thought that she must stable her companion, poor Yori, who now seemed like her only friend, and climb up the wide steps and meet her sister and then the children, whom normally she spent hours of every day with, if she were not travelling around her realm, then she could not believe that she could go through with it. She was an impostor. That was what she felt. And between her and Ben Ata the bond lay heavy and strong, and it was as if she could feel his thoughts thrumming and vibrating. He was waiting for her to come back to him, and at the same time felt a helpless despairing anguish at the knowledge that she would. He was in their pavilion, not with his soldiers. He was sitting there, alone, thinking. Or striding up and down. He was trying to understand, trying to come at what they should both be understanding. And she should be there, with him. But the drum was not beating. She knew that. She could hear the soft splashing of the fountains. She could hear the cries and the clash of the soldiers at their exercises on the plain. But the drum was silent, though Ben Ata was listening for it and longing for it as much as she listened for it and longed for it. And dreaded it.

The nature of Zone Four—it was conflict and battle and warring. In everything. A tension and a fighting in its very substance: so that every feeling, every thought held in it its own opposite.

When she reached the palace, which filled two sides of our central square, she dismounted, and looked, as always, to see who would be waiting for her on the wide white stone steps. No one and nothing was there. She walked to the trees in the square where there were always attendants ready to take horses of people who had come from the regions, and one took over the responsibility of Yori—but did not greet her as Al·Ith. He was polite, but almost perfunctory. She walked back to the great steps, and mounted them slowly, feeling her yellow skirts swing out around her ankles. She had never, ever, approached this entrance to the palace without people running to meet her from everywhere, not only the building itself, but from the gardens behind, and other parts of the square. "Al·Ith," they would shout, "Al·Ith is here." In a profound silence, deepened by the doves' contented crooning from the trees, she went up into the apartments and chambers of the ground floor, walking swiftly through them to see who was at work there, what was happening: in one a Council was in process, and her sister sat there with twenty or so people. No one looked up as she stood in the doorway. They were discussing a mysterious ailment that afflicted the cattle in the western ranges—so things had not improved, were not yet improving. Though of course they were going to. Her sister sat with her back to her, but usually this would not have prevented her from sensing her presence and turning to greet her. A young girl Al·Ith knew well, one of the orphans she had mothered, did at last look up and see her, but her eyes at once moved away, as if Al·Ith were not there at all.

So Al·Ith left and went up into her own rooms. They were flooded with a heavy yellow light from the westering sun, and Al·Ith sat at the window, immersed in yellow, strong and sustaining, but did not feel anything but a shadow and a ghost. Into these rooms, so simple and light and pleasant, with nothing in them she had not chosen because of her affinity with shape or colour, she came always as if into her own self, her self expanded and displayed there, smiling . . . but now its very refinement of tone and texture, its subtlety, refused to admit her: she had become heavy, and unfit for it. She should not have come at all, very probably.

Up she went on to the many levels of the roofs and walked there watching the sun sink down and set the mountains alight. All our capital was spread out below, with its familiar streets and gardens. There was not a house, or a square, or a public place that she did not know—often from inside and very intimately, out of friendship with its inhabitants, but at least in appearance, its frontage, roof, pattern of windows—all part of the habits of her own mind. But she was not welcome there now.

Thinking that high in the belltower she might reach to the heights

of herself from which she had so far sunk away, she climbed up and
up and up the winding stairs and stood dizzyingly high, mountains
and clouds and snow fields her peers, and the birds swinging past at
eye level, and looked up and out towards the gap in the peaks where
the blue fields lay waiting, but she was muttering: Far. Too far . . .
and she could not believe that it was so recently she had stood there
feeling she had only to allow herself to be drawn into that cerulean
to be translated into something other than anything she had known
or imagined, feeling even that she had only to step out of the tower
and run across the sparkling skies, lighter than air, to vanish into
blue as the clouds do when the sun's heat dissipates them. Now
she was encumbered and clogged and felt that she was wrong to
stand here, unwelcome.

And she went down rapidly to her rooms to find her sister there.
Murti· was startled. She had not expected her. This astonished and
dismayed both. Never before had either been unaware of what the
other did or was at any time, even if they were at opposite ends of
the regions.

Al·Ith sat down in the window and so did Murti· but at a distance. The two women examined each other, with pain, and like
strangers. Al·Ith saw Murti· as ethereal, all fire and brilliance, like a
fountain renewing itself at every moment from springs quite un-
imaginable to Al·Ith now, in her dragging state, who, to Murti·
seemed as if a light had gone out of her.

"Have the children been asking for me?" enquired Al·Ith humbly,
pleading.

And Murti·, wincing at this new suppliant's tone, said with difficulty, "No."

"They have not missed me?"

"They talk as if you are dead, Al·Ith." And she leaned forward
and took Al·Ith's hand, from old habit, to renew the currents that
had always played there between them. And slowly let the hand fall,
with a sigh.

"Do you tell them I am not dead, but will come back again?"

After a while Murti·'s bright kind eyes fell before Al·Ith's, and
she said, "It is different. I don't know why. Al·Ith, *it is hard to
remember you.* Do you understand that?"

Al·Ith's anguish held her pain contained, so she did not weep. And she contained her anguish, this sensation that was no part of her lovely realm, where pain and suffering were signs of illness, to be treated with patience, compassion, and determination that this foreignness would not infect others.

Al·Ith stood up. The flaring light from the sun was sinking again, and the streets and alleys lay in shadow, while light warmed the rooftops. The cries and voices of the town rose up to them: warmth, living, vitality.

Al·Ith clasped her two hands close into her waist as if she should keep them safe and their touch must not contaminate others.

"Are things any better with us? Are the animals still sorrowing? Are they still lonely?"

"Are they lonely, Al·Ith?" The two sisters stood close, but not as they had always been in the past, their hands and arms together, sometimes cheeks touching, so that each could feel the rhythms and life of the other, like her own. They were close but not touching, and their eyes talked, but with reticences.

"Yes, they are sad and they are lonely," Al·Ith was whispering. Both whispered, yet they were alone and no one could have heard them. "A mare in a herd of horses will be overcome with loneliness, but not know what it is, but stand shivering, believing there must be a word she could hear, or a voice, but there is nothing but silence. A stallion will surge from one end of a prairie to the other, driven by emptiness. A whole herd of cattle will lift their heads all at once and cry out that they are suffering . . ."

"I've heard them, Al·Ith, I've heard them," whispered Murti·.

"Suddenly on a hill a thousand sheep will move away, running, the shepherds after them, calling and soothing. They feel some terrible loss, Murti· . . . but is it getting better, is this pain being lifted from our beasts?"

Murti· shook her head, and sighed. "I do not think so."

"And is there still a lack of hope with us all? Are the children not being born?"

"Things are as they were. Al·Ith, it is a very short time since you first were taken to the other Zone. Does it seem to you a long time?"

"A very long time. Oh, such a long, long time." And tears fell from Al·Ith's eyes in floods.

"Are we going to have to accept tears and grief as part of the normal functioning of our Zone?" demanded Murti·, fierce.

"No, no, you are right."

"If it is your part, in this series of events, to go down into that other place and know tears and grief and . . ."

"You do not know, Murti·, you cannot imagine!"

"No. But it is not I who have been ordered to make this marriage, Al·Ith! I am sure that this duty is something very high, much finer than anything we can imagine—but you must not poison us with your grief."

She was hard and fierce and angry. Al·Ith could see that her beautiful sister, her other self, was as firm in her protection of the realm as she herself had ever been. It was Murti· now who was this land, this realm. It was she who embodied and contained it.

Al·Ith whispered, "Our beasts were grieving and low and restless before I ever went to Zone Four."

"That is true. But now when you come back from there, you come in a cloud of black. If you could see it, my sister! No. You must not come again until—"

"Until what? And I am not obeying my will, but theirs."

Murti· nodded. "That is not my business. But I can tell you that you are bringing with you a contagion. It is not your fault. Nothing is our fault, Al·Ith. How can it be? But you have been given a part to play. For the sake of all of us."

Al·Ith nodded. Without looking again at her sister, she went into her cupboards, and began cramming necessities and clothes of all kinds into saddle bags.

"And is the song and story festival being taken care of?"

"Is it important?"

Al·Ith turned swiftly, and faced her with emphasis. "Yes, indeed it is. Very."

"Then I shall see to it. Do you know why?"

"That you must understand for yourself," said Al·Ith, on precisely the humble pleading note that had distressed Murti· before. "There is something there we can grasp. Murti·, I know this, I know this absolutely. . . ." And she came close to her sister, forgetting their new distance from each other. But it was dusk in the apartment now.

The tall oblong of the window showed a fading inky light, and the stars were there.

Murti· took one step back, away from this presence she felt as contaminating. But then stood fast. "What is it?"

"There is something we should have been doing. But we have not done it."

The two could hardly see each other's faces now. They leaned forward to gaze.

"You don't know what?"

"Yes. It is to do with the blue realm beyond the peaks in the northwest. But *what*, Murti·? What? That is the point. And that is what we must find out. *We must find out what we are for.*"

And Al·Ith turned and ran out of the rooms, and down the stairs to the lower floors and the Council Chamber and down again till she reached the wide white steps and she fled down these and then, in the square, around the edge of the palace into the alley that led to the stables, where she found her horse. And she leapt on to his back and was off through the town and rode all night, reaching the top of the pass by dawn, and then rode across the plain through the morning, and reached the frontier by early evening. But the drum was not beating. She knew that. So she dismounted, and found a stream and grazing for her Yori, and sat there alone through the dark hours, watching the stars move. She could not go forward into Zone Four: it was not time for her. And she was not wanted in her own land.

And that was how our queen, Al·Ith, wandered in the between places, unknown, ignorant of what was needed from her or what her future was to be, hungry, cold, quite alone, except for her kind horse. And before morning Yori lay down in a patch of grass, and Al·Ith curled up against his warm side, and waited for the sun to rise.

She was singing to herself.

> "*Sorrow, what is your name!*
> *If I knew your name I could feed you—*
> *Fill you, still you, and leave you!*
>
> *Grief, if I knew your nature,*
> *I would lead you to pasture.*

What is the path I should lead you?
Which is the food I should feed you?"

When Al·Ith woke in the early sun she was lying bundled in the grasses of the riverside like a leveret whose mother has abandoned it: her horse was feeding nearby. She pulled the thin seeds from the grass heads and ate them for her food, and drank water from the stream and sat watching the mountains of her realm. She dreamed of her journeys around and through her country, to the north and the west and the south, where the vineyards and the oil grew, and to the east again, where she now loitered. How various and rich and wonderful was this land of hers, from which she was now banished, where she was now unwelcome. For how long had she roamed in it, summing up and accomplishing in herself all its potentials. She, Al·Ith, the beautiful, now a fugitive, unwanted anywhere, sat by the river, trying to remember for how long she had enjoyed all that richness. But she could not remember for how long.

All day she waited, her face lifted towards the high ranges of her peaks, and at night her horse lay down again, and she close to it, for shelter from the searing wind that started at sundown from the low places of the east. She laid her head to Yori's side, and listened to the strong heart beating there, and imagined that she heard the drums beating from the pavilions of Ben Ata. But she did not. Ben Ata was alone, striding through those empty rooms and around and through the fountains, waiting, as she did, for the drum to begin.

But it did not.

Days passed.

During the hours of light she wandered by the stream, watched the birds splashing and skimming, or sat gazing at her mountains. Sometimes the light massed them strong and lowering and with every ravine and rocky spur defined and clear. But sometimes they seemed to float there, shining or shadowy, and their tops and outlines merged with the blues of the sky. At night she sheltered near her horse, and did not sleep, but sang her plaints of exile, and listened for the drum.

And still she could hear nothing from the pavilions of Ben Ata.

Now she lost her sense of how much time had passed, was passing. She wondered if perhaps she was mistaken about her path and direction. Perhaps her sojourn in the realms of Ben Ata was completed, and she had failed, and had been thrown out to linger here until she died. But then she remembered that there was to be a child, who was still no more than an act of belief for her, since the new life had not made itself felt. If she was not important or necessary to the Providers or the Necessity, then the child was.

Or perhaps she was being punished. . . . When this thought came battering at her mind, she pushed it away, for she was still able to remember that in her land, if some little person allowed such ideas to enter the mind, then it was a sign of mental illness, of a monstrous and shocking egotism.

But the compulsion to believe she was most fatally in the wrong kept pressing in on her. After all, it was in Zone Three that such ideas were mistaken, not at all in Zone Four—and that was, or so it seemed, where she belonged! If she did belong anywhere now—but how could she know? If she was guilty, then of what was she guilty, and why was this punishment the fit one for her? These thoughts—or were they emotions?—ground around in her head—or was it in her heart they seethed and simmered?

Sometimes she called Yori to her, and stood by his head, gazing into his mild and intelligent eyes. "Yori, Yori, am I wicked, then? Do you know what it is I have done?"

But he looked his love for her, and his kindness, and soon, as a horse has to, lowered his head to graze.

He was lonely here with her. One day a herd of wild horses, their manes flying, came chasing across the savannah, and Yori called to them and galloped off, his hooves making the hard ground ring. For all of a long happy day Yori ran races with them, and rolled over and over the earth among the warm-smelling grasses, and once raced away with them quite out of sight, so that she thought he would not come back at all. But he did come back, alone, at dusk, and she saw that he was sad and would have liked to stay with his companions. But he put his soft nose into her neck in greeting, and patiently lay down again, because the gales had already started from the east, and it was time to shelter her.

Days passed.

One evening as the light was going, she saw, on the other side of the stream, but far off, a man who seemed to resemble Ben Ata. She crossed the stream on stepping-stones, and ran up the bank and towards this man, who was on the other side of the frontier line. She stopped when she had to, as the tensities of the air changed, and saw that this could not be Ben Ata, for it was a lean desperate man with none of the stolid oxlike quality of the king of that low Zone. Yet she longed to rush towards him, and understood by this that it was Ben Ata. Separated by impossibility, they stood, gazing, and then she called out, "Ben Ata!" And he, after a wait, called gruffly back, "Al·Ith!".

Their voices were strange to each other, reminded both of their differences, and how abrasive was their actual contact. Yet they remained there, while the dark came down, and they could see nothing but shadows.

She did not call again, and nor did he, but later they found that both had stayed staring and leaning into the dark, for many hours. She returned to her stream and her horse's sheltering side when the wind grew too bitter to bear. That night she felt in her lower abdomen the creeping flutter that announced to her the child was more than a bundle of accumulating cells. She put her hand to cup the place, in greeting, but was divided and in conflict.

As for Ben Ata, who had been in torments of wanting and not-wanting ever since he had left her at the frontier, when he had seen her there, in the half-dark, a little burned-out fragment of a woman in her flame of a yellow dress, he had suffered an overturning of himself, and had ridden back to the camps, bypassing the pavilions, where he had been all these days, as little conscious of their passing as Al·Ith was, and feeling again she had stolen his good senses away. But back in his own camp, his own tent, with Jarnti and the other officers tactfully welcoming, he was possessed no less than in the pavilions . . . *but by what?* He could not sleep. He did not eat. He could not keep still. Dabeeb, washing the family's clothes in a great tub at her back door, saw Ben Ata jump the little fence, and stride towards her as if he was going to overturn her, the tub of water, and the wet wrung clothes in their basin. He stopped in front of her and, taking her chin in his hand, lifted it and gazed into her eyes, and at every bit of her face. He was frowning with the immensities of the comparisons he was making. Dabeeb could see this, and grudged him not at all. Poor old king, he's certainly got it bad, she was thinking, while maintaining a smiling but decorous pair of smooth dusky cheeks and eyelids that shuttered her real thoughts. Hmmm. Not done him any harm at all, thought she, as Ben Ata, without apology, turned and strode off again. And she smiled to herself, congratulating Al·Ith, imagining how she would use the man's desperations and his anger.

But Ben Ata quite simply could not stand this turmoil another moment. It was time for another campaign. In a fever, he called for the latest reports from all his frontiers, and found—hardly to his surprise of course—that there had been skirmishings on the border with Zone Five. "Time they were taught a lesson," he muttered, together with other ritual and routine incantations, and went out into the officers' mess to share these around and raise the temperature a little. As usual all were delighted at his announcement of a new campaign. Meanwhile, he was sitting in his tent, thinking of Al·Ith, and her scorn of him, his wars, his campaigns. He was thinking of the last campaign, and for the first time since he could remember, of the dead and the wounded, for until now he had not been ever prompted to do so.

He could not cancel this campaign, for this would make him seem soft and vacillating, but neither could he face riding out, in front of his army, "going through all that palaver," he was muttering, dismally, and then "putting up with it all for days and weeks on end." These thoughts struck him as quite treasonable, and he let out a sort of muffled roar of anger, which was heard by his orderlies, who looked at each other, silently sharing comments that it would have been too risky even to whisper.

Ben Ata rushed out of his tent, bounded on to the first horse he could see in the corrals, and rode off towards the eastern border, which lay adjacent to Zone Five. He had not left any of his unhappiness behind!

"What am I going to do?" he kept muttering, as he alternately switched his horse to make it go faster, and then checked it, and patted it briefly . . . the horse's mouth was lathered, the bit was uncomfortable there . . . Ben Ata thought that Al·Ith, and everyone in her country rode without bridles, without saddles, without beatings, without everything that here, with them, was found necessary. He lessened the grip of the bit on his horse's mouth, and even mut-

tered a few words of pity for the beast—but as he did so, felt himself
to be a traitor again. And what was he doing going towards Zone
Five at all? He loathed the place and always had. Long before the
actual frontier, the heavy deep soil, the good rich fields, the canals,
and the ditches and the ponds and the interminable flat perspectives
of Zone Four, which he had always—or had until recently—felt was
the proper way for a country to be, gave way to scrub and sand and
a thin high air that tasted always of dust. He had never penetrated
far into the hateful place, but the captives and girls his soldiers
paraded before him, or flung into his tent, were thin scraggy things
and the dust always powdered their limbs and faces and hair a dingy
yellow. He supposed that this dust, this dryness, was general for
them, but did not know. He had not asked. Now he came to think of
it, he had not ever offered more than words of command to girl or to
prisoner, had never questioned them, only punished or used.

Ben Ata did not go as far as the actual frontier, but only where he
could see slopes of rippling sand, ridges of stone and low bitter
brush. He sat on his horse, caressing its neck without knowing that
he did, and thinking of the poor creature's torn mouth, and remembered the feel of the captured girls, the gritty acridness of their bodies as he held them, their tears and their anger.

Ben Ata wept. He knew perfectly well that he was not going to
order any war on this luckless place: he would countermand his
instructions as soon as he got back to camp. He knew that his soldiers would say that he was a woman's victim and was not fit to be a
soldier. He thought they were right. He did not want to go back into
his own land, where it seemed any thought he was likely to have was
bound to be discordant or seditious.

He decided to stay where he was. He dismounted, relieved his
horse of saddle and bridle, and with his face turned inwards to his
own land, and his back to Zone Five, he sat in his cape, in a vigil.
And so it was that Ben Ata, king of the terrible Zone Four, was
sitting far from his armies and his camps, all by himself, when the
drum began beating again. He did not hear it.

After a night of solitude, and sleeplessness, he rode back in again.
He heard the drum from the camp, as he arrived, and was going to
ride straight on to meet Al·Ith when it occurred to him that it might

be too late. He strode up the hill to the pavilions just as she rode up from the other side.

The two entered their room from opposite arches, and stood examining each other. As usual it was their difference that had to strike them first: both, matching the long days of questioning and wanting and longing, with the reality of this stubbornly self-contained individual, felt only a sort of exhaustion.

Both were manifestly and at first glance, worn out. Both were burned dry and brown and lean. Both raged inwardly with need and restlessness. The eyes of both burned in new hollows. They were consumed as they stood there by hungers neither in the least understood.

And, together at last, they sank down, side by side on the couch, and looked close into the other's eyes, face, and ran their hands up and down each other's arms, and limbs. And, being assured that he, she, was there, truly and absolutely there, the long tension snapped. They sighed, yawned, and fell back and slept in each other's arms. They slept for a day and a night and hardly moved.

How long were the days that followed, every thought and movement slowed and heavied with self-awareness, and questioning. For this place, this phase, was being experienced for the first time by both, so that everything said and done had to surprise them.

For one thing, they were alone together and suspected that this would be so for a long time, because for both of them their ordinary —their former and now lost?—lives seemed forbidden to them. They had become exiled, and the realms that were excluding them were created and sustained by the companionship, the bonds and needs, of others. Neither had ever been alone with one other person for days . . . and days . . . and days. And nights.

They were making love as neither had before: serious and prolonged, as if coming to an end must mean the end of a possibility in understanding, as if this were a task they had been set in self-exploration, as if their being joined in this way made a strength, an unassailable place that was withholding doubt and worse—hostility of some kind and from some source—calamities, even chaos. And as they wrestled, or clung, or sheltered, each cast upon this scene, much more often than either would have wanted the other to know, a cool dispassionate eye which concurred completely in any judgments that anyone—who? that hostile unknown?—might be pronouncing on them. Yet against these judgments they rebelled, and protected the other, in thought and in action, too, for what did it mean, this need —and an increasingly frequent one—to hold Al·Ith, to hold Ben Ata, inside strong arms felt as, perhaps, the barricades built up outside a cave where some small and infinitely vulnerable and brave thing had taken cover.

But from outside there came not one word, and no sign. The drum beat steadily, on and on. And they knew it must continue to beat. For a time at least.

Al·Ith would lie on the couch, on piled cushions, quite naked, her hand lightly held over the place where this hybrid of a child of theirs was hatching its way out of the realm of possibilities, and she felt that the infant was pulsing there in response to the drum. And Ben Ata, quite naked, would come over to her, having seen from the frowning concentration of that face that was now close and beloved to him, so that he would not have been surprised to see it when he looked in a mirror, that she was in communication with the future lord of this Zone, and gently pushing aside her hand, substitute his, listening through his palm and fingers. Or he would press his ear there, shutting out all the other sounds from this dear and familiar house of flesh, so that he could hear only the drum, the drum, beating into his ears and setting the tides of his own blood.

Now they were naked most of the time, for their being bare there together was like being clothed, so various and speaking had these two bodies become. He would look at the damp light from the fountained garden moulding her shoulders and think how well it suited her to stand just there, this slight Al·Ith of his, as slender and taut as the springing arch of a pillar she leaned against; and she would watch the fine moulding of his back and loins and believe she could watch the play and the tension of those muscles without tiring for all the rest of her life. And he put his hands into the black fall of her hair and marvelled at his past and dead life, when he had not even noticed—or so it seemed to him now—the infinite complexities of one small woman's head, with its world of differences his fingers explored, tress by tress; and she let her arm lie across his strong brown shoulders and knew that the languages and messages of two skin surfaces, lightly touching or sliding on the other, would suffice her for ever.

If she put on a dress from some whim or need for coquetry then soon the dress was off again, for coquetry seemed quite insulting to this serious state they were both exploring for the first time; and if he pulled his dark soldier's cape around him, when the wind blew in cold from the hillside that sloped to the camp, then he felt uncomfortable in it, almost as if he had no right to it. And instead they sprang back together again under the covers of their great couch, back into their world, their time . . . which did not change, could not change . . . but did change, nevertheless, and soon, for one day sitting at their little table under the arch from which they could look down the hill into the bustle of the camps, they summoned food with their thoughts and nothing at all happened. But even as they sat there, wondering, they saw Dabeeb come climbing the hillside, bent forward because of a cold wind that tugged at the old cape she had wrapped around her, and she was carrying covered dishes and jugs. Which she laid down quickly and carefully on the edge of the portico under the outermost arches, and ran off again quickly, without even glancing in towards them.

They wrapped up their nakedness, and went out into the portico to retrieve this food, which was from the officers' mess, as Ben Ata was able at once to see, and which consisted of stewed beans and bread.

He noted, as he himself began to eat, and with relish, that Al·Ith was eating it hungrily, as if she did not miss her rose-scented confections, and her fruit and her syrups.

This pavilion of theirs, this magical building, had become quite prosaic to both. Once it had seemed to Al·Ith like a rather inadequate representation and reminder of the elegances and subtleties of her own land. Not long ago, to Ben Ata, it had been a charming—certainly—but irritating place, effeminate, which he had no alternative but to put up with. But now there was nothing in it that he even thought about much. The airy room with its springing fountain of a central pillar, its shadows, its high spaces and shapes under the moulded ceilings—the rooms he used for bathing, or changing, and through which she wandered as freely as he did, the rooms that were her quarters, and where he went in and out just as she did—all this was, simply, his home now: his and Al·Ith's home. He had once lived in tents and not wanted anything finer. He supposed he would again . . . reminded of these distant obligations, he retired to his room and, seated stark naked at the simple table he had ordered to be brought up for this kind of use, he wrote an order that the armies must engage themselves in manoeuvres and some mock war or other, because he had remembered that he had promised them a war, and had failed them. This would "take up the slack" a little, he muttered, and was wondering as he sat there, head in his hand, which part of this country of his would be best, at this time of the year, for a mock war, and whether . . . but his staff could deal with all that perfectly well, he decided at last, with the oddest mixture of regret at this relinquishing of his own participation in this war, and relief that he would not have to go through weeks and weeks of tediousness, pretending that inventions and masquerades were real, with a real purpose . . . and, thinking thus, he remembered that Al·Ith did not believe that any of this occupation of his had any purpose at all . . . yet when he thought of this son of his, being incubated at this moment in Al·Ith's delicious body, it was always as on a horse, with him, at the head of the armies.

It was a son of course. Al·Ith knew it, and so did he. Because it was necessary and consistent that this union should bring forth a son. The marriage of Zone Three and Four needed to bring forth a son: that was evident.

He returned to find Al·Ith dressed, and for the first time in many days.

The cupboards in her apartments were filled again with dresses that were the product of this country and not hers. She did not disdain them now. This was partly because the women were producing more apt and simpler clothes, as a result of pulling to pieces and studying every stitch and fold of the dresses she had given Dabeeb. And partly because Al·Ith had changed, and no longer considered the products of this land as impossible to her. She was wearing now a rose-coloured robe that fitted her well, and outlined the soft slope of her pregnancy.

She was sitting at the table, head in hand, in thought.

"Ben Ata," said she, as he had known she was going to say, "there are surely things that we ought to be attending to!"

Before answering, he sat down opposite her. He did not intend to agree too quickly. Looking back at that time—and it seemed long ago—when her visits to this country had been so short and irregular, he remembered most that they had quarrelled. It had been his fault for not standing up to her. She was bossy. He liked the state they were in now. Married. That was how he put it to himself. We're married now, and she can't have her way as she did.

As for her, she remained silent, because she, too, was remembering how things had been. Oh, not as they were now . . . not as *she* was now . . . Between Al·Ith now and her own high realm, there seemed a curtain or cloud. She could remember that things had been very different. This difference was *felt* by her, as an ease, a lightness, a sweetness, above all a marvellous friendliness in everything. She remembered all her children, and the sense and competence of their being together. She remembered she had a sister, the beautiful one, and they had been used to sit together in the evenings watching the evening sky as the light faded, or to walk on the roofs . . . recalling delightful wanderings on those roofs was painful to Al·Ith. She could not do that now—it seemed to her that she was afraid of high places and of being on the level of birds and mountains . . . and there had been something else, a tower, and from there—but at the memory a pain of longing attacked her and with it, a feeling of such urgency that she sprang up, wringing her hands. She sat here, she was loitering here, but meanwhile, this was not at all what she should be doing. . . .

"What is it?" enquired Ben Ata, calm and magisterial. "You shouldn't jump about like that, should you? It's bad for the child."

Considering the strenuosities both committed daily and nightly she decided to ignore this altogether. But she did sit down, slowly, and did calm herself. For what she felt was that if she could not communicate to Ben Ata the nature of the superiority that subsisted in her memories and her past substance—even if that was not what she was now—then there was no use in insisting on anything.

"That's right," he said, in a kindly, but perhaps absentminded way.

He was thinking that when this child of theirs was born, he would order celebrations and festivities of all kinds. So it was essential to make sure the mock war was well over by that time. He took out the paper he had written his order on, and made an alteration in a date.

"And I think, when we have the celebrations," he remarked, as if she had been kept informed of all his plans, "that the other children should act as attendants. Or in some such capacity."

Al·Ith already knew that Ben Ata had fathered innumerable children, in the course of his soldiering, and that these were put into children's regiments as soon almost as they could walk. The Children's Army was quite a feature of life here. She had been indignant when she had first heard this—but her indignation had been absorbed into the need to understand.

She had not replied. Ben Ata now realised she had been silent a very long time and, having amended his order and pushed it into his belt, looked up and smiled.

"Are you all right, my dear?"

"I would like to see something of the country, Ben Ata. No, it would be all right now, I am sure. I have become acclimatised."

He was instantly enlivened. "Oh, good. You could travel with me on manoeuvres. Would you like that?"

Al·Ith was thoughtful. She had the look of one tasting a new food, or experience. "I don't see why not . . . but what I was thinking was this—I'd like to ask the women to make a festival of their songs. We used to do that, I seem to remember. At home. Something like that."

"Oh, they wouldn't like that, my dear! They have their own ideas, you know. No man can go near one of their ceremonies—not if he values his manhood." And he sat back on his ridiculous little chair and roared with laughter, enormously amused.

"I wasn't thinking of you, actually. I could go. As a woman."

"So you are fed up with me already!"

"We might perhaps bear to be separated for an evening?"

Here they reassured each other with some small nibbling kisses, but there was a tinge of the perfunctory in them, there was no doubt of that.

"I'll write a note for Dabeeb, when she comes to bring our next meal."

"I'll speak to her myself."

"Oh, no, it is always much better to put things into writing, there's no possibility of misunderstandings then."

Al·Ith did not contradict, but merely determined, privately, to attract Dabeeb's attention, and have her say. She smiled gently at Ben Ata, as if in total agreement.

Shortly, they did in fact see Dabeeb come up the hill.

Ben Ata strode to the arch and on to the verandah and prevented her from simply setting down her dishes and running away again.

Al·Ith heard him giving her the piece of paper with the orders for the mock war, and instructing her that next time there would be an order regarding Al·Ith's wishes, but he had not yet written it.

"Oh, what a nice thing," Dabeeb was cooing, "it would be so nice to do something to please the lady. But meanwhile, could I have a word with her myself?"

"Come in," said he, stepping aside, and off he went to his quarters to write out Al·Ith's wishes for her.

The two women were alone. Al·Ith got to her feet, and they went rapidly to the farthest point away from Ben Ata's apartments.

Al·Ith whispered to her what she wanted, and Dabeeb understood at once and said, "The women will be pleased. In fact they were talking about asking you. They asked me to mention something of the kind—and now there's no need."

At this point in strode Ben Ata, the picture of uxorious benevolence. But as he came towards them, he had time to think that one of these days it might be pleasant to have Dabeeb to himself for an evening or two: he visualised himself astonishing her by all that he had learned in this long period of—but he hastily censored the word *imprisonment*, and substituted *pleasure-making*—with Al·Ith. This thought appeared on his face as a self-congratulatory smile, and both instantly understood it.

He handed a written chit to Dabeeb, who opened it, read it, and remarked soothingly, "It is always so much better to have a thing written down. But there is one thing, Ben Ata, sir, it isn't a question of having a singsong any time we have a mind to it, it's just our foolishness, don't think anything else, but we have them at times and seasons."

"Very well then, next time it is a time or a season, just invite Al·Ith, and I'll see that she runs along in good order."

"Thank you. We will all be very honoured." To Al·Ith, as she turned to go, she gave the fleetest of winks, and wishing them a good appetite, she ran off down the hill.

They spent a fond night, and then, in the morning, Ben Ata confessed that he did not believe that these new war games could possibly get under way without his supervision and begged leave to go off on his kingly affairs for a few days.

Al·Ith found herself first in a state of tender desolation at the thought of spending even an hour without him, then a flash of panic, which alerted her to consider her state pathological, then indignation that he should want to leave her, and then, unmistakably, relief. Oh, what a wonderful thing, to be given an opportunity to locate her own self again—which seemed so far from her she doubted whether she could recognise it—and then to dwell for some time at least inside it, with her own, her real, purposes . . . whatever they might be. For she could not remember.

Meanwhile, Ben Ata, believing her silence to be sadness, and dreading that she might weep or plead with him, announced that he would make arrangements for her to accompany him on at least some part of the way towards the war but, of course, she must return home before the games actually started, because it would never do for her to get overexcited.

Al·Ith agreed to everything, sending him off down the hill with a warm and lingering kiss that she could not remember ever having given anyone before, for it seemed to have in it far too much of the suppliant.

And, having waved to him for as long as she could see his broad figure marching energetically off towards the camps, she returned to her apartments, bathed and perfumed herself, and dressed in a white woollen dress embroidered all over in colourful flowery patterns, and was just about to take herself out of the other door into the gardens that were full of the fountains, and where the drum kept up its beat—but from where? everywhere, now this place, and now that—when Dabeeb suddenly appeared again, whispering that Al·Ith should go with her now, for it was the exact night when the women held their ceremonies, but of course she could not have told Ben Ata, since no man ever knew when the women congregated. They were not told, and the one man who had infiltrated their secret meeting place wished very much that he had not.

Al·Ith flung Ben Ata's cloak around her, quite in the style of Zone Four and, hand in hand with Dabeeb, ran down the damp hillside through the lines of the tents, no one seeing them, since all the soldiers were too busy with the war that was to begin in precisely four days' time, and out into the fields beyond.

There they ran without stopping through the short damp grass, disturbing herd after herd of melancholy cows, and crossing innumerable small bridges, and jumping over ditches and canals until, quite drunk and elated with all this fast movement even though it was through the enervating and unresisting air, came to a great stone building that looked deserted. It was an old fort, the relic of some past and gone war, for it was partly in ruins.

But when they had dodged past some thickets, through some bushes, and beneath a great arch, they were in a large stone hall, and this was quite filled with women of all ages, who were sitting on benches around long wooden tables, with food and vessels of wine in front of them. There was a cleared place in the centre of all this, and there a group of young girls was singing as they made all kinds of movements with their arms and bodies. Everyone was laughing, and enjoying themselves. Seeing Al·Ith, they rose to their feet, held up their hands above their heads and clapped vigorously to indicate she was welcome, and then sat down again to continue watching the girls. Al·Ith was shown a place at the head of a long table, and without further ceremony she seated herself, with Dabeeb beside her. She did not at once take in her surroundings, because she was too interested in the girls, five of them, vigorously acting out these words, which they were singing solemnly, and with concentration, to get them exactly right, so that there was the oddest contrast between their demeanour and what surely had been, at least to start with, some playground counting game?

All together they sang:

"*I found a string of beads,*
I hung it on a tree,
A prettier string of beads,
You did never see."

And then, each taking a line:

"*They didn't come from you,*

> *They didn't come from you,*
> *They didn't come from you,*
> *Beads as nice as these,*
> *Are very far and few."*

Together again:

> *"I found a string of beads,*
> *I hung it on a chair,*
> *Beads as nice as these*
> *Can only come from there."*

And separately:

> *"There is where they grow*
> *Where we have to go,*
> *Though the King says No.*
> *Where the clouds are snow,*
> *We have no beads like these,*
> *Made of clouds and snow."*

And the five girls, in the full coloured skirts and low-necked bodices that were the usual dress of the women, whirled around in a quick dance, whose steps were, Al·Ith could see, most precisely and minutely prescribed. And then, they stopped, all at once, so that the skirts swirled about their legs. And, as they did so, every woman and girl and girl child in the place stood up and ran from their benches out into the space with the dancers. And now Al·Ith saw that the western side of the great hall had been carefully removed at about two-thirds of the way up, to give a view of the mountains of Zone Three from one end to the other. Here the tops were not visible, but even so, this crowd of women, lifting up their arms and performing some act of worship or of remembrance, had to bend back their heads to see the mountains. It was early evening, the light hung there with a sad and meaningful density and Al·Ith, amazed, realised that for all the time she had been shut up—as she now felt it—with the king, she had not once gone out to gaze up at her own realm, at her own mountain heights. She simply had not thought to do it. And, standing there, letting her head fall back and back on the tension of her neck, she found it difficult, and the muscles complaining. It was clear, too, that many of the women could not sustain this pose for longer than a few moments and were glad to let their heads fall level again. But others were not only maintaining their own difficult posture, but had their hands out and supporting the heads of others, mostly younger ones, by tilting them back by their chins. Some of these protested a little, and stood firm, then were pleased when released, and sat down at their places, massaging their necks. All at once, the whole company returned to their seats.

Into the empty space now came a dozen mature women, in the same colourful skirts and blouses that the girls had worn, but they were large and one or two even gross, but all good-humoured and smiling, with the kind of shrewd knowingness that they seemed to feel was due from them, for it was this expression they adjusted on their faces as they energetically belted out this bit of doggerel, swinging their hips and making all kinds of suggestive gestures, so that in no time the whole company was howling with laughter.

> "Who fell in the canal last night
> Giving you such a nasty fright?
> Pick up your skirts and pick up your cape
> Pick up your skirts and run.
>
> Who got under your skirts last night,
> Giving you such a nasty fright,
> Up in the snows we'll climb and go,
> Up to the snows we'll go.
>
> Who woke you up from that dream last night,
> A dream of clouds and snow and light,
> Coming from far away,
> Coming from far away.
>
> Who told us that the road was there,
> Plain as your arm and always there,
> Going to far away,
> Going to far away . . ."

And again, as the end was reached, every female clattered out from her place and into the dancing place, and stood with her head back, gazing at the mountains which were now dark, their shapes

and heaps outlined by a bluish luminousness that must be starlight—
but no stars were visible, for the whole vast window was filled with
the mountain slopes. Al·Ith went with the women, and stood there
in the crowd. Her neck muscles ached and resisted, and she could see
that again some of these who were having their heads supported back
by others had tears in their eyes and bit their lips with the effort of
it.

And then, after only a short time, for it was clear that this exercise
could not be sustained for longer, all of them crowded back to their
seats. Platters of food were being brought out from some kitchen at
the end of the hall, and girls went around replenishing the jugs of
wine.

The festivity, or ceremony—for it was that—went on, through the
night. As soon as one game, or song, or counting rhyme was finished,
everyone rushed to join in the act of stretching their muscles, and
keeping them stretched—for by now it was clear that this in fact was
the intention behind these rituals. And all the time new groups of
girls and women went out to contribute their song, and each one
was, obviously, a repetition of something done many times before.
For often the words and their sense had nothing to do with the
gestures that accompanied them. Lewd gestures and nods and winks
could illustrate verses whose words were innocent, and the other way
about, too. Yet every woman there knew exactly what words or
gestures to expect at every moment, for more than once the singers
and actors were corrected, by someone calling out: "No, you put
your arm out there," or "You don't smile there, it's in the next
line."

A ritual. A rite. And that there was an especial vigour and energy
in it tonight because she was there, Al·Ith knew, for she was aware
that all watched her, openly or covertly, according to their natures,
to see how she was taking it all—and with such hope!

Long after midnight, when the mountains were already beginning
to pale, Dabeeb, on a signal from someone who had been acting as
mistress of co-ordination, walked out by herself into the centre of the
empty space, and stood waiting for silence. No one else had sung, or
danced, alone.

There was a close, attentive silence.

She sang:

"If I said to you, you are a man,
　You'd pick up a stick,
　Throw it for a dog to fetch:
　And so you went to school!
　Very well, let's play the fool!

And everyone echoed: "Let's play the fool."

"I say to you, you are a man!
　Is there no work for you?
　Were you not set a task to do?
　That's not your rule?

And everyone came in with: "Then—play the fool!"

"I watch you, man and man and man,
　Throw stones from off a shore,
　To see who throws them short, or far:
　And so you go to school:
　To play the fool."

This next verse was anticipated, for everywhere Al·Ith could see angry, bitter, reddened faces, leaning forward, and now the company took up the words and sang them with Dabeeb:

"Oh, little boy, dear baby,
　Why are you slow and silly?
　Swaggering and silly . . .

[This was hissed out, with bitter intensity.]

　Was that your school?
　To play the fool?

And now Dabeeb again, alone:

"The mountains mass and fill the sky,
　Yours to hold and know,
　You loiter here below,
　This is your rule,
　To play the fool.

　Match your women, men and man,
　Without you they can't,

Without you they won't,
Bend the rule
That plays the fool.

Man, are you man enough to man
And make the road, the rod, the tool?
No?—"

[And now every female there hissed out, in a frenzy of anger and bitterness]

"—Then play the fool!
Very well, let's play the fool!
We'll play the fool!"

And as Dabeeb's deep soft voice fell silent, everyone got to her feet and rushed, not to the centre place, as before, but clean out of the hall. And Al·Ith and Dabeeb came after them. Outside the hall was a court, surrounded by low buildings. The mountains were now visible from their foothills to their topmost peaks. The brilliant stars shed their blue gleam, but the sky was softening and becoming gold in the east. So the mountains were looming there illuminated as if from within, and their peaks seemed not much lower than the zenith. Everywhere the women stood, their necks stretched back, some shaking and staggering with the effort, some cursing their inability, and some, as always, being assisted by others. And now they stayed a long time, compared with the brief efforts within the hall, fighting and struggling with themselves to get their heads back so that they could see everything in those wonderful mountains that seemed to float on a bluish mist, their peaks wreathed with cloud that was snow.

Al·Ith was weeping, like them, but it was for her faithlessness to them, and she was supporting her neck on her two clasped hands. And then, again, and all at once, the women let their heads fall forward. She saw an astonishing thing: a number of them, mostly the younger ones, picked up heavy metal helmets from a pile against a wall, and fitted these down on their heads. The weight and clumsiness of these helmets could be seen by the effort the poor creatures had to make to keep their heads up at all. And they peered from strained eyes, filled with tears, trying to keep their gaze level. They looked at Al·Ith, and with such longing. All came quickly up to her whispering, "Al·Ith, help us, help us, Al·Ith," and then, with the suddenness she now knew was their way of doing things, they began running out of the court, but in twos and threes, while a woman who had climbed up on to a low roof acted as sentinel and called out as she thought it safe for them to leave. Al·Ith and Dabeeb went out last, and already it seemed that they were looking out into a deserted dawn landscape, so completely had the women been absorbed by the misty half-light. But Al·Ith saw one girl, holding her head up with both hands in its heavy metal case, weeping and swearing as she staggered forward. And she heard the words float back: "Help us, help us, Al·Ith . . ."

"And now we must run for it," said Dabeeb, in the cool capable way she had, and the two went back as they had come, taking advantage of every bit of cover and running through the herds of animals wherever animals were to be seen. Dabeeb gasped out bits of information, such as that this ceremony was held four times in the year. That it was held not always in one place "for we are not short of fortresses and forts, whatever else!"—and that the men of course knew that these ceremonies took place, and tolerated them. They saw them as a safety valve. "For if one of us did break her promise and tell her man what we do, then what can they object to? Not one of us would tell about taking off the punishment helmets, and looking up at the mountains in secret. Not one! For she would know we would kill her . . . it's in all our interests, you see, for it is a long time since the men reminded themselves of what it is they should be doing . . ." and now they had reached the foot of the hill on the top of which the pavilions stood, graceful and white in the early sun. "I'll leave you here, or my husband'll give me a hiding if I'm any later . . ." and she swerved and ran off home.

Al·Ith climbed the hill slowly, listening for the moment when she would hear the drum, and feeling that the child was wakening with the day: she fancied him yawning and stretching in there, as she held her hand close over him.

What was it Dabeeb had said: *what it was the men should be doing.* . . . Of course! It was all perfectly simple! And she could have seen it all long ago, for there was nothing very difficult to see.

What the men should be doing was not making war, in reality or in pretence. That was a displacement of something else, some other aim, or function, something enjoined that they had forgotten . . . and had not only forgotten but now forbade. But why? What had happened? And above all, *how*. That was the word. The men were supposed to . . . supposed to . . . but *how*.

In all the singing and the dancing and the games of the night, not one girl or woman had even hinted at that. If "to climb the mountains" was the proper activity of men, then what did that mean? She knew that if she said to Dabeeb, "Very well then, what is the proper activity of men?" Dabeeb would point to the mountains. Yes, but what did that mean?

And now I propose to interrupt this narrative to return briefly to Zone Three.

This business of the song and story festival Al·Ith had asked for, believing that she would find there information, or at least hints and suggestions of half-forgotten sagacities . . . she had been right. But wrong about *where*. Which was, in fact, the ceremony, or commemoration, of the Zone Four women: in their rituals, their acts of deliberate preservation. While she had so energetically been participating that night she had been thinking, too, of how one may be so right about a thing, but only half right . . . for now she knew—but did not know why she did—that the Zone Three festival would not be likely to yield up anything useful. And so it was.

Murti· did not neglect her sister's request.

But she did have difficulty with it.

For one thing, as I've said, we had festivals of this kind at least once a year, and there were the regional festivals, too. So how was Al·Ith's need actually to be made effective? Were we to allow it to be understood everywhere that in our old songs and verses, and even the most silly and worn out of them, there might be use, and that they were to be presented with this idea in mind? My experience has always been that an overdirect approach to such matters usually defeats itself. No, it is through the unexpected, or the sidelong, or the indirect that truths come our way . . . so I brooded, *had* to brood, since I was much concerned in preparations: Murti· left it to me in the end. Was it perhaps a question of us listening in a different way? That seemed to me to be getting near to it. It was certainly true that our songs, our stories, had not changed very much for a long time: perhaps truer or more to the point that we all took this for granted, and did not look very far. . . . I am stating here baldly what has already been hinted at—that the general malaise, or stagnation (but such a word was hard to use of our beautiful land) was well established among us, the Chroniclers, the makers of pictures, the songsters . . . though as is usually the way it was not until later we were able to use words like stagnation.

Our festivals were very beautiful. I use this word after thought. That is exactly what they were. They had a rich, rolling, *plumpness* about them. They were reassuring. Attending one was like eating one's way through a long and abundant feast. But there was no sting or surprise there. No moments of shock. They did not stimulate.

This is certainly not the place for a discourse about what festivals are for. Discussions on this theme were plentiful during that phase of preparation and on the whole were fruitless. My experience is that discussion is fruitless. What sets forth and demonstrates is the sight of events in action, is living through these events, and understanding them. . . .

The preparations for this special festival went awkwardly. No one knew what was demanded of them. Al·Ith wanted it: and so of course it should be . . . but she wasn't here, was she? Did she intend to return for this occasion? If not, what was the point of it? Had it been commanded by the Providers? But we believed not.

When the festival took place, it went on for a week, and it was the largest and best attended for years. All our regions sent their singers and tellers. As usual everything was most lovely and—luscious. I use the word wryly. . . .

I, and others of us—professionals, the organisers—had to be wry. Dry. And disappointed. Nothing happened that had not happened a thousand times before. Each song, each set of verses, each tale, came out so pat and smooth and smiling, and no matter how we listened, trying to borrow Al·Ith's ears, we heard nothing that suggested more than we already knew.

Murti· was there throughout, of course, and she was in a sense

Al·Ith . . . but there was no conviction in it. She was lackadaisical, even perfunctory, as one is when performing a duty that has no heart in it.

And when the festival was over, that was the end of it all.

And I do not think I am being fanciful when I say that this was at least partly because it had already taken place—but elsewhere. After all, this story of Al·Ith has taught us all that what goes on in one Zone affects the others, even when we believe we are hostile, or forget everything that goes on outside our own borders. We share and exchange even our times of sluggishness, insularity, self-applause. When those women strove and struggled to lift their poor heads up so they could see our mountains towering over them it was as if they were secretly pouring energy and effort into springs that fed us all. When Al·Ith made her forced descent to that dreary land it was for us all . . . paradoxically one reason for our festival not being much of a success was that things were improving in our Zone. This was being felt, though it had not been acknowledged openly. For instance, the animals that came in from all the regions and were pastured together outside Andaroun—they were far from melancholy, but all gave evidence in their own way of the highest of spirits. Gambolling and playfulness, all kinds of games, went on, and watching them we joked that the occasion would result in a fine crop of youngsters. And of course we watched among ourselves for signs of a new spirit—and believed we were finding them. Though not much was said . . . the tide had turned . . . we already dared to look back at a *past* bad time. And Al·Ith was being connected in the general mind with that time, and as we already found ourselves reluctant to think of it, so Al·Ith was being talked of less. Her visits to us of course had been discussed: different accounts of them were circulating. All made her sound bizarre. As it were tainted and contaminated. In my experience it is a rule that people anywhere will refuse to open their minds to the damaged, the hurt, unless they are forced to. Fear is the root of it: that they might be brought low themselves. I have to record that as the atmosphere of Zone Three lightened, and the confidence and morale of ourselves and our animals returned, so Al·Ith was less remembered, was thought of, even, with distaste. I am afraid that is the exact, the proper word.

One of the motives for this chronicle is an attempt to revive in the hearts and memories of our people another idea of Al·Ith, to re-state her in her proper place in our history. It is not enough that a minority of us seek her out, identify with her, try to live near her, when such a large majority think of her only as we do of those who represent places in ourselves we find it dangerous to approach. . . .

Al·Ith entered the pavilion slowly, feeling that she was tired and would shortly need to rest—and there sat Ben-Ata, on the bottom of the couch, his sandalled hero's legs sprawled, gazing at her with a white, set, wounded face. He rose to his feet and came tragically towards her, and she could see that in a moment he would strike her.

"And where have you been, Al·Ith?"

"At a festival. With the women," she said, in the coollest, most amazed voice in the world, throwing water on his flames, and she saw his fist, which had been raised, lower again.

"And why should I believe you?"

"But why should you *not* believe me?" she enquired, in the reasonable voice of her real self, which only a few hours ago she had believed she had lost for ever.

Suddenly he caught her to him and buried his face in her neck, her hair—he, she realized, was smelling her to see if she reeked of some man or other, Jarnti perhaps? But presumably Jarnti had been with him all that time making war plans? And Al·Ith could not help feeling pleased, as if with a promising pupil. For Ben Ata would no more have been capable of the simple physical common sense of sniffing at her to see what she smelled of, when they first knew each other, than he would have been capable of doing what he did now, which was to take her hand, sit her beside him on the bottom of the couch, and, looking—still white-faced and burning-eyed, it is true, but sane enough—into her face, say, "Al·Ith, you must not do that again! I've been tormented out of my wits with worry for you."

Al·Ith, returning forbearance for his, refrained from reminding him that in her own land it could not occur to anyone to be worried about her, and indeed it was getting harder for her to remember that this had been the case—but harder, above all, to revive in herself the reasons for it. For she had been surrounded for so long by the signs of rank, or hierarchy, that she was beginning to rely on them herself, thus allowing real faculties of discrimination to become dulled.

She now assured Ben Ata that to alarm him in any way was the last thing she wanted to do, that his peace of mind was her first concern—and said all these things with the more ease because they were true, but not perhaps as he believed them. Besides, inside this shadowy and delightful place, alone with him, the Al·Ith who was Ben Ata's other self, had returned. She could see as she examined a face she had learned to study as if her mirror had suddenly taken to supplying her with his image, insisting it was her own, that he had truly suffered that night. His temples seemed marked with thought, and the way he held his mouth spoke of a real suffering. She saw him leaning forward to search her face, to look into her eyes as if there was a mystery in them he had been sentenced by a most inexorable judge to study. With a sigh that she refused to deepen into a groan, she again saw him as her fellow prisoner, and marvelling that this taut, grief-marked man could be the gross and fleshy Ben Ata of their first days, she enclosed him, as he did her, and their lovemaking was all a consoling and a reassurance. When his hand felt for their child, now responding quite vigorously to their lovemaking, as if wishing to share in it—as if it were the promise of a festival—it was with a respect and a promise not to an extension of himself, or of her, but a salute to the possibilities of them both: a considered and informed salute, at that, for Al·Ith, feeling the delicately contained strength of those enquiring fingers, knew that the potentialities he acknowledged were for the unknown and the unexpected, as well as for familiar delight. For this union of incompatibles could not be anything less than a challenge.

Al·Ith felt that she loved this man utterly, and it was this that united her finally with the women she had been with during their ceremonies of remembrance.

But with what a sinking of the heart did she acknowledge this commitment to him—she could not now remember what she had felt for the men she had been *with* in her own realm, but she knew it had been nothing like this. It was as if she were relinquishing light and air for bonds that tightened as she breathed, growing into her flesh.

When they rose from their submersion in each other, there was a new task for her.

She was to parade, with him, in front of his armies.

First, Ben Ata came with her into her apartments, and with a frowning care and concentration, looked at her dresses, one after another, bringing out from the cupboards at last a gown of gold tissue that was ornate and magnificent. There was a skill in this choosing that was even dispassionate, for it did not relate to her, or to him, but only to her role as the queen of this place.

And, of course, as mother of the heir.

She fitted the gown on, while he watched, leaning against the wall with arms folded, considering possibilities. He then turned her about, frowning. She allowed herself to be passive, and his subject. At last he nodded, but indicated with his eyes that her flowing hair would not do. She braided it, and massed it around her head. Since he still seemed unsatisfied, she pinned on a little square of gold tissue, which had the effect of seeming to confine even more those subdued masses where, during their lovemaking, he had been plunging his hands, his face, and wrapping him and her together as if these tents of glossy hair could hold off the world from them both for ever.

Outside the pavilion, among the fountains, her Yori stood waiting, and he had a bridle in his mouth, which he champed and tried to ease, and layers of gold stuffs underneath a heavy leather saddle that was tooled in gold. Ben Ata was waiting for her to challenge him on this, and she did, but only insofar as her eyes told him that the imprisoning of poor Yori was for this occasion only. Yet Ben Ata, standing there, arms folded, feet apart, was not expecting her to rebel against necessity, for he did not show the uneasiness of a false position; and she was not petulant, nor aggressive.

He lifted her on to the horse, and arranged her dress, smoothing it down so that the curve of her pregnancy was well shown. And she assisted him.

He led the horse through the fountains, by the bridle, while she pressed her hand on Yori's neck, telling him that this indignity and discomfort would soon be over.

At the foot of the hill, near the corrals, he shouted for his horse, which leapt the stone walls and came running to him, already saddled and bridled. Up leapt Ben Ata, and the two, king and queen, cantered off down to the meadows where the armies were marching and deploying, making patterns of scarlet, of blue, of gold, over leagues of misty green, among the steaming canals.

As Ben Ata and Al·Ith rode up all movement stopped, the shining trumpets sounded, as they flew up to the lips of a hundred or so trumpeters, the drums beat, it seemed hundreds of them, a great massy earth-shaking drumming quite defeating the soft signal drum of Ben Ata's and Al·Ith's solitude, and to all this commotion and clamour was added the sound of cheering that began as the two sovereigns reached the edge of the parade ground and did not cease till they left it, which was a long time later. The soldiers could not get enough of the sight of Al·Ith, the queen of the legendary Zone, high on her black horse which long ago had become part of their songs and tales. There she was at last for all of them to see, so beautiful in her gold dress, and there was the evidence of this marriage, the strong triumphant curve of her stomach.

The cheering was like a storm that comes racing across fields and woods, it was like rain pouring down, it was like a steady wind blowing from all quarters of the sky at once.

And the drums went on beating, and the trumpets raised fanfare after fanfare.

There is of course always—there has to be!—a difference between the way their artists and ours portray the various incidents in the tale of our queen and their king.

There have never been lacking scholars only too willing to devote their lives to the analysis of this or that picture or ballad, and while this exercise does not seem to me useful, I must confess I have always been a student of the different emphasis given by the two realms. Scenes popular with us are indifferently received by them, for instance: and of course, the other way around as well.

This scene of Al·Ith parading herself before the armies has always been the favourite one in Zone Four. In fact it would be easy to believe this was the only event of importance in the marriage, judging from the number and size of the pictures: the ballads, the songs, the tales. It is not too much to say that if there is any picture at all in a home or a public building then it is this one.

Usually it is not far off the truth—for why should there be any need for Zone Four to distort or embellish what could be seen that day?

Ben Ata rode first. As was always his custom he was dressed no more elaborately than the humblest of his foot soldiers. He wore a leather tunic, which came to mid-thigh, and sandals on his bare feet. Over it was a lighter tunic of glistening silver material: the "invulnerable" vest. He carried his famous sword which no one but he could lift—so went the story, though of course plenty of the strongest soldiers knew they could use it as efficiently as Ben Ata did. In an army where the slightest grade of difference was marked by braid and trappings and ornaments of all kinds, an army hierarchical in every detail, Ben Ata's simplicity was shrewd. For one thing, it protected the lowest ranks. In this mass of men, never at war as much as they liked, where campaigns were rationed like extra food, where sometimes mock wars and exercises were the most they could hope for in a year, of course there was always fighting among themselves. And no soldier coming on another in the dark, or impelled to start a fight in a bar, could do so without wondering if this unknown might not be Ben Ata himself. That was one thing. Another was that in so firmly identifying himself with the humblest, his proudly competing officers knew that he was for ever above and apart from them, and they in his eyes not worth more than the least of the new recruits. Ben Ata was always under pressure to design for himself a magnificence of a uniform, but he would not.

When he rode out in front of his armies the sight of him was never anything but provocative of emotion. All focussed on him, the king, sitting so straight and firm, his great brown legs like tree trunks, his grey eyes all benevolence.

Behind him, and half his size, on her black horse, is Al·Ith. Her horse's neck is arched under a tight rein. She is sitting sideways and is very pregnant. Sometimes the child is born and is held in front of her: a large child, dwarfing her. Her face is conventionalised, has the blunt solid look of their people. She is smiling, and holds out one hand palm upwards: in the palm is a small object meant to represent Zone Three—a mountain.

With us this scene has never been popular, as can be imagined. For a long time it was not represented at all. This was not only because it was felt to be painful and demeaning. Not only that. There was an ambiguity in it that all of us could feel, even though there are so few of us who are capable of understanding—who are prepared to make the effort to understand—what it meant to Al·Ith to descend to that Zone in the way she did.

But later on our more adventurous artists did try and tackle it—and this precisely because of its difficulty.

Soon the early, cruder representations lost favour: some of them had even showed Al·Ith with bound hands, or a chain around her neck. But most concentrated on the soldiers rather than on Al·Ith, who was reduced to a pathetic doll-like figure on her horse. We had instead the faces of the soldiers, exuberantly cheering, rather like animals contemplating an imminent feast. In short, these first pictures all tended to caricature.

In the end a more serious school of artists took to showing the scene not very differently from how it was generally shown with them in Zone Four—a fact not without irony, and of course appreciated very much by some of us.

The pictures were of, above all, Al·Ith's gold dress—of her decorated and opulent dress, and her bound, trapped hair. She dwindles under the weight of stuff and jewellery. Her pregnancy is not ignored, but not made much of either. Her face is only indicated. She rides between ranks of men in uniforms which are shown in the greatest detail. These pictures came to be known as "Al·Ith's Dress"!

And there were some rather funny verses current, too, all about Al·Ith's dress, and its adventures, as if Al·Ith were not inside it.

And yet all these representations failed to come to terms with Al·Ith's real feelings as she rode behind Ben Ata, for hour after hour after hour, in that steamy dampness, in the clashing thumping noise which was making her feel faint.

The fact was that she was watching Ben Ata closely. She did not smile or wave at the soldiers, for she knew this was not expected of her—she was not anything more than a symbol. It was Ben Ata's function to show himself through the look on his face, and his eyes. He did not miss anything. She saw how he took in, at a glance, every detail of a company of men as he slowly rode past. She knew that he was storing up what he had noticed to deal with it all later. She knew that when he was with his officers everything he had seen would be brought up and attended to.

She tended to forget him in this role, which was after all his real one, his purpose and his being—the representative and leader of his men. This she understood and respected, from her own knowledge of herself, and of her function.

She found, watching this Ben Ata, that he was absolutely and every bit in command of what was needed from him.

She respected him for this. She loved him.

She might be feeling inside that appalling dress of hers that she was being asked for *almost* more than she could bear but then, obviously—and it was quite clear to her, just as much as to Ben Ata—it was necessary.

Al·Ith, on that steamy, damp plain, among thousands upon thousands of Ben Ata's soldiers, was no captive as she watched and approved Ben Ata.

I do not believe that any of our artists, or our ballad-makers or songsters, have got anywhere near the truth of that scene. And in fact perhaps those Zone Four pictures that have the child already born and sometimes even on his own little horse riding in front of both Ben Ata and Al·Ith have got nearest to it.

When at last the parade was over, and the plain full of companies of men marching back to their camps, the two were a long way from their own pavilion, and it was evening.

Not far was an old fort, and they rode there, side by side now, and in good understanding with each other. He was not grateful for her compliance, for gratitude is not in order when something necessary has to be done, but he knew the day had cost her a good deal. Besides, she was pale, and confessed to a headache. At the fort, he helped her take the bridle and saddle from poor Yori, before untrapping his own horse. Both were set free for the night, having been told by Al·Ith that they were to be waiting here in the morning. The beasts raced off in the dust, tossing their manes and neighing in relief at their freedom, and then rolled in the soft grass, while the two watched.

"All right, Al·Ith, don't say it," said he.

"There is no need," she said, soft and fierce, "no *need* for it. Why make slaves of creatures who will do what you want for love?"

At which he clasped her, with a sort of groaning apology, and pulled down her hair so that he could sink his face in it. And so they stood until they felt a coldness and saw that the mists were already as high as their waists. They went into the fort. Both were happy to accept hardship when it was necessary, and in fact they were welcoming this holiday away from the ease and delights of their pavilion. This great stone hall, with its bare flagged floor, and the roof through which stars shone because it was going into ruin, suited their mood very well. They sat together with no light except starlight, and refusing thoughts of food and drink.

In the middle of the night, hearing the horses whickering and talking outside, they went out to them and petted them. It was chilly, and the sky was ablaze with stars. Both gazed up into the snowy masses of the mountains that hung there, filling the sky. Ben Ata said suddenly, fierce and sad, "Oh, Al·Ith, you will be pleased to be home again, I know that but . . ." And again he held her close and she clung close to him.

Of course she knew that this sojourn in his Zone could only be temporary, and of course she longed for it to end, but neither had said this for a long time: that she would have to leave him. She wept. She was drenched with sorrow and with loss.

That this could be the truth was more than she could understand or accept. It seemed that long ago she had floated away from anything she could understand: buffetted back and forth between such oppositions in herself.

And so she clung to him, feeling that without him she couldn't be anything. And he held her, thinking that without her he would be only half of himself.

As soon as the light came, they got back on to their horses, and rode on, Ben Ata's saddled and bridled, but hers not.

He had promised her a tour of at least part of his realm, and this was a suitable time for it, before she got too large to be comfortable for long hours on a horse.

Not all of this land was so low and damp. Soon they left the central lowlands behind and ascended into a dryer wooded country where there were sparse villages. These were not large, and were poor, surrounded by fields of quite good earth that had been indifferently farmed.

In the fields worked women and children, and old men—the young men were in the armies.

All stopped as the two rode by. There were no cheers here, not even an acknowledgement. Al·Ith saw that these people did not know that this was their king, did not know, very likely that they had, even if briefly, a queen.

They wore brown, coarsely woven garments, and used the simplest of tools. With us, such implements had been in museums long ago.

As they rode through the huts and houses of the villages, Al·Ith looked for marketplaces, for meeting places, for dancing places. She looked for the warehouses and the storage sheds; the artisans' shops, the manufactories.

Recently, how things were in Zone Three had rather faded in her mind, but what she was seeing now revived her memory. She was shocked and sorrowful, contrasting the riches and the comforts of her own country with this poverty which was not even conscious of its thin bareness.

She at first kept glancing at Ben Ata, to find out how he saw it all, but realised from his glances at her, which he tried to hide, that he was hoping to learn from her. And then she did not look at him, for fear her eyes would say how very poor she thought his country. She did not want to wound him. Yet as the day went on, and they kept riding through woodlands, where the soil, she could see, was good and could be fruitful, and then coming out on the bare windswept patches of marshy field that edged the villages, and then riding through the villages which were only associations of dwelling places for—presumably—safety, she became heavier and colder in spirit.

She asked if she might see inside a house. This was in one of the better villages, where some attempt had been made to lay stones along the road that bisected it—other villages were in swamps of mud, or in hard rutted dust.

An old woman, in a thick brown skirt and a sort of ragged leather jerkin that showed her withered arms, was sitting in front of her doorstep on a tree stump, and stood up as the two rode towards her. She peered and puzzled. It seemed that she knew these must be important and powerful, if not that she was in the presence of her sovereign, for she attempted a smile, and then even a sort of bob, in the course of which she nearly fell. Ben Ata leapt down from his horse, and steadied her, and said, "May we enter your house and sit down?"

She had never had such a request made of her, they could see that, for she was having to work it out in her mind. Then she nodded, and went in before them to a room that was not too small, but was clearly the home of at least ten people. For on a corner of the floor were piled skins and woven blankets, to leave room for the day's occupations. The roof was thatched, quite strongly, but not with any art. The floor was flagged. There was a fireplace in which hung hams and joints to dry in the smoke. There were strings of vegetables and herbs hanging from the rafters. A single door at the back led into a room where jars and vats showed that this family, or tribe, had food enough, if nothing much else.

In the main room were no more than a couple of benches, and a loom.

The old woman followed them, gazing, and smiling uncertainly, and from time to time she hastily smoothed her thin white hair, as the idea came to her that something of the kind was due. Then she smiled and bobbed again as they thanked her, and without sitting down, went out again, got on their horses and rode away, past doorways where children came out to watch, and some old people.

And so it went on all that day. In the evening they found a small town, where things were better and Ben Ata seemed ready to show pride, if she felt it was indicated, but she was despondent, and not able to smile. There was an inn there, of a sort, which consisted of a large room where travellers might eat and doze away the night sitting up on benches. Here they were recognised and the whole town came out to stare and admire. They ate broth and bread and roast fowl with some travellers who were too much in awe to eat, and when the meal was done, they thanked the townspeople and rode off again into the forest, where they again spent the night wakeful, but sometimes dozing a little.

He did not ask her what she was thinking, and she did not tell him. But she was secretly planning a visit for him to her land, so that he could see for himself: if she could acclimatise to this heavy lifeless air, could he not get used to the atmosphere of Zone Three? But would it be allowed? Would the Providers encourage such a thing? Wondering if similar thoughts were in his mind, she sat within the strength of his arms, under the great tree that they had chosen as shelter, and smelled the rich loamy soil all around them, and knew that there was nothing in her realm that he could not achieve in his. If that, in fact, was part of what was ordered.

They kept up this tour for several days. There were sometimes larger towns, but mostly small ones, and all had that exact and limited functioning which means that a centre serves its locality—no more. There were very many villages. Everywhere had the same stamp of on the edge of poverty. And nowhere could be seen young men, or men in the prime of life, or even middle-aged men. The women were formidable, and very strong, as if they had been forced to swallow iron very early in their lives and had never digested it. The old people stared from eyes that had learned to expect nothing. The children did not seem playful or lively, but had a hard watchful stare and were suspicious. Al·Ith was now remembering everything about her own country, even though each thought of it was painful to her, and she half wished that she could forget it all again. There was a really dreadful restlessness in her, a grief rooted in conflict. Everything in her was rent and in argument and fighting against itself. Above all she was thinking that it was this graceless and impoverished land the child in her womb was destined to rule—and the thought was cold and heavy, making her feel an alien to him. Usually she liked to put her hand there and greet the little creature. She enjoyed feeling him stretch and prove himself. She needed to feel that she was feeding him strength and confidence. But now this friendly hand of hers was inhibited, and wanted to keep away from the child, as if her touch could only send doubting and undermining messages. Nor could she imagine how this future of theirs was to be: a mist lay between her and what was to come, and she could not remember ever before not knowing what she was to expect, so that she could prepare herself for it.

The Al·Ith who at length said to her husband that she had seen enough, ridden enough, and was ready to return "home"—to their pavilion, she meant, not her own realm—was very different from the one who had ridden out to show herself off to the armies.

They turned their faces towards the central lowlands, and rode slowly back, taking their meals in the towns that had inns, but always spending their nights in the forests, or in some fort or ruin.

Al·Ith was thinking all the way home of what could have happened to this place to make it as it was, of how it might conceivably have been in some long distant past before war became its function —and of what Ben Ata could be persuaded to do that might change it.

And Ben Ata was restless and longing to get back to his armies.

For he had seen during his close inspection of the troops that day that they would not be content for long with reviews and tattoos and parades—he would have to allow them something along the lines of a war, or he would not be king for long.

Besides, he now knew perfectly well, from everything that Al·Ith had not said, but could not prevent herself from showing, that his country was a very poor place indeed.

He was out of his depth, faced with a problem beyond his powers, and unsure of himself and his purposes.

A new phase began for them.

Looking back afterwards both saw that their ride together through his realm was when they had come closest to each other, the culmination of their marriage. For now he turned out again towards his men, and she found that the women were claiming her, and that she spent more time with them than she did with Ben Ata.

Soon the child would be born, and there was not a woman in the Zone who did not know of her visit to them, one who was not implicated with every moment of this adventure.

Ben Ata came in late every night, usually mud-besplattered, and often tired. Food had been brought up for them from the camp kitchens, and when he had bathed he sat with her to eat, often preoccupied, but ready to respond if she asked him for his news and always willing to hear what comments she had to make. But war was not what she understood, and while she was interested to hear details of this life that was foreign to her, she could not contribute much. So it was that often he did not talk at all when he came in. He was ready to go to sleep early, since he was always up with the first light. And she at this time was heavy and uncomfortable and did not sleep well. Yet, wrapped together on their couch, it was in friendliness, and for mutual comfort. He liked to lie with his strong lean hand on her stomach, feeling the movements of the baby, until the weight of it grew too much, and then he turned her so that her back was towards him, and he laid his arm just under the curve of her stomach. They made love gently. Al·Ith had not made love much before when pregnant—or she did not think she had. She had certainly spent the time of her pregnancy with the Fathers, much more than with Ben Ata now. It seemed to her that her days had been spent with the men who were the parents of the child, in sustaining and feeding and reassuring, and that this being together at such a time was of the utmost importance. Yet it was a concept too far from Ben Ata's life for her to mention it.

And so, when Ben Ata had bathed and dressed and had kissed her, and said that he looked forward to being with her again in the evening, and had gone off shortly after sunrise leaving her still curled up on her couch, it was to the women who would shortly come up the hill from the camps that her thoughts turned. This child of hers was being sustained, through the daytime at least, by women, by the talk of women, the love of women, who longed for him to be born almost as much as for the birth of one of their own. And this, too, was not anything that Al·Ith could remember—not this fierce identification with the birth of a child as if it was some sort of a self-fulfilment. More: as if a birth was a triumphing over a threat or even a wrong, meriting the wild exulting yell of a warrior over a defeated enemy. Her children, in the past—those she had borne personally—were viewed more as a summing up or a confluence and a strengthening of influences and heritage. A child, born, was greeted as a fellow spirit, a delight, a gift—but had there ever been this passionate need to have and to hold and to exult? Well, perhaps it had been like that. . . .

There was another thing that was quite different here. It was that she was never alone at all. While in her own land of course the Fathers, and the women who would be implicated in the child's upbringing, and who would be considered Mothers, were close and often with her, she remembered long hours of solitude in communion with herself and the child. But now any such wish on her part was considered as an evidence of weakness or faintness of mind. She must be sad, perhaps? Or frightened? For they all behaved as if this was her first child, and she could not bring herself to tell them of how her life had been as the Mother of so many children, her own and the orphans, because they were unable to understand anything but the possession of what belonged to them—as they saw it.

Yet this child was felt to be Ben Ata's son. Not her son. She was seen as a channel or a vessel. It was most strange and awkward and she was many times in any day thrown off her own precarious balances and made to wonder if perhaps she was quite wrong and they altogether right? But how could they be? This *mine, mine, mine* about a child paid every kind of reverence to the flesh, but where was the acknowledgement of the high and fine influences that fed every child—each child, that is, who *was* supplied and fed with them? Anyone could lick a child all over as if it were a puppy or a kitten— but where had that thought come from? What a strange thing to come into her mind! And anyone could clutch at a child and mark its features: "This nose is mine, and that his, and that my mother's, and that his father's . . ." Anybody, even a horse or a dog, could calculate streams of inheritance in that way. And all that was pleasant enough, and of course no one would refuse the delights of watching for the appearance of this or that trait in a child. But that was not even the half of it . . . one might not, most definitely *could* not, say of a child, "mine, mine," or "ours, ours"—meaning, only, parenthood. For what was real and fine and precious in this new being was in relation only with . . . somewhere else . . .

Where? Al·Ith's mind dizzied and swam. "Blue . . ." she muttered. "Yes. Blue . . . where, though?" And she would put her head in her hands and shut her eyes and try to remember . . . she saw an infinity of blueness, an azure field shimmering between tall peaks. But where? And now she felt hands on her shoulders, and she was being gently shaken. "Al·Ith, Al·Ith, what is the matter, what is wrong?" And just as she was surely on the verge of *really* remembering, she was claimed back, pulled back. All around her were concerned, affectionate women, and Dabeeb was holding her, and they exclaimed and exhorted and would not be still. Chatter, chatter . . . that is all they would do. And yet she loved them and was grateful for their support. For she was giving birth, after all, in this land of theirs and not her own, and she did not know what to expect.

While Al·Ith spent her days thus, Ben Ata was furiously busy. He set his armies complicated war games, and visited them frequently, inspiring them with rousing speeches and exhortations, which, however, were beginning to shame him, make him feel embarrassed. More than once he found himself muttering that it was a good thing

Al·Ith wasn't in a position to be there. Otherwise he was riding back and across and around and everywhere through his realm. He wanted to see how it struck these new eyes of his—a vision that was the gift of Al·Ith. And besides, there were districts that Al·Ith had not visited on that long journey of theirs: he had been careful that she did not. For they were worse than anything she had seen. He saw the deprivation of his people clearly, and with pain, and wondered often how things might be up there, in her Zone, to make her so silent and anguished about his. He could not imagine a country without armies. Even the thought of one caused him to feel contempt —which at first he did not recognise as such. Then, realising that when the thought of Zone Three came into his mind he was feeling a cold dislike, as he did when his armies had won a victory—even of one party in a war game contrived by him—over an enemy, he was forced to acknowledge that this was contempt. And so he became confused, and diminished inwardly—because this emotion of doing-down, of superiority, was the fuel for his energy. Which was for-midable. From one end of his Zone to another, the king was known as a man who could stay in a saddle all day and a night, or work at matters of organisation, practically sleepless, almost indefinitely. And why was this? He had not known it, but he did now: because at such times it was as if he ground some enemy into dirt with his heel. Was he really willing to feel such a thing for Al·Ith and her people?

When this idea first came to him, was rejected completely, came back, was tentatively admitted, and thrown out again, returned in-exorably, presenting itself four-square and face-on—he felt ill. He was dizzy, and sick. As it happened he was riding through woods that not so long ago he had traversed with Al·Ith, his other self. Riding there alone, it was as if he saw before him in a deep green glade all singing birds and loamy richness, himself, Ben Ata, with Al·Ith, radiant in her golden robe, her black hair flowing down her back, her small supple hand talking to her beloved horse.

And suddenly Ben Ata found himself weeping. This was just silli-ness! It was even shocking. Yet he flung himself off his horse and stumbled choking with sobs to a slender birch that stood at the edge of the glade. He embraced this tree and wept. "Al·Ith, Al·Ith," he was saying, over and over again, kissing the white skin of the birch, as if Al·Ith were dead, or already vanished from his realm.

But how could he sustain this welter of emotion without her! How live! He was no longer himself, not a warrior, a great soldier. He had become one who disliked his own deep motives, watched feelings spring up inside himself as if they were bound to be enemies, a man whose purposes had gone.

"Al·Ith!" he moaned, mourning her—and it occurred to him that she was a day's ride away. All he had to do was to turn his horse around and tear across the fields and ditches till he could ride up the hill, and stride into their love-pavilion where the soft drum beat, and beat, and beat—and take her in his arms.

But if he did, he would find her in her apartments, leaning back in a low chair, her great stomach seeming to confront him with its strangeness, surrounded by—it seemed—half the women of the camps. Dabeeb would be sitting close to her, perhaps fanning her, or stroking her arms, or rubbing her ankles. Al·Ith would be distressed, flushed, and moving her head irritably from side to side as one of the women—perhaps Dabeeb again!—brushed out those gorgeous black tresses he loved so much. So he had seen them yesterday. He had stridden into the room, and found them there. Al·Ith had lifted her head and smiled—exactly as a prisoner might who did not hope for release. Yet who had imprisoned her? Not he!

He had backed out of the rooms with a hasty apology. Dabeeb's smile at him had been rich and reassuring, like a comrade's.

Al·Ith's beauty, the challenge of her vigorous good sense, being denied to him, he thought of Dabeeb, almost as if she were Al·Ith. He imagined himself walking from his mess tent, perhaps, or to his own tent, and finding Dabeeb in his path, smiling. And he felt sustained and soothed. He was smiling as he left the birch tree, and swung himself back on his horse.

He would not be in any hurry to return to the women. He would ride on through his country, seeing everything he could, not hiding anything, and keeping Al·Ith's face in his mind's eye as a gauge and a reminder—the face of Al·Ith as it had been during their journeying together, alone, through the woods and fields and forests, sitting together all night in each other's arms, or hand in hand. Had such a happiness really been his—theirs? For now he could only see—if he thought of Al·Ith as she was now—a hot, rather swollen face with eyes that asked—and asked. What for? Did she not have everything?

And in any case, how could he get anywhere near her, with those blasted women crowding around her?

He found a town large enough for a garrison, and instructed the officer in charge to send messages by drum back across the land to the camp down the hill, that he would not be back that night. Or even, perhaps, the next—or the next—or the next. Smiling, he rode on, thinking that Al·Ith had said in Zone Three messages were sent by tree. Yes, by tree. There were trees everywhere in her realm that were known as transmitters of any message that needed sending. A late traveller, or someone not able to be home at a promised time, would seek out such a tree, which Al·Ith described as always being tall and well-grown, with a certain configuration in its branches, and whisper what had to be said to the trunk of this being—for in this way did Al·Ith talk of the transmitting trees, as if they were sentient and knowing. The tree's thoughts, or feelings, accepted the thoughts, or feelings, of the sender and wafted these across as many distances as were necessary to reach a husband, a child, a waiting family. Often had Al·Ith, she said, a long way from her palace, her children, her sister, and, of course, her men, muttered Ben Ata, hotly, feeling himself suddenly red and sweaty with jealousy, found a tree and whispered her news to it.

And now a quite unforeseen anger and discomfort swallowed all his gentle thoughts of Al·Ith, and he found himself raging against her.

Oh, yes, it was all love and love and kindness, all smiles and kisses, but he was just one of—he did not even know how many! Al·Ith, when he had asked—but only in their early days—how many, who, how often, and that kind of thing, had laughed and called him a savage, a barbarian, a dolt—there had been no end to the names she had had for him. But not now. Now she was only too ready to curl up inside his arms and lie there, resting. But what would happen next—or later? Anything at all, with such a creature, who could become anything as the occasion was!

And so Ben Ata raged and sorrowed his way across his realm, from village to threadbare village, from town to town, always secretly comparing them in his mind with villages and towns of Zone Three that he could not even imagine. What could it be like, a town where there was no garrison, no soldiers in the bars and taverns, no bugles to mark the coming and the going of the light? What could a village be where the men were all there, doing *women's work*—and here he heard Al·Ith's laugh. Al·Ith was laughing at him! Oh, yes, probably she always had, inwardly, she very likely laughed but concealed it from him. Oh, she was sly, the great Al·Ith, of that there could be no doubt at all.

Reaching a town as the light drained from the sky, he paused on its edge and looked up at the mountains. The mountains of Al·Ith, he was murmuring, suffused with longing for her. It was those mountains that had made her, the lovely Al·Ith—and he imagined her coming to him with her arms out, smiling—and, cursing, he flung himself off his horse, ordered a passing soldier to stable it, and went into the nearest inn. There he found a woman whose soldier husband was off at the exercises, in whose face he could see something of Al·Ith as she had been when she had first come to him, lithe and light and supple, not as she was now, hostile to him, behind her enormousness, and he went to this woman's bed. But he could not take this woman as he had always in the past, without thought for her, not considering her as an individual creature. He was asking about her, her children, who were asleep in the next room, about her husband, and what he thought of the new exercises—dissatisfied, Ben Ata gathered, because they were only exercises and not war, with chances of loot—and when he made love to her, he had to watch himself so as not to call out Al·Ith, Al·Ith.

Never had he been so afflicted. Never had he thought of one woman while he lay with another. And he did not sleep at all during that night, lying with this companionable woman in his arms, she absolutely asleep, because she was worn out, she said, her youngest child being difficult at the moment, with new teeth coming in. Ben Ata did not know about children's teeth. He did not know how old this brat was likely to be, and feared to betray ignorance by asking. But he felt his palms wet in the night, and understood that there was milk in these comfortable breasts, and felt only revulsion and annoyance. Why had she not told him? Warned him. How could she be so importunate and needy as to agree to sleep with him, her king, and not first confess she had milk in those great breasts of hers . . . it occurred to him to think she might not see it as a fact that needed confessing. He thought that Al·Ith's breasts would soon be milky and wet under his hands. He was disgusted anew, and at the same time longed for Al·Ith . . . and so the night went on, with Ben Ata tormented every minute of it by new emotions and thoughts that he was convinced were probably effeminate. Even demented.

Meanwhile, Al·Ith was giving birth to their son, the new heir, Arusi.

She found it all very tiresome. Not difficult or even particularly painful, for after all, she was an old hand at the business. But certainly she did not recognise any of this bustle with the wise women, and admonitions not to do this and that, but to do that and this, and the baby being dandled by everyone but her, as if she were an invalid, or in some amazing way weakened by a process that it had never occurred to her in the past to think of as anything but satisfying.

She could remember clearly that with her other children, she had gone with her sister to her own rooms, leaving the Fathers together —they having been summoned to support her with their presence and their thoughts—and there she had crouched down, squatting, over spread pads of soft material. Almost at once the baby had sprung forth into the hands of Murti·, or into her own hands. The two women held the child, welcomed it, wrapped it, and when the afterbirth appeared, the cord was cut. Murti· helped to wash and cleanse Al·Ith, and then the two women had sat together in the window enclosure, with the child, introducing her, or him, to the sky, the mountains, the sun, or the stars. This was always a time of gaiety and friendliness, while the child looked at them with its new eyes and they reassured and held and stroked. Happiness! That was what Al·Ith remembered. A blessed, quiet happiness, and she could not remember any like it. And then, when both were rested, and the baby accustomed to their touch and their faces, all three went out to where the Fathers were waiting, and there was happiness again. The other women came in, too, those who would assist with the child. Women and men, and then Al·Ith's other children, all together, welcoming this new creature . . . that was how it was in her own realm.

Nothing like this.

Al·Ith was quite possessed with exasperation, at all the fuss, and the concern for her.

And there was not a man in sight, nor, obviously, was there likely to be. How could it be right or sane for a child to be born into this clutch of women. Where was Ben Ata? And there came a message from the camps that he was travelling far from here, and would not be back immediately—the drums had said so. Not their own drum that beat softly outside among the fountains. The army drums . . . none of the women could see anything untoward in this, but on the contrary, one or two, Dabeeb among them, said that: It was just as well, this was no place or time for a man.

Al·Ith gave up trying to understand the ways of this barbaric place—for it was again seeming to her as backward and crude, and insisted that it was she who was the right person to hold this child— for so far the women had seemed to believe that the right to dandle and exclaim was theirs. The baby was fretful and cried. Al·Ith could not remember any one of her babies ever crying when it was born. Why should they? But these women seemed to delight in Arusi's discomfort and found it a proof of strength.

Al·Ith got out of her bed—they had brought one in from outside, since she refused to use her marriage couch for this purpose—and took the baby, and sat with it in a chair, and asked them, rather peevishly, to leave her. Even her ill-temper seemed to them proof of something to be approved of and expected. They exchanged looks and nods that quite astounded Al·Ith, who was ready to be ashamed of herself. They went off, with smiling yearning looks at her sitting there holding the baby, who was not now crying, but looking intelligently about, being a fine strong boy with everything right about him. Dabeeb stayed, but seemed to feel Al·Ith's need for quietness, and busied herself with what seemed to Al·Ith a myriad of quite unnecessary occupations to do with clothing and washing the child.

Who she wanted was in fact Ben Ata. She longed for him. It was time the child saw his father. Time he was held by his father. Fed by the thoughts of his father. This was why, probably, he was looking around, continually—he wanted his father. Al·Ith had not longed before for the presence of a child's father—there had not been a need to.

Al·Ith was being rocked by all kinds of emotions that she most heartily disliked and found out of place. While Dabeeb urged her, delightedly, to have a good cry, if she felt like it, Al·Ith was flaming with irritation, and controlling it. While Dabeeb told her to put the child to the breast, poor lamb, Al·Ith shook her head—for to feed the baby now would be to feed it annoyance and need.

But she did not want to anger or disappoint Dabeeb, who had been kind and patient, nothing like her own sister, Murti·, but as good a substitute as was possible in this benighted place.

Dabeeb took the baby later, while Al·Ith bathed and dressed herself newly, and arranged her hair in the mode of this place, braided and confined. Then she told Dabeeb that she would like to be alone now until morning. Dabeeb had absolutely no intention of going off and leaving her mistress alone—this was obviously the whim of a poor woman under stress—but she pretended to agree, and took herself out of the pavilion onto the verandah that overlooked the camps and settled herself there with her back to a pillar. It was a mild night, if damp. She would be able to hear Al·Ith call, if she did call, but she meant to creep in frequently so as to make sure that all was well.

Which she did. She found Al·Ith walking about her rooms, singing to the child, and talking to it—a difficult sort of talk that made Dabeeb uneasy. And then she saw that Al·Ith had crouched with the child in her lap, near a window that looked out and up to the great mountains. She was showing the mountains to the baby! And Dabeeb took time off from her duties to run down the hill and tell this news to the other women.

When all that was done, Al·Ith, with the light coming up gold and rose on the snow peaks, took the swaddling layers off the baby, with the intention of wiping it gently clean, as she had always done before —but she found herself licking and nuzzling the child, like a mare with a foal, or a dog with its newborn young. She was quite dismayed and surprised, but at the same time found herself enclosed in a loving spell with this new child, and licking it clean, as an animal does, seemed to be the most natural thing in the world. And the child seemed to think so, too, for he responded to her face moving close to him, and the touch of her hair as she licked him all over, and even quite roughly, as an animal might do to start the blood and the vitality moving more swiftly.

And, all that done, she covered the child up again, and held it close, thrilled through and through with the wildest emotions of love and possession—but she had not felt anything like this before, and was most uneasy that she did so now. It was not what she ought to be feeling. She was faint with loving and wanting this child, as if—as she had heard one of the women croon earlier—"she could eat him all up."

Well, this was Zone Four, these were Zone Four ways, and so, presumably, there was nothing to be done about it.

But where was Ben Ata? Where was Ben Ata? Where was he? How could he leave her and betray her thus? How could he abandon and starve his child? What sort of a monster was he, to go off just at the moment when she, and the child, needed him most?

Meanwhile, Ben Ata was riding back across country, unsatisfied in every way. His night with the woman had left him only the more curious about Al·Ith, whom he was seeing as a creature of secrets kept deliberately from him. If he had been in any state to narrow down his unease to a definition, he would have said that he could not reconcile an animality (though that was not a word he would use to Al·Ith herself) felt, obviously, as a source of strength and rightness, with an intelligence that he knew overmatched his. But he was not analytical, only tormented with contradictions. His night's companion had told him—simply through the fact that he had for the first time allowed his understanding to inhabit an impulsive coupling —that throughout his apprenticeship to this marriage he had been, simply, a brute, and he was not in the habit of accepting such words about himself. He had seen that he had fathered children more casually than a beast does. He had been quite proud of the Children's Army, in which his own offspring had been placed together with those of his officers. He would often, on parades, or on similar occasions, allow his eye to sweep over those young faces, and try to pick out those that resembled him. He expected these boys—some of them young men now and in every way fulfilling expectations—to become ornaments to his armies.

But he had not been a father.

He had not suspected that there could be a different view of the matter.

It seemed to him that he had spent most of his life blind to his own nature.

And more, and worse, many things said or suggested, by the

woman from whom he had parted when light came and she left him
to attend to her children, had told him that his kingdom was in every
way poorer and more brutal than he had ever suspected, and his
people more dissatisfied.

Yet it had never occurred to him to even wonder about it.

He had done and behaved as he had always done, and as his father
had, and his father—for all he knew, but then he had not thought
about that either.

It was dusk when he arrived back in the camps at the foot of the
hill, and he saw that the soldiers and the wives and children were
looking at him with smiles and showed every sign of being inclined to
cheer. This he saw, in his mood of bitter dissatisfaction with himself,
as hypocrisy or even treason. He did not respond but rode unsmiling
up the hill, his thoughts full of Al·Ith and his intention to understand her, meaning by this that he would not in the future be deceived by her. Yet he longed for her—longed for something that was
more than what last night's woman had given him. He was not
thinking of the child at all.

On the verandah that framed the pavilion, he saw a woman with
a baby in her arms, and thought wearily that before he could be
alone with his wife he would have to get rid of all those females.
Then he thought that this particular woman must be Dabeeb, and his
annoyance softened: he had every intention of making love with her
at the first appropriate opportunity, for he wanted to understand her,
too. Dabeeb nearly always had a baby or a child somewhere about
her: so he had become accustomed to seeing her. Then, as he approached, he had a moment of dizzying confusion, for he thought
this was not Dabeeb but Al·Ith.

In fact it was Dabeeb. The last few weeks of continual attention
on her mistress had thinned her and refined her. Her joy at this birth
had lit a flame in her that had its source in the belief of all the women
that this child would in some way redeem them all, and through
them, the kingdom as a whole. And, being close to Al·Ith, she had
taken into herself something of the higher pulses of that land which
towered over this one.

She was radiant. But as Ben Ata bent over her to grasp her, to
look into her face, and demand—in one shattering and truthful
moment—that Al·Ith reveal to him everything she had been keeping

back from him, he saw that this was Dabeeb. Even more confused, he went on past without looking at the baby she was holding out to him.

A woman stood in the archway into the main room, arms folded. Again cursing inwardly that his life was filled with women, women, women, he was about to go past her when he saw this was Al·Ith. He was stopped dead, and could not speak.

Al·Ith was heavy, lightless, even coarse. Her eyes puzzled and narrowed at him. There was about her an aroma of blood. Only her black glossy hair recognised him.

"Where have you been," she said, in a voice that he could not accept from her. Having swung back and forth from emotion to emotion, each unwelcome, he could not now face another one, which was a suspicion that this female had in some way given up her charm, her light, her fire, by some magical means to her servant Dabeeb.

Then it occurred to him that she was no longer heavy and pregnant. Then, slowly, that she must have given birth. And then, that the baby he had just passed was his own.

All this was too much, and he strode straight through into his own apartments, and sat at a table with his head in his hands.

Al·Ith did not at first move. In her mind she was back in her own land, trying to match anything at all in her experience with what had just happened.

She did not meet Dabeeb's eyes, which were urging her to go after her husband and to take the baby with her. She had seen that Ben Ata had approached Dabeeb with an urgent desperation, a query, that she now believed, having seen it so often, was due to herself. This was "love," in this Zone: desperation, questioning, an unfulfilment.

Al·Ith was being possessed by a sharp searing pain she had never felt before. It was as if she were being deprived of air, or as if she had been made to step out over a cliff. She did not know what this amazing new anguish was, but it made her dizzy. She abruptly went into her own apartments and, like Ben Ata, sat with her head in her hands.

She did not like what she felt, though she did not recognise it.

There was no end to the miseries and humiliations of this nasty place.

The pain she was feeling squeezed her heart, shortened her breath, and made her reluctant to open her eyes, for the room swam around her when she did.

Now it was dark outside, and Dabeeb brought the child in, because he was hungry and needed feeding. She pulled at Al·Ith's sleeve, and Al·Ith listlessly took the baby. He began to cry. Dabeeb expected Al·Ith to bare her breast, but Al·Ith did not. She was thinking that the pain she felt—an evil one, she knew—would poison the baby, who was not only deprived of the food of his father's presence, but would be additionally ill-influenced by herself. She could not say this to Dabeeb, who was a savage in these matters, for all her kindness. She stood up, with difficulty, for she felt ill, and walked up and down with the baby, to quiet it. But he cried miserably.

Dabeeb was wondering if she ought not to go to Ben Ata to tell him to come to his wife, when he appeared. His face, as he saw Al·Ith walking there with the baby, was that of a child. He had been stunned, shocked, with a pain of complete loss and deprivation. But now to him Al·Ith seemed complete and perfect holding the baby, and he thought her exhaustion and even her drowsiness beautiful and right. If he had approached a doorway into a building that held everything he had ever wanted in his life, expecting to be made welcome, but had found it shut in his face, he couldn't have felt worse. He leaned against the arched entrance, folded his arms, and moodily watched his wife, his face white, and thin.

Dabeeb was not in the slightest discomposed. She knew exactly what was happening. Both were jealous. It was all quite in order. Her understanding of natural things being in every way as complete as Al·Ith's in a higher region of nature, she trusted perfectly that all would shortly be well. With every one of her own births, her dear husband had found some woman, usually the nearest to the birth, irresistible—and she had been jealous. And he had seen her as completed by the baby, and was like a small boy in consequence. Surely Al·Ith could see this for herself? Sometimes this great queen was quite remarkably slow-witted, though it was not her place to say it or even think it.

Reposing on nature, humble in her faith in it, Dabeeb discreetly bade the pair good night and departed down the hill to tell the women that everything was normal.

"Why won't you look at me, Al·Ith?"

"Because you have betrayed me, betrayed me—and the child!" said Al·Ith in her new tight shrill voice, which quite astounded her.

He believed, of course, that in some dark way she had come to know about his escapade of the last night, and at once looked sheepish, which she saw—and *then* understood the reason. For she had long ago understood that this bumpkin look of his went with guilt about sex. Now she quite simply loathed him, and even more loathed herself for caring anything for him. She had sunk so far away from anything she really was that she could not stop herself listening to see if the drum was beating—if it had by some supremely good timing chosen this moment to stop, so that she could simply call up her horse and ride away out of this realm of low and seething mists.

As for him, he could feel that he was writhing about like a country urchin, and was amazed, because he did not feel guilt at all. On the contrary, he was now quite proud of what he had learned by spending a night with a woman even if it was just once, as though she were deserving of equal respect with himself.

Al·Ith said, "Your child . . . this is your son . . ." in a choked, feeble voice.

Ben Ata understood that this was indeed a son, as of course he had fully expected, because nothing of this enforced marriage could make sense otherwise, but although he had known it, he was flooded with joy. He did not know how to express it, though he wanted to take them both together in his arms. He strode across, and clumsily put his arms around mother and baby. He was beaming. The baby, however, set up a yell, and Al·Ith simply pulled herself away and sat down with her back to him.

"All right," he said bitterly, "you do things differently in your country."

She did not reply, but exposed a breast, which the baby at once fastened his mouth on. Silence. Ben Ata walked around to the other side, ignoring Al·Ith's back, which was meant to shut him out, and beamed down at the sight. He was now so happy, that he could not believe Al·Ith really meant her coldness.

And after a few minutes she sighed, and seemed to soften.

"With us," she said, "the child's fathers are present to greet the child. To . . . to feed him. . . ."

The words "the child's fathers" had simply fallen flat. As if the very air of this place refused them. As soon as they were out Al·Ith regretted them, fearing that he would see them as a deliberate provocation. But it was worse than that. He was staring at her in bewilderment. "But surely even in your country, it is a woman who feeds the child?"

"Not with milk," she said, in a cold sarcastic voice she really could not believe was hers. "There are other foods, Ben Ata. Believe it or not. This child isn't just a—lump of flesh."

The feeding was not going well: so much anger and reproach and irritation were surging through the room and reaching Arusi through the air, and through the milk he was imbibing, and through the body of his mother. He kept letting go of the nipple to cry a little, and to writhe uncomfortably about, and when he did this, Al·Ith's large breast—which Ben Ata could not recognise as Al·Ith's at all, and could not own as his—spurted milk, which soaked Al·Ith's already jaded blue dress. All this Ben Ata found quite appalling. Yet he was still smiling, and longed for her friendship.

"I suppose you all sit around together," said he, attempting sarcasm, though in fact he was interested, "and enjoy happy memories?"

"Oh, go away," she said, "just get out of here. Go to—Dabeeb!"

This surprised him: he could not understand how she had seen this intention in him—after all, he hadn't shown it. He was also a little afraid of her, as he had been in the beginning.

But he did not go. He turned his back on the scene for a little while, staring moodily out of the window up at the massed, now dark mountains, which seemed ominous tonight, and hostile. He listened to the gulping sound of the baby, which after a while stopped. Silence. He turned at last, cautiously, to see Al·Ith sitting peaceably, the child asleep on her lap, and now her look at him seemed pleasant, and even welcoming.

"Come and see him," she whispered.

He approached eagerly and, to achieve a level with Al·Ith and his baby, knelt down by her chair. They were both smiling. She freed the baby from a wrapper that was tight around it, and let the little limbs fall free. Together they minutely examined this child of theirs, feature by feature, limb by limb.

Arusi was a solid, strong baby. His hands and feet showed he would be big, and tall. He already had a soft thatch of glistening brown hair.

"He will be built like you," she whispered, "but he will have a look of me—he has the eyes of our country."

And then she exposed him entirely, so that he could see he was a son, and that he was in every way whole and good.

Then she wrapped him up gently, only his face free, and said, "Now hold him."

His teeth clenched at the enormity of this challenge, he took the little creature, and, then, smiling with pride, because he was able to do it, stood up.

"Now walk with him," whispered Al·Ith, beaming herself now, delighted, all confidence.

Ben Ata walked up and down for a while, and when he seemed inclined to hand the child back, she said, "No, no, hold him. Think of him. Make him know you are there, with him."

Ben Ata understood, and did as she said. Later, after they had eaten a little—for neither had eaten, so they felt, for days—and the baby had fed again, she put the child between them in the bed and insisted that this was necessary, for this night. "So that he can know us both," said she.

And so the two of them spent that night, sleeping soundly, with the baby between them both, and Al·Ith felt restored again, because at last Arusi was being nourished by his father.

And that night was quite wonderful for Ben Ata, who felt that he was being admitted to the ways of her Zone and her thoughts, which he knew he must aspire to—for the sake of all his people.

But next day was a different matter. For one thing, all the women were back again, overrunning everything, and their beaming smiles at him, as if he had accomplished something marvellous, made him think about the other children he had fathered—after all, this was hardly his first child! And then, Al·Ith alone with him, wanting to share the child, was not the woman who seemed harassed, and worried and preoccupied, and even ugly again—for he had to acknowledge that in order to believe her beautiful he was forced to remember her as she had been during their ride through the forests, and this now seemed a long time ago.

Yet while she seemed busy every minute of the day with the child, she was looking for him all the time, her eyes always searching for him: where was he, what was he doing?

What he was doing was, in fact, dreaming of how he could escape, and he did go off to his troops in the afternoon, listening to her shrill accusations with as much shame for her, as she was feeling—and he knew it, and was sorry for her—on her own account.

Besides, he wanted to see Dabeeb. He did not know why this was, nor much care. He told himself he would like an account of the birth from the chief midwife, but really he did not care about that very much. He found Dabeeb, as he fully expected—she had not come near Al·Ith all day—in her own home that evening, when he re-turned from the war games where, of course, since he was a great general, Jarnti was fully occupied looking after everything. Ben Ata and Dabeeb, having made sure the children were asleep—sharing in this concern made him feel most responsible and adult—at once went to bed, where they enjoyed each other with relish. Dabeeb did weep a bit, and moan that she was wicked, and better still, that he was, and that men were all alike—but this being very much what he had experienced all his life, in one form or another, he was reassured and felt exonerated. Above all, he was not being made to feel guilty because of insensitivity or lack of proper feeling: he had been begin-ning to believe that this new Ben Ata who had been given birth to by Al·Ith had destroyed in him all joy for ever.

And in the morning he went off to the war exercises, and looked Jarnti in the eye as a king does his general, and did not return until that evening. That is, he had been away for two days. He expected to find Al·Ith vituperative.

But instead she was wearing a dress he had not seen before, of a pink shining stuff. Her hair was done in the matronly way he did not much care for. He thought the dress unfortunate, because it seemed to him to signify fleshiness and it made her look plump. He saw that she was trying to be attractive to him, and this dismayed him, and made her unlikable: it seemed to him quite improper to make love at this time, when she was still unhealed from the birth. But, when the baby had been fed and put to sleep—not in their marriage bed, but in a cradle next to it—he did in fact make love with Al·Ith, whom he did not recognise at all. She clung to him, she was a suppliant, she was also aggressive, and this was because she was ashamed.

He could feel she did not really want him, not from her own need, but she wanted him to prove something—to her, or to him, he did not care. She seemed to him, in her flesh, unresponsive and slack, and he could not rid himself of a mental picture of this body stretched and opened by that child asleep in his cot who seemed, viewed from this perspective, as quite enormous. Pushing into Al·Ith, Ben Ata could think only of the child pushing out. It was awful, in fact. He hated it.

As soon as he could he turned away and, pretending to sleep, he slept, his last thought being that what he was feeling for Al·Ith now was pity. He would have liked to be allowed to hold her like a child and comfort her. But obviously that was not what was needed.

As for her she was tortured with shame. She knew that she had never done this before, nor could have done. She did not recognise herself in this harried, shrill-voiced woman who was jealous. Yet, hearing one of the women use the word in some other context—as of course words do arise in a scene or a situation, informing us when we need it, of some truth or other—Al·Ith knew she was jealous. As soon as that word had been used, she accepted it. She had never been jealous before. She had not known it was possible. If such a feeling had been described to her, at home, with her peers and her real companions, she would have refused to believe it.

Yet she had dressed herself to attract Ben Ata, in a way she had never done before—nor even had an impulse to—and had needed him to make love with her. What for?

Al·Ith lay awake, listening to her husband's deep breathing, and the light uneven breathing of her child, and listened to the soft drum beating, beating outside, and longed for only one thing. That it would stop beating and release her.

In the morning, Ben Ata made several casual references to Dabeeb, who had not arrived, and Al·Ith knew exactly what had happened. With part of herself she raged: it was not just, it was not fair, she was disadvantaged, she was deceived—a gamut of feelings that she, with the other part of herself judged as lunatic. Such was the conflict that she was relieved when Ben Ata went off back to his armies. And when Dabeeb came up, Al·Ith reassured her with a kiss, as much for her own peace of mind as for Dabeeb's, because she could not stand herself in the role of jailor, possessor, and accuser.

And besides, she had been wrong to want for this child what the children of her own land had by right. Arusi would be nourished in the flesh, and by what she could bring to him, *had* brought to him, by virtue of her own realm. He would not know the nurture of father-hood, as she understood it. There was nothing to be done. And perhaps she had been wrong even to wish for it, and to attempt it, that first evening, with Ben Ata.

She was seeing very little of Ben Ata. He spent days at a time, then weeks, with the army. She heard—but did not challenge him on it—that he was planning a real campaign against Zone Five. If he did come in late at night to join her in their bed, she made it clear that she was tired, or even that she preferred to sleep on a couch in her own rooms, for fear of the child being restless and disturbing him. They were at that time like strangers who have been forced together by circumstances, but are determined to be courteous.

She did not even wonder whether Dabeeb had again enjoyed her husband. She refused to think about it, because she so much despised the creature inside herself this kind of thought invoked.

The child being healthy and strong she was thinking of weaning it.

It was at this time she had a dream. She was sexually initiating Arusi. He was simultaneously a small boy, a half-grown boy, and a young man, and it was a dream of intense pleasure, and of *rightness*, since this was the closest intimacy there was or could ever be, being expressed in the most natural way. And it was full of an intense regret, too, since in this act he was being set free from her to go to other women. And of responsibility, for this was not a guilty act, but a ritual and a necessity, sanctioned by everyone. When she woke, the switch from *that* world, where it was proper for a woman to initiate her son into sex, and this one, where such an act was inconceivable, wicked, harmful, was so great that she seemed to be wandering for hours in a between place where neither state was real, had validity.

When she saw Dabeeb coming up through shrubs on the hillside from the camps, catching at the tops of branches to release the scents of the leaves, her cheerful and energetic solidity seemed to challenge

Al·Ith, who felt herself perverse and shameful for having even dreamed such a thing, and so strongly that she was still in the dream's atmosphere.

Al·Ith was sitting on the floor on a large red cushion, and the baby was lying on another, a blue one, asleep. Dabeeb as usual beamed with fond pleasure at the sight of them. Then, acute as always, she saw that something troubled Al·Ith, and she stood, hands folded, by the central pillar, in a pose of willing service, looking concerned.

The contrast between that sturdy earthy woman, and the exquisite slight curves of the springing pillars, seemed to Al·Ith a summing up of her thoughts.

"Dabeeb," she said, "I have had a very disturbing dream."

"Have you now, my lady," said Dabeeb, in her usual soothing nursery voice.

"Do sit down, Dabeeb. Will you never learn to be my friend instead of my servant?"

Dabeeb sat on the edge of the marital couch, since she did not take easily to floor-sitting.

"Yes, I dreamed that this boy here was grown, but at the same time he was quite young, about seven. And a baby too. And I—it was my task to teach him sex." Al·Ith looked quite shocked at herself, because she was having difficulty in bringing this out. Prudishness was a Zone Four quality. . . .

But Dabeeb seemed unmoved, though she glanced nervously at the arch that led into Ben Ata's quarters, where the curtains were drawn back.

It happened that he had come in a short time before and was working at his military plans.

He had in fact observed Dabeeb coming up the hill, and had heard what Al·Ith said. He now appeared in the archway, and leaned there, looking at the two women from a distance. He was preserving an expression of detachment.

Dabeeb showed signs of wanting to escape, and got off the couch, but Al·Ith nodded that she should sit down again.

"Ben Ata, I had this extraordinary dream."

"So I heard you say."

He found the proximity of these two women of his upsetting. He often wondered how he had got himself into this situation, one which offended his every instinct for discretion and order. He would have preferred that they had never known each other . . . that they did not know each other now . . . that Al·Ith should make scenes and throw Dabeeb out—anything rather than this quite appalling intimacy.

Dabeeb's instinct to get up and go seemed to him admirable: Al·Ith's casualness—as it appeared to him—indecorous, offensive.

"Well, Dabeeb, aren't you going to say anything? I can see that you do have things to say!"

"I have had that dream myself, Al·Ith," said Dabeeb, in an embarrassed but stubborn way.

Ben Ata made an impatient movement, and reddened.

Al·Ith saw this and smiled. "There you are, Ben Ata, I'm not alone in being perverse!"

"I didn't say you were perverse," he protested at once.

She laughed.

"I have had that dream with every one of my sons. I've got four boys," confessed Dabeeb. She was laughing, but uncomfortable. "The first time I thought I was a wicked woman. But now I know . . ."

"What do you know?"

"When you talk to the women, all of them turn out to have had that dream. It is when the child is very small, but in the dream he is any age. Usually seven or about twelve."

Ben Ata now left the arch into his quarters, drawing the curtains across firmly behind him, as if insisting on proper boundaries, and he walked to the arches that overlooked the camps at the foot of the hill. There he stood with his hands linked behind his back, his feet planted well apart, in a characteristic pose. His whole person said that he was suffering an assault which he proposed not to submit to, proposed to endure.

"I wonder where the dream comes from?"

"Why did you say that, Al·Ith?"

"Well, it certainly isn't your practice, Dabeeb, is it!"

"Heavens, how can you say such a thing! How you must despise us," said Dabeeb, offended.

"I was joking, that's all."

"Ask her if it is a Zone Three practice," suggested Ben Ata, his back still turned. He was doing his best to sound good-humoured.

Al·Ith, sorry for him, said soothingly that until she had the dream such an idea had never entered her head.

Ben Ata could not prevent a quick sigh of relief, and he shifted his position as if a burden had been taken off him.

"Surely you didn't imagine . . . oh, Ben Ata, you have known me for so long now, and even now you do imagine the most extraordinary things about us!"

"Why should you be surprised? You forget, some of the things you *do* get up to, and which you see no reason to be ashamed of, seem bad enough to me. Of course I am just a barbarian."

"Well, you can take my word for it."

Dabeeb was looking quickly from one to the other during this exchange, as usual showing pleasure and relief that they were getting on instead of quarrelling, for when they did she was made miserable, since she could not prevent herself from thinking that it was her fault. Partly, at least.

"It is a funny thing, you should say that, Al·Ith. Only last week one of the women, it was her first son, she had this dream, and she was telling some of us—very shy she was about it, and someone else said just that same thing: where does the dream come from? Because certainly we would be ashamed here to do any such thing, we would never think of it, it wouldn't ever come into our heads if we didn't have these funny dreams. But we do have them."

"Probably it is a record of the past," said Al·Ith.

"I wouldn't like to think it was this Zone," said Dabeeb virtuously. "Not ever. It isn't nice, is it, even to think about."

"I don't know about that," said Al·Ith. "That is exactly my point. The dream wasn't only pleasurable, but what makes it hard to understand is that it was a ritual. Something ordained. Expected of me . . . it is only now that I am awake again I feel it is wrong."

Ben Ata gave a half groan.

"I don't think you ought to be talking like this in front of the king. It isn't very nice for him, is it? It must be upsetting."

"Why? He had a mother!" said Al·Ith, and Ben Ata groaned again.

"Oh, Al·Ith," protested Dabeeb.

"It is no good, you always shock me. I know that neither of you will understand why, but you do. How is it that you women can be content to treat your men as if they were enemies, or idiots you can't trust or small boys."

Silence from Dabeeb and Ben Ata: the stubborn silence of those preserving integrity against heavy and baffling pressures.

"If I had had that dream in Zone Three, I can tell you that all of us would have talked about it and wondered about it, and we would have called in the Memories and the historians, everybody, and we would have found out everything we could. It could never occur to us to keep it a secret just for women."

Silence again. Then Ben Ata said in a gruff hurt voice, his back still turned, that he was sorry he was so backward, but it would take a long time to get used to such ideas. "Perhaps I prefer to be treated like an idiot and a small boy." And now he turned and came over to the couch, smiling, having set himself to smile and be friendly, and not to go off in a huff, which every instinct he had was urging him to do.

Thinking as well that he might as well be hung for a sheep as a lamb, he even sat by Dabeeb, who was still ensconced on the couch, making a pair with her, while they both looked down at Al·Ith and the baby. She sat smiling up at them. All three were, in fact, disturbed. But containing it.

"Perhaps the dream comes from Zone Five," said Dabeeb. "We all know what those savages get up to down there."

"I've never heard anything about it," said Ben Ata, thinking that he had never given himself the opportunity to hear anything much that wasn't of fighting and loot.

"It has to come from somewhere," insisted Al·Ith. "It is in the minds of the women of this Zone. So strongly that now I am down here with you I dream the same dream. So that means it must be somewhere in your mind too, Ben Ata."

"If you insist, Al·Ith."

They laughed, but it wasn't easy. This was a hard moment for all three of them. Ben Ata was fighting his distrust of the whole thing, the dream being only part of it, for he simply could not like this business of the three of them being so close and adaptable— seemingly.

And Dabeeb was guilty, but telling herself that she had not sought out Ben Ata, but he her, and it was not her place to refuse her king, and that since Al·Ith continued to show every sign of liking and esteem, she was not being blamed by her.

And Al·Ith was jealous. But not in a straightforward way. She was lonely. As she saw the two, her husband and the woman, sitting there so alike in build and sturdiness and a quality of strong endurance, she felt an alien, excluded. Somewhere inside Al·Ith wailed a little child she had known nothing about until now: oh, I am unloved, I am shut out, *they* love each other better than they love me.

When I leave here, Al·Ith was thinking, Dabeeb will be with my husband, and I shall even be glad of it, for I won't want to think of him as lonely, but the truth is they have more in common together than either has with me . . . she was wrung with anguish. Yet smiled, as friendly as she could make it.

"Al·Ith," said Dabeeb, "that dream means with us that the child should be weaned."

"Is that how you take it?"

"Yes. We wean our boys, if we haven't already, when that dream comes. It means that inside yourselves, though you don't know it, you have grown apart. He begins to feel himself a man."

"Very well, I shall."

Dabeeb got up and went off to Al·Ith's rooms, tactfully leaving them. And Ben Ata, after waiting a little, and making some suitable remarks about the healthy appearance of the boy, made his excuses and left: he was not able to stand too much of this dreadful tugging and pulling. Dabeeb, Al·Ith, then Al·Ith, Dabeeb—over and over again. And also he was partly afraid that Al·Ith would want him to make love to her again, and for some reason he simply did not want to, not at all.

So he soon went back down the hill, and much later that night found his way to Dabeeb. He was by then in a state of anxiety, because he was thinking of Al·Ith's dream, which was bad enough, but worse that Dabeeb spoke so easily of all the women having the same dream. It was as if all the dangers he had associated with Zone Three, to be summed up as a sort of smiling treachery, which could never be condemned or refused, since in some extraordinary way it was judged higher and better by *them*, the Providers—as if they had come close in Dabeeb, and permanent, and could never go away again. It seemed to him that half his realm, the female half, was a dark dangerous marsh, from which monsters might suddenly appear. And this dangerousness had been suddenly and recently presented to him: he even regretted his previous state when he never wondered about women at all. He found himself hoping that when Al·Ith at last went his mind would be restored to its previous wholesome condition—but he feared not.

Dabeeb, that night, at his half-willing insistence, talked of all kinds of women's dreams, beliefs, ideas, only hinting however at the nature of their secret gatherings, and it seemed to Ben Ata as if he was being gathered into a place of infinite comfort and reassurance —Dabeeb's large and competent body—and when there he was being repeatedly given shock after shock of unwelcome knowledge. Between the two of them, Dabeeb and Al·Ith, he was being thoroughly done in! Who would have thought that this Dabeeb, the soldier's wife, so sane and comely and ordinary, should turn out to be such a nest of trouble, like feeling grass seeds in his undervest when he was on parade and could do nothing about it but smile. Because where was he now going to find the real dark, real comfort, real oblivion, which was how he had only recently been taught to think of women: he could have no belief now that he could come on a woman who would not, suddenly, present him with problems and thoughts and comparisons that even went right back into history, into the far past. . . . "Where does this dream or that come from?" the women asked each other, talking about such things, but never telling the men what they thought and wondered. So mused Ben Ata, with Dabeeb, lying awake that night and other nights during the time when Al·Ith and he were as if they had an invisible barrier between them.

Meanwhile Al·Ith weaned the boy, and found herself restless and full of new energies.

She did not have enough to do. In her own realm she did so much, and so variedly! She could think of nothing but reviving her wardrobe, an occupation that the best part of herself found tedious, and she ordered new dresses from the dressmakers in the towns—thus at least stimulating manufacture. She was slender again and full of fire and did need clothes to match this new Al·Ith—as she saw herself, and as the women saw her, joking that it would be time soon for a new baby.

But Al·Ith felt that another baby was not what was wanted of her. Oh, no, she had done what she had had to do . . . and yet the drum beat, and it beat: perhaps it *was* intended she should have another child with Ben Ata?

Ben Ata came in late one night and saw her, and he was drawn to her all over again, as if she were quite new to him. And she certainly did not refuse him or discourage him. On the contrary. She found herself craving for him. This, too, was something she had not known: she put it down to the way she spent hours of every day on her appearance, studying dresses of this kind and that which would emphasise a line, or breasts, or legs, or arms, arranging her hair under the skilled supervision of Dabeeb, who adored helping her mistress to become beautiful again. If one devoted one's energies to self display, to the exact disposition of parts of one's body, and always with one idea, that one should be seen, and attract—then presumably that was enough to call forth this raging desire? Cause and result. An energy spent thus will be answered thus . . . so Al·Ith diagnosed her condition, but this did not stop her taking Ben Ata into herself—as if she were starving for him.

And he, enjoying it all, nevertheless said to her, "Do you remember how we used to make love?"

"And how was that?" she asked, knowing quite well.

"Don't you remember that time . . ." for now it seemed as if it had gone on for a long time, had been never-ending, a lost paradise. She had been not at all as she was now, but light, and delicate, and funny, too—thus shielding the grateful Ben Ata from her world which he knew was shadowed by the unknown, the difficult, the immanent, the threatening—she had known how to be subtle and to dance, as it were, from one delight to another, until their unbearable separation roared up in a fire that consumed them both, and in a way that never happened now. How could it, when the approaches to the act were so different.

"And how were we then?" she asked, practically. But knowing quite well.

"Ah, you were different then."

"And now?"

"Now—I plough you in. I plough you under!"

"Ah, yes," she breathed, in a sort of shudder. "Yes, you do. I have to have it. You must. I need it."

"Oh, I'm not complaining," he said, good-natured, like a husband, looking her over with complaisance and appreciation. "Don't think I am complaining."

"But you are!"

"It is as if you need me to extinguish you. Put you out. You lie there groaning away, and I . . . plough you under."

"Yes. Yes. Now, Ben Ata. I get so tense, so . . . I could fly apart. I need you to . . . fill me. To . . . just *do it*. Now. You must. I need it."

And he did. He ploughed into her, long, steady, on and on, while she groaned and died under him.

But that was not what he remembered, not what he looked back on as an experience so far above anything he had ever had with any woman, anywhere, that sometimes he doubted it had ever happened.

But it had. That was how they had been together. A marvellous subtle answering, touch for touch, glance for glance, a challenge that used chords and responses they had now, it seemed, forgotten entirely.

Could this desperate and necessitous woman be the laughing Al·Ith who had taught him delights he had never even imagined?

"Why can't we be like that again now?" he asked, and asked again.

"But that was when I was from *there*, Ben Ata."

"But you are still from there! Where else are you from?"

"Oh, no, Ben Ata, I am not. I assure you no, I am not."

And she held him as if she were drowning and could only be saved by his driving body.

She felt as if he did not do this, extinguish her, knock her out, sink her deep, drive out of her all the tensions and the electricity, that she would go crazy, explode. Why? she had no idea. This was Zone Four! This was how it was.

And yet, always, she listened to the drum, and wondered when it would stop and she could ride up again to her own country and be her own real self.

One day, it would stop and she would be free.

She even imagined how, after being restored in the high cool fresh airs of her own self, she might meet Ben Ata again and they would be able again to "do it" as he remembered with such admiration.

Yet, while she thought like this, it was impossible for her to believe this could be.

And then this is what happened.

Ben Ata strode up the hill from his armies one morning, and, not finding Al·Ith in the pavilion, went through into the gardens. She was with the child on the round raised white platform, or dais, at the other end of the long pool. Between him and her were jets of splashing water, and the sound of the drum filled his ears. Beyond her was the oval pool full of fountains. The spice trees shed their scents. The sun was shining, and all the wetness and dampness and green of the gardens was glistening. Light came from everywhere. The drumming seemed to echo and sound. And there, in the middle of this golden beat of sun and sound was Al·Ith, with her son, who was lying on a spread of blue cloth on the white. Al·Ith seemed to be all light and dazzle herself. Her yellow dress showed thin brown arms, and her legs, where it was pushed up. She was leaning over the child, in intense concentration, which shut him and the world out. He was able to approach without even lightening his heavy soldier's tread, because of the noise of the waters and the drum. He stood quite close, unseen by her. She was absorbed, lost, gone in contemplation of her son. The child lay waving his little limbs, and making soft noises, aware of his mother's adoration—if that was the word for it!—Ben Ata's bitter heart supplied it, in default. The baby seemed to glow with contentment and love. Al·Ith touched the small feet, enclosed them in her hands, slid her hands up and down the small legs. She looked into the child's face, bending forward to do so, with a close, stern intentness that Ben Ata had not seen in her before. She had certainly never looked at him like that! Then, as he stood there, almost holding his breath in his determination to understand what he was seeing—for he knew he must do that, since jealousy was choking him—she slid off the baby's garment, so that he lay naked. He was a pale child, beside his mother's alert slim brownness, and seemed slow and heavy in comparison. Ben Ata was at once forced to acknowledge something he had not wanted to: he felt an instinctive antipathy towards the nakedness of this son of his. Perhaps not an antipathy so much as a curiosity whose source he did not understand. A curiosity about what? He felt as if something inside him said *no* . . . the boy was beautifully formed, a normal healthy child. The genitals, Ben Ata supposed, were his own, he recognised them. But they made him disturbed, and uncomfortable. Why did she expose the child thus? Al·Ith was examining every part of her child, peering close, with the same intent stern gaze.

Every little part, every crease and fold . . . and she touched, and stroked and slid the limbs up and down inside her hands. Ben Ata was aching, and it was with loneliness . . . was she going to handle the boy's genitals? He watched, frightened. But she did not, though in this inspection—as if she were looking for evidence, Ben Ata found himself thinking and not without surprise at himself—she buried her face in the child's body and laughed, and he grabbed at her hair and kicked vigorously and laughed too. It was a love scene Ben Ata was witnessing, and he told himself that she did not handle him with such delight, did not bury her face in his own belly . . . he could imagine the touch of her lashes on his skin, and a forlorn rage began to drum in him. But she *had* made love to him like that— once. Oh, a long time ago. Yes, she had, but did not now. Now she would clutch only and cling as if begging to be saved. She turned the little boy over onto his front, where he strove to raise himself onto his knees, though could not, and Al·Ith continued with her long, loving ritual of inspection or devotion. Or was it passion? She laid a forefinger gently on the backs of the knees, as if searching for a pulse, or at least some announcement of the flesh there. She cupped her palm over the little buttocks. She kissed the back of the child's neck. She stroked the small shoulders with the sides of her palms. And she seemed to be enclosing the child entirely, possessing him, as she leaned over him, a lithe tawny girl in her sunny dress, her hair iridescent in the sun. This pale long child seemed not hers, but an impostor's—and to Ben Ata there was something wrong, even perverse in her owning and having him as she was doing . . . and still she did not hear himself. Though he was standing over her now and his shadow stretched almost to the edge of the round white platform. On which, it now seemed to him, he and Al·Ith had made love a hundred times. It was the plinth or setting for their love, theirs, the two of them. . . .

And suddenly Arusi, striving to get his knees under him to take his weight, succeeded—instead of slipping away under him, they held, and he was on all fours, like a little white dog, thought Ben Ata. He was choked and crowded with emotions. He was so vulnerable that baby! Why, he could kill him by picking him up and dropping him head down on the white marble. As he thought this, the baby clutched Al·Ith's hair and pulled himself up—he was standing. Ben Ata's eyes were full of red anger. He held on to himself, steadied, and as his sight cleared saw that Al·Ith was looking up at him, smiling.

The smile seemed to him brazen. There was no guilt in it at all! Yet she had just betrayed him, a thousand times over.

She was still smiling, a warm close smile that surely was for the baby, not him, Ben Ata! She held out her hand, and laid her palm on the side of his knee, just as she had done with the baby. Shameless, thought Ben Ata, feeling the shock of that touch go up him in flame. She smiled. She wanted him to sit down by her and the child and share in their love rite. There was not an atom of remorse or guilt in her, he saw, with amazement. . . . Ignoring the child, he picked her up and began to carry her into the pavilion.

"Ben Ata," she shrieked, "the baby, the baby, we can't leave him there."

But the shriek had summoned Dabeeb, who was already approaching through the pillars of the pavilion, and had seen that she must fetch the baby and guard it. Her face was all knowing smiles and shrewd guesses, as if, thought Ben Ata, averting his eyes from hers in an instinctive need to shield their privacy, his and Al·Ith's, she had at some point in her life been issued with instructions for reactions suitable for every occasion. When the master carries off the lady to their marriage bed, then the faithful servant has to put on a certain face. In the pavilion, he set Al·Ith down. She was laughing. So was he. By now his anger had all gone, charmed away by the light warm strength of Al·Ith's body in his arms as he carried her. They stood on either side of the great couch, on guard, watching each other like fencers, in an amused, laughing antagonism. Equals. A balance . . . their lovemaking now was set to be a different thing from what he had been thinking of recently as "married" love. A lightness, an impulsiveness . . . a grace.

And so it was, just as it had been "all that time ago"—as Ben Ata had been thinking.

And they woke together in the dusk, close, healed as if of some frightful and unnatural separation that had afflicted them, unforeseen and unforeseeably, and now had vanished away, leaving them breathing together lightly and at peace.

And in silence.

They could hear the water splashing outside.

What a silence . . . it seemed to fill them, slide along and around their limbs, submerge them in itself.

A silence.

The drum had stopped beating. And, suddenly, at the same moment, they sat up, looking at each other, and both let out a sighing breath like a groan.

"Oh, no, no, no," he muttered, clutching her to him. And she had her two hands in his hair, half pushing his head against her body, to keep it there, but partly to hold it away . . . her whole body was shaking with sobs.

And he now held her close, rocking her. They rocked each other. They were kneeling beside each other on the couch, consoling and holding, in a terrible grief. They held each other's faces in their palms and looked into each other's eyes as if there would be an explanation there for this sentence passed on them.

To be separated *now* . . . no, it was not possible.

And it was at this moment that Dabeeb came in from the hill entrance, holding the child, and having cleared her throat gently said, "I have to give you both a message."

And at this the two, Ben Ata and Al·Ith, sank away from each other, to either side of the couch, already apart, and knowing that what Dabeeb was going to say would be some final thing that they would not be able to bear . . . the pounding of their hearts told them.

And Dabeeb's face showed she was stricken. Hurt on their behalf. And at the same time, uplifted.

"Who gave you the message, Dabeeb?" he asked.

"It was a child."

"You did not know whose child?"

"Never seen him before, and it is dark, I couldn't have seen him, and he went off down the hill at once."

A silence. They heard each other's breathing, coming broken and fearful.

Then Dabeeb said, "I beg for your forgiveness first—for what I am to tell you."

"You are forgiven, Dabeeb."

"My lady, you are to return to your own land . . . but you know that already, since the drum has stopped."

"Yes, we know that."

"And you, my lord Ben Ata, are to . . . are to . . . you are to marry the lady who rules that country to the east. You are to marry Zone Five, my lord."

Al·Ith had slid by the couch, and was sitting with her head in her arms, making herself breathe evenly.

She asked, "Is that the whole message?"

"No. The child is to stay here. With us. But you will spend time with him. Six months in every year."

At this Al·Ith wailed and flung herself face down on the couch and drummed with her fists on either side of her head.

Ben Ata stared at this bringer of—what could only be seen, at this time—bad tidings, and seemed to want to speak. But at last he shook his head, helpless, and Dabeeb, in tears, went out.

And so these two were left.

They clung together through the night, weeping, trying to comfort each other.

And in the morning both listened straining for the drum—for perhaps it might start again with the light. But there was silence, only the sounds of the water.

And soon Dabeeb came in with the child, and gave him to Al·Ith. Who sat with him for a moment or two, gazing at him, and handling his limbs, but briefly; and with her touch and gaze already—not indifferent—as it were averted. She did not kiss the child, but handed him back to Dabeeb who of course was weeping bitterly.

Ben Ata was standing with his back to the room, gazing down into the camps.

"Goodbye, Ben Ata," said Al·Ith, sternly, and dry, and almost cold—and she went out into the gardens where her horse was waiting.

And so did Al·Ith ride away from her child, her adopted home, and her husband, Ben Ata.

Al·Ith, riding on her beloved horse towards the heights of Zone Three, was a very different person to the one who had ridden that road the last time she left Ben Ata. She could hardly remember herself. She knew she had been glad to leave. Was that possible? Yes. She had left this watery place as if set free.

She had returned to her own land like a returned exile. And now she was thinking only that her body was so heavy a lump with grief it could not absorb, that she could have slid off the horse, and into the canal and drowned there, without complaint. Raising her eyes to the moonlit mountains, where the snows glimmered, she felt she could never, ever, have the strength to climb up there again. And what was she returning to? She seemed to remember that last time she was there she was no loved and welcomed inhabitant; on the contrary, she had felt herself not to be part of the place—more, it was as if she had been invisible. How could she now just ride back into that life, as if nothing had happened.

Even though in half a year she would ride back along this road— to find her husband married to this unknown queen from the east.

But that was impossible. Neither she nor Ben Ata could take it in . . . how *could* he marry that girl, whoever she was? Why, they two, she, Al·Ith, and he, Ben Ata, were so married now that they made one person.

And yet, he *would* now marry someone else, and the child Arusi would be brought up part-orphaned. No, how could that be? How was it allowed? The Providers, surely, had erred, been wrong in judgement . . . so Al·Ith, as she steps her horse soberly towards the frontier. She had at least remembered the shield. She would not be able to enter her own country without it. Why, she was so much an inhabitant of this Zone now, that she literally could not remember the Al·Ith of Zone Three. But she had to. She must try. . . .

Through the long dark night goes Al·Ith, seeing the gleam of the canals beside her, the white shimmer of the peaks of Zone Three ahead. Her horse is slow and careful under her. And all night the tears run down her face.

So she is pictured. And so she was.

She had been for some time inside her own land before she realised it. She seemed to remember sudden and indeed even painful effects at the crossing point, but the shield was dangling unregarded from the saddle, but why was there a saddle? She got off, flung the saddle and the shield away, talked a little to Yori, who was lifting his head and sniffing and letting out little whinnies of welcome to this remembered place. She was not feeling any ill-effects at all. In the dawn light, the great peaks seemed close, and not difficult and harassing as they had yesterday.

Al·Ith stood quietly there, watched the sky lighten, watching thoughts she had not had for a long time creep back into her mind. She was greeting and recognising them: Why, you there! I had forgotten about you! Welcome! What a lot of herself had been put aside while she had been down there, in Ben Ata's land—and yet she still ached for him.

She wandered about for a while, among the small bushes and ferns of the plain's edge, and Yori did, too, and now she was consciously waiting for her long-forgotten self to come back and re-establish itself. She wanted the heavy anguishing woman of Zone Four to vanish and be forgotten. But it seemed that what was happening was something different. Soon she was regarding her stay in Zone Four quite equably and calmly, but from a distance: she was able in her mind to move all over that land, as if it lay open before her. She knew everything about it, she understood it—and the Al·Ith of that place was there, too, visible to her, and she could look at her without repugnance or regret.

She jumped back on Yori, and rode slowly on, waiting gently to be at home with herself and her land again. She was remote from it. An onlooker. One who rode through it but did not belong in it.

Al·Ith was beginning to feel a little frightened. Never mind, soon she would meet some people, and their reactions to her would tell her . . . and soon she did. A group came riding towards her from the mountains, and they lifted their hands to her and called out a greeting. And rode on. They had not called her name. So she was visible to them now. Yet she was not Al·Ith to them either.

She rode up through the pass, she met many different people, and no one called out to Al·Ith, though all offered her the usual courtesies, which she returned.

Al·Ith was riding through this beautiful land of hers recognising every turn in the road, every new glimpse of the peaks, feeling as dry and light as a leaf. There was a part of her that knew what was happening, and understood it, and was feeding into her a resignation that was like a contained grief.

She was not going to be accepted back into her old self, or into her land. She was separated from everything she saw. The joyous oneness with soil, and tree and air, the being part of her people so that she knew instantly all there was to know about them, since she was them, as well as being herself, this had drained away. And she was not part of Zone Four either, and would never be again—to visit there for six months knowing she must come away again—and to visit a son who was its child—and a husband married to that strange woman whom she had yet to meet—no, even as she thought of it all, of how her life was going to be, it was as if she was being made distant from everything she had been—lighter, dryer, more herself in a way she had never imagined. But doomed always and from henceforward to be a stranger everywhere she went.

When she arrived at the palace, she took her horse around to the stables, and the men and girls working there at first stared, doubtful, then whispered, and then stared again. She had changed a great deal, and they could not accept her. They were glad when she left the horse to them, took herself away.

Up into her palace she went, along the great stairway, past the rooms where her people were living their lives so comfortably without her, and into her own quarters. But there she saw at once that this, her place, was not hers any longer. The low couch she slept in was in use. The great cupboards had clothes in them not hers.

She sat herself in the window enclosure and waited for her sister, who of course now had taken her place. And did not need her.

When Murti· came, she was not surprised—for this whole affair, dictated as it was by the Providers—was not one for surprise, but Al·Ith could see from the change of the set of the muscles of her sister's face that her being there meant something that Murti· had to deal with, to make allowances for.

The sisters sat together in the window and watched the sky darken towards evening, and tried to come close again. But there was nothing in Al·Ith's experience of Zone Four which she could communicate to Murti·.

And she belonged there now. So Al·Ith understood when she saw her sister's reception of the news that for six months she would be away down there, with her family . . . who were not her family! And so it was with everyone in the next few days. They knew this was Al·Ith. She was, or had been, their queen—for Murti· was in that place now. She had been gone from them, sent away by the invisible rulers of all their lives, and would go again. She was a stranger to them. And the way they looked at her, spoke to her, drove this home in Al·Ith. She went to stand in front of a mirror, and remained there, for hours—she wanted to catch that thing in her which told everyone she was no longer a citizen of this, her own land. But it seemed to her she was the same. No, not entirely . . . there was an animal gleam there, was that it? No, that was not the right word: when she had travelled through her husband's land it was the word earthy that she had been whispering to herself: a heavy, lightless people—clods. With nothing of the easy warm quickness of her own people. Had she then become earth? A clod? She turned herself around, looking at her body. She bent into the mirror, trying to see herself as it were unobserved . . . her eyes, what did they say when not on guard, or observant? No, she did not seem to herself cloddish. But there was some kind of leanness there, an angularity. Where was the smilingness and quick response of these her people who were no longer her people? Not now. Not any longer. Murti·, finding her there, and knowing at once what she was doing, came to her and stood by her. The two women looked together into the glass.

"What is it?" whispered Al·Ith to Murti·, her eyes at last filling with tears.

"Oh, Al·Ith, you are a long way from us now . . . a long way." And that was all it seemed she *could* say. The two women did cry for a while, together, in their window seat, but it was not as it had been. And soon Murti· had to leave for her duties—Al·Ith's old duties. And Al·Ith knew she was not going to be asked to take them over again, nor even share them.

And her "husbands"? Her other selves? Wandering about her

rooms, her palace, her old riding places, the streets of her town, she met them, she was greeted, news was given to her—but what news could she give to them?

If she were to tell them of her marriage to the warrior king, they would not believe it.

So it seemed as if the links with them were broken too. And those with "her" children. And Al·Ith took to wondering what those links and bonds could ever have meant, if now someone else could stand where she had, and she was not missed at all. They greeted her, her children: "Al·Ith, Al·Ith, where have you been all this time?" And they came crowding around. But as she stood silent, unable to respond, for she was thinking of that dark painful bond with Ben Ata, and the son who would grow up to—presumably—general the armies of Zone Four, they soon lost their smiles, and their interest in her, who stood so silent and apart from them, and ran off back to the other women, their other mothers, and to the delightful, the lovely Murti·.

"I do not belong here, I do not belong anywhere, where do I belong," Al·Ith was whispering to herself as she strayed among her old memories.

She was repeating to herself Murti·'s "You are a long way from us now . . ." and one day she climbed up to the flat roofs, and from there up the little winding stairs and stood high in the tower, turning herself around to see her mountains, her snows, and then—the faint blue distances of Zone Two.

There she went now, day after day, filling her eyes with that blue.

And soon she went to fetch her Yori from his place with the other beasts, and telling Murti· only that she was restless and wished to wander by herself for a while, she set off towards the northwest. Along roads and paths which of course she had often ridden before. Passing people whose faces she knew if they did not—it seemed—know her. Passing villages and farms and towns which she was contrasting with the meagre poverty of her husband's country, and wishing he could see them. What plenty there was here! What safety! What healthy peaceful faces . . . and Al·Ith saw in her mind's eye the pale unfed faces of the poor of Zone Four and . . . suddenly found these she was looking at fat and mindless.

This shocked her, brought her back into herself. No, it was not that she wished for this land anything of the deprivations of that war-country. Not that she wished these faces any less rosy and warm and quick to smile. Not that she wished to see roofs where gaps showed in the reed-thatch, or holes in the slate, or rutted or mired roads instead of these paved and well-kept ones. Not any of that . . . but, as she hungered and craved herself—though she did not know for what, she wondered how it could be that these people here, *her* people, could live all their lives through without ever wanting anything more.

She was leaving behind the parts that she knew, and her horse was labouring under her, as he climbed a steep and little used road to a crest that was cut, once, by a pass. By the pass that led, she knew, to the gap in the blue mountains . . . hearing her Yori's breath come harsh and slow, she remembered he was old now, he was an old horse, and she slipped off him and walked beside him, her hand on his neck. He turned his loving eyes towards her and asked why she was so restless, always moving, never at rest. He seemed to ask if he might not be allowed to live at peace, with his friends, in his own quarters. . . . Al·Ith stroked him, and praised him, and called him her only friend, and they went on together, up and up . . .

What she had seen was blue, always blue, distances speaking in colour, but now she expected to see closeness dissolve the blue. And yet it did not. There was a soft blueness about everything—ahead of them, where the road turned around a clump of rocks, a bluish air seemed to beckon them on. The hills here were purple, and the vegetation had a blue tinge. Above the turn of the road ahead the sky was blue not only with distance, but because the air everywhere was blue in essence. And small purple mists lay among the trees.

The air seemed different from what she had ever known. She knew that she, like her poor horse, was breathing harshly. And her mind was not as clear as it could be, and as she relied on it to be. It seemed almost as if a blue falseness was claiming her mind. What falseness?

Looking around, carefully, holding tight to her consciousness of how things should be, she thought the blueness was only the underground of something different, as yellow flames have a blue base to them. The blue was only what she could see—was able to see. Probably, with different eyes, the eyes of someone set much finer than Al·Ith's, this world she was walking through would show itself as one of springing flames. An iridescence of flames over this dull blue base. . . . Yori came to a stop, hung down his head, and trembled. Al·Ith told him to go back along the road until he felt comfortable with his surroundings, and there wait for her. She would not be long . . . she watched him turn and go walking slowly and uncomfortably back, grateful to her for releasing him, but not able to show it in a thankful gallop, or a canter, and when he was out of sight, she turned and went on into Zone Two. Though of course she did not know when it would start. She thought that coming and going from Zone Four had needed shields and adjusters and here she was venturing on without any sort of protection. She thought that no one had told her to come here . . . and yet, it seemed a natural thing to do. Why did not people venture here occasionally, or even make it part of their lives? Why did Zone Three live without ever thinking of this neighbour of theirs, separated from them by nothing, not even a frontier. . . .

She really was feeling very . . . ill? No. But she was not at all herself.

She was stumbling through a thick blue air which her lungs were labouring to use. It was like milk dyed with blue, or like . . . at any rate, more a liquid than air . . . air was not far off a liquid . . . air had its own heaviness, its moments of lightness . . . it rolled and it gambolled . . . made visible as cloud air had a thousand freaks and movements . . . air was . . .

Al·Ith went on stubbornly.

She lost her senses. Coming back into herself a long time later, she was alone on a vast plain, whose air was the same blue, but light and sparkling. Nothing here was familiar to her. She did not know this earth—if it was earth, this crystalline yet liquid substance that held her on its surface, while it was able to move and slide and resist. She did not know these trees or plants, which seemed more like flames or fires. The skies were not hers, being a wild flowing pink. Yet the strongest feeling in her was that she did know this place, it was familiar to her—she was at home, even while she recognised nothing at all.

She knew that the surging and churning emotions she felt were of no importance, only the reactions of an organism stretched or provoked by unwonted stimuli. She knew that the thoughts that fled through her mind like the wisps and shreds of—cloud?—that continually came into existence overhead and disappeared again, were not to be relied on because they were the creatures of this unfamiliar place. And yet *she*, Al·Ith, knew this place. And she was waiting for—who, or what?—to come to her. To explain? To warn? To give her advice?

Al·Ith stayed where she was. In this dream she was dreaming, or idea she had stumbled into, it did not matter if she sat still, or tried to press herself against barriers and boundaries she could not see, to make them give way . . . she had already gone beyond boundaries to be here at all.

Someone would come.

It seemed to her that all around her, above her, were people—no, beings, were something, then, or somebody, invisible but there. She was in the middle of a population that could see her, observe her, but whom she could not see. Yet they were there. *Almost* she could see them. Almost, in the thin blue of this high air it was as if flames trembled into being—flames big and small, frail and solid and wild and steady. One moment she could see them—almost. Then could not, and there was nothing there.

Voices. Could she hear voices? There was a whisper of sound, of voices, just under the silences of this realm, but as she strained her hearing, it kept snapping off and out, leaving her deaf for a while, to recover. And her eyes, straining, seemed to go dark. Al·Ith slept there, worn out with attempting what she was not fitted for, and when she woke, it was to exactly the same landscape, empty, and peopled with the invisible multitudes that seemed to press and whisper about her. But now she knew more than she had when she had fallen asleep.

In her sleep she had been taught what she should know.

"Al·Ith, Al·Ith, this is not how, this is not the way, go back, Al·Ith, you cannot come in here to us like this . . . go back, go down, go. . . ."

Al·Ith pulled herself up, and staggered back off the crystal airs of that plain with its swirling pink skies, and into the thick blue mists that surrounded—or guarded—it, and down along the road she had come.

She knew that she must come back. But that she must come differently. Prepared. But how?

As she went on, and down, her mind seemed to clear, and she began to think of her friend Yori. For some reason the thought of him brought no consolation. On the contrary, she was wild with anxiety . . . she saw him in her mind's eye dying, dead: he longed for her, was waiting for her so that he could take leave of her—and as she came around a bend of the road and out of the blue country into the ordinary light of her own realm, she saw Yori lying in the grasses by the road. She ran forward, and was in time to see him lift his head, with difficulty, and give her a friendly glance—goodbye, Al·Ith—as he died.

She sat there by him on the warm clean grass of that high pass, and feeling on her cheeks a sudden fanning wind, looked up knowing she would see an eagle fly past—but the great bird was settling himself on a tree almost overhead. And she looked about her and saw eagles and birds of prey perched on the rocks and the trees, and even on the ground.

She waited by her friend until he was quite cold, and she was sure his spirit had gone, and then she stood up and called to the birds: "Come, take him, take him back, return him to our earth"—and she went on down the pass by herself, not looking back.

When she reached the easy flowing airs of her own country, Al·Ith found a little stream, and sat by it. She was thinking of how long before, or so it seemed to her now, she and her horse had waited by a stream, keeping each other company, and her heart ached. Her heart seemed all ache, for she could not stop thinking of Ben Ata who—presumably—was engaged in marrying this new woman of his.

She had no one.

She sat the night through there, wondering at the stars, and their brilliances, and thinking of the skies of Zone Two, just there, so close, available beyond a few turns of the road, skies which did not know—or so she believed, from her short acquaintance with them— stars at all. Or at least, not these stars. Or not in this shape and guise. But stars of course there had to be, since stars are what we are made of, what we are subject to—stars there must be in Zone Two, though she had not seen them . . . and she had been there, she realised now, for a long time. She had gone up into the pass with Yori in early spring, with fresh green plants and grass everywhere, and the birds building, and now it was nearly winter, and the grasses were dead and broken and the water of the stream was thickened with cold.

Into that Zone she had taken the senses of Zone Three and, of course, of Zone Four, whose citizen she now was, but had tried to take in, to assess, that high delicate place but without what was needed to assess it. Who could tell her what in fact she could have seen there, if differently tuned, if more finely set? How would those raging pink skies look to someone else, a citizen of that realm? Perhaps not a swirling fleeing mass of magenta and pearl and flame at all. Perhaps what she had seen there were stars, through eyes not tuned to see them! The stars of Zone Two—well, one day she *would* see them, as she saw these here, now, tonight—the friendly, familiar stars of her own life, cold, frosty, enormous, the winter stars of Zone Three.

And those eyes would soon see the springing cold flames that fed on the blue base that was all she could take in . . . and she would see. . . .

Al·Ith, sitting by her cold stream, under her brilliant stars, locking her arms around her knees in an attempt to hold in a little warmth, dozed off, or was tranced, and in front of her eyes on her lids danced shapes and figures she had never seen in life. Dreaming there, she believed them to be the invisible ones of Zone Two—and how many of them there were, and how different, and how fine, and how strange—and all of them, she knew, or seemed to know, and it was as if she stretched out her hands to them and pleaded: This is Al·Ith, Al·Ith, take me, let me come . . .

But the barrier between them was absolute, and this barrier was the thick clumsy substance of Al·Ith.

What shapes did she not see there, that night! Some seemed to her as familiar as Murti·, or her own children. Some came straight out of old tales, and songs, and stories: the storytellers, too, described these as if they had known them intimately themselves! And perhaps they had, thought Al·Ith, sitting there, rocking herself back and forth under the stars, because of the sting of the cold that was creeping into her through her bones. When storytellers say: And then there appeared a dwarf with a hump or an exquisite girl made of the wind—well, their audience always thinks that this is a manner-of-speaking but perhaps after all these storytellers, or their ancestors, *did* see little gnarled strong men and women who live deep in mountains, or a race of people so rare and fine they could pass through walls and who were at home in flames or in the wind . . . or at least such beings were part of the consciousness of the lower Zones, to an extent that the thoughts of these minds, or the words of the storytellers, could bring them to life—there they were now, vivid, alive, moving in Al·Ith's mind's eye, perfect and created, yet so far away, yet she could see them, and yet she might not touch them. And there were the strange beasts of the realm of the storytellers, and the familiar beasts, too. Who knew that when at last she, Al·Ith, returned to Zone Two, but properly and soberly prepared, she would find her Yori there, but a transformed and translated version of him . . . so dreamed Al·Ith through that frigid night, while she sat hunched and huddled among the frosty grasses.

And here I must raise my voice, say something—not on my own behalf of course, for there is no "I" here, can only be the "we" of equals and colleagues. Al·Ith sat dreaming of us, the song-makers, the tale-tellers, wondered if we see what we tell . . . and what are we to say to that?

Suppose that Al·Ith, at that moment, shivering with arms around her knees, and her head full of fiery beings not herself, was in fact—and no less than any one of us who are supposed to be different and gifted and specialised—herself a storyteller, ballad-maker, Chronicler: herself and on her own account? What are any of us when we call ourselves Chronicler or song-maker, queen or farmer, lover, tender of children, the friend of animals? We are the visible and evident aspects of a whole we all share, that we all go to form. Al·Ith was, for most of her life, queen . . . the substance of Zone Three expressed itself in her in that shape . . . queen. Or at other times mother, friend, animal-knower. And when she went down to Zone Four how may we assess the way Zone Three squeezed and forced itself in there, as Ben Ata's wife, queen of that place with him, Yori's protector, Dabeeb's friend . . . yes, but what are all these guises, aspects, presentations? Only manifestations of *what we all are* at different times, according to how these needs are pulled out of us. I write in these bald words the deepest lessons of my life, the truest substance of what I have learned. I am not only a Chronicler of Zone Three, or only partially, for I also share in Al·Ith's condition of being ruler insofar as I can write of her, describe her. I am woman with her (though I am man) as I write of her femaleness—and Dabeeb's. I am Ben Ata when I summon him into my mind and try to make him real. I am . . . what I am at the moment I am that . . .

We Chroniclers do well to be afraid when we approach those parts of our histories (our natures) that deal with evil, the depraved, the benighted. Describing, we become. We even—and I've seen it and have shuddered—summon. The most innocent of poets can write of ugliness and forces he has done no more than speculate about—and bring them into his life. I tell you, I've seen it, watched it . . . no, it doesn't do to take these things lightly. Yet there is a mystery here and it is not one that I understand: without this sting of otherness, of— even—the vicious, without the terrible energies of the underside of health, sanity, sense, then nothing works or can work. I tell you that goodness—what we in our ordinary daylight selves call goodness: the ordinary, the decent—these are nothing without the hidden powers that pour forth continually from their shadow sides. Their hidden aspects contained and tempered. I have not written here, for example, much of those facets of Ben Ata's realm that made it a place of terror not only for the regions along its eastern borders, but also for places and people within itself. I have not done so because I am reluctant. I rely on us all knowing what the extremes of poverty and deprivation breed: always meanness and spitefulness and cruelty and threadbareness of spirit . . . except for the few in whom poverty flowers in giving and compassion. Ben Ata's people's poverty bred monsters— as it had to do.

We do not know what aspects the dark forces wear in our own Zone Three. In lethargy perhaps? The stagnation that afflicted us until Al·Ith freed us from it? And what of Zone Two—no, that we cannot even begin to imagine. Yet we may be sure that in those high places there is a dark side, and who knows but that it may be very dark and frightful, worse than anything we, with our limited experience of the lower Zones, may imagine. The very high must be matched by the very low . . . and *even fed by it* . . . but that is not a thought I can easily accommodate or that I wish to write much of. It is too difficult for me. I see myself as a describer, only that; a writer-down of the events which pass . . . and so I record here only that when Al·Ith sat and dreamed of Zone Two, she was Zone Two, even if in the most faint and distant way, and her imaginings of its immaculate fire-born beings brought her near them, and when she thought of us, the Chroniclers, she was us . . . and so now, in this footnote to Al·Ith's thoughts on that occasion I simply make my cause and rest it: Al·Ith am I, and I Al·Ith, and every one of us anywhere is what we think and imagine. No more and no less. We are the dull blue base to the wildest subtlest flames. Al·Ith dreamed all night of people known and unknown, creatures real and imagined, saw and did not see events and phenomena she had not experienced herself.

And in the morning, alone, all one vast hungry ache for her Yori, and for her husband—but she had to keep suppressing that ache, and putting it from her, thinking it unbecoming to hunger and ache after a man who was after all not likely to be thinking of her—she got herself up, and walked the stiffness from her limbs and set herself off to find a village or some place where she would be fed.

And as she went she was muttering: A song. What I want to find is—a song. There must be one. Songs and tales, yes, they tell. They talk. They sing. Instruct . . .

Oh, if only she had her Yori to . . .

I shall ride my heart thundering across the plains, she was muttering. Yes. My heart shall ride thundering . . . yes. That's it. My heart . . .

When she came to a village, and asked if there was an inn, expecting to be invited into the house whose gate she stood at, as Al·Ith, she was not known, but taken as a mendicant—a shocking and untoward thing, for this country does not understand the extremely poor. She was given a loaf of stale bread and it was suggested that if she wanted work, there was a place in the manufactory where stones were set and polished. Or in the storehouses where fruits and nuts were prepared and were kept through the winter. Or she could work, if she felt up to it—for the woman was giving this thin and ill-clothed beggar at her gate doubtful glances as she considered her in the light of a field worker—if she felt strong enough, she could find work with the horses or the cows.

And so it was that Al·Ith came to work with the beasts of this village, caring for them, feeding them, exercising them along the lanes and the fields.

What she was waiting for—and not with any hopefulness or pleasure—was the summons to return to Zone Four. For it was six months since she had left it.

She knew that in some way or another she would be told, instructed, and there was no need for her to do anything but wait, alertly, and on her guard.

And now we must go back half a year to the moment when Ben Ata found himself alone in the pavailions of his love with Al·Ith, she having ridden off without looking back—and yet with the tears streaming down her face.

He was not alone, as she was, for he had Dabeeb there, and he had his little son.

Dabeeb did bring in the baby to him, and Ben Ata laid him on the couch, and played with him for a little, even quite consciously trying to copy, if not able to feel, the relish and knowledgeableness he had seen in Al·Ith with the child. But all he could feel was pity, a need to protect and guard. But luckily here was Dabeeb, who was really a kind of mother. Arusi was not going to be deprived, not really . . . so Ben Ata's thoughts went, while he held a small foot in his great palm, feeling it tug and pull in efforts towards freedom and self-definition. He bent to look into the baby's face, into the eyes which, Al·Ith had said, were "Zone Three eyes." It was true they were Al·Ith's eyes that looked back at him from the baby's small face, but they did not have Al·Ith's soul in them . . . and as he thought this, Ben Ata was struck through and through with a cold longing. Bereaved in every part of him, in every cell, he knew that half of himself had been torn away with Al·Ith. And that what he had to do now was something he had no heart for, no, nor ability for either.

What did it mean, to marry the woman ruler of Zone Five—that barbarous and backward place? What was he supposed to do? How was he to locate her? Would she simply arrive here? Or would he have to send soldiers again to escort an unwilling and angry woman to share his life. His bed, at least. As if the struggle to adjust to the great queen of Zone Three had not been enough! Why, it had practically done for him, that struggle! And just as he and Al·Ith had seemed to reach some plateau or plane of balance, in an understanding that was neither his savagery with her, for now he recognised it had been that, nor her awful and avid need of him—for he was quite simply unable to recognise that use of him (so he saw it) with decency, order, and proper feeling—no sooner had everything come into balance between them, all based on the lovemaking that was a marvel of lightness, gaiety, wit, and fire, than she was off. Gone.

It seemed to Ben Ata now that what he wanted, what he wanted now and for ever, was simply to sit by Al·Ith, and to hold her face between his palms, and to look into eyes which held in them everything he could possibly want to learn . . . eyes that had taught him everything, not these baby eyes looking at him so happily and so emptily.

Dabeeb, hovering as usual to catch what was needed from her, came and lifted the baby away. Her look at him was sober and comradely, and told him that he could rely on her absolutely.

For she loved him, Dabeeb did. He knew it. In a sense, she was his wife.

Was she Jarnti's wife as well? Did he and his great general then share a wife? Such thoughts would not have been possible to him before the advent of Al·Ith. He would not have sat, empty-handed, for hours, on the edge of a rumpled couch that smelled tantalisingly with the skin and the flesh of the lost Al·Ith, wondering what a wife was, a husband was . . . *what did it mean?* What made the difference between him when he was a young soldier, barbarous with casual lusts—so he described himself now—grabbing some poor girl and having her and then never thinking of her again, and *being married*, as he had been with Al·Ith? And as he was with Jarnti's wife, Dabeeb, who loved him and who was now guarding and loving his child, just as, of course, she did with her own children—Jarnti's. What did it mean that he should *marry Zone Five?* There was something in all this that was a mystery, too much, his brain did not take it in. Where was Al·Ith, of whom he could ask the question, and then she would laugh and scorn him, and then explain, or if not in words then with her eyes and her flesh?

Oh, Ben Ata was low and lost and empty, he bent his great handsome soldier's head, and he grieved and he sorrowed, and when

Dabeeb had put the baby to sleep and had fetched food from the camp kitchens, she set it before him and stood by his chair, hands folded, and he was ashamed to weep in front of her.

"But what am I to do, Dabeeb?" he asked her, and she replied, "They"—meaning the Providers—"showed you with Al·Ith, and they will this time. Wait, and watch."

She stayed with the baby, that night in Al·Ith's quarters, while he paced and grieved, and so it went on, for several days. In his mind he was with his wife, wondering how she was finding her own land—and thinking, too, of her "men" and her "husbands" who doubtless would be claiming her again. And yet he did not make approaches to Dabeeb. The three of them remained quietly in the pavilion, waiting. For instructions. Which did not come.

But the impetus of already unfolding events carried him forward, for a message came from Jarnti that the war on the frontiers with Zone Five needed him.

Since he didn't seem to be good for anything else, so he was muttering, Ben Ata strapped on all his soldier's gear, and he rode off to the frontiers.

His heart was not in it at all. All the way he was looking at the poor villages and sullen towns and wondering how to change things for the better.

When he arrived where the army was camped all along the frontier, he reviewed some troops, as he supposed he had to, and then retired to his tent. It was a fine tent, of a dazzling white, embroidered with gold; it had two rooms in it, one a bedroom; and in the living part of it were his working table, a good strong chair, which had been with him on a thousand campaigns, and a chest for his accoutrements. There were no guards on the door: Ben Ata prided himself that he did not need them.

Late at night, he wrapped himself in a black cloak that everyone knew as the king's garment—he even joked with Jarnti that when they saluted, it was the cloak they paid homage to, not him—and he went wandering by himself through the camp. The tents of his soldiers seemed to stretch endlessly: they covered a long high ridge that overlooked the frontiers with the enemy Zone. Sentry after sentry stiffened and peered, and then, recognising the king, presented arms and remained motionless, watching him pass. There was no end to this camp . . . how many men lay sleeping here, ready for the battle which, presumably, though Ben Ata could not remember why, was going to take place tomorrow.

What was this particular war about? Oh, yes, of course, there was the disputed territory, which stretched from this ridge here, to that ridge there, on which he could see a sort of dark clustering and thickening like flies. The soldiers of Zone Five did not lie snugly in tents, but wrapped themselves in their cloaks—which were of animal skins. They were not supplied with proper soldierly meals, from the mess tents: they carried with them pouches of dried fruits, and dried meats. Ben Ata found himself envying the leaders who did not have to think of supply waggons and mess tents and all the palaver and annoyance of striking camp and dismantling it, and the lines of soldiers with their mess tins three times a day . . . but that was nonsense, the armies of Zone Five were barbarians, it was no army at all, and there were even women fighting with the men, and sometimes they were worse than the men . . .

So Ben Ata, strolling among the innumerable tents in a soft half-moonlight, a sombre figure . . . and sombre-minded he was, reviewing all the thoughts he ever had had about Zone Five, so that he could make up some picture of this woman he was supposed to marry.

Meanwhile, the sheer weight and mass and presence of those thousands of tents was subduing him . . . yes, he had often done this before, the midnight stroll among his soldiers, but he had not recently . . . he was thinking of the men there. And of various conversations he had with Al·Ith. And, too, with Dabeeb.

"There is no need to send an embassy to our country. It isn't that you don't have all the arts and crafts in Zone Four—but you don't practice them. You don't develop them. How can you when all your men from eighteen to sixty are away playing war?" Al·Ith, of course.

"But Ben Ata, can't you see? In the villages and towns there are no men. There are old men and women and the sick and the children. The boys are brought up by women. Then when they are ten or eleven they are put into the boys' companies, and turn against their mothers and sisters. Surely you can see that, Ben Ata? Boys have to turn against women when they have known nothing but women, in order to become men at all—there is too much of women in them . . .

to be brought up by women is to bring up a nation of soldiers. Men without softness for women, only contempt for them, and hardness." That was Dabeeb.

"But, Ben Ata, of course your country is rich. It has everything ours has—certainly as much water! But wealth isn't wealth until it has been through the hands of people."

"Well, obviously, Al·Ith."

"Not *obviously* at all, Ben Ata. Because you don't practice it. Your women can't do everything while your men play games. And so your wealth stays in the earth and the rocks and in the thoughts of the people, who know perfectly well how things should be. Why don't you ask them? A man who can cut a strip of leather for a helmet's chin strap from a badly cured hide is already one who can make a saddle—if you insist on using saddles—that will last a hundred years or more. A woman who brews some rough beer for the camp feasts has it in her hands and her instincts how to make fine wines and liqueurs. Yes, it is true, Ben Ata—in your realm it is all potential."

"And in yours it is all ease and comfort and *fat nothing*"—so that quarrel had gone.

Suppose he sent home—let's say—half these men? All over his poor meagre land would flow strength, locked up now in the armies. Strength would flow into the arts and crafts of Zone Four. Roofs would be mended, ditches dug, fields properly ploughed. Harvests would fill barns and women would make preserves and pickles . . . and there would no longer be pinched unhappy faces to see when he rode through his country. Yes, tomorrow he would discuss with Jarnti how it should be done . . . not that he could expect that great general who had been a soldier since he was six years old, to agree with him. No, it would have to be wrapped up, in some way. Presented. Made to look as if dismissing half the army's soldiers would in some way and in the long run benefit the army . . . so Ben Ata was thinking as he strode back to his tent that glimmered there so beautifully on a slight eminence.

He strode in, dashed water over himself, and sat wrapped in his cloak, legs stretched out in front of him. Thinking. He was thinking of Al·Ith. It seemed to him now that he had had offered to him a treasury of thoughts and experience he could have used, availed himself of—but he had let the opportunity go past. How much she knew! How much she had taught him—and now it was all gone. For his heart told him most finally that when she returned for her six-monthly sojourns their relations would not be at all the same. No, of course not. He had been forced to marry Al·Ith, and had hated it, and had come to love her, and now could not do without her—oh, he was not grumbling, one did not complain or grumble at the ordinances of the Providers who of course knew best—but when he had married this other woman, presumably it would all happen again in some way or another. So he could not expect, not ever again, Al·Ith to come cantering up the hill along the road from the mountains, so that the two of them could live their marriage in the pavilion. All that was over.

Would he have two women in the pavilion, two wives? He could not imagine that. Al·Ith was not Dabeeb, born to adapt and present herself for every new need and occasion. And there was this savage woman, this queen . . . there had been no word at all from *them* as to how he was to go about the new marriage.

It occurred to him that what Dabeeb had said, when announcing the message from the unknown small boy was: Al·Ith was to spend half of every year with her son. Up to this very moment, he had believed this would mean that Al·Ith would return to his Zone, here. And he knew that that was how Al·Ith had seen it. Yet perhaps that was not what had been meant at all? At the thought that *his* son was to be taken away from him to spend six months in Zone Three, he was struck and ravaged by a violent jealousy, a *no* that possessed him entirely . . . but one did not say *no* to such ukases.

The thought came to him that this was a way to enable Arusi to learn all the airs and graces of Zone Three, and thus equip him to teach Zone Four what it could. . . . Ben Ata was sitting there, all fierce black concentration, wrestling with his thoughts new and old, when the tent flat was pulled back, and a couple of soldiers who had been on a raiding party thrust into the tent a young woman who was panting, scratching, and as vicious as a wild cat that had its paws tied together.

The soldiers were grinning, as was obligatory. They stood with arms folded just inside the tent flap, waiting for him to be pleased with them. He put a smile on his face, thanked them, added some of the necessary winks, leers, and knowing looks, and tossed them some coins he had in his robe's pockets for just such occasions.

The young woman had fallen on the floor of the tent and was unable to right herself. The soldiers went. He thought, first of all, that she must be uncomfortable, if not in pain. He was about to throw her skins to lie on, and even to cut her bonds, when he realised that this was an occasion of moral crisis. It was his right to rape this girl. Worse, it was his duty. Whether he wanted to or not. He had never not wanted to before—or rather, he had not thought about it. Now he *was* thinking about it, remembering drearily how these girls of Zone Five were always so dusty and gritty to the touch. And he thought, too, of Al·Ith, of Dabeeb, and the woman of the night his son was born.

Lust was in fact flickering and licking its lips—but not very much.

He realised the girl was not struggling.

He glanced quickly at her, and away. She was a splendid girl, tall, large, with masses of bright yellow hair bound back from her face. Her eyes were the fierce bright grey of Zone Five women. She had strong long limbs. She wore trousers of rough skin, and a tight jacket of fur.

While he postponed a direct gaze at her, she looked at him calmly with her unafraid eyes, and waited.

The idea of raping this wild creature, who reminded him of a hunting hawk, quite revolted him, whether his soldier's honour was involved or not. On the other hand he had to do something. If he loosened her bonds she would run away and that would make him a figure of fun throughout the army. He looked covertly, for fear of being observed to show weakness, to see if her bonds were too tight. They did not seem to be cutting into her wrists or ankles.

As he was not sure what to do, he went on sitting there, wrapped in his black garment, staring straight out of the tent flap, which the soldiers had forgotten to fasten, into a very dark night. A soft scented breeze flowed into the tent and stirred—though he was not looking at her directly—the girl's flowing hair.

He was again thinking of Al·Ith, who had taken his old heart out of his body, and who had not given him anything in its place. How was he going to live, a half-man, not a soldier, not a man of peace, not a husband since he was bereft of her, not properly even a father, since it seemed there was at least a possibility of his losing his son to Zone Three for half of every year . . . these messages from the Providers . . . it was not that they were ambiguous, but that you had to wait for events to interpret them.

Who was he? What was he going to do?

It occurred to him that this was how poor Al·Ith had been made to think and suffer as she sat in her palace waiting for his soldiers to come and bring her down by force, to him. She had known that her life, her ways of thinking, her rights, her habits—everything—were about to be torn apart, destroyed, re-framed and re-assembled by some barbarian, and there was nothing she had been able to do about it.

And there was nothing he, Ben Ata, could do about it.

Al·Ith had been savaged—yes, he was quite willing and able to use the word now—by him, the barbarian, and he was now going to have to be the same with a dirty primitive queen . . . it occurred to Ben Ata that in the corner of his eye, where the girl was, he was seeing something he had not before taken in. Still only half looking at her, he turned his head slightly, and noted that on those magnificent arms were heavy gold bracelets, on the legs barbaric but beautiful gold ornaments, set with all kinds of coloured stones, on the fingers rings, of gold again and one in particular, so heavy and ornate that it could only announce some position of power or prestige, and around the girl's strong white neck hung a massive sigil or scal or symbol on a gold chain.

The truth came to him suddenly, and he said, "You are the queen of Zone Five?"

"Yes, of course," she said.

He laughed. He had not known he was going to, but it was an event so apt, coming so pat and right, so magnificently challenging and even—so he recognised in his innermost self—expected, as if nothing else could have happened, that he could only laugh. And she, in a moment, laughed with him, showing her beautiful strong teeth.

So it was that as the camp came to life all around them in the dawn, what those soldiers heard first who were near the king's tent, was Ben Ata laughing, and with him, an unknown woman, who, the word went around, was some female soldier caught in the dark of the opposite ridge and flung into the king's tent for his enjoyment.

"They are having a good time, those two," the soldiers said to each other, half admiringly, half enviously, as is the way of the underdogs. And when, shortly, it became known that it was the queen of the enemy Zone who had been captured, and that she was going to marry their king, their natural and proper disgust that there was not going to be a battle that day turned to feasting and enjoyment.

On the opposing ridges in Zone Four and Zone Five the two armies feasted and danced for a week. They visited each other's camp, made all kinds of joint forays and sorties and even raiding parties among the unfortunate local populations, for the sheer joy of it—and generally became a good deal better acquainted. For it was a remarkable fact that these two countries had been at war off and on for generations, yet they knew practically nothing about each other.

Meanwhile, what went on in the king's tent was not as the soldiers' uproarious imaginations had it.

The queen's bonds were of course immediately removed, refreshments were brought for her, and another tent, almost as fine as the king's, was set up near his.

Her attitude and manner were not that of a captive so recently ignominiously flung down like a sack full of captured fowls. Ben Ata, who was after all a soldier before anything else, knew from the start that all was not as it seemed, and before the queen had dismantled her second roast chicken she had most willingly confessed—as was her way she was laughing so hard she could hardly keep her seat on a chair which it was clear was not her most usual form of seating— that she had got herself captured because she wished to meet the king and—it was she who put it forward first—marry him.

Ben Ata learned from her that the methods and habits of his soldiers and sentries and raiding parties were such that her fighting men "knew everything they were going to do days before they did it"—that the discipline, order, martial correctness of his army provoked nothing but derision in his opponents who, in their own eyes at least, did exactly as they liked and when they liked.

"But if this was the case," he most politely enquired, "how was it that this war of theirs had not been over long ago?"

"But why should it have ended?" enquired the queen, rummaging in her chicken carcasses for titbits and licking her fingers in a way which both shocked and tantalised her bridegroom.

There followed a long and amiable discussion between these two ancient antagonists from which Ben Ata learned a good deal, though he feared she did not . . . the style, or mode, of their being together was already established, and would not change for some time.

She sat sprawling, and lounging, raising her arms to yawn and stretch, moving and swinging her legs as if the chair she sat on was a stone on a hillside, or perhaps a horse—at any rate, she was quite magnificently unable to subdue her wildness to this strictly sober military tent. She laughed continually, and with the utmost good-nature, at *him*, his ways of speaking, of thinking—but this became her.

As for him, the more she displayed—as he felt it, *flaunted*—this careless and sensual confidence of hers, the more he straightened his back, and reminded himself of duty, and self-discipline.

He was able to observe himself in this scene with an eye which he knew was Al·Ith's—or at least, was her gift to him. Certainly before knowing her he would not have been able to enjoy an inner smile at this situation.

For one thing, he already suspected that he would have done better to rape her at once, as protocol demanded: that this was what she had counted on. For he could not help believing that part of the reason for her wild and exhilarated manner was nervousness and even uncertainty. Possibly—he wouldn't be at all surprised—contempt of this man. Who, though, she surely could not consider unmanly, for she had already said that she had often watched him at the head of his troops from some hiding place on a hillside or an animal's hole, and had found him attractive.

Now there was certainly no case for flinging her down and getting it over with, a set of words which, coming to his tongue and finding themselves examined, at once dismissed themselves. Yet she was quite dazzlingly attractive. But he did not know how to behave, now that the natural order of things had been upset. And his own instincts were confused, because he was after all still married to Al·Ith, and that in itself forbade any casual or instant lovemaking with this queen.

He supposed that probably what must happen would be restraint until the marriage itself—which she had announced should take place soon, and there would be a wedding night of the formal kind. But before that, he knew he must prove himself in some way. The queen of Zone Five, he had already been informed, rewarded the victors of certain contests among her soldiers with a night in her tent, and he would be expected to do as well as any of them. And he could already see, from moments when she speculated on his possibilities both militarily and otherwise, with long cool insolent looks of which she was of course unconscious—for she had no self-consciousness at all—that she was doubting him. It was this mien of his: so tight, and orderly, "so very Zone Four," as she already was putting it.

Meanwhile they discussed military matters, each defending his and her way . . . which in fact defended itself, by the sheer fact that neither side had permanently gained from the other so much as a stone's throw of territory in all those generations of fighting.

It was becoming evident that if Zone Four had seen the war with Zone Five almost as an obligation, a necessity whose beginnings no one could remember, then Zone Five's attitude was not dissimilar.

War—of their own kind of course—was a way of life for the queen and her people. It was their means of testing themselves, preserving their honour and self-respect, their chief amusement.

Why then did she want to put an end to it?

About this she was vague, rather carelessly and obviously so, which Ben Ata found amusing, as with a would-be clever child.

It took him some days to put together a picture which satisfied him and which he felt he could rely on.

Zone Four believed Zone Five to be a place of deserts and thin scrub, where a few nomad tribes moved their tents and herds to find sparse food and water. This was because nothing but rocks and sands and scrub could be seen from their side, and they had never seen any other kind of people. But these sandy wastes were only part of the Zone. Eastward were lush pastures, farmland, villages, and even large towns—a realm that had got rich and soft and could not defend itself against Vahshi and her horsemen. This girl had not inherited her position as leader of her tribe, though she was a chieftain's daughter, but had fought for it. Under her had been consolidated a federation of tribes who called her queen. The war with Zone Four had continued, as always, but she had seen very quickly that it was foolish to waste resources there: to plunder the farmlands was obviously more sensible. And then, with the farming country brought under and owing allegiance, her bands of ragged men who could live for weeks off the milk of their mares and a few handfuls of dried provisions, terrorised the towns. She had called representatives of every part of Zone Five together in a great palaver or assembly and had had herself crowned queen before them all.

Why should she bother with Zone Four? She looked forward to a reign of plenty, exacting tribute from those maggots of townsmen, and capturing what she needed or had a whim to take.

And where did her marriage with Ben Ata fit into this plan of hers?

Her magnificent grey eyes slid a little, her face put on a look of frank confession, she smiled invitation and seduction . . . but Ben Ata saw at once that the marriage had no importance for her, except as it could secure her frontier and leave her free.

In the late evenings, when he dismissed her—politely of course—to her tent, he braved her glances of laughing scorn with a self-command he knew would make the subject of all kinds of jests and camp songs when she went back to her own people to arrange the wedding feast.

Then he lay awake in the dark, arms behind his head, thinking. Of this savage girl, with whom he promised himself all kinds of pleasures, the more satisfactory because she would not be expecting them.

Of Al·Ith, whose thoughts seemed to be flowing there around and near him . . . and there was more than a little anger in him. He knew that he was for ever caught up and bound, if not to her, then to her realm, her ways—so that he could never again act without thinking, or be without reflection on his condition. And he did not regret it, not that, yet even now there was a part of him that said she had put a spell on him—and that she must be exulting, knowing his new queen was at this moment laughing at him in her tent.

He could no longer be as he had been, the Ben Ata who had never doubted what he should do; nor could he yet react from any higher or better centre or state. He was in between, and horribly uncertain.

From thinking of Al·Ith, and her unfair and sly enchantments, he thought of the Providers, and for the first time in the way of trying to put himself into their minds . . . yes, he knew it was foolish and probably even punishable. But he could not stop himself. He believed he was beginning to see the outline of their plans for Zone Five, if not for Zone Three—which was quite beyond him. And he was thinking that "if he were in their place" he certainly wouldn't let those desert savages ravage and raid and plunder. Vahshi's gold ornaments, for instance, all had been stolen from the workshops of the cities. The grey furs which set off her blond beauty so well were not the workmanship of her people, but from the markets she thieved from. All the women of the tribes now swaggered about in gold and precious stones and even the horses wore gold chains and the dogs gold collars. Every group of tents had store tents heaped with silks and fine cottons and robes that the women wore for feasts, though not in their ordinary tent lives, and there were festivals every time there was a raid. The lives of the tent people were now not hard and meagre and self-sufficing, but full of indulgence. Ben Ata had said to the queen that it would not be long before the tribes were as soft and rotten as the people they despised, but those eyes had slid away, in that way of hers, and her smile had been uncertain for only a moment before she had flung back her head and challenged him with: But how, soft?—you'll see how soft we are!

And it was not long before the wedding feast, when he did see.

The black tents covered what seemed to be miles of the desert, but they were in groups rather apart from each other—solitariness and separation being the ground of their natures, as desert people. There were herds of horses thousands strong. There were platters containing whole sheep or calves, even two or three at a time. It seemed as if the whole valley was one vast offering of food, and Ben Ata and his attendant soldiers were given a reception they could have been undone by. For during the days while the queen had withdrawn to prepare her people for this marriage—and of course Ben Ata knew that the picture they were being given was not at all the same as his—he had been preparing himself for the moment when he would have to outdo her champions. He was a fine horseman, but it was a long time since he had proved this to himself or anyone else. Once no man in his armies could have outwrestled or outfought him—but that was not recently. The finest and most cunning wrestlers and horsemen were called from every part of Zone Four, and Ben Ata put himself in their hands, and between them all he was restored to his youthful skills and strengths.

Ben Ata had little doubt that he could defeat her champions wrestling—and so it turned out. On an open place outside the swarming black tents, surrounded by watching women and children and the horsemen who were headed by the queen, Ben Ata wrestled with, and threw down, one after another, a dozen men who were as wily, tough, and lean as any he had seen.

The queen had not expected this, and—as usual unable to control her facial expressions, or the attitudes of her limbs and body—sulked quite obviously while commending him.

She was hoping, he could see, that he would be outdone in the horsemen's race, which meant every man on the tribe starting at a certain point, and going on until either he was obviously outridden, or he had won. The only condition of this race was that no horse should be ridden to its death or to permanent weakness. Ben Ata's horse was the best in his kingdom—he had no doubts on that score. But as he sat waiting for the signal to be given (a certain wild ululating cry from the women) he was examining the contestants and could not prevent self-doubt. Some of them were like whips or like snakes for leanness and litheness, and all had been put on horses before they could walk. Ben Ata shared the queen's obvious expectation that he would be defeated, but in his mind he was holding on to a single thought, which was that the Providers—the way he saw it—must want him to win, and if this was the case, he would. And he did. It was a very long, wearying race, over many miles of desert, in a hot dusty late afternoon, the sun on his left hand, and it seemed to him that it was not his own will that carried him, but a high nervous energy that was being fed steadily into him. One after another he left behind the desert riders, and rode back alone into the place on the sands from where he had started off.

The queen was not sulky now, but thoughtful, and even seemed ready to be submissive. Everything in her heredity bade her honour this man—now her husband by right of victory—while her calculation was reinforcing her instincts.

She had not for one moment expected anything but defeat for him, and while this would not have prevented the marriage which was necessary for her plans for her people, she would have made her gift of herself to him an act of contempt.

As the custom was, the two were accompanied to their wedding tent by bands of ululating women, and riders who raced their horses around the tent, and who jumped over it until the queen raised her voice from inside in a great yell of dismissal—part of the ritual, and was to inform her people that this man was what she had expected.

As a matter of actual fact, Ben Ata, still insisting on his own earned rights—as he felt it, his experience with Al·Ith had earned him certain superiorities—had indicated to his bride that until these savages of hers had gone away, he had no intention of doing anything at all, and he was seated at ease on a vast pile of rugs, boring her to the point of hysteria with a blow-by-blow account of the race he had just won.

When he at last was prepared to fulfil her expectations, he found things to be as he had had no doubt they would be: she had as little finesse in her as he when first he loved Al·Ith. To begin with she found him quite inexplicably devious, and then saw that she had in fact no need to despise Zone Four.

And so these two were married, and the festivities and feasting and racing and wrestling went on for a month. Babies were conceived by the tentful, and Queen Vahshi announced that she, too, was pregnant, and the child would be an earnest of the eternal alliance with Zone Four. This was partly to soothe her new husband, also to hasten him back to his own home, for she could not wait to get back to the enjoyable business of draining the fat lands of Zone Five of their wealth.

But Ben Ata did not seem in any hurry at all to leave.

Far from being a token king, in a marriage for strategy's sake, he showed every sign of wishing to influence policy. This was not at all what she had planned for. The way she saw it, he wished to make the lives of her people as dull and as ordered as those of his own. He did not approve of her warlike ways, he refused to support her in her plans for perpetual plunder, and he warned her day and night that if she did not change course, she would be the ruler very soon over an army of degenerates who lived only for their bellies. . . .

And—yes—while he argued thus with his new queen, Ben Ata was fully conscious of the ironies of his position. For with half his mind he was busy with plans for making sure his own people would be much more preoccupied with improving their lives than ever they had been. Three-quarters of his army had been sent home "on indefinite leave"—with instructions to raise the level of their villages and towns. Jarnti sulked, then even pleaded and begged—he could not understand it, he, too, was convinced that the foreign witch from the high lands had put a spell on his king. And of course he saw through that "indefinite leave." Armies were not maintained in condition in this way . . . he suspected Ben Ata of losing any interest in the martial glories of Zone Four. He suspected a good deal—but his mind, immersed in war all his life, could not follow Ben Ata's. He was reduced to trying to find out from Dabeeb, and everything she said only confirmed his fears.

There was more than one irony in the mind of Ben Ata.

Zone Four, once returned to peace and plenty, was to be no less policed and orderly, he was determined on that. No anarchy! No relaxation of the disciplines which Ben Ata respected from the bottom of his heart.

Yet he was exhorting Vahshi not to abandon all wild and desert ways entirely but only to stop thieving and grabbing from others. But if she were to return to the traditional life of her people, this meant —to Ben Ata's way of thinking—an ordered anarchy. Each tribe, or even group of aligned tribes, owed to the members of it a fanatical and fantastic loyalty, even to death. A man claiming protection from a fellow tribesman might ask for that man's life, if necessary, and was bound for always to return the same if asked. There was an absolute honour, trust, giving, between members of these tribes and groups— but between groups, tribes, no limits to deception, treachery, guile, dishonour. The tribes preyed on each other's herds and flocks, stole each other's women, whom they nevertheless thereafter treated as well as they did their own: and these were free, proud women, with rights and privileges. They slit each other's throats for the matter of a stolen sheep, or slaughtered men lying asleep in the sand wrapped in their ragged cloaks for the sake of the water they carried. This was the state of affairs which Ben Ata was recommending to his consort as one preferable to the new one, which had armies of fighters joyously rampaging from one end of Zone Five to the other, taking everything they could find.

It was only relative, Ben Ata comforted himself, unable quite to believe in this new role of his. And continued amazed as he returned again and again to the same argument: that the *healthy* desert way of life was doomed unless the tribes were kept to frugality, hard living, hard riding, discomfort.

There were moments when he longed for Al·Ith to share astonishment with him—share, surely, amusement? How had he got into this position? Was he doing as he ought, as he had been expected to? What were the Providers thinking of him—were they pleased with him?

Ben Ata would sit, while Vahshi was out ordering her realm, alone among the sand dunes, or in his tent, thinking. Had he gone wrong somewhere? Yet everything had seemed to happen as if following some invisible but powerful plan. Was there something more expected of him that he had not seen? For he was prepared to believe that he was being blind to evident and obvious potentialities. So he brooded, so he pondered, while Vahshi, catching him at it, might in her turn sit quietly and allow the beginnings of thought to live in her mind. She had never imagined before Ben Ata that one could respect a man like this one, and yet she did: he was beyond her, she could acknowledge that, even if only secretly and to herself.

His cautions about the degeneration of her people, yes, he was right in the fact, if not in the reasons for it. She could see it herself: there was a slackness and a loosening among them and she did not like it.

She was thinking that when he went back to his own land, she would miss his counsels. He was stolid. He was slow. But he was not stupid. They were a balance for each other, yes, that was it. Well, perhaps she would visit him—after all, there was this child coming. They had no doubt at all it would be a girl: she because the strength of her wild femaleness could only give birth to itself, he because he felt the same fitness and appropriateness as when he and Al·Ith expected a son. He had told her this girl child would be as much queen of Zone Four as of Zone Five, but in partnership with an already born son—about whom he was somewhat vague. Vagueness was not his style, and so here she suspected him. If there was treachery then it was to do with raids and looting—so her mind could not help but work; and visions of herself as mother of a ruler of that profitable Zone to the west mingled with those of plunder. Besides, she had been informed by her tribes along the frontier that Ben Ata's garrisons were still there from one end to the other, and this made her wonder if he had some means of seeing into people's minds, for she had been considering how she might contrive raids into Zone Four— only sometimes, of course, not often, and more in the way of reminding herself of alas forbidden pleasures. She had intended to make amends by saying that the frontier people had been raiding there so long they could not be expected to change overnight.

Ben Ata left her suddenly. He woke one morning from a dream of the pavilion and the drum beating. Propped up on his elbow beside her, gazing out of the tent door where nothing could be seen but blowing sands made yellow by a dusty sun, the drum still sounded in his ears—and through his whole body, in a pulse of grief and loss. He leapt up, embraced her, summoned his soldiers, and was off before she had properly understood he was going.

And when he had left she sat alone in her tent for many days, admitting thoughts that were not dissimilar to his when Al·Ith had been ordered away from him. There was nothing in this marriage that she had wanted, or expected—she certainly could not say she had enjoyed it, for there had been too much uncomfortable newness in it for that. And yet everything in her was changed, and she felt set apart from the life of her people, and responsible in a way she did not understand. For what she did, the choices she made, she would have to give an account—but to whom, though? Ben Ata spoke of those he called the Providers. Who were they? How did he know they existed? It made her uncomfortable to feel she was overlooked and watched, and even, so he suggested, directed. Ben Ata had told her that Zone Four was not the end of it—there was Zone Three, and one of his women had even come from there. And beyond that, too, other realms, of which he knew only the names.

Her people said, and sang, that the queen was grieving. She let them. Oh, no, she was not sorry that Ben Ata had gone. She was glad—he had been a weight, a heaviness, something she could not push away so as to be herself. She longed for one thing: that she could go back to being as she had been before that night she was thrown into the tent where the soldierly Ben Ata sat—thinking. She had not known that one could think. She did not want to! She had been perfectly content before he had introduced her to these awkward, slow, brooding ways . . .

Ben Ata rode up to the pavilion, and found his son with his nurses, supervised by Dabeeb. The boy was walking. Ben Ata's immediate thought was that he would like to put the child in front of him on a horse and then ride up and down before his armies—but there were no armies to speak of.

Dabeeb seemed to have everything well in hand. Jarnti was busy with keeping up the hearts of the remaining troops.

Ben Ata thought that he would go on an inspection of his kingdom to watch life and strength flowing into it, with the return of the men.

But meanwhile he found himself with his son, in the garden among the fountains. He sat with the child on the raised white marble plinth and lifted his face so that he could see the mountains of Al·Ith his mother, and he spoke to him of Zone Three and of how one day he would go there, and learn all its ways.

Through a window Dabeeb was watching, and in no time all of Zone Four knew that the king was teaching his son to look upwards. The punishments for people who watched the snows ceased, and everywhere they openly gazed up at the forbidden realm that was out of their reach no longer. And the women's ceremonies were wild and victorious, and for the first time men joined them. This new spirit flowing through and around the Zone gladdened Ben Ata, and made the child confident and strong. But he was waiting for the drum he had heard in his dreams, and it remained silent.

Ben Ata began talking of a visit to Zone Three, with his son, to visit Al·Ith. But this was not what had been ordered—as the silences of Dabeeb reminded him. Was it then that he, Ben Ata, was forbidden Zone Three? And yet it seemed that his son would visit there. . . .

He observed that Dabeeb and a band of women were making preparations for a journey, and he knew before he asked where they were going. He, the king, who would not long ago have had the lot of them in prison, or with punishment helmets on their heads, heard that the women were going to visit his wife, in her own country, and they were going to take Arusi.

And how did they know that this was what was needed and intended? he demanded of Dabeeb.

She replied that it seemed to all of them—meaning the women—that it was their place and their right to go, since it was they who had kept the old knowledge alive for so long.

But had they been told? Ordered? Been sent a messenger?

At this, Dabeeb bridled, with an air of being in the right, and right in a way he ought not to challenge. His inner purposes having been so thoroughly overthrown and re-directed, he did not stand against her.

The child was two years old when he left with the women. Their send-off from the watery plains that had once been the scene of such military proficiency was an occasion, though not an official one. Mixed crowds shouted and sang the women's songs that had now become adapted everywhere for general use, and showed how proud they were of these gratified women who seemed to express even in their appearance the new Zone Four, where so much was changing.

There were twenty women, mostly in their early middle years. They wore dresses they had copied from Al·Ith's, for her stay with them had inspired new materials, new and subtle colours, and ways of fit and cut never even imagined before. They wore their hair flowing loose, in proud and self-conscious defiance, looking their not entirely happy men firmly in the eyes, and laughing from the strength of their being together. And they were all on horses that they refused to saddle or bridle. Skilled as Al·Ith was they were not, and their handling of the beasts earned doubting comment as they rode off, but they did well enough. Such was their confidence in their welcome by Zone Three that at first they refused to take shields, or even protective brooches and clasps, but when they began the climb up to the frontier Dabeeb had to set up her shield in front of her, and the others followed suit.

They were a handsome, strong, good-looking company, with the little child there in front of Dabeeb, and there were other small children there, too, for the women claimed that these "should take the opportunity of learning the new ways."

They passed up into the high sparkling airs of Zone Three without feeling other than exhilarated, and crossed the great plain before nightfall and the start of the punishing wind.

Halfway up the pass to the plateau they stopped at a large inn, and asked for hospitality, in the name of Al·Ith. People pressed out to look at them, and stood about watching as they were admitted, and their horses led away.

They had been sure of an especial reception because of Al·Ith, but they saw that it was not because of this name—which in fact seemed not to impress their hosts—but because it was the way of this realm to give hospitality to strangers, that they were treated with such courtesy.

It seemed to them, though, a cold, or at least indifferent politeness.

They were set around a very long broad table in the main room, and were served attentively, while the ordinary users of the place watched them, though not impolitely, from where they sat separate. The women began to talk and laugh rather too loudly, and to shake their hair back, and make a great thing of their liking for each other, while their inner confidence ebbed. What had they been expecting? Of course, to be welcomed *home*. From an exile. That is how they had been feeling all these long months of preparation. But it was easy to come to terms with this in themselves, and to say: Wait, when we actually see Al·Ith it will be different—what was really undermining them was their understanding of what rough figures they cut here. The best, the finest, the most daring of their land were clumsy here. Well, that they could suffer and withstand, for after all it is what they had been doing for generations, knowing always that they were cut off from the best and from their own potentiality.

Their surroundings afflicted them, made them begin to realize their deprivation.

Of course, in their own land were inns and hotels of various kinds. And some did not look, at first glance, so very different from this one. It was when they were at ease, sitting, able to look and touch, that they began to see.

There was no inn with them that did not have a large main room, a fire of some kind, seats, or tables . . . ah, but what a difference . . . yet, had they entered *this* room, there, they would not, not at once, have noticed—what? Detail. It was the variety, the loving inventiveness of everything.

The fireplace's great mantel was carved cunningly, and amusingly, too—there alone was enough to keep them absorbed for half an evening. There were not merely benches, but chairs, and forms and settles, and stools, and the chairs had cushions and they were embroidered and the embroideries, like the mantelpiece, were as good as an evening full of stories and songs. The plates they were served on were china, which they hardly knew existed, and these were beautiful in an unfamiliar way. There was no end to it all—and this without the foodstuffs, which every one of these skilled housewives knew to be far above anything that even the king was served.

This, then, was peace. A realm at peace. They had all been impressed and encouraged by the changes going on at home—roofs thatched properly at last, houses rebuilding of stone or good brick, fields tilled that had been growing rushes and frogs, or stones and weeds—this, they had been telling themselves, was what peace meant.

They were put, in twos and threes, in great bedrooms where none of them slept at all because of the excitement of examining quilts and pillows and rugs and even the beds themselves, whose elegance and solidity they had not been able to imagine. They were running from room to room across the landings, no less excited than the children with them, and exclaiming, and trying to make sure that what they saw would stay in their minds, until the innkeeper came and most politely asked them to let the other guests sleep.

In the morning, after a breakfast they were not used to, and did not know that people needed, they all went to the stables, expecting to be astonished. And came out soberly, sighing and whispering to each other that many of Zone Four's citizens would be better for living as those horses did.

And very soberly did they ride onwards under the towering snows that seemed, now they were so close, to mock them because of their distance—but were distant in another way. They rode quietly past the people they met, waiting to be greeted, and all the elation and excitement had gone from them. They were moving on slowly, too, because they wanted to see everything they could, and stopped at midday in a little town on the verge of a stony upland where beasts were grazing, since the soil was not being used for agriculture. The animals were well covered, and strong, and none of them had ever been overworked.

The town was made of stone, and built high of tall houses, some of them ten or twelve stories. But they were not regular or uniform, but spread themselves about, with many corners and stretches of roof on which people could be seen sitting and passing the time and looking out over the high lands to the mountains. Squares and oblongs and circles all over the surfaces of the buildings glittered and reflected the sky and even clouds and passing birds—like water caught up and spread and held there . . . they had marvelled at glass the night before in the other inn—not the fact of it, for there was glass in their own land, but they had not imagined its use like this, to make windows whose setting and proportions gave pleasure, or to make a whole town seem as if sky had been woven and knitted into walls or water was spread over the sides or roofs of towers . . . they were standing in the leafy little central square gazing up open-mouthed . . . they were yokels and knew it. Again they made their way to an inn. It was different from last night's, so much so they would not have known it as one. Covered terraces surrounded a great central room which itself was open, but able to be closed with sheets of glass. People were sitting out at tables arranged on the different levels of these terraces, and eating and drinking at their leisure, and children played around them. The snowy peaks above them were reflected in the glass, as if mountains, snows, and windy skies were part of their own substance. This so ordinary scene, of people at ease, was nevertheless punishing their poor overwhelmed hearts. Taken detail by detail there was nothing in it so remarkable: a man telling a small child how to sit well at the table, a woman smiling at a man—her husband? If a husband, certainly not like one from Zone Four!—but looked at as a whole, it all seemed suffused with a clear fine pale light that spoke to them of the longing that is the inner substance of certain dreams: it was the knowledge of a bitter exile.

They told themselves that they were looking at—pleasure. This is what they saw. Well-being without purpose or pressure or reproof. But the word pleasure had to be dismissed. Dabeeb said to them that Al·Ith had had this air of ease, at least when she first came to them: this is what had struck her, Dabeeb, at first and immediately: Al·Ith's largeness and freedom of being. But that had not been pleasure, had not been, even, delight: though what Dabeeb had taken back to her own bare little house from that first meeting with Al·Ith had been an awed, even triumphant, conviction that happiness was possible. But Al·Ith's strengths had stemmed from something—*somewhere* —else . . .

What they were looking at, the inwardness of this scene, was not pleasure or happiness, words which—no matter how far they had seemed from them down in Zone Four—now seemed paltry and even contemptible qualities—but something they could not begin to understand.

They were most powerfully and bitterly crushed down. The gap between this and what Zone Four could even hope for was— hundreds of years. Was—time, but time that beat a higher, finer measure. Oh, yes, Zone Four could build tall houses like these, and even lace their sides with glass, if they were shown how. They could learn to make the dishes on their tables speak through designs and patterns that were like a new language. They could clothe their servants in garments that had these languages of pattern woven into them. But as for the real differences, they would have to learn to feed from this other dimension that they had only just begun to think of. For one thing: the easy and casual ways of these serving people here, equals and partners—how long would it take Zone Four to learn this absolute equality, individual to individual, when divisions and classes and rank and respect for these—*servility*—had been stamped so long into its deepest substance? Even this partial aspect of Zone Three seemed impossibly distant, so that a smiling enquiry from the girl who asked if they would care for this dish or that, seemed to be emanating from a realm far above them.

They left this inn, or, rather, were driven away from it by their own feelings, and rode on and away from the town of lovely glowing stone that had sky and water and snow and light and mountains as part of its fabric, turning their heads continually and lifting up Arusi and the other children so that they would see everything and be impressed and remember—and be the first individuals from Zone Four to have in their inner selves the knowledges of Zone Three.

And at evening they rode into Andaroun, and, having again asked their way, into the small square with its trees and gardens. And stood together on the broad white steps of the palace, asking for Al·Ith.

At the name they were given curious but not unfriendly glances.

After a long wait a young woman came slowly down towards them.

Dabeeb at least knew at once that this was the sister Al·Ith had spoken of, because she was Al·Ith, fair-haired and white-skinned.

Dabeeb repressed an impulse—because of this marvellously beautiful palace, its airy heights and breadths, its balconies and colonnades, its delicate bright colours—to go on her knees, or supplicate: my lady! For she knew that these were not the ways of this place.

When she used the name Al·Ith, Murti· nodded and said simply, "But she is not here."

This, it was evident to the women, was a final statement: meaning that they were not going to be given what they had expected.

"This is her child," said Dabeeb, holding out the boy.

Murti· took Arusi, held him a little, in a way which said that her arms were seldom without a child in them, and said, "My sister is not here."

"Is she not queen here now?"

"You don't understand, I think," was the reply. "I do her work for her now, if that is what you are asking. You will find her there . . ." and Murti· pointed away to the northwest.

It seemed that that was all she meant to say.

But, just as they turned to go, she asked, "Why are you here?"

And now they were clumsy, and flushed, and were ashamed, because they had been asking that themselves. Murti· was enquiring, as Ben Ata had, if they were here by right.

"You must ask my sister what to do," said Murti·, and with that she handed back the child to Dabeeb, and ran back up the steps into the palace.

The women again found themselves an inn. They were now low in spirits, and even full of forebodings, though no one was anything less than courteous. They were fed and housed for asking, for they had no means to repay what they were being given. And what they were thinking was that they could return home with news of what they were seeing, and even if they were believed, it would do no good, for they could do no more than explain, and say again, that if the fat and the fullness of a land were not continually poured away into war, then everything, but everything, would start to fill, and flower, and grow lovely and lavish with detail. In hands and in minds lived skills and cleverness that had only to be fed and given room . . . patience.

This building they spent the night in was one that offered gardens and plants to its guests. There was every kind of garden, and set among them were pleasant blocks of rooms. They were all put together in one, and food brought to them. This evening they did not examine bed covers and door handles, but walked through the gardens. They had believed those arranged among the fountains of Ben Ata's and Al·Ith's pavilion were grand and fine, but knew now that they were only a token or a symbol of what could be made.

And so it was for several days. They rode on quietly and observing everything, trying not to be despondent, or self-demeaning, and spent their nights in different kinds of inns, for it seemed to them as if there was no end to the varieties of pleasure and interest this place offered its travellers.

They asked for Al·Ith as they went, and sometimes were even met with blankness. As if Al·Ith had been forgotten. Though generally people replied that "it was said that she was somewhere over there."

And so they went on until they saw a range of mountains that had a gap in them, where blue mists curled.

One evening they came into a small village meaning to ride through it again, but, enquiring for Al·Ith, were told that she could be found in the stables.

And so they did. She was bringing in some horses from fields into their sheds. When she saw them she seemed surprised. But welcomed them. And took her son into her arms with an eagerness and a regret that told them everything.

But they knew now, quite certainly, that they should not be here.

For one thing, to judge events by how they went, well or ill, then that was answer enough: for here they were, with Al·Ith, and there was no place even for them to sleep, for this village was too small for an inn.

She went to the people who on behalf of everyone decided the affairs of this village, and asked if the women might sleep in the orchards, since it was still the end of summer. It was agreed that they should, and also take what fruit they needed.

Thus it came about that the twenty women, and their several little children, and Al·Ith's son, spent that night in the grasses of the orchards, under a warm sky.

It could be said that this was the first time since the women had left home that they were in surroundings that were familiar—but even that was partially true. For there was nothing in Zone Four like these old rich orchards, and even some of the fruit was new to them.

They talked of the new dispensation in Zone Four, and of Ben Ata, though tactful about what was said of the new queen, with whom after all Ben Ata had spent a long time. They described how the worst of the land's poverty was being soothed away, and how the granaries and storehouses were filling. They described how the child Arusi, now asleep on Al·Ith's lap, had grown and his various ailments and small accidents.

But it took them a long time to talk of Al·Ith herself and ask what she was doing here, an exile from her old life. This was because they knew already, and understood.

If they yearned for this land, for Zone Three, then they believed it natural for Al·Ith to long with all her heart for the higher lovelier place whose entrance they could see simply by lifting their eyes.

Strange it was to these women, to sit there among the low sweet-smelling grasses, and to gaze up, with Al·Ith, as they had done, for so long, at the wonderful peaks of Zone Three. They did not even feel ready and right yet to enter this place—which she had had her fill of, and wanted to leave. All this they knew. Though they would not know the day-by-dayness of it.

This is a scene particularly loved by our artists who embellish it with a vast yellow moon positioned so that it is close to, or behind, Al·Ith's head. Or there is a delightful crescent set off by a star or two. And they often add a large peacock, whose shimmering tail fills the orchard with reflected lights.

But it is on the whole a realistic depiction, and I am saying this because it is the last of the truthful scenes. For now there is something in the tale of Al·Ith that goes beyond popular taste. What we are dealing with here is the account of a great and loved queen who—but no, she does not turn her back on her realm. She does not repudiate it. Easier, more dramatic, if she did. But it is as if she is already living, at least with part of herself, somewhere else. And this is a bleak truth. Arid. Even insulting, since it is hard to believe that everyday warmths and satisfactions are not being despised altogether by this person who, seen from outside and by the uninstructed view, does not give much evidence of the change and growth within—any more than the growth and ferment inside a chrysallis is suspected by the ignorant. No, it is necessary, it is forgivable, in us, the songsters and the Chroniclers and the portrayers, when we soften certain facts.

For instance—her horse Yori. The *fact* is that Al·Ith did not return to Zone Four. Never again did the drum beat for her. For a long time she waited for it, expected it—or half expected it, being at the same time fearful—believed all kinds of things, such as that she had made a mistake in being here on these higher borders, had fallen away from responsibilities. But she was, after all, so she comforted herself, always ready to leave. And she still longed, with what was left of her heart, for her husband. But all these conflicting hopes and wants came to nothing at all, for what actually did happen—and much later, after certain vicissitudes—was that her son came for long visits to Zone Three. But his visits to us were really to spend time with Murti·. So did events cheat her expectations . . . or half expectations . . . or none, for she felt more and more that she was due nothing.

One of the most popular pictures of Al·Ith is of her riding down into Zone Four with the boy, aged about six, in front of her. Ben Ata, smiling and amenable, is behind and below her, so that she dominates the picture. These are heading a troop of Zone Four's children, returning after an educational visit. They are portrayed as little savages willingly tamed. The horse Al·Ith rides is Yori. No, not exactly, for the artists are careful to make small differences, in case they are challenged. It can be said that Yori never died: there are deaths that are not accepted in the imaginations of the ordinary people. And of course horses by the thousand are named after him.

Another figure that has never achieved realism is Dabeeb, who is shown most often as a singer, as if this was her profession.

In the early morning, when most of the women had fallen asleep, and Al·Ith was dozing, curled in the grasses, Dabeeb, who was too sad to sleep, was singing quietly to herself:

"I shall ride my heart thundering across the plain,
Outdistance you all and leave myself behind—

Who am I on this high proud beast
Who knows where I should ride better than I do?

Oh, I do not like to look back at myself there,
Little among the stay-at-homes, the restabeds.
No, sting my self-contents to hunger
Till up I ride my heart to the high lands
Leaving myself behind.

Teach me to love my hunger,
Send me hard winds off the sands. . . ."

"What are you singing?" said Al·Ith, sitting straight up.

"It's a new song."

"Yes, I know. I haven't heard it. Where is it from?"

"It is from the desert. From Zone Five," said Dabeeb, apologetic.

"From *there*. . . ." Al·Ith was kneeling, leaning forward, hands gripped together in front of her. And Dabeeb could not help smiling.

"Oh, you have changed so much, Al·Ith!"

For she could not stop herself remembering Al·Ith as she had been when she first came down to them—as if this memory had a claim over the present.

As if the smilingness and charm of that queen had the power to condemn Al·Ith as she was now, kneeling in the grasses, the snow peaks behind her all flushed red and wild, a worn thin woman who seemed as if she was being burnt through and through by invisible flames.

"Sing it all!" begged Al·Ith.

"But Al·Ith, they don't have songs the same way we do. You know our Zone Four songs—they have different words at different times but we know what those words are. And some we teach to our children, word by word. And some are only for our daughters and we tell them they will get a good hiding if they get the words wrong by a syllable. Yes, that is our way. But down there, so they tell us, the songs are made up as they go along. They ride across those sands of theirs—and that's a terrible place, so they say, dry and not enough water and hot enough to bake you brown—we shouldn't complain in Zone Four, not really, though we do. Down there it is lizard country, and there's a snake under every stone and you can shake scorpions out of your skirts. Yes, I am sorry, the song, I am coming to it . . . about their songs, a whole troop of horsemen go out riding together and one will sing out a line, and then another take it up and add a line, and so they go on, making it up as they go, sometimes all day or night. And when they have feasts, there are prizes for those who can best make up songs as they stand there. Someone will throw out a line, I don't know what, let's say, 'Here we sit in the middle of the orchard,' well, no, it wouldn't be orchards for those poor things, more likely sandstorms. This song came our way when Ben Ata's bodyguard came back into the villages. It became popular. We all sing it. But I wouldn't be surprised if down there they hadn't forgotten it altogether. They'd be on to something new by now, I should expect."

"That it should come from *there*," Al·Ith was whispering, "*there*."

It was agreed that the women might spend a few more days, but should remember that the weather was due to change soon. In return, there was work for them with the harvest.

Al·Ith, her son, and Dabeeb rode up into the blue pass together. Halfway up Al·Ith dismounted, to show Dabeeb white bones in the grass.

The three stood enclosed in a curdling blue mist. Dabeeb found it frightening. She was having difficulty breathing. The little boy, who was brave and strong, seemed as if he wanted to cry, but would not let himself.

"Ben Ata says men do not cry," he announced to his mother and to his nurse.

Al·Ith said that they should stay and wait for her. "I can go up by myself. I go farther every time . . . I can stay longer now. But today I won't stay . . . oh, Dabeeb, if you only knew how I long for there, how I hunger to be taken in . . ."

"But I do know, Al·Ith!"

Dabeeb sat with Arusi near the strong white bones and told him stories about the kindest and most loving horse that had ever lived, until Al·Ith came back. It did not seem long, but Dabeeb could see from her eyes how far she had been gone from them.

Al·Ith sat and took her child in her lap and bent and gazed into his eyes and fed him with what she had brought from there.

"Take it back," she was whispering. "Take it to your father. Give it to Zone Four—feed, strengthen, nourish, endure . . ."

"What is it that you see up there?" asked Dabeeb.

"I am not *able* to see. But I do see more and more . . . there are beings like flames, like fire, like light . . . it is as if wind had become fire, or flames . . . the blue is only the matrix of the real light, Dabeeb, and if I shut my eyes—" and she shut her eyes—"I can see images, pictures, reflections . . . they are high and fine, Dabeeb, they are not like us, to them we are just . . . they pity us and help us, but we are just . . ."

So she babbled.

And Dabeeb said, "Yes, to them we are just . . ."

Subdued, Dabeeb was. While Al·Ith, who she felt was her heart, her self, her sister, her lady, her friend, was already slipping away from this her realm and her home, she, Dabeeb, was preparing herself to return down, down, down—and it was as if she had been sentenced.

Back in the orchard she said to the women that they must go home, and they did not disagree. She said to Al·Ith that the boy should be left with her, in the manner of one suggesting a reparation, but Al·Ith's face reminded her how badly she had gone wrong.

"I'm sorry," she mourned. "I don't know how it happened that I was so sure we should all come—but I do see now . . . what got into me? And I have done harm, yes, we can all see that."

The mother and child were separated, and it was dreadful. Like a grown-up person he was silent and held his grief in, and went riding away in front of Dabeeb, who held him very tight, and rained tears onto his soft head. He did not look back at his mother, who stared after him, her face dead.

The band of women who rode back home were not in any way as they had been while coming from the lowlands, but were silent, and seemed not to want to be observed.

And the looks they were getting along the roads were critical, and in the inns their reception was courteous, but in a way that chilled them.

The results of this mistake of theirs were indeed severe. In Zone Three—and we had never regarded "down there" with kindliness—everyone talked of the ill-mannered and bumptious women. Their coming at all was sensed to be ill-judged. Much worse damage had been done by them than by the officious and doltish soldiers who had come to fetch Al·Ith at the beginning. And what was wrong with the place anyway, that women had to come in a company by themselves, just as soldiers, the men, had come—as if it were the most normal thing in the world—without women. Their clothes—that they had been so proud of—their hair, everything about them was condemned, and this reflected badly on Al·Ith, who in any case seemed to be in the wrong about something, or to have been affected by her marriage. All of us questioned the marriage again, and felt undermined: some were even wondering about the Providers—if they had made a mistake, or had been careless in allowing themselves to be wrongly interpreted. Such thoughts were new with us, and an uneasy troubling current was set at work throughout the Zone.

In Zone Four, the reports the women brought back were not useful to the work of slow repair and regeneration. Many people did not believe the talk about that high, fine, subtle way of living. And no one understood it. What the women said was not untrue, but there was nothing yet in Zone Four that could reflect and explain what they had seen. Rumours about the decorations and colours and patterns and cleverness of "up there" resulted in Zone Four suddenly breaking out in all kinds of garish clumsiness. Ben Ata actually had to pass a law forbidding unnecessary extravagance, and there was ill-feeling on the lines of: Why should they have it when we can't?

And the marriage itself, and the child, who was heir to both Zones —though in a way that was not yet understood—was for the first time criticised. Al·Ith was judged to be standoffish and capricious, and public feeling turned in favour of the new consort, who was paying a visit to Ben Ata in the pavilion. All over the Zone people were laughing at the gossip that the serving women brought from the pavilion. The new queen was giving Ben Ata a right old time of it! She was a real wild one, she was! And this kind of talk did them good, because they could feel superior to those sand-eaters "down there," instead of the oppressive incapacity and inadequacy that came from reports of Zone Three.

But I am anticipating . . .

When Dabeeb rode back up the hill to the pavilion with the little boy, who was still sorrowful and bereaved, clutched before her, she found it empty. The women who acted as nurses to the child were in their homes and Ben Ata was with her husband, Jarnti, organising a smaller, more pliable army.

So she took Arusi down to her own home, and put him with her children. In any case she knew that the boy had been damaged by her ill-judged visit, and needed comforting and the security of someone he had always known.

Ben Ata came back, hearing the women were there, and found Dabeeb with the boy, who knew him, but seemed disposed to distrust him, as being one who was bound to come and go unpredictably.

An older child took Arusi out of the room, and the two were alone.

Dabeeb was thinner, with a solitary suffering look. Ben Ata found her beautiful, in a new way—which both held him off and reminded him of Al·Ith.

The two sat quietly in the bare little room which as yet showed nothing of the new spirit that was raising Zone Four. Looking at it, Ben Ata resolved to do something to help this bare frugality—little knowing that she had seen wonders and beauties that would make her forever indifferent to what could be done here, for nothing would seem to her worth bothering with.

"I have been very wrong," said Dabeeb, facing him with it, bravely.

"Yes, I think you have."

"Ben Ata, you simply cannot imagine how wonderful . . ." and she talked on, in a heavy, painful, needful way of what she had seen, which succeeded only in communicating that she had suffered some inward blow or wound.

"Al·Ith," pleaded Ben Ata, "how is she? How does she seem?"

And now Dabeeb sighed, and shook her head.

"I don't think I can explain. We can't understand, you see . . . but, Ben Ata, there is something wrong, or so I feel. Not all the women agree—some believe that the way she is is right, because she was always a strange soul, wasn't she?"

"But, Dabeeb, *what* is wrong?"

"It is as if she were being punished. That is the feeling . . . it is her sister. Oh, she is a hard one, Ben Ata!"

"Murti· is hard!" he protested, remembering what Al·Ith had told him of her sister who was "her other self."

"I've already said—what you learn there is that they are above us, and we don't really understand . . . but I'd swear to one thing. Murti· is turned against Al·Ith. Or, at any rate, she is pleased she isn't there."

"But *where* is she?"

At last he got a picture of it all, and could only end by agreeing with her that they were not able to judge.

He was dismayed by Al·Ith's strangeness. That she was changed —"oh, you wouldn't know her!" That, "she's gone a long way from us, Ben Ata, and we can't expect to know where."

But immediately, he was worried about Dabeeb whom, after all, he loved, too.

It did not occur to him now to slap affable kisses on to her cheeks and neck, while she protested, and then tumble with her on the bed, having pulled a chest across to hold the door against the children coming in.

He brought his chair close to hers, and took her hands, and smoothed her hair, and held her while she wept, and so they stayed until it was time for her to feed the children. Including his Arusi. And it was arranged that for the time being the little boy would remain with her, so that he could be loved and feel himself part of her family.

And so Ben Ata comforted Dabeeb; and visited her often, to see his son, to hear more about Al·Ith, and to discuss what should be done next.

For if Al·Ith was not about to visit him, then he wanted to visit her.

But nothing happened. The drum was silent. No messages came from anywhere. The child, who was after all the heir to two realms, was flourishing in this common household.

When the drum did beat, it was for Vahshi. She did not want to come. He had to go and fetch her. The two returned with a double escort—troops of her wild desert horsemen, and Ben Ata's soldiers in formation. The desert men skirmished about, communicating in wild yells and shrieks their surprise and dislike of this safe, domestic, and tame little kingdom, while the soldiers marched on stolidly, looking straight in front of them.

While Vahshi stayed with Ben Ata, the desert men rode all over the Zone, for it was not their nature to stay in one place. What they told the women they enticed, and the dazzled boys, added to the ferment and the change, and by the time Vahshi returned to her own place, a company of young men had formed itself, who had success-fully petitioned Ben Ata to go with her and learn the adventurous ways of the desert.

And then—nothing happened. Al·Ith did not come. And there was no summons for Ben Ata. Dabeeb knew, and so did the king, that plans had changed because of the untoward effects of the wom-en's reckless excursion. The uncertainty was hard on them.

What a hard time it was for them all!—as well as its being an exciting, demanding time, everything new . . .

Particularly for those men, mostly the older ones, or the middle-aged, for whom the army had been life.

Jarnti, for instance.

It was not that he had nothing left to do in the now dwindled armies, but that the glory had gone out of it.

He was at home a good deal. In the little married quarters' house with its patch of allotment it seemed that a dozen children of all ages were crammed: there was no room for him and no occupation unless he was prepared to mend doors, paint walls—that kind of thing. He did these tasks, sharing them with the older boys, but while they enjoyed this closeness with a father they had so seldom seen, he worked always with a baffled incredulous air that said he could not believe in himself in this role. And Dabeeb, watching him at it, and grateful, nevertheless shared his unease, for she knew what it cost him.

Or he would stride restlessly about the little place, making it shrink and become paltry and flimsy, that great military man who even in old uniforms long since relegated to civilian use and stripped of braid and crispness was a soldier.

A front room's windows looked up at the rise where the pavilion rose, graceful among its gardens, and beyond that to the mountains of Zone Three. He would bring a camp stool there and sit staring ahead: for his head could not lift itself on those so long-punished and brought-down muscles.

Dabeeb might come into the room and see him striving to get his head up and back—and failing. And she would creep out again, for fear he would know she had seen his failure. It was his pride she was nursing now, for she was so very sorry for him.

"Dabeeb, do you understand that my whole life has gone for nothing?"

"No, how can that be, my dear?"

" '*How can that be*' . . . don't use that tone of voice to me! But what have I been all my life? And what am I now?"

Dabeeb, standing behind him where he sat straddling the camp stool, staring dully and painfully ahead, made sympathetic noises.

"Do you know what it feels like? I've been one thing all my life. That is what I am."

"Not all you are perhaps," soothed Dabeeb.

"I will not have you using that tone of voice! How is it you can't tell me apart from those spoiled brats of yours?"

"I am sorry, but I don't think . . ."

"It doesn't matter what you think! My life—it's gone, cancelled, wiped out. Once we were proud of our army. We could hold up our heads with the best . . ." But here he stopped, and the silence vibrated because of the unfortunateness of that phrase. "At any rate, we knew where we stood. But suddenly, from one day to the next, everything is its own opposite, black is white."

"I'm sorry, Jarnti."

"What difference does it make whether you are sorry or not! And my father? What does this make of my father's life! He did his duty as he saw it all his life. And *his* father—what does this switch-about make of us all? Nothing, that's all we are."

"Well, my dear . . ."

"Don't you dare offer me a cup of hot milk now, or a nice bite to eat . . . I'll beat you if you do . . . and that's another thing. How is it you've suddenly become too delicate to touch. You'd think you would fall apart if I laid a finger on you. *I'm not your child, Dabeeb,* I don't understand how it is I've only just seen that you treat me like a child."

Dabeeb said nothing. She was bursting with the need to comfort, uphold, soothe, reassure. Both their occupations were gone!

Sometimes she would come quietly into the room where he sat day after day, trying to lift his head up, against the habits and training of lifetimes—his and his ancestors—so that he could gaze steadily at the once forbidden peaks. And she sat herself by him, saying nothing, hoping that he at least was comforted by having her there.

Meanwhile, she quietly taught her children that they must respect their father for what he had been, and even more for his valiant attempts now; and that for their part they must train their minds to dwell on that higher land always hanging there above them, so that when opportunities came they might partake of its influences. And she was a kind stepmother to Arusi. And all the time she thought secretly of Al·Ith, identifying with her; for while Al·Ith was being consumed away from her land, Dabeeb was inwardly taking leave of this one.

When she sat close with her old husband—for he had aged very much after that blow of seeing his great armies suddenly demeaned and demolished—she would put out her hand to him, hoping he would not see this as the sort of approach one makes a child, and sometimes he even took it, and leaned forward to stare wildly at her, as if he had not really seen her before.

"Dabeeb!" he might demand, broken but stubborn. "Dabeeb, you talk of the Providers. You talk of them . . . one'd think you knew them the way you talk! But they take everything away. That's what they do . . . they lead you one way, or they let you go all your life one way, and you feed yourself on it and you think that it is everything and then—pouf! It's gone! Gone . . . Dabeeb, what do you say to that, eh? Tell me!"

"We have to believe they know what they are doing, my dear."

"We do? Do we? Well, I'm not so sure." And he would turn away his blunt, stubborn soldier's face, so that she would not see his eyes had tears in them. "Don't you see, Dabeeb? It's not just that now we are told that the army is nothing, and that all our old ways we were so proud of were nothing and that the great thing is to build barns and make drains. But that makes all the past nothing, too. Don't you see? Just puffs of air and old rubbish."

"I don't see that, Jarnti."

"You don't? Well, I do."

It was not until five winters had passed since Dabeeb's return, that Dabeeb went to the king and said that a message had come for him to go to Zone Three. He was on his horse and off almost as she spoke.

At the frontier he found his way challenged, not by his garrisons, his sentries, but by a company of young men and women from Zone Three who were armed, and who threatened him. Ben Ata was too surprised to do more than sit silent on his horse, gazing. First of all, that he *could* be prevented, after the Providers had given the Order. And secondly, at the arms. For he had seen nothing like this out of ancient illustrations of obsolete weapons. The young people had truncheons. They had catapults. They had sticks which had thin ropes tied to one end, with weights or stones on the ropes. They had large rocks in their hands. They wore the ordinary garb of Zone Three, and their appearance was utterly civil and civilian. It was not that the weapons were contemptible: they were enough to incite the soldiers and their king. . . . Not so long ago Ben Ata would have laughed and his soldiers would have guffawed derisively with him. Then they would have enjoyed chasing these poor people, would have made them prisoners and tormented them as ignorant children torture animals. But now Ben Ata restrained his soldiers, and sat quietly on his horse thinking. Then he sent the soldiers off, and rode straight back to Dabeeb.

"Was there anything else in the message that you left out?"

Dabeeb said that there was. "But it seemed so ridiculous, Ben Ata . . ."

The message had been that he should go with his army.

Dabeeb and Ben Ata sat soberly together. They talked it over, and Ben Ata went off to talk to Jarnti. The arrangement now in Zone Four was that all young men should do two years' military service, and should consider themselves thereafter on indefinite leave from the army: this to ensure what Ben Ata thought indispensable—that every youth should learn discipline and orderly ways. He asked Jarnti for three companies. There were a hundred men in each. They were armed with guns, and with swords and knives. But it was their appearance that Ben Ata was counting on, and to this he devoted his attention.

When Ben Ata again arrived at the frontier, it was in front of soldiers who were wearing fighting gear, weapons all over them, helmets glittering, lances at the ready, and the famous reflecting jerkins. A drum beat and pipes flourished.

The bands of young people with their stones and sticks made a show of standing their ground, but their amazement undid them, for they had not really understood that an army could be so inexorable and unrelenting. And they had not known that three hundred men could become one—that individual wills could cease to be entirely, absorbed in this larger, terrifying will.

And Ben Ata himself, the husband of their Al·Ith, was a large and appalling figure, with his great legs bare from above the knee down, his arms like blocks of wood. His leather jerkin, tightly belted, seemed to them so hideous that it must have a punitive or sadistic reason. And his metal helmet was a sign of inner brutality.

Thus it was that all the way from the frontier, up the pass, and across the plateau to the capital, these marching companies of soldiers caused all movement along the roads to cease, and they passed group after group of people who had believed themselves to be martial and indeed even cruel figures, but who stood limp, staring, disarmed by their innocence.

They camped for one night. In the middle of the next day Ben Ata's army arrived in the little square. Ben Ata did not dismount, but rode his horse to the foot of the flight of steps up to Al·Ith's palace, and sat there, waiting. Faces appeared at windows, people came from everywhere and stood about, looking, whispering, staring.

At last Murti· came down the steps, as she had for Dabeeb, alone.

Ben Ata was nearly undone at the sight of her. For she seemed to be Al·Ith over again, all her slender charm and enchantment, but translated into the blondness of the savagely magnificent Vahshi, who so delighted and exasperated him.

"I see you have come with all your armies, Ben Ata," said she.

"Hardly all, Murti·."

"But armies. Armed."

"Like your young people at the frontier."

"They were doing their best."

"And I am doing what I am ordered."

He looked straight at her. She, at him, but her eyes fell away and she sighed.

"Are you no longer obedient, Murti·?"

"When I am sure of what I am supposed to do."

His horse was shifting about, tossing its head, trying to free itself of the metal piece in its mouth.

Murti· watched this, and smiled, a small scornful smile.

"Yes, I know," said he. "We have different ways. But in one we must be alike."

"Ben Ata, this realm of ours was once at peace. Content. No one had thoughts of change and destruction."

"Murti·, content is not the highest good."

Again their eyes encountered, held—and held. She did not look away.

He was smiling—ruefully.

"I do not find anything to smile at."

"I was thinking of the combats between me and Vahshi, of Zone Five. But she argues for unrestrained freedom in all things, licence—anarchy. As I see it. To her I represent the law. Self-satisfaction. Contentment. Not to say—smugness."

She allowed herself a brief smile, and was sober again.

"And what is this great new queen of yours like, Ben Ata?"

"The great queen in Zone Five is the tribal leader of several hundred people, who because she is skilled, and very brave, was able to dominate fifty other poor tribes, and they all live in a narrow desert strip that borders Zone Five where it joins our country. Zone Five is a rich trading country that grows as many different crops and trees and fruits as you do. But this girl was able to make them all pay tribute to her because they were lazy and self-satisfied. And she was able to rob them and plunder as she liked."

"You certainly like variety in your wives."

"But Vahshi no longer terrorises all the rest of the Zone, because I won't let her. Because I am stronger than she is."

"A salutary story, Ben Ata."

"I take it you are trying to prevent me from seeing Al·Ith?"

She said stubbornly, "It is more that I am trying to prevent Al·Ith from—well, it is not so easy to explain."

"Creating disorder?"

"Yes."

"It would appear to me, Murti·, that whatever the effects really are of this marriage of ours, it is now too late to alter anything."

"We can prevent worse—as for instance when those stupid women came making fools of themselves."

"Yes. That was a mistake. *That was disobedience.*"

Murti· did sigh now. She stood silent for a long moment.

"I can't stop you from going to Al·Ith," said she. "You are stronger than we are. I had no idea! Until I saw this army of yours today I simply did not know. And I don't admire it, Ben Ata."

With which she turned and went indoors.

Ben Ata and his troops rode on towards the northeast.

What had happened was this.

Soon after Dabeeb went home, a woman arrived at Al·Ith's village, asked for her, was directed to the stables. She pleaded to be allowed to stay and work. She wanted to be with Al·Ith, she said. Work was found for her. Soon came another—a young boy. By the end of the winter a dozen people had come. There was really not room for any more. But the spring brought others. It was being talked about in the near villages, then farther afield—until one day Murti· arrived, by herself, and sat in the orchard with Al·Ith. It was painful for these two to meet—so estranged were they now, when once their thoughts had run side by side, and they knew what the other was doing, or meaning to do, even when apart.

Murti· was changed. She was sterner, older, more judging.

Al·Ith was a wisp of a woman, burnt out.

"You must move from here, Al·Ith," said Murti·, sounding abrupt and harsh, because of the difficulty of it. "And you must not come back into this realm."

"Then where am I to live?"

"Where you do now—it seems. I hear you are closer to *there* than you are to us."

"You don't understand."

"I can understand what I see."

"That isn't much, Murti·." Al·Ith said this softly, but stubbornly, and Murti· was silent for a time.

Then: "I have to ask you something, Al·Ith. And I know you will answer honestly. Suppose, before your marriage with Ben Ata, when we were all untroubled and things were as they ought to be . . ."

"But, Murti·," said Al·Ith reproachfully, "you know perfectly well . . ."

"No! You must listen to me. Listen! Once you were our Al·Ith and we were yours. Suppose then that you had come to know that there was a wild restless troubling spirit in our Zone, that people

were talking of all kinds of change and challenges that none of us
had ever heard of, so that everything was different, and even the
animals were perturbed, would you then have taken steps to put an
end to it?"

"Of course," said Al·Ith. "But . . ."

"Then that's all," said Murti·.

Murti· had already begun to run away, quite desperate she was, as
if Al·Ith were hunting her and even meaning harm. She had reached
her horse when Al·Ith called, "Murti·!"

Murti·, in the same dreadful haste, was jumping on her horse.

"Murti·" said Al·Ith, but in a soft commanding voice.

And she checked her horse and turned towards her sister and
listened.

"You have forgotten, Murti·! Things were very bad before I was
sent down to Ben Ata. We were sorrowful and despondent and ail-
ing. We were not giving birth as we had, and the animals were in the
same state. . . ."

"Oh, I don't know anything about that," said Murti· in a hasty,
angry voice. But she was still there, listening, compelled by Al·Ith's
strength over her.

"But it was so. And now, instead of lethargy, and listlessness, and
sorrow, instead of a falling birth rate and animals who will not mate,
we have the opposite. The opposite, Murti·!"

But this was as much as Murti· could take, and she turned her
horse and raced off as if Al·Ith had sent hostile and vicious animals
after her.

And here I am going to interpose an observation on a phenomenon which is not exactly unknown to us all:

When two people have been very close, as Al·Ith and her sister
had been, and then one of them moves away into a different experience that seems to be very different from, or even destructive of, past
balances and understandings, then the surviving partner will often
seem to close up, or perhaps even go retrograde, as if protecting a
wound, or an exposed and vulnerable place . . . yes, but this was
Zone Three, and this particular reaction was not undergone by us
in this form: not so crudely, in a word. We who were watching
thought that while Murti· had not been subjected to Zone Four, she
was nevertheless being exposed to it through her sister, who was after

all her other self: Murti· had not escaped from the "going down," though it might seem as if she had. Simply, this level of unreflective, cut-and-dried, even revengeful behaviour, was not what any of us expected from Murti·.

We have pictures of Murti·, showing her with a harsh and bitter face, sitting on her horse gazing down from that height at poor Al·Ith, the outcaste among her humble beasts.

Well, it certainly happened, and is honestly recorded as far as it goes. But I for one have brooded often enough on the scene, and I am sorrier for Murti· than I am for Al·Ith. This is not Murti·'s story. There is no time here to tell it. But it is enough to suggest that if she suffered in an indirect and difficult way from Al·Ith's sojourn in the watery Zone Four, she was bound to experience, too, at a remove, something of what Al·Ith did—and would—feel in her slow osmosis with Zone Two. Murti· was our lovely and loving and entirely delightful ruler for a very long time—she still is, in fact, though old now, and has long ago retired into the background to give place to others, Arusi among them. But there has always been something enigmatic and distant and above all, solitary, about her, since her separation from Al·Ith—and I believe that if we were able to know what she undergoes, we would find that she is not very distant from Al·Ith now, in her own way.

The day after Murti·'s visit to Al·Ith there appeared a band of our young people, armed in their amateurish but certainly painstaking way, and they insisted on Al·Ith going with them. They were not embarrassed at what they were doing. Al·Ith could hardly believe that these were the same people among whom, so recently, she had moved like their sister, or like some invisible part of them known and acknowledged by both sides—everything she thought transparent to them, their thoughts open to her. There was a barrrier between them and herself now: they saw her, but *she* was not being seen. . . .

They took her to the foot of the pass that led up to the blue mists. There was a little shack or shed. She had room to grow herself some vegetables, and there was a cow in a small field. They had put in the shed, on Murti·'s instructions, some ordinary comforts. They retreated a little way and took up positions. There a guard was maintained, from then on. It was not a terrible or an ugly guard, far from it—merely a line of young people, always different ones, for they were not expected to spend their lives at it. But a guard nevertheless, who prevented her from going back into her own Zone, and—too— prevented those friends who had wanted to be near her from coming close.

She watched her friends gathering on the other side of the line of young people. There were about fifty of them. They gazed up towards her little shed, and she waved at them. They talked to the guards—and were refused. Having discussed matters among themselves, they dispersed. What happened then, though Al·Ith did not know it, was that they all found places in the farms and villages close to, and as more and more of such people, those who were similar to Al·Ith and felt a pull towards her, came to find her, they too settled in the northwestern parts of our Zone. So very soon all the farms and villages for a long way around were occupied almost entirely by them.

When Ben Ata came riding towards her, he learned all this at the place where she had been. And he stopped to talk with the many people who had come to be near her. All had the same characteristic —not visible at all at first, but then, as you got to know them, it was like a brand. Each one suffered from an inability to live in Zone Three as if it was, or could be, enough for them. Where others of us flourished unreflecting in this best of all worlds, they could see only hollowness. Fed on husks and expecting only emptiness, they were candidates for Zone Two before they knew it, and long before the road there had been opened up for them by Al·Ith's long vigil.

Ben Ata dispersed his soldiers among these friendly souls, left his horse with them, and walked up along the pass to the little shed where his wife was.

She was sitting on a stool at her doorway, and as he came near, jumped up, looking hungrily for—as he could see at once—her son.

"I'm sorry, Al·Ith, but they said nothing about Arusi."

She nodded, smiled, and stayed waiting for him. He came close, and took her hands, and sighed, and then they sat beside each other on the doorstep very close, smiling.

"Oh, Al·Ith," said he, "it is just as well I have come to look after you."

At this she laughed irrepressibly, in the old way, so that they were both at once laughing together.

"But you are a prisoner!"

"I used to mind—I minded terribly. But now I don't."

"Well, you aren't going to be a prisoner any longer. It seems to me that Murti· was pleased that I am stronger than she is—in this, at least."

And he told her everything, shared with her the news of years, explained all that had happened.

He did not mention Vahshi, until she asked. And then he laughed, in a way that combined pleasure and amazement and anger and told her everything—so that for a moment she had tears in her eyes. Which she firmly wiped away.

"She's like a child," he said. "You have no idea. She thinks that if she wants anything, she's got to have it! But she's better than she was—I think. And she has fits of temper—you've never seen anything like it! But she's better in that too—well, a little . . ."

He kissed her, seeing her face.

"Well, Al·Ith, I had to love her—after knowing you!"

This she took as it was meant, and smiled.

They sat within each other's arms, cheeks laid together, and looked up the pass at the hanging blue mists, and thought that they were still married, for all that they were so finally separated.

Ben Ata stayed some days on that visit. He dismissed the guards, who were ready enough to go, since they were finding their task tedious, and indeed, harder every day to believe in. He was ready to set Al·Ith comfortably in some house or suitable place in a near village, but she said she loved her little shed now and did not want to go. Her friends—for they thought of themselves like this—were able to come and talk to her, and she visited them.

Later in the same year Ben Ata came again, without soldiers, and bringing her son, and also Dabeeb. When the time came to go home, Arusi was left with Murti· to learn the ways of Zone Three.

This state of affairs continued, but not for too long. One day when Al·Ith climbed the road to visit the other Zone, she did not come back. Others of her friends disappeared in the same way—just as, not often, there were always some—people from Zone Four came to our Zone after being attracted to it, sometimes for all their lives, and found a place with us, and stayed. Dabeeb was one.

There was a continous movement now, from Zone Five to Zone

Four. And from Zone Four to Zone Three—and from us, up the pass. There was a lightness, a freshness, and an enquiry and a remaking and an inspiration where there had been only stagnation. And closed frontiers.

For this is how we all see it now.

The movement is not all one way—not by any means.

For instance, our songs and tales are not only known in the watery realm "down there"—just as theirs are to us—but are told and sung in the sandy camps and around the desert fires of Zone Five.

A NOTE ON THE TYPE

The text of this book was set in Electra, a Linotype face designed by W. A. Dwiggins (1880–1956). Although a great deal of Dwiggins' early work was in advertising and he was the author of the standard volume *Layout in Advertising*, Mr. Dwiggins later devoted his prolific talents to book typography and type design and worked with great distinction in both fields. In addition to his designs for Electra, he created the Metro, Caledonia, and Eldorado series of typefaces, as well as a number of experimental cuttings that have never been issued commercially.

Electra cannot be classified as either modern or old-style. It is not based on any historical model, nor does it echo a particular period or style. It avoids the extreme contrast between thick and thin elements that marks most modern faces and attempts to give a feeling of fluidity, power, and speed.

This book was composed by The Maryland Linotype Composition Co., Baltimore, Maryland. It was printed and bound by American Book–Stratford Press, Saddle Brook, New Jersey.

Typography and binding design by Camilla Filancia.